The
ENEMY
BESIDE
ME

The

ENEMY
BESIDE
ME

A Novel

NAOMI RAGEN

ST. MARTIN'S GRIFFIN
NEW YORK

First published in the United States by St. Martin's Griffin, an imprint of St. Martin's Publishing Group

THE ENEMY BESIDE ME. Copyright © 2023 by Naomi Ragen. All rights reserved. Printed in the United States of America. For information, address St. Martin's Publishing Group, 120 Broadway, New York, NY 10271.

"All I Ask of You" from *The Phantom of the Opera*. Music by Andrew Lloyd Webber, lyrics by Charles Hart, additional lyrics by Richard Stilgoe © Copyright 1986 Andrew Lloyd Webber licensed to The Really Useful Group Ltd. International. Copyright Secured. All Rights Reserved. Reprinted by Permission of Hal Leonard LLC.

www.stmartins.com

Designed by Steven Seighman

Library of Congress Cataloging-in-Publication Data

Names: Ragen, Naomi, 1949– author.
Title: The enemy beside me : a novel / Naomi Ragen.
Description: First edition. | New York : St. Martin's Griffin, 2023.
Identifiers: LCCN 2023016834 | ISBN 9781250840905 (trade paperback) | ISBN 9781250293077 (hardcover) | ISBN 9781250840912 (ebook)
Subjects: LCGFT: Novels.
Classification: LCC PS3568.A4118 E54 2023 | DDC 813/.54—dc23/eng/20230414
LC record available at https://lccn.loc.gov/2023016834

Our books may be purchased in bulk for promotional, educational, or business use. Please contact your local bookseller or the Macmillan Corporate and Premium Sales Department at 1-800-221-7945, extension 5442, or by email at MacmillanSpecialMarkets@macmillan.com.

First Edition: 2023

10   9   8   7   6   5   4   3

For my mother-in-law and father-in-law, Shirley and Manny Ragen, may their memories be blessed, who survived the Holocaust and the worst human beings can do to others, and remained the best that human beings can hope to be

He spoke very deliberately: "We do not hate the Jews. But the Jews—*ja?*—the Jews hate us, perhaps not even unjustifiably, perhaps I would hate us too, but the time has come for this hatred to end . . . There is only one way. We must love the Jews until they stop hating us, regardless of how long it will take."

—"The Right Nose" by Doron Rabinovici, translated from the German by Dagmar C. G. Lorenz, from *Nothing Makes You Free,* **edited by Melvin Jules Bukiet**

ONE

MILIA GOTTSTEIN-LASKER SWEPT into her office, as always, as if the ground outside were on fire and she was seeking shelter. Running her fingers through her thick, shiny mahogany hair—crying out for the cut and blow-dry she couldn't waste time on—she slammed her huge black purse onto her desk, turning to her long-suffering secretary, Shoshana, with her usual greeting: "Where are we up to?"

Unlike other enterprises, which had a beginning, a middle, and an end, or at least a way of measuring progress, hunting for Nazi war criminals who had escaped justice was a never-ending process of effort and almost constant disappointment. There was no problem finding them; they were all over the place, even now, seventy years later, having escaped via the infamous routes dubbed "ratlines": There was the Nordic route, through Finland and Sweden to Argentina. The Iberian route through Spain via Rome or Genoa. And then there was the Vatican route—provided by friendly churches and clergymen and sympathizers worldwide, the Croatian priest Krunoslav Draganović, and the Bishop of Austria, Alois Hudal. It was the one Adolf Eichmann had used, Milia discovered, and he was apparently so grateful that he said he considered himself "an honorary Catholic." Which, Milia was sure, must have been just lovely for the Pope.

Others, she'd found, had been equally helpful: the International Committee of the Red Cross had provided false identity papers, and the Americans, via the CIC, or Counter Intelligence Corps, the precursor to the CIA, were only too delighted to generously host Nazi war criminals who were willing to turn informants, like the infamous Klaus Barbie, who happily chatted away about Communist activities. Through their Military Intelligence Service, the Americans had gone so far as to actually set up a secret camp within the United States where Nazi scientists who had spent the war years diligently working on missiles to annihilate the West were allowed to sunbathe by a pool and play tennis—that is, when they were not being feted with trips to Jewish department stores where they could buy their wives and mistresses expensive lingerie for Christmas—all the while being pampered by American GIs (almost exclusively Jewish refugees who spoke perfect German) obscenely forced by direct military orders to "make them comfortable." The US rocket program had been grateful.

Judging by the sheer number of Nazi octogenarians and nonagenarians spread across the world, the fugitives had taken very good care of themselves. Money, after all, had not been a problem; their victims had seen to that. But then, even when you found them and produced live witnesses to testify against them (miraculous in itself—the survivors, alas, had emerged penniless and ill), governments *still* declined to extradite or prosecute, claiming the murderers were unfit to stand trial, or that their identity had not been proven beyond a reasonable doubt.

And when, finally, they'd been forced to put them on trial, they suspended their sentences, or allowed them to appeal until they conveniently died peacefully in their beds at ninety-eight. Even worse were the ones actually sentenced to terms more appropriate to shoplifting eye shadow than smashing babies' heads against rocks. More than once, Milia had come to view her work as a Sisyphean task, in which the only people actually getting punished were the pursuers themselves, people like herself, her father, and her grandfather.

Despite everything, her grandfather, Marius Gottstein, founder of the Survivors' Campaign, had refused to give up. His experiences as a Palestinian Jew fighting alongside the British against the Nazis in the Jewish Brigade; his shock as he entered concentration camps at war's end; and the shattering discovery of the fate of the family he had left behind had given him a vision. In it, he saw the petty clerks, the failed small businessmen, the untalented lawyers and doctors, the low-level civil servants, the career criminals—who had been proud of their shiny boots and spiffy Nazi insignia and willing to commit mass murder if they got a tablecloth and some earrings out of it—finally exposed to their neighbors and family and the world for what they were and what they'd done. It was not about revenge, but about educating young minds to inoculate them against such poison that, once ingested, turned ordinary people into heartless, soulless monsters.

That was enough for him. He'd never expected to achieve anything as grandiose as "justice." For what would be a just punishment for such unprecedented and unthinkable crimes?

She remembered visiting her grandfather in his office—small, crowded rooms full of file cabinets and windows that faced walls. Her memories of him were the opposite of what most people imagined him to be. With her, he was always jolly and generous, a large-faced man with a quick smile. Sitting on his welcoming lap was like being enthroned in a private kingdom where sweets and toys flowed up out of bottomless pockets. He was of such formidable girth—testifying to a very low resistance to sweets, especially Austrian cream cakes—that she had found it impossible to imagine him as the lean, muscular soldier he had been at war's end.

But once, watching him on a television news program

interrogating a suspected Nazi collaborator—now the mayor of a small German township—she'd caught a glimpse of another side of him. She'd watched, mesmerized, as his blue-green eyes (the ones she'd inherited) darkened to a muddy gray, flashing with lethal threat, his stance as still as a leopard ready to pounce.

Unlike his famous counterpart, Simon Wiesenthal, and despite a relentless work ethic, he'd only been modestly successful, accomplishing the arrest of mostly minor Nazi officials: SS concentration camp guards, Gestapo interrogators, Hungarian police officers involved in roundups and deportations, and a handful of Einsatzgruppen shooters. His biggest fish was Aribert Heim, called Dr. Death for his "work" at Buchenwald, Mauthausen, and Sachsenhausen, where he was credited with particularly gruesome methods of medical torture. Following numerous dead ends, Marius had managed to track down Heim in 1962, living under everyone's nose right back in Germany. Heartbreakingly, Heim managed to flee to Egypt hours before arrest, tipped off by one of his many local friends. While the Egyptians were more than happy to host people of that ilk, under pressure they eventually produced a death certificate for Heim. Her grandfather hadn't been convinced.

The Heim case had broken him. She remembered her grandfather bedridden, his smile gone, in deep discussion with her father, his arms swinging with deliberate, even dangerous, abandon to underscore a point. He had died soon after.

No one could fault her father for the dedication he'd brought to the role he'd inherited. Yet his connection to the Survivors' Campaign was never the same as his father's. For he had, as the French intellectual Alain Finkielkraut wrote in *The Imaginary Jew*, "inherited a suffering to which [he] had not been subjected."

It was an irony that oppressed him.

Unlike his father, who had experienced so much evil firsthand, Moshe Gottstein had grown up in Israel among free, proud Jews who knew not only how to protect themselves, but also how to exact revenge from their enemies. By the time he was a young man, the Israelis had put Eichmann in a cage. Moshe had watched Eichmann on television, grimacing and twitching as he crookedly pressed his stingy lips together when forced to listen through headphones to eyewitness testimonies of the unimaginable human suffering his work had put into motion. A normal human being who knew he was guilty of such crimes would have grabbed the gun from his guard and put a bullet through his own head, her father once told her. But not Eichmann. He wanted to live and was not too proud to grovel, fantastically claiming that he "was only following orders." Considering the boastful recordings he'd left behind in Argentina crediting himself with being the chief architect and supervisor of the Final Solution, this must have cost him.

In the end, he might just as well have admitted the truth. The Israelis weren't fooled, nor had they been squeamish about putting a noose around his lying throat, then turning him into ashes, which they cast far out at sea so as not to pollute their land. This, her father often said, was the only just punishment for Nazis and their collaborators. Unfortunately, except for the Jews, no one else in the world seemed to agree. "Let's face it," he told her, "most countries have zero to gain from show trials, which expose their own complicity and bad national character, let alone the spectacle of evil old men gasping their last at the end of a rope."

He had more than ample reason for this conviction. After her grandfather's death, her father had flung himself against the locked doors of ministries, government agencies, and justice systems all over the world, desperately battering away, consumed by his passion to see some kind of justice, however token. It was a quest that in the end separated him from his family, carrying him to the ends of the earth for months at a time.

Her mother, Judith, also a child of survivors, had been sympathetic at first, even proud, first of her father-in-law's and then her husband's tireless efforts. But eventually she lost patience. There were no screaming matches, just a swift, almost silent uncoupling as her parents' marriage calved off, floating away into the unknown. Soon after, her mother remarried. Both her parents lived only blocks from each other in the same leafy Tel Aviv neighborhood, walking distance to the beach. Her stepfather, an orthodontist, was a blank to Milia, defined by his punctuality, demand for neatness, and love of soup. But she had to admit, even in her resentment, that her mother seemed not only content with his predictability, but positively enamored of it: "When he comes home, at least you know what you're getting," she'd say. "With your father, you could never tell. His days were one long horror story."

With such memories, taking up the torch after her father's sudden death had never been a clear-cut choice for Milia. By then a doctoral candidate in English literature, wife of Julius Lasker, a busy surgeon, and the mother of three active children, she'd struggled to decide which of her obligations made the morally superior demand upon her time and dedication. Julius had not been happy, to put it mildly, demanding to know how they would manage with two such formidable jobs. He wasn't wrong. It had been exhausting, a life of constant compromises, which she had had no choice but to shoulder alone. He, after all, was saving the living, while she was representing the already dead.

In her mind, the pendulum often swung up and back, sometimes going so far as to embrace her mother's view that the only thing her father's work in the Campaign had accomplished was to destroy yet another Jewish family: his own. But whenever that idea overwhelmed her, she remembered how her father had answered her when she'd confronted him with such a bitter assessment. Wordlessly, he'd handed her a brown manila envelope. "Read it" was all he'd said. She had. And it had changed everything.

TWO

❧

As ALWAYS, BEFORE sitting down behind her desk and turning on her computer, Milia went to the window and looked out
into the quiet street. The unchanging familiarity of the old pines
and towering eucalyptus trees swaying gently in the barest wind
always calmed her mind.

Shoshana, a religious woman nearing sixty, adjusted the short,
constantly too-tight brown wig that piously covered her graying
hair, her expression one of slight dread as she waited patiently for
a sign that Milia was ready to start the day.

"Well?" Milia asked with characteristic impatience, suddenly
turning back and sitting behind her desk.

"There is an invitation. From Lithuania."

Milia took off her sunglasses, releasing a puff of exasperated
air between her teeth that lifted the sweat-moistened bangs from
her forehead. She hadn't slept well. Black-and-white images of
mass graves from a case she was working on kept sneaking into
her dreams. Why couldn't the invitation be from Denmark? she
thought. Or Sweden? Instead of a country whose mere mention
was like prying open the rusty doors to a house of horrors?

How often had she heard the stories about her Lithuanian

relatives—the three sisters and four brothers, their children, their in-laws, and all the cousins? The obscure, strange-sounding names of their villages were burned into her memory until she sometimes forgot she hadn't actually been there, too, inside those neat wooden houses near the big lake, joining in the enormous, rollicking Friday night meals; milking the cows; watching the timber carted in from the deep black forests.

Shoshana cocked her head sympathetically. "So, do you want me to politely decline?"

Of course she wanted to decline! But then she thought better of it. Lithuania had been her grandfather's and father's obsession. And as much as she wished it weren't so, ever since opening that manila envelope, had become hers as well.

"No. Wait."

Dear Dr. Gottstein-Lasker,

I am writing to you on behalf of the European Commission, which, as you know, on 29 November 2018, acquired a Permanent International Partnership with the International Holocaust Remembrance Alliance. The participation of the EU in this international body allows for closer cooperation on combating Holocaust denial and preventing racism, xenophobia, and antisemitism.

As part of this year's annual Holocaust Remembrance Day in Europe, we are organizing a special program to involve young people throughout Lithuania in remembering Lithuania's Jewish communities, titled Our Neighbors, Our Friends. *As chairman of Lithuania's Holocaust Remembrance initiative for the coming year, and initiator of this event, I would be honored if you would consider accepting our invitation to be our keynote speaker. Your important work as head of the Survivors' Campaign has given you a particular prominence in our country, which would be extremely valuable in drawing interest and participation in this year's activities.*

Of course, all expenses would be paid as well as a modest honorarium. Please let us know if you would consider this proposal. We are hopeful for a positive response.

Sincerely,
Dr. Darius Vidas, Chairman, Algirdas University

Milia sat up straight in her chair, as if someone had appeared at her door with a shotgun. Keynote speaker! In Lithuania! *A particular prominence!* And then the strange fear suddenly left her, replaced by a sudden uncontrollable desire to laugh. She felt it climbing up the back of her throat almost choking her before she finally gave in to it. And once she started, she found it almost impossible to stop. She laughed deeply, helplessly, until her throat ached and she was blinded by tears.

"Everything all right?" Shoshana asked, her eyes wide. Milia, unable to speak, shooed her away almost rudely, as she valiantly attempted to control herself.

"*Honored,*" she whispered to herself, in between hiccups. And the title!! *Our Neighbors, Our Friends!!* Since Lithuanians had murdered all their Jewish neighbors and friends seventy years ago . . . She wiped her eyes, studying the signature at the bottom of the page. Vidas. Dr. Darius. She considered whether it was someone she or her father had come across over the years. But it didn't ring any bells. *He's probably new and someone is playing a trick on him, suggesting my name. It's a practical joke,* she thought, feeling a tiny spark of reluctant sympathy for the hapless Dr. Vidas.

For years she had been considered persona non grata in that Baltic backwater. Someone had once even called her Lithuanian public enemy number one! Even though she knew that wasn't true (Dr. Efraim Zuroff of the Wiesenthal Center in Israel deserved that crown), she'd considered it a badge of honor to be placed alongside Dr. Zuroff and Dr. Dovid Katz, whose *Defending History* blog was a daily thorn in Lithuania's side, shining a relentless light on the continuing, infuriating moves of the Lithuanian government and its institutions to distort its history of joyful collaboration with Hitler to achieve the Final Solution.

And then there was Grant Gochin, who was in a category all his own. Born in South Africa, the descendant of a large Lithuanian Jewish family mercilessly butchered, he had taken it upon himself to sue all those in the Lithuanian government attempting to turn "partisans" with Jewish blood on their hands into national heroes. Despite constant setbacks, and the fury of the establishment, he was relentlessly pursuing his agenda through Lithuanian courts like a Jewish Don Quixote.

But perhaps bravest of all were the rare non-Jewish Lithuanians fighting against their country's distortion of history. Silvia Foti, granddaughter of Jonas Noreika—widely honored by Lithuanians as a partisan martyr and hero—had bravely published an eye-opening memoir outing him as a notorious antisemite, Nazi collaborator, and mass murderer. And bestselling Lithuanian author Rūta Vanagaitė had collaborated on a remarkable book with Dr. Efraim Zuroff titled *Our People*, underscoring with deadly accuracy the long-buried secrets of Lithuanian-Nazi collaboration. Silvia had been accused of disloyalty, while Rūta had seen her successful career implode; her publishing house not only dropped her, but also removed all her bestselling books from the shelves, intending to pulp them.

Milia was proud to be counted among such people. If you were a Nazi hunter and no one hated you, you weren't doing your job.

But it wasn't easy.

She remembered sitting beside her father twenty years ago in his roomy, almost too-modern private suite in Tel Aviv's Ichilov Hospital, when everyone was still running around getting recommendations for physiotherapists, convinced he was on his way to recovery. "Please, Milly, get out of the Shoah business," he suddenly implored her, taking her hand with surprising firmness. "It's thankless work, better left in God's hands."

She was stunned. "*Sha*, Aba. Don't strain yourself."

He sat up straighter, shaking his head. "This is not coming from weakness, from being sick. It's coming from the idea that life is short, and I shouldn't have dragged you into this mess, the way my father dragged me."

She pressed her lips together. *Dragged?* "But I thought it was *your* idea. That you *wanted* to take over."

He shook his head. "It wasn't, and I didn't. But he needed help, and there was no one else. He had suffered so much, how could I abandon his dream? But it's different for us. We are part of the new life Jews have built for themselves. Besides, the perpetrators are all dead, or dying. The ones still around have one foot in the grave." He shrugged. "Nobody cares anymore."

"*We* care. Since when does a murderer get a pass because he's escaped justice most of his life? Remember that manila envelope you gave me?"

She saw the doubt roll over his forehead, creasing it. He breathed in deeply, squeezing her hand one last time and nodding as he closed his eyes. "Do what you can there, in Lithuania. Then close the office and go back to teaching Virginia Woolf."

To everyone's surprise and horror, he had only lasted another twenty-four hours, a second stroke accomplishing the complete devastation of which the first had simply hinted. The result had left no room for false hope. She'd thrown the earth over his plain pine coffin in the hills of Jerusalem, devastated that had been their last conversation.

Do what you can there, in Lithuania. Now it had become a death-bed wish. What power it held over her! And while her mother had implored her to close up the office or find a replacement, she found she couldn't ignore that wish, just as she hadn't been able to ignore the contents of that manila envelope, which had ousted her from her neat, pleasant academic life into the horror-filled trenches of Holocaust research and Nazi hunting.

Besides, despite his misgivings, in his will her father had trans-ferred the complete assets, offices, and research of the Survivors' Campaign to her, naming her as his executor and successor. What was she supposed to do with all that? Burn it? Find some hapless relative to foist it upon, since her sister, Ruth, and her brother, Shalom, had zero interest?

Often she daydreamed about doing just that. How cool and delicious it would be to spend her days in a classroom or an aca-demic office where she would have nothing more urgent to deal with than D. H. Lawrence's attitude toward the male element in woman or Virginia Woolf's use of color. The phone would seldom ring, and the texts she'd deal with would be the creamy, unillustrated pages of literary criticism or fictional stories written by ordinary men and women about their ordinary lives.

Sometimes (actually, often) she fumed at how fate had tied her hands, imagining the intrusive, judgmental eyes of her relatives—living and dead—upon her, reading her thoughts, staring her down. She fought against them. Why did another generation have to be tainted, destroyed by the knowledge of what had been done, all the sickening details? Hitler and his monsters had been vanquished but still there was no peace. Why was that so? Why couldn't all of them—every last Jew—simply let it go?

But then it came to her: It was not the Jews gripping the past, it was the past gripping the Jews. It would never let them go until there was some kind of reckoning. And that, she realized, had to take place in Lithuania.

For in no place else in Europe had almost the entire Jewish community (96.4 percent) been slaughtered. But more than that, in no place else in Europe had the killing, raping, and pillaging taken place with such enthusiasm, such ferocity, and, yes, such joy. And it had been done not by indifferent strangers in far-off death factories, but by neighbors—the farmers and their sons, the town constable, the butcher—people with whom the Jews had grown up, traded goods and stories, and gone to school. Every strata of society had taken part, not just a few "thugs."

Even so, she, her father, and even her grandfather had wanted to believe reconciliation was still possible. They had even felt on the verge of it when the Lithuanian president Algirdas Brazauskas had stood before the Israeli Knesset in March 1995, declaring: "I ask for forgiveness for those Lithuanians who ruthlessly killed, shot, deported, and robbed Jews. These are not easy words to pronounce. Not only Israel and the Jews need them. They are likewise needed by Lithuania and the Lithuanians. That is so because the Holocaust of the Jews was also the misfortune of Lithuania. That is so because the only way to achieve reconciliation and coming to terms with history is through an acknowledgment of the truth. It is not enough just to ask for forgiveness. It is necessary constantly to be aware of what occurred. That is our path to the world of civilized European states from which we were severed for over fifty years, first by the Nazis and then by the Soviet occupations."

If only two years later Brazauskas hadn't made a similarly stirring speech as he enthusiastically granted Lithuania's second highest honor, the Grand Cross of the Order of Vytis, posthumously to Jonas Noreika! As for acknowledging the truth, Lithuania had done just the opposite, doubling down on their infuriating refusal to accept responsibility.

It wasn't us, they told whoever was listening; it was the Germans. It wasn't us; it was the Communist Jews. It wasn't us; it was just a few bad apples. And besides, haven't we also suffered? Didn't the Communists—many of them Jews, after all—take away our farms and our businesses? Didn't they execute our partisans? Exile us to Siberia in the thousands, where we starved and died? Why, it was exactly the same as the Holocaust, they'll tell you. And now, they declare, we are even.

Oh, the Lithuanians had it all figured out. Along with the rest of the Nazis who survived, they had been able to make their way to the peace and freedom that had so far eluded the victims and their descendants.

Milia's first trip to Lithuania had been back in graduate school when she was working part-time at the Campaign. The idea of the adventure excited her, as well as the chance to see up front what the work of the Campaign could accomplish. They'd gone in order to witness the trial of Aleksandras Lileikis, the chief of the Lithuanian Security Police, who'd turned over thousands to Lithuania's homegrown volunteer death squads, Ypatingasis būrys.

Thanks to the ever-helpful CIA, Lileikis had been allowed to make a comfortable home in Norwood, Massachusetts. That is, until in the 1970s, when the New York City congresswoman Elizabeth Holtzman—outraged by books like *Wanted!: The Search for Nazis in America* and the feeble response of the Immigration and Naturalization Service—used all her political power and considerable savvy to help create the Office of Special Investigations in the Justice Department. Over a hundred cases were opened, most resulting in Nazi war criminals being charged and many deported, including Lileikis, who didn't wait to be thrown out, instead dusting off his Lithuanian passport and catching a flight to Vilnius.

Instead of seeing the prosecution of Lileikis and the other deportees as an opportunity to disassociate their country from such criminals with a swift trial and harsh sentencing, Lithuanians were outraged, protesting against the "Jewish plot" to harass

"Lithuanian patriots." It was ironically Lileikis himself who got closest to the truth, declaring that if he was guilty, then so was the rest of the country: "All of us were collaborators—the whole nation, since it was acting according to Nazi laws."

The matter would have no doubt rested there if the then vice president of the United States, Al Gore, hadn't made it crystal clear to Lithuanian politicians that membership in NATO required evidence of "Western values," including the prosecution of Nazi war criminals.

A full two years after he'd arrived home in good health, Lithuanian prosecutors finally charged Lileikis with genocide. It was the first Nazi war crimes prosecution in post-Soviet Eastern Europe.

Milia and her father arrived early to the courtroom and had good seats for the trial. But the only thing they saw was a sharp-featured old man who theatrically "fainted" upon entering the courtroom and was subsequently removed in a stretcher to an ambulance. It was two whole years before he finally testified via video link, and then he conveniently died. If anything had encouraged her to pursue an academic career, instead of becoming her father's assistant, it had been the disappointment of that experience. Only three Lithuanian Nazi collaborators were to be indicted in independent Lithuania. None of them would be punished.

She'd found Vilnius a surprisingly attractive city, surrounded by high green hills and winding silver rivers. Left with nothing to do before her flight back, she'd spent the afternoon wandering in the rain through the crooked streets of Old Town with its squares, parks, and secret courtyards. She touched the walls of the old buildings, glistening in the shafts of light that traveled through the narrow alleyways, wondering at the ancient, towering redbrick gothic churches, the white renaissance facade of Vilnius University, and especially the overdone Baroque Jesuit buildings, almost comical in contrast to the soul-deadening ugliness of Soviet-created apartment blocks. Surprisingly, some of the loveliest private homes and businesses, instead of being cherished, were disfigured with graffiti.

"Why is that allowed?" she later asked their translator, who shrugged. "After the repression of the Communists, we view graffiti as freedom of expression. We welcome it."

Milia was shocked. How could scarring some of the only treasures left in a city invaded and destroyed again and again be welcomed as a gesture of freedom? There was a great deal she didn't understand about these people and their history, she realized.

The morning before they flew home, she'd walked with her father down to the old Jewish quarter. Right outside was a park. They'd sat quietly side by side, disappointed and confused by what had happened, considering their next move. She tilted her head back, enjoying the warmth, the gentle breeze, the rolling grass, when suddenly her eyes spotted something white and round sticking up out of the ground. She got up and moved closer, only to realize in horror that it was the top of a tombstone that had risen up out of the earth after the rains, refusing to stay buried. The park had been created over a graveyard. It was, she thought, a metaphor for the entire country.

Now she printed out the letter from Darius Vidas, then held it in her hand. Was this a rare opportunity to be grasped? Or an invitation to be part of throwing more obscuring dirt over the facts? Who was this Dr. Vidas and what was he really after?

THREE

DR. DARIUS VIDAS was having a wonderful day. First, as he walked from his enviably comfortable apartment (by Lithuanian standards) around the corner from his office at the university, he was stopped no less than three times by people who recognized him from his recent television interviews on TV3 and LNK promoting his new bestseller, a novel based on the true story of Wiktoria and Pawel Burlingis, who had selflessly taken in Getele, the two-year-old daughter of David and Lea Gitelman and one of the last Jews left in Vilnius after the Nazi destruction of the ghetto.

"I was moved to tears," a middle-aged woman in a stylish leather jacket told him. "And when the child started singing a Jewish song in front of the neighbors . . . I thought for sure they would be caught. I just couldn't put the book down."

He smiled at her, reaching out to shake her hand and thank her. She blushed red as she timidly put her hand in his, making him wonder if attributes other than his writing skills were earning him such unexpected popularity.

He was a tall man, close to six foot three, with dark blond hair graying handsomely at the temples, a straight nose, and large, expressive blue eyes; a man who women of a certain age found irresistible. That is, until they got to know him.

Justyna, his ex-wife, had long ago thrown in the towel on their relationship, finding him utterly unpredictable, foolishly impulsive, and impossible to pin down. He was all over the place, she often complained. How was novel writing going to advance his academic career and get him tenure? she'd badger him. Why couldn't he just do what his department chair was asking of him, put aside the nonsense, and write the definitive history of the Soviet repression of Lithuania's legitimate dreams of independence?

"No one will read it. No one cares. I don't care," he told her with a yawn, sick and tired of being nagged. "Funny, you have no complaints when it comes to cashing and using my royalty checks!"

She'd seethed. At that time, he remembered, composing her still-pretty but rapidly aging face into practiced lines of righteous wrath had become her favorite new hobby.

She was one of those Lithuanians who had to display their patriotism whenever the opportunity arose in the form of selective outrage against past injustices committed against their country. But only those. Injustice in general, however, didn't move them at all. The country was still mired in its misogynistic, anti-gay, anti-Jewish past.

That didn't mean she wasn't on to something. All he needed to nail down his tenure and secure a permanent place for himself to wither and die in academia was to write that "definitive history." If only the very thought of it didn't make his head hurt and his stomach queasy!

Imagine saddling yourself with years of dumpster diving through KGB files and old Soviet newspapers, reading all those half-hysterical secret partisan newsletters shot through with vicious antisemitism! No, thank you very much. Life was far too short. And he was having too much fun.

After writing three rather steamy romances, this latest novel, titled *The Kindness of Strangers* (okay, not an original title, but luckily titles weren't copyrightable), had been a fluke. He'd come across a copy of *The Righteous Among the Nations*, by Mordecai Paldiel, published by Yad Vashem—the Holocaust Martyrs' and Heroes' Remembrance Authority in Jerusalem—on a visit to the Vilnius Jewish Public Library. It caught his eye because it described only acts of kindness by gentiles during the Nazi reign of terror, non-Jews who had often paid the ultimate price to help save Jews. Quite a departure from the usual horror stories with which one was bombarded, particularly as a Lithuanian!

While only five Lithuanians had found their way into this remarkable text, he was convinced there were many, many more who deserved it. There had to be. The ones listed were only those brought to the attention of the authorities by survivors. The Jewish family who had been saved from certain death by his own grandfather, for example, had never either publicly expressed their gratitude or alerted Jewish organizations. Why was anybody's guess.

It was surprising and disappointing. One thing about Jews, they had long memories both for good and for bad. They never let anything go. Every year, for example, they had a holiday in which they booed a Persian courtier who lived 2,500 years ago for his failed plot to kill them! A courtier who had been hanged, along with all his children! And they were still angry!

He himself had been schooled in his grandfather's story, which his mother never tired of repeating: how her father, the mayor of J—, had hidden an entire Jewish family, the Kenskys, in the secret alcove above his office in the municipality, bringing them food and making sure they were warm, right under the noses of the Nazis who were using the same building! It was almost a miracle no one was shot.

Why hadn't the Kenskys alerted Yad Vashem? It couldn't be that they didn't remember or were ungrateful. In fact, they'd gifted his grandfather a precious necklace right before he arranged to secretly spirit them out of the country—at mortal danger to himself and his family—using all his official connections to make it happen. His grandmother had never taken that necklace off, and now his mother treasured it, keeping it under lock and key, wearing it proudly only on special occasions.

He could remember fingering it around his grandmother's neck when he was four or five, fascinated by its flashing diamonds and blue and green emeralds. Where did Grandpa buy it? he'd asked her. In response, she'd told him the story of the Jewish family, even retrieving an envelope from a box high up in her closet covered with foreign stamps, which she told him was a thank-you note from the Kenskys, who were all now safe and happy in America. They lived in a city called Denver, she explained, in a beautiful home overlooking the snowy mountains. All their wealth from their prominent shirt factory had no doubt been sent to them, she conjectured, for how else had they been able to afford it?

At the time he had been too young to read, particularly since the letter was in a foreign language, and later in high school when he expressed an interest in seeing it again, it was nowhere to be found. His mother blamed the careless "helpers" who had cleaned out his grandparents' large country house after they'd moved into a small apartment in the city. "How could something so valuable be misplaced?" he'd fumed.

Still, it was a story of which he was very proud. Lithuania suffered from a terrible image problem in that area, not receiving the credit it deserved for the selfless acts of local people like his grandfather, who, under Nazi threat no less than the Jews, had made such daring attempts to thwart their sickening agenda, just as the partisans had given their lives to get rid of their Soviet oppressors.

Squeezed between two fanatic totalitarian regimes, the Lithuanian people had been between a rock and a hard place at the outset of World War II, when, under the thumb of the hated Soviets, they were invaded by Hitler. That many had viewed the Nazis as saviors, he thought, was more an indication of how despised the Communists were than of how depraved the Lithuanian people were.

When he began his university studies, he chose to study history. But soon he got restless.

Dead ideas about dead people and old events. He wanted something that bubbled with new discoveries, new ways of looking at the world, at the past. He soon switched from the history department to the department of philosophy and cultural studies. He did his senior thesis exploring the changes in sexual mores among Lithuanians during occupation and its aftermath, which he presented at an international conference organized by his department in 2013 called Human Relationships during War and Oppression: Communication, Intimacy, and Stress. While the conference garnered a great deal of attention and was viewed favorably by the foreign press, he personally had been roundly criticized by his department, as well as local media pundits, both hauling him over the coals for "catering to populism." As if that was a bad thing!

So when a local publishing house offered him a nice advance to publish his paper, on condition he "take the academic starch out of it," he was thrilled and only too happy to comply. The book sold surprisingly well. "Why not a novel next?" suggested his editor—a chubby man who smoked stinky cigars and blew smoke in his face the entire meeting. At first, he and Justyna had laughed about it. But when the editor offered him a surprisingly large advance, even she reconsidered.

Both of them hated their *khrushchyovka* apartment, a third-floor walk-up in a depressing Soviet-era concrete block in Šeškinė consisting of forty-five square meters: one cubbyhole bedroom, a living room with barely enough space to stretch out your feet in front of the couch without knocking over the television, a small dining table, and a "kitchen" consisting of a wall of rotting Soviet cabinetry and appliances that should have seen the bottom of a dumpster a decade earlier. The bathroom was even worse: two tiny closet-like rooms—one holding only a toilet, and the other a sink and shower that you could only get to if you squeezed past the washing machine. Both rooms were so narrow you couldn't risk having any overweight friends to visit!

Subsidized, it was all they could afford.

They'd done their graduate-student best with the place. He'd undertaken to sand and paint the peeling cabinets a cheerful sky blue while Justyna stood over him, complaining every step of the way that he wasn't following the DIY instructions from their friends precisely enough. It had come out the way all DIY projects explained by friends come out. Of course, like all Soviet-built apartments, there were no closets. Luckily a neighbor on the fourth floor was getting rid of one, so they'd taken it apart and hauled it downstairs and installed it. It was not only a truly dismal shade of brown, but much too big, taking up almost the entire bedroom wall, turning the small room positively claustrophobic. To cheer themselves up, they'd splurged on a gently used secondhand Teka oven from a colleague returning to Sweden. When they were done, they walked through their new domain hand in hand, staring at each other wordlessly, then burst out laughing.

After four years there, it was no longer a laughing matter.

"If I take the advance for the novel, we could move," he tempted her, knowing Justyna was obsessed with moving.

She shook her head adamantly. "You're already on thin ice with this 'Sex in Lithuania' stunt you pulled. A novel will destroy you."

She hadn't been entirely wrong. After two decades of being one of the most popular teachers in his department, he *still* didn't have tenure. Whatever. It had still been worth it, allowing them to rent a larger, renovated place near Old Town, something their combined salaries—his as a university instructor and hers as an elementary school teacher—would not have done.

To everyone's astonishment, his first novel became a runaway bestseller, opening the door to even more generous advances and even larger book sales for subsequent books.

Eventually, with the windfall money from the books, help from both their parents, as well as a sizable mortgage, they were able to put a down payment on a dream apartment on Šiltadaržio Street in Old Town, a two-minute walk to Bernardinų Park, five minutes to Gediminas Castle and Kempinski Cathedral, and a brisk twenty-minute walk to the university. Originally, the owners had renovated it as a bed-and-breakfast for tourists. But the slowdown in tourism and a personal financial emergency had forced them to put it on the market. Such a great buy! Both of them had been thrilled. Why, Justyna had occasionally even gone so far as to smile at him!

It was there they had finally found some peace, he remembered, wondering if it had been the apartment or the arrival of his babies, two strapping boys and a delicate little girl. So long ago. What did it matter now anyhow? He shrugged. His children—Domantas, Jurgis, and Karolina—were all grown up now. Domantas took advantage of the free tuition offered to students from the EU to enter the PhD program in biology at the University of Gothenburg, Jurgis had graduated with a degree in communications from Kaunas and was working at a local newspaper, and Karolina . . . ?

A swift, stabbing pain in his stomach wiped the smile off his face. What had started out as Karolina's backpacking trip after high school, scheduled to end when university began in September, had turned into a permanent relocation. At the end of August, she'd sent a curt email informing them that she "had met some people" and was now in Paris, and staying. Both he and Justyna had hurried off to haul her back but found she had no intention of leaving. Ever.

That had been four years ago. They spoke sporadically on FaceTime and WhatsApp. He knew she was still working as a bartender in a Paris nightclub. He couldn't bear to think of her petite frame, her delicate blond, blue-eyed beauty surrounded by predators every night. She'd already gotten Covid, a mild case, but he knew people who'd had it more than once. Although she made a great show of how nice people were to her, especially her boss, he knew this was her fourth job in Paris. He pondered what had happened at the others.

Sometimes he wondered if deep down she courted danger, as if putting herself in precarious situations was her way of sucker punching fate, almost a religious ritual, like walking over hot coals.

He had no idea what experiences had made her this way. They were hidden to him. Was it drug-related? Or was it simply a millennial thing together with her fierce independence, disdain for all her parents' values, especially her mother's patriotism, which she snidely dismissed as a useless relic of a disgusting bygone era best left to rot in the dust? Often, he conjectured about the mistakes he and Justyna had made in bringing her up; what they'd neglected to do, to say, to teach.

While her absence was a chronic ache in his heart, he had realized long ago how helpless he was to do or say anything that might lure her home. Of course she preferred the City of Lights! She was twenty-two, beautiful, and full of ambition. What opportunities could her native land offer her that could compete? Oh, Karolina, Karolina, his beauty, his heart . . .

He prayed for all of his children, hoping his love and their mother's could keep them safe in this dangerous world. Life was so complex, so extraordinary. No one really had a handle on it, no matter their beliefs or child-rearing methods. It was all a crapshoot.

One thing was not confused in his mind: when, six months after Karolina absconded, Justyna had announced she was leaving him for a balding optometrist, he knew it was the apartment he would miss most. He didn't even try to talk her out of it, accepting the divorce as inevitable, along with the fact that she was never giving the apartment up, no matter how much he offered in order to buy her out.

Surprisingly, even that hadn't been the end of the world. Pretty quickly he'd come across another great find in the same perfect area, a little smaller, perhaps, but so what? It was just him, after all. It even came furnished—lots of brown leather and dark wood, just his taste, if not Justyna's, he secretly exulted. Best of all, it had floor-to-ceiling windows that brought in beautiful light from a private inner courtyard with a fountain and fruit trees.

Anxious to close the deal before anyone else snapped it up, Darius made a one-time offer to Justyna and her optometrist, who could thankfully afford to pay through the nose for absconding with another man's wife—and even worse, as far as Darius was concerned, his perfect piece of real estate. One of his conditions was that they didn't involve Justyna's cutthroat female attorney, who would have gummed up negotiations indefinitely if she'd any idea just how much money he stood to earn from his latest novel. And since no-fault divorce didn't exist in Lithuania, and he had grounds to accuse Justyna of adultery and have the courts take months to divide their property, his soon-to-be ex was uncharacteristically cooperative. Luckily, Mr. Baldie-Eyeglass-Maker was in love, both with Justyna and the apartment, though not necessarily in that order. He was in a great rush to put a ring on Justyna's finger and his name on the house deed. So despite the great chagrin of Justyna's lawyer, who wanted a fight, as it turned out, Darius succeeded not only in getting the money he demanded without a peep but in dissolving a marriage he didn't want, and buying a lovely new home he did, with startling and most convenient swiftness.

The latter turned out to be fortuitous. With ready cash, he had been able to negotiate an unbelievable deal on a completely renovated town house months before a shocking rise in real estate prices sent Old Town property prices soaring. Every time he thought of it, he exulted anew, indifferent to Justyna's bitter complaints that he had deliberately set up house practically around the corner from her and her new husband to torment them.

Honestly, there wasn't an iota of truth to that accusation. But he would have been damned to let this bargain slip through his fingers just to appease Justyna's pettiness. Besides, her mood swings weren't his problem anymore. For that, he was honestly grateful to Mr. Baldie, who'd not only released him from a dead relationship but conveniently taken the social onus as well.

Of course, the divorce was hardly Mr. Baldie's fault, or Justyna's either for that matter. In his marriage, as in his university work, he had always gone his own way, ignoring demands, obligations, and partnerships, a stubborn streak he had inherited from his mother, who had been the first person in her family to go to college. He and Justyna, who had been university students and colleagues when they met, had never been able to incorporate the equality of their early relationship into their marriage, and the constant aggrievements on both sides as they negotiated their relationship had turned acidly bitter with time. Parting was sweet, without any sorrow, he thought, butchering Shakespeare.

It was a week before Christmas and so deadly cold that he actually felt his fingertips icing up inside his thick woolen gloves. Still, he smiled as he put his hands into the pockets of his down coat, whistling as he crossed the street to the park. The trees looked charming, like iced holiday cookies, but the path was treacherous with ice and dirty snow.

Sometimes, he daydreamed about a future where he would escape the university and Lithuanian winters forever, living an undisciplined and immoral life on the beaches of Hawaii or Ibiza. As he often told his close friends (only half in jest) and the women he was serially dating over beers or white wine, his ambition was to become a beach bum.

But his present life also had its rewards. He thought about the EU conference he was in charge of planning. It was a great gig, working with the EU. Not the money—that was always sparse—but the freedom. All you had to do was come up with a topic that ticked off all the boxes: gender neutral, virtue signaling, and humanitarian. This Our Neighbors, Our Friends idea was brilliant! It not only met all those criteria in spades, but also had the added benefit of addressing Lithuania's harshest critics, the ones who called his country "a graveyard of Jewish bones."

Horrible! But the country, his country, was so much more than that! If only they could find a way to accommodate their critics, whose voices were growing shriller every year. Tourism was down. Almost a fourth of the population had left the country. Things were going downhill, all right, after all those years his people had dreamed about a free democratic sovereign nation, and now that dream was drowning in the undammed waters of criticism that flowed incessantly from every direction, condemning them en masse for something that had happened decades ago, brought about by invaders, people who were almost all in their graves, or on the brink. Come to think of it, most of the people doing the condemning had not even been born, let alone experienced any suffering at the hands of his countrymen! But like it or not, Lithuania had a Jewish problem. It's true they had no more Jews, but they were more trouble, it turns out, dead than alive.

He paused, taking in a deep, frigid breath that chilled him to the bone. That was crude, he thought, and not at all how he really felt. Deep down, he was far from callous about what had happened during the Nazi era, his dark humor masking a sense of deep shame.

Just recently he had read books written by Lithuanians that had made a profound, even shocking impression on him. *Our People*, by Zuroff and Vanagaitė, had taken him on an eye-opening journey throughout his country, unmasking the hidden horrors so nearby! Even before the Soviets showed up, the Germans themselves—afraid they would lose the war and terrified of others discovering the vastness of their crimes—had forced Jews and Soviet prisoners of war to dig up and burn over sixty-eight thousand corpses from eight pits in Ponary. Yad Vashem estimated that the pits held one hundred thousand people, almost half the Jewish population of the country. All this a short ride from the university where he studied and taught!

But it wasn't just the vast scale of the murders—civilian deaths, after all, are endemic to wars—it was the brutality and the fact that his own countrymen far outnumbered the invaders in perpetrating these senseless crimes.

Silvia Foti's book actually made him feel sick.

If these books had had this effect on him—a Lithuanian patriot who deeply loved his country, a loyal citizen—what would they do to outsiders? That was why he must publish his own book about *his* grandfather, and why he must hold this conference. He must show the national shock, the sorrow, the desire for reconciliation deep in the heart of every Lithuanian, as well as the desire to compensate for crimes that had, after all, occurred before he had been born. What more could their critics ask for? In addition, he must do his best to educate young Lithuanians to take responsibility, to slough off their prejudices, to inform their ignorance. If not, then Lithuania would always be a backwater with a dark, ugly history; a place where the native-born, like his daughter, wanted only to escape and live somewhere else.

For the first time, he thought he understood Karolina. Who would want to be burdened with such a nasty history, particularly one neither acknowledged nor repented by the nation's official representatives? From what he could tell, the only way to dig the country out from under the guilt and horror was to literally and figuratively dig up the bones of the victims that lay scattered outside every single town and village and reinter them with dignity, respect, and true sorrow; to finally stop hiding the truth, however painful.

That was the true, underlying reason for holding this conference and why he had refused to invite the usual Lithuanian Holocaust distortionists and apologists on the approved list handed to him by his department. He wanted not only to stir things up, but also to actually get at the undistorted truth. Which was the reason he'd decided to invite Milia Gottstein-Lasker.

She wasn't his first choice. To everyone's shock, the first person he had asked was Dr. Efraim Zuroff, whom many viewed with hatred as a tool of Putin, out to ruin Lithuania's reputation. A large, imposing figure, Zuroff took no prisoners, his friends and colleagues warned him. In fact, the last time Zuroff met in Jerusalem with a delegation of Lithuanian teachers, the group had burst into tears halfway through his talk! But Zuroff had a prior commitment. Besides, he had been a keynote speaker at a conference not too long ago organized by Rūta Vanagaitė, a fellow Lithuanian writer who was always one step ahead of Darius on the bestseller lists. That is, until *Our People* was published. Now she was an outcast. As warm as his down jacket kept him, he suddenly shivered. But his own book about his grandfather would be nothing like hers! It was a safe project, one that would fill every Lithuanian with pride, he told himself.

It was actually Zuroff who had suggested Milia. From what

Darius could gather, *she* was Lithuanian public enemy number two. Everyone, but everyone, he spoke to was as appalled by Gottstein-Lasker as they had been about Zuroff. She was the plague, they warned him, and he, Darius, was unvaccinated. He'd listened politely, then sent off an email inviting her.

From photographs, she seemed harmless enough: petite, dark haired, about his age.

While she had been born in Tel Aviv long after the war and had inherited (somewhat reluctantly, he had read somewhere) her role as a Nazi hunter, her reputation for ferocity and Israeli chutzpah was entirely of her own making, belying her charming, feminine appearance. Once, on an academic panel in Belgium, she had slapped a Holocaust denier upside his head. When all hell had broken loose and he threatened to sue, she had patted her backside, inviting his lawyers to kiss it, then stormed off!

He chuckled to himself. Just what he was looking for. *That* would keep everyone from falling asleep in their Styrofoam coffee cups! Besides, having her as keynote speaker would give the entire project the legitimacy it so badly needed, proving this was not just another self-serving Lithuanian Holocaust distortion festival, but a signal of real change.

He hoped she would say yes.

Once that was nailed down, he was not yet entirely clear about what the rest of the program would look like. He was thinking in terms of a monthlong series of activities around the country at high schools. He already had some ideas. He'd call it To Walk in Their Shoes. All those pictures of shoes piled up from Jewish victims would be featured. And then he'd get busloads of high school students—always happy to get a day off from the grind of their studies—to follow a typical day in the life of Vilnius's Jews: the morning synagogue prayers, the little workshops and study houses—all through photographs and staged rooms, since except for the one remaining synagogue, none of that existed anymore.

Maybe he could get the chef of the kosher restaurant Rishon to serve a typically Lithuanian Jewish meal: peppery gefilte fish, stuffed cabbage, potato pancakes, or vegetarian dishes from famous Vilnius restaurateur Faina Lewando's *The Great Book of Vegetables*. Perhaps the bakery Beigeliu Krautuvle, which was already "promoting tolerance" by baking challah and bagels every day but Saturday, could bring over some of their stuff?

But what else? How were they going to segue seamlessly from munching to the inevitable somber talk about the Ponary forest massacres? Perhaps instead of buses, they'd take the groups out there in open-air trucks, just as the thousands of residents of the ghetto had been transported before being shot in cold blood and thrown into mass graves? There was nothing bagel and cream cheese about that! And what would they do once they actually got there? Jews said a prayer for the dead at such places, called kaddish. But wouldn't that be cultural appropriation?

Rūta Vanagaitė had taken groups there. She'd had a whole moving program. His was suspiciously similar, he worried, not wanting to be accused of copying her. (He was, of course. How many other ways could you approach this? It's not like there were endless possibilities.) So okay, no "Tumbalailaka" group sings and toasting on the bus with kosher wine after visiting mass graves. Maybe just reading from the latest bestseller, the book everyone was talking about, *When I Grow Up*, the 1939 YIVO contest entries of Jewish teens talking about what they hoped for in life, just two years before they were all murdered, many by their Lithuanian neighbors. That would certainly wipe the silly, sarcastic grins off their pimply adolescent faces!

It wasn't so much the actual event he was concerned with as much as the spirit of the whole enterprise. He wanted it to be raw truth for once. The country's leadership, the politicians, the teachers, were constantly muddying the waters, giving mixed messages. He would do his best to go (he tried not to even think of the words "dig a little deeper"!) a little further, without getting his program banned and himself boycotted and thrown out of the university. He was sure someone like Ms. Gottstein-Lasker would point him in the right direction, even if he had to be careful to stop short of hurling himself over the cliff as Rūta had done.

So many years after the fact, it wasn't easy to figure out a way to make the terrible story of Lithuania's behavior during World War II understandable and meaningful to young people. First of all, the story was so hard to believe. Even he himself, who had studied the subject, found it almost impossible to connect to such ghastly crimes. They would have to make it clear that not all Lithuanians had been involved. There had been many—if not most—who had been opposed but helpless to stop it. The picture needed to be fair and balanced. You didn't want the next generation hating their own country and their own people, now did you? And the current attempt to tear down all Lithuania's partisan heroes, uprooting their statues and wiping their names off street signs and plaques, also had to be halted. Young Lithuanians had to have people to look up to. Not all Lithuanian heroes had lead feet.

Perhaps he would make a speech himself about his new passion project, or, if he made enough progress in the research, even quote passages from it. The story of Tadas Vidas, savior of his Jewish neighbors, was exactly the story Lithuanians needed to hear right now.

He had taken all the material scattered in boxes from his grandparents' home and had even interviewed his grandmother and mother about what they knew. He had left the KGB files about his grandfather's interrogation over partisan activities for last, as well as whatever was left from the documents at the J— town hall. Both would be painful, he had no doubt. It all happened during the nightmare years.

But most of all, he wanted to involve the Kensky family; he

hoped they would agree to attend the conference and personally tell their story. How wonderful that would be! It would finally be real proof that the *entire* story of what had happened in Lithuania during the war had not been fully and truthfully explored from all angles, and that his countrymen had been unfairly maligned.

He stamped the snow off his boots as he entered the university, unzipping his coat. He sighed in pleasure as the warmth of the building defrosted his body, already feeling more hopeful, less confused, as if he actually had a handle on what he was hoping to accomplish.

He turned the key in the lock of his office door and entered the familiar room gratefully. Boxes were piled up everywhere, a reflection of the chaos that reigned in his academic pursuits as well as his personal life, having just broken up with his latest girlfriend.

He would have to find time to sort it all out, he scolded himself; to give both some order and meaning. He switched on his computer and opened his inbox, anxious to see if there was an answer yet from Milia Gottstein-Lasker.

FOUR

THE DRIVE HOME from the office was ridiculous, Milia told herself for the millionth time as she inched her way through rush hour traffic. Whatever had possessed her and Julius to sell their Tel Aviv apartment and buy a house up on a hill overlooking the sea in sleepy Zichron Yaakov, a forty-five-minute commute even at the best of times? It was wildly impractical. Stupid, even.

But it had seemed a good compromise at the time, when Julius accepted the position of chief surgeon at Rambam Hospital in Haifa. At least it was a nod in her direction, a place in between their two offices, although her commute time was still roughly double his.

She turned off the road, passing the familiar giant wine barrel that welcomed you to the little township, home to several wineries. As always, she was tempted to turn into Kibbutz Ma'ayan Tzvi to pick up some luscious baked goods, rivaled only by bakers in Paris. An anomaly, that wonderful little bakery in the middle of nowhere, with its heavenly baguettes and croissants. She'd gained at least ten pounds since the move! Determinedly, she pointed the car straight ahead toward home.

She parked in the empty driveway, disappointed but not surprised that Julius wasn't home yet.

He seldom showed up before her. Sometimes he even spent the night in Haifa if there were emergencies, or localized terror attacks, or Hamas rockets being launched from the Lebanese border. As the wife of an Israeli doctor living in Israel, she'd grown used to it, both his absences and the attacks.

She opened the ironwork gate, letting herself through the tall fence surrounding the house. As always, she caught her breath at the luscious scarlets, yellows, deep purples, and blues of her garden, whose only hint to passersby was the wild riot of white bougainvillea that rose in tangled, wedding-veil glory above the fence. Inside, a stonework staircase with terra-cotta pots full of petunias and roses led up to a carved wooden door painted turquoise. The color had been her idea. She'd wanted a house filled with reminders of the sea, a place that would wash her mind clear of the horrifying, colorless images that were her daily fare and the mainstay of her work.

As she unlocked the door, she glanced over her shoulder at the majestic olive tree that stood like a sentinel in the center of her lawn, its branches finally emptied of fruit. It seemed to greet her with a dignified rustle from the gently buffeting winter winds. But even now, in the middle of December, it wasn't a very cold wind, barely enough to encourage grabbing a sweater, let alone a winter coat. The rains, too, were usually short and sweet, the sun emerging in strong, summery warmth to smile down on you as soon as the clouds parted, even on the shortest winter days. As for snow, it was only to be found far away, if at all, on the highest mountaintops in the Golan Heights. And on the rare, magical occasions it found its way to Safed or Jerusalem, it was actually cause for celebration, a huge, excited whoop of delight arising from the throats of children all over the city. And while conventional removal equipment was available, it was usually the sun that took care of it, taking it off the streets before it got to be a nuisance. She couldn't imagine how people coped with months of real winters, snow up to their doorknobs, and iced-up windshields.

Inside the house it was ironically colder than outside, she thought, shivering. Built of stone, the house had cool marble floors and faced west and north to avoid the ferocity of the summer sun. It had no central heating. People simply used their dual air conditioning-heating units or a fireplace to take the chill out of the air. She hesitated to turn on the oil-based fireplace in the living room, hating the *boom* when it caught fire. She'd wait for Julius to come home and do it, she thought, turning on the air conditioner to a toasty twenty-eight degrees.

She kicked off her shoes and put her purse on the kitchen counter, boiling water for chamomile tea. When it was ready, she tucked her feet beneath her on the blue velvet couch, pulling a soft wool blanket over them and warming her hands around the cup. Before she knew it, her eyes had closed.

She was, she realized, exhausted. There was that interchange with the prosecutors in Riga about the extradition of one of the last living members of the Einsatzgruppen, a man who had murdered thousands of people and who had been living his life since as a jolly and well-respected baker in a small Argentinean village until retiring to a country house. He was almost ninety-four years old. Let him live and be well, she thought grimly, until she could get him extradited to face the public calumny he so deserved.

No one agreed with her. The authorities in Riga, his birthplace, were hemming and hawing, as they had been since he was eighty, waiting for her to give up. And the Argentineans wished she would disappear from the face of the earth and stop bothering them with this and many, many other cases. The country was a garbage dump of old Nazis.

She had no intention of pleasing either of them. But these endless struggles took their toll, she thought. How was it that these people were not also enraged by the material she was sending them? Photographs of frightened young children, pregnant women, mothers with babies in their arms, humiliated in their nakedness and summarily killed without mercy? So you didn't love Jews, so what? Were you really as heartless as all that to have no feeling at all, no human empathy, for your fellow human beings? It was so hard to assimilate, this inhuman disregard. It was enervating to try to find rational reasons for this kind of human failure.

And then there was that Lithuanian thing, this Dr. Darius Vidas. She'd looked him up on the internet. He seemed a perfect product of Lithuanian miseducation. He was going to inform people of the facts of Lithuania's murder of its Jews, when he himself was ambivalent, or so it seemed to her, about whether his country was even responsible. This EU farce he was planning, it was like soft-core porn, she thought. "Our Neighbors, Our Friends"?! Who was he kidding? In a country where gravesites were fanatically honored, their remains had been treated like dog shit.

But still, she found it hard to turn his offer down. After all, Lithuanians hardly ever invited her to such forums anymore. And although Vidas might be clueless and/or misguided, his offer seemed sincere. Besides, wasn't it in her job description to point him in the right direction, or at least to pierce his comfortable little balloon of self-congratulation and virtue signaling? But was it worth the effort? And what about the time away from home? Especially now?

Julius had of late turned up the volume of his usual complaints about them never spending any time together, including the fact that they hadn't taken a joint vacation in three years. This surprised her. After all, wasn't it Julius who was constantly saying he couldn't get away? Wasn't it her husband who worked all hours, holidays, and weekends? But in arguments between couples married for decades, the truth seldom played any part. She sighed. He was feeling neglected, and she knew she needed to fix that. Flying off to the Baltics this summer wasn't the answer, particularly since the date of the conference was around their anniversary, just the time she'd hoped to surprise her husband with a romantic cruise to some exotic locale.

There was nothing to stop them now that the children were all grown and on their own. Amir, her eldest, was married to the beautiful artist Renee Shusterman and had become the father of two sweet little girls. He was working at a high-tech firm just about to go public. Although they lived relatively close by in Herzliya, with lockdowns and Covid, she hadn't been able to hug her granddaughters for close to two years. It was heartbreaking. The baby, whom she had held in her arms briefly when she was four months old, was already in nursery school, singing songs in both English and Hebrew! And she had missed it all!

Her daughter, Karin, was starting her residency in internal medicine at Soroka Medical Center in Be'er Sheva and married to Solomon, a fellow medical student. They were wildly busy between their work and their son, Tal. Just thinking about her one-year-old grandson's chubby little knees and enormous cheeks brought an immediate smile to her lips. He was in a cuteness class all his own, just as Karin had been. Milia had also been planning to offer to take Tal off their hands in the summer, allowing them to take a well-deserved vacation, a way of compensating for her living too far away to help them with any babysitting chores during the year.

And then there was Gilad, her youngest, but by no means that young anymore . . . What could you say about him? A kind, gentle soul, he was always slightly out of sync with reality, and suffered for it.

A talented writer and guidance counselor who had published a number of books, why was it his life was going nowhere? Nearing thirty and still single, here he was, once again uprooting himself, taking a job in the most remote desert outpost in the country, after a year of excellent work in a school near Haifa whose pupils adored him. True, the principal of the school was certifiable, telling him to "ignore the garbage kids from the garbage families" and to spend more time filling out paperwork for the Board of Education. Being Gilad, he had written it all up in exquisite prose and sent it to his supervisor at the Board of Education, who—as anyone less innocent than Gilad would have known—was not prepared to do anything, certainly not to remove the principal. They never fired anyone.

"Why not just do your job and forget about the principal? She can't fire you, whatever you do. Ignore her and keep on doing excellent work. The kids love you," Milia had urged him, which—being Gilad—he had resented and ignored, quitting in a huff before securing another position, leaving him without a job and necessitating a midyear move to an out-of-the-way place no one else wanted to go to, all desirable positions in the country having already been filled. Why hadn't he just quit six months earlier, she fumed, shaking her head. It was so Gilad: impractical, impulsive, but with a heart of gold. Her heart ached for her darling, quixotic boy and the difficult path he always chose to walk.

She sighed, shifting her thoughts back to the question at hand. How then to respond to Darius Vidas? But somehow that question refused to be uppermost in her mind. Instead, she found herself focusing on getting away for a few days. Maybe this weekend? There was that bed-and-breakfast in the Galilee in that vegetarian village they both liked, with spectacular views of the mountains, the one with the Jacuzzi surrounded by glass walls looking out into a thick forest of pines. Or the one with the rose petals on the bed and candles burning in the bathroom and on the night tables . . . It had been so long. She felt a sudden ache of longing for their old, lost intimacy.

Later, she would not remember that had been the last thing on her mind when the phone rang and she picked it up and her life nose-dived into depths she had never yet experienced.

FIVE

SHE GOT UP the next morning as if drugged. No, not "as if," she admitted to herself with grim honesty. She had taken not one, but two sleeping pills. Still groggy, she reached over to Julius's side of the bed, strangely surprised it was empty, even though it was she who'd ordered him not to come home. In the light of day she regretted it, missing his familiar warm, solid body next to hers, his shuffle into the shower that lent the silent house a sense of habitation, breaking the bitter solitude she now felt as she got up and looked out the window. It was still raining. A drive into work, in the rain, she thought, until she realized there was no way she could get behind the wheel in her present state. Luckily, there was an alternative, one Karin and Gilad had been urging her to take for months: the train into Tel Aviv. It was a ten-minute drive away and would take thirty minutes tops to get her into the city. What had stopped her in the past was the impossibility of finding parking near the station. But now there was no choice. She would just take taxis there and back.

She walked shakily into the shower, her toes feeling slightly numb. Her fingers, too, didn't seem to be working properly any-more, the soap slipping to the floor half a dozen times. The last time she bent to retrieve it, she hit her head on the metal soap caddy getting up.

"OW!" she bellowed. And then the tears started in earnest when she realized no one would hear; no one would care or ask her if she was all right. She slid down to the soapy warm tiles, hitting bottom, letting the water pummel her breasts and shoulders and knees as she sobbed, her tears salting the water streaming down her face.

"What am I going to do?!" she said out loud, her fists tattooing her thighs with a painful strength until she saw the welts rising. She stopped. Why should she punish herself? Was she the guilty party here? She didn't have an answer, feeling defenseless against any and all charges that might be leveled against her. It was always the woman's fault, her grandmother used to say, quoting some misogynistic Yiddish wisdom about how "the wise woman builds her house, and the foolish one destroys it." A home had partners, both of whom could build or destroy, she protested silently, the way she had always protested vocally when her grandmother was still alive. She hadn't believed it then, and she didn't believe it now. But the roots of your understanding of life and your place in it, planted firmly during childhood, were almost impossible to dislodge, their tentacles spreading throughout your character, squeezing out any attempts at replacement with hard-fought wisdom.

It had been twenty years since her grandmother passed, and her memory was slowly fading into a generic portrait with sepia overtones. Only occasionally did she remember something specific that brought back the unique flesh-and-blood human being she had known briefly as a child.

Her mother, on the other hand, whom she had lost only five years ago, was more vivid.

She didn't actually miss her, the way you don't miss a place where you once lived but hadn't been particularly happy—as much as she missed being mothered, craving unconditional love and a kind, supportive word for that soft place inside that was still so needy.

Truthfully, her mother had never filled that role very well anyway. She was an intelligent woman, but a harsh critic and a demanding mentor. And when you didn't live up to her expectations, she made it clear what a disappointment you were. On the other hand, when you *did*, she filled you to bursting with self-satisfaction, until pleasing her almost became a dangerous addiction.

Her long-silenced voice still echoed inside Milia's head, demanding her father leave the Survivors' Campaign and go back to his previous job. His responses had vacillated between appeasing cajolements and furious condemnations. Remembering always made her feel like that abandoned ten-year-old hiding under her covers in her bedroom, her head crushed between two pillows to drown out the noise. She had vowed never to become her parents, to do anything she could to fix her relationship with the man she married rather than leaving, as her mother had done.

Despite her unending work and obligations, she had tried her best—letting Julius be the head of the household, the CEO of domestic bliss; being considerate of his time and obligations, and taking up the slack with household chores and child raising when he wasn't around (which was often). He had never bussed a table, washed a dish, boiled an egg. He had been served first, the tastiest tidbits, the best cuts from the roast, the first piece of the pie. Both of them took that for granted. And if things went awry, then it was her task to fix it.

How, Milia thought, *can I fix this?*

She stood up carefully, steadying herself with one hand against the sea-green tiles. She rinsed off her shampoo, applied a dab of crème rinse, then rinsed again before shutting off the water and reaching for a towel and terry-cloth robe. She sat on her bed, hugging herself as she dried off, trying desperately to focus. Should she call someone? The children? She shook her head in alarm—God, no! A lawyer, perhaps . . . ?

The truth was, she didn't feel like speaking to anyone, because she honestly had no clue what she planned to say. If she had to name the emotion most dominant in her at the moment, it would have to be humiliation. She was embarrassed, most of all for herself, but, yes, also for him. Such a cliché! The middle-aged man taking on a lover, a married woman who was a friend of the family, whom they both knew socially. The powerful saying "Don't shit where you eat" came to mind. And suddenly the chagrin she felt turned to anger.

The shmuck! What was wrong with him?! And did he really think he was going to get away with it?

Haviva Melnick, a hospital administrator, and her husband, Nadav, a businessman, had been in their circle of friends for more than five years, both of them Haifa natives. They'd gone on vacations together, met for dinner, and stayed for the weekend at each other's homes.

Her mind pictured the cheerful, middle-aged woman with long, curly, bleached-blond hair and a ready smile. She was taller than Milia and, yes, slimmer. But she couldn't imagine *that* was the attraction. It was the smile, she suddenly realized, and the easy laughter. Everything amused her, including her job, her children, and even her husband. She had never seen the woman angry, never heard her say a negative word about anyone or anything. Politics, history . . . these things didn't upset her because they didn't interest her. At all. When Nadav got on his soapbox, she simply sat back with an indulgent look on her face, letting him bloviate, her eyes checking out the view from the window, the state of her nails, the clothes other women were wearing. This was something Milia noticed about her immediately, and one of the reasons they had become friends. Who needed more passionate speeches about saving the world when you spent your day examining atrocities and trying to hold the perpetrators to account?

The world, Milia had decided long ago, was not savable. Because human beings were so flawed. Even the best of them could change in a minute. Given the right circumstances, there was bottomless evil in everyone. Or so she had come to believe. The people who behaved morally under pressure were truly angels, or freaks of nature. One of the things she constantly wondered was how she herself would have behaved had she been a young gentile woman in Berlin surrounded by people both terrified and inspired by Hitler. Would she have watched the Jews being loaded onto cattle cars and slunk back into the shadows, thrilled not to be a Jew? Or would she have joined the underground and risked her life for people she didn't know, and in so doing risked the lives of all the people she did know and held dear? It was not a question that came with an easy answer, or even an honest one she could swear was consistently true. It was a question that tortured her.

But Haviva wasn't tortured. No, she was merry, like Santa Claus, Milia thought, outraged. She was the go-to friend who knew where to get your nails and toes done just so (not necessarily the same person or the same place, something else Haviva knew and no one else did). She knew the nicest hand creams and the most effective wrinkle removers. And she was into Feldenkrais (whatever that was) and health spas that used electrodes to tighten your stomach and thigh muscles and get rid of your cellulite. Or was that another kind of spa? Milia could never keep this information straight, not only because she had zero interest in any of these things, but because the treatment, or exercise, or spa, or pill that Haviva had sworn by the last time they'd gotten together had usually been replaced by another, even more effective one, according to her by the next time they met. There was always something better when it came to improving your body, your attractiveness, your youthfulness, according to Haviva. She was as dedicated to discovering it as oncologists looking for a cure for cancer. And what can you do, it f—ing showed! Milia raged.

Haviva looked good, very good. Younger than her age, for sure, but *still not young*, she comforted herself. In fact, she was actually a year older than Milia. So it wasn't like Julius was going to be anyone's sugar daddy. *That* she could have understood. A young nurse, perhaps, or (even more nightmarish) a thirtysomething, attractive apprentice surgeon. That she could have gotten her mind around. But Haviva? Why? Why, why, why, why?!

And even if he'd decided to make this imbecilic move, then why not have the decency to call her himself? Why allow it to get to the point where that unmitigated bore Nadav was the one to pick up a phone, forcing her to endure his endless indignation about how they had both been betrayed, and what was she planning to do about it, et cetera, et cetera, ad nauseam? That was almost more unforgivable than the affair itself, Milia thought bitterly.

She'd called Julius as soon as she'd hung up the phone, hoping Nadav was mentally ill and the two of them could have a good laugh about it. Dr. Lasker couldn't come to the phone, they informed her. He was in scrubs. But they would give him the message.

"Tell him his wife called and our house is burning down," she informed the person on the other end, then listened to her sharp intake of breath before hanging up. Then she sat on her hands on the edge of the couch and waited. It didn't take long.

"What happened?!" He was short of breath.

"Hello, Julius."

There was a sudden silence as she realized the brutal calmness in her voice must be forcing him to recalibrate what he thought he knew.

"Is the house fire out? Are you all right?"

"There is no fire. And no, I'm not all right. Thanks for asking."

Now he was angry. "Then why leave such a message? I am scheduled for surgery in five minutes, so stop playing games."

"Why? I thought you liked games. Fun and games with our dear friends, Haviva and Nadav."

There was silence on the other end.

"Hello?"

"How did you find out?"

"Find out what, darling?"

"So, you are going to make me suffer every inch of the way, right?"

"You don't think you deserve that, huh?"

"No. I don't."

This surprised her. The matter-of-factness of it, his tone, suddenly relaxed, the panic gone.

"Well, Nadav disagrees with you. He called me. Wanted to know what I'm planning to do."

"True to form," he sniffed. "Idiot."

"No, *I'm* the idiot. The woman who didn't suspect a thing."

"I'm sorry you had to find out this way. I was planning . . . actually . . . Listen, they are calling me. I have to go. We'll talk tonight."

"No. We won't. Don't you dare come home tonight."

"This isn't going to help, Milia, but okay. Whatever you say."

Then the phone went dead.

Maybe it was a mistake, she reconsidered. Maybe if she had seen him, if they had spoken face-to-face, she would understand what she could not at the moment comprehend. Perhaps it wasn't what it seemed to be; perhaps there *were* reasons; perhaps it was different, better. Now she was facing a blank page where the story should have been written. That and a terrible emptiness.

Overnight, the fury and hurt had drained away, she realized

with surprise. All that was left was an aching tiredness. *All I want,* she admitted to herself, *is to go on. For the day—for my life—to go back to normal.* If she couldn't control anything else, she could at least control her own actions. She went to the closet and picked out an office-appropriate outfit: gray slacks and a black sweater topped by a black-and-white houndstooth jacket.

By the time she was ready to leave, the sun was shining. She stepped out into her garden, lifting up her face and closing her eyes, allowing the distant but powerful rays to kiss her forehead and cheeks. Instead of calling a taxi, she impulsively put on her sneakers, got into the car, and traveled down the short road to Nachsholim, the most beautiful beach in Israel.

She parked in the empty lot, then walked to the beach, which in the summer was engorged with young families, surfers, and retirees. Now, in the middle of winter, only a collection of seabirds had marked the sand with their tiny footprints. She found a large piece of driftwood and sat down, careless of what would happen to her good clothes as she stared at the waves.

As a child, she had always found this comforting, the endless back-and-forth of the foam, now crashing down, now lifting itself skyward. Nothing interfered with that. As urgent and varied as our lives may be, it has absolutely no effect at all on the waves that were this way before we were born and will be this way long after we die. In the large scheme of things, human beings' individual lives aren't that important. The earth absorbs the villains and the saints alike and keeps on going. It is infuriatingly unjust, and also a cause for rejoicing, limiting the gargantuan egos of the human species, allowing us the humility we need to keep on trying to get up every morning to do our very best for that day and the next and the next after that, no matter how inadequate or compromised by our own weaknesses and failures. Being human is the problem, encompassing all we just can't solve. This includes making the world a just, kind place. All we can hope to do, she comforted herself, is to make it a tiny bit more just and a tiny bit more kind within the limits of our human abilities and our short time on earth.

And then it hit her. Of course he preferred Haviva. How could he not? Anyone was preferable to a woman whose whole life was steeped in tragedy and horror; an endless (useless?) quest for a justice that could never be achieved, but along the way embittered everyone around her. Even now, in the midst of a personal crisis, she was being philosophical!

You have always kept your life separate from your work! something in her protested feebly. She shook her head. *No, I haven't, because I can't. It's impossible. My work is my life, just as it was my grandfather's and my father's.*

She thought about her grandfather, who had left his studies at the Technion in Haifa behind and enlisted in the Jewish Brigade, hoping to help save the family he had left behind in 1937 in Telzh, Lithuania. After fighting the Nazis as part of the British Army in Italy, surviving several suicide missions with his comrades, his strong, brave heart had been smashed to pieces from the rare oral testimonies of sparse Lithuanian Jewish survivors. No one in his large family had survived.

Mad with grief, instead of returning immediately to Israel after the war, he had joined the clandestine Jewish revenge squads, or as they were called in Hebrew, *chulyot*, who had decided to hunt down SS officers among German prisoners—identifying them by the tattoo beneath their armpits with their blood type—as well as camp guards, and other war criminals identified by the army. The *chulyot* dealt with those they caught in a most direct manner: putting a bullet through their heads or throwing them off precipices in the Alps. They made sure a few hundred at least never lived to enjoy cushy lives with their stolen Jewish wealth. They never felt a moment's guilt. But after a while, they all realized it was a drop in the bucket. Truthfully, they were tired of killing in cold blood, a great taboo in Jewish history, culture, and education. Most of all, there were more important things to do at the moment: survivors who needed help, all those children hidden in monasteries who had to be returned to the Jewish people and taken to their home-land, all the displaced persons desperately looking for family, for a home, for someone to listen to their stories. To his surprise, he found that the desire to be heard and the longing for justice were often even more important to survivors than either food or shelter.

The Survivors' Campaign had been born to do just that: to interview the precious remnant who had defeated Hitler's plans, and to find out exactly what had happened to them and who was responsible. To get the names, the dates, the acts. To make sure no one escaped Jewish scrutiny and Jewish justice for Jewish victims. To make sure no one deluded themselves that it was all going to go away or be swept under the carpet and forgotten.

Enlisting the help of an American rabbi, a chaplain to the US army, they organized the first Survivors' Campaign in 1945, inviting all those he had come across in displaced persons camps to bear testimony, telling their stories to one another, and to the world.

But soon he found talking about it wasn't enough. Along with many others, including the esteemed Nazi hunter Simon Wiesen-thal, he came to believe that the enemy of yesterday would be-come the enemy of tomorrow if they were allowed to live. And so began the endless search for the enemies not only of the Jewish people, but of all mankind.

She remembered something else her grandfather had read to her from the memoirs of Wiesenthal: "The crimes of the Nazis were so terrible and unbelievable that we'll be busy with them as long as our generation lives . . . Day after day we hear about their crimes. But the whole truth will never be known, nor will all the criminals be caught and tried. We lack hundreds of pounds of German documents which were destroyed and before all, we miss the testimony of eleven million murdered people."

That was the ground zero she had inherited from her grandfather and father.

Wiesenthal had closed his documentation center in 1954, when he couldn't get the funding to follow Eichmann to Argentina. He dispatched his findings—all 532 pounds of boxes—to Yad Vashem in Jerusalem. But he kept the file on Eichmann. People, he said, were becoming resigned to living among murderers. It was Wiesenthal's courage that gave her grandfather the idea to keep up the work he had started after the war.

Not everyone felt that way. Otto Frank, for example, the father of the famous diarist Anne, who died in agony in a concentration camp along with her sister, was a "forgiver and forgetter." He even once said about the SS officer who had arrested Anne and the rest of his family that he was acting correctly.

Many agreed with him. But many others condemned this attitude, as well as Frank's willingness to allow the distortion and exploitation of Anne's legacy into the comfortable fictional summation that "people are really good at heart." In truth, Anne's diary was the opposite: the ferocious death cry of a talented Jewish teenager, a girl murdered out of boundless, blackhearted fanaticism and racial hatred of Jews. There was nothing ecumenical about it.

No, we are not *all in this together,* she thought. Although the Nazis were surely against everything decent mankind had ever produced, they waged a unique, singular war against the Jews that never let up, even when the general war was acknowledged as lost. Anne was a special victim, not a universal one. To pretty it up, to make it palatable to the gentile masses, was disgusting revisionism, like the German burial of Dachau victims in graves marked by crosses, and like Lithuania's "double Holocaust" narrative, proclaiming its equal victimhood under the Soviets. It was a message that left the door open for antisemitism to rear its head once more.

And that was exactly what was happening.

She didn't agree with Elie Wiesel that only those who had suffered through the camps and ghettos had a right to write about it, to get involved. For if that were true, where did that leave all future generations? She had not lived through it, but she, like every other Jew, had been seared by it. Jews would never again live in the world easily, with untroubled faith in their neighbors, their governments, the rest of mankind. Never. No matter how many Nazis were caught and tried, no matter how many collaborators were brought to justice, the damage was done. What was the point, then, of keeping going, especially when it was taking such a personal toll on her peace of mind, and now her marriage?

She sat silently, watching the ocean, the clouds swinging across the bluest sky, feeling the sun's warmth on her arms and eyelids, for a moment wishing she could just pitch a tent and stay there forever, detached from the past, the future, and especially the present, wishing she could find unadulterated happiness. She took a deep breath, then slowly got to her feet, brushing herself off.

No, she really didn't want that. First, because no matter what she personally chose to do, it wasn't over. There were still plenty of survivors alive, and even more criminal perpetrators.

Second, because this was what she was good at. It was, in a way, a "golden cage." She would never be as skilled in interpreting Virginia Woolf as she was in discovering the clues leading to Nazi criminals and their collaborators. It was a unique education she had received, and a unique skill set few others shared. And third, because this work had chosen her, and it wasn't about to let her go anytime soon. But most of all, because she was alive and she had a voice and a worldwide audience who tuned in to what she had to say. And her voice and her words were all that millions of victims had left with which to cry their keening prayer for justice to those who would rather stay deaf.

On the ride to Tel Aviv, she slipped in a cassette of the Gipsy Kings and let the rhythm of another culture distract her.

* * *

She opened the door to her office and slammed her purse down on the desk.

"Your shoes," Shoshana said.

Milia looked at her questioningly.

"They are full of sand."

Milia shrugged, closing the door behind her.

She opened her computer and sifted through the emails. Another one from Darius Vidas, just a polite reminder that they were looking forward to hearing from her. She stood up and walked around the room, feeling the sand squishing between her toes. She sat down and took her shoes off, trying to empty them out into her wastebasket, then peeled off her socks and shook them out.

What was she going to do? She thought about her husband, her life, her job. But it was only the last one she had any control over. She pressed the intercom: "Shoshana, can you get me Dr. Efraim Zuroff at the Wiesenthal Center in Jerusalem?"

SIX

DR. EFRAIM ZUROFF had been a mentor and a friend ever since she could remember. A large, formidable man, he often joked that his dream had not been to be a Nazi hunter, but the first religious Jew to play for the NBA. He had done an astonishing amount of work in the area of bringing Nazi criminals to justice, and his special expertise for the last few years had been in the Baltics, especially Lithuania. Zuroff's family had lost four precious members during the Holocaust, including his grandfather's brother, after whom he was named. As the director of the Israel office of the Simon Wiesenthal Center, he was known and feared in that part of the world. His Operation Last Chance, offering monetary rewards to people willing to provide evidence that would bring Holocaust criminals to justice before they died of old age, had been launched in 2002 and relaunched in 2008.

It was Zuroff who had encouraged her from the first to take over her grandfather's and father's work, convincing her that their generation owed it to the victims. "There is no country in the world that exonerates criminals because of age," he said. "Besides, in all my years of finding and arranging for the prosecution of war criminals, I have never, ever come across one that expressed any regret for what they had done."

She thought about that often. All they needed to say was: *I regret so much what I did. I was pushed into it by circumstances, by the regime, by the times, I was young and stupid. It was such a mistake . . .* But they didn't, because they weren't. If anything convinced her to keep going after them until the moment God finally took their rotten souls, it was that.

She sat across from Zuroff now in his little office on the ground floor of an apartment building on a leafy Jerusalem street, where stacks of files and books revealed that time had made few incursions into his disciplined, unceasing efforts. He was in his seventies now but was clearly not retiring anytime soon.

Looking into his friendly, open face, she suddenly felt immensely comforted that she wasn't alone in this sacred work. She handed him a printout of the invitation from Vidas.

"What should I do?"

He looked it over, then slid it back toward her.

"As you can imagine, after all our conversations about the rampant Holocaust distortion in Lithuania, this is not an easy decision to make."

She nodded. "Exactly. At first it seemed like a joke to me. But I've heard from them again and they are dead serious."

He nodded. "On the one hand, this could be a terrific opportunity to publicly tell the whole unvarnished truth about the massive Lithuanian participation in Holocaust crimes. But that all depends . . ."

She looked up expectantly, her face questioning.

". . . on whether or not they will let you deliver an uncensored speech."

"Right. Of course," she said, ashamed that that had not even occurred to her.

"Did they say anything about submitting a draft before the event?"

She perused the letter once again. "I don't think so. But maybe it just hasn't come up yet."

"Okay. Find out. And then you have to take into account the unpleasant encounters and reactions you will have afterward with your hosts, journalists, and maybe even people on the street." He smiled. "You might find yourself having to hitch a ride back to the airport."

"Sounds wonderful," she said glumly.

"It's a real dilemma, but it could also be very important. I would advise you to ask for an itinerary of the whole visit, as well as whether they want to see the text of your speech before the main ceremony. Think it over! As I've told you many times, to do your job, you need a thick skin and a lot of determination, but that is exactly what this is all about."

"Thanks so much, Effie. I will give it some thought."

"Good luck and keep me posted. If you have questions or doubts, you call me night or day."

"This means so much to me. This job we've got . . . it can be very, very lonely sometimes." She felt sudden hot tears come to her eyes. She quickly took out her sunglasses and put them on, hoping he hadn't noticed.

Driving back to her office, the vision of herself being chased through the cobblestone streets of Vilnius Old Town by a pack of furious Lithuanians holding cudgels and torches like a scene lifted from *Frankenstein* went through her mind. She shuddered. The first time she'd visited, her father had been there to hold her hand. Now she was completely on her own.

"Hold the calls," she told Shoshana as she rushed through the door to her office. She closed it behind her, going straight to her computer.

Dear Dr. Vidas,

*Many thanks for your kind invitation, and for your efforts to
participate in the vital work of commemorating Lithuania's Jewish
victims of the Holocaust as well as educating Lithuania's young
people to the truth of their history. As you know, in no other country
in Europe was the Jewish community nearly wiped out to the
extent it was in Lithuania, and with the help and participation
of many ordinary local citizens who collaborated with the Nazis'
Final Solution.*

She lifted her fingers from the keyboard, clasping them together. Too harsh? she wondered. Well, if he chose to feel offended, what was the worst thing he could do? Rescind the
invitation? Probably the best thing that could happen to her, all
things considered! It would take the decision out of her hands.
She pressed Save and continued.

*Before giving you my final answer concerning my participation, I
would need to have further information. For example, I would need
your word that my speech will not have to be vetted in advance,
and that I will be allowed to speak unhindered and uncensored the
entire time I am in Lithuania. I would also need the full itinerary
of my stay, as well as the complete information about what other
events will be taking place under the auspices of Our Neighbors,
Our Friends.*

*If all these requirements can be met, I will be happy to seriously
consider becoming part of your initiative.*

Sincerely,
Dr. Milia Gottstein-Lasker
Director, The Survivors' Campaign

She looked it over, changing a word here and there, correcting the spelling of a few others. She had to admit, it was extremely unfriendly. But if Darius Vidas was sincere and not a fraud, he should be able to handle it. And if he wasn't, and he couldn't, best to find out now before sinking any further into the quicksand. With mixed feelings, she pressed Send, wondering just what kind of response she should be hoping for.

Shoshana opened the door. "I'm leaving, if you don't need anything else . . ."

Milia looked up, startled. Was the workday over already? To her surprise, it was almost six, an hour later than her secretary—or she herself—usually worked.

"You didn't have to stay, Shoshana . . ." she said guiltily.

Shoshana smiled in a motherly way. "I have nothing more exciting waiting for me at home than vacuuming the carpet and emptying the dishwasher." She hesitated. "I hope you don't mind my asking . . . but . . . are you all right, Milia?"

Milia began a quick, simple, businesslike response but found herself unable to speak.

"I . . . I . . . don't know," she finally managed.

"Can I do anything?"

Milia turned off her computer, leaning back in her chair. "Some days, do you ever just feel you can't do anything right?"

"You do everything right, Milia. You are a treasure," said the older woman, her kind face radiating honest admiration, concern, and affection.

Milia stared at her, feeling that place inside her that was empty suddenly fill.

SEVEN

DARIUS VIDAS SAT staring at the screen. He blinked. At the same moment someone knocked on his door. "Come in."

It was Paulius, another associate professor in his department and one of the few people at the university Darius trusted and considered a friend. He leaned against the doorpost, jiggling his leg with impatience as he pushed the thin, dark bangs out of his narrow, dark eyes.

Unlike most of Darius's academic colleagues, who had long ago given up their bodies to the consequences of bloating sweets and Lithuanian meats, which were slowly building up their cholesterol and getting ready to kill them, Paulius was lithe and slender, with the hard, athletic body of the professional cyclist he had once been. He, too, was divorced and living it up.

"Listen, about that party Friday night . . ." Paulius paused, suddenly noticing his friend's dazed face. "Hey, what's wrong with you? You look like you just got disappointing results from an STD test."

"Worse. I got an email from Milia Gottstein-Lasker."

"Wait . . . head of the Survivors' Campaign? *That* Milia Gottstein-Lasker? You wrote her?" Now it was Paulius's turn to be dazed.

"I did more than that. I invited her to be the keynote speaker at our conference."

"That's insane! You know the Czar is not going to be happy with you." The Czar was what they called their loathed department head, an unbearable, domineering lout and flag-waving patriot everyone was waiting to either retire or, better yet, die, preferably of some slow, debilitating disease whose progress they could gleefully track.

"When has the Czar ever been happy with me?" He gave a lopsided grin.

There was actually nothing funny about it. The man's favorite hobby was thinking up new tortures for him. He gave him twice the teaching workload as everyone else and was fond of making up fake complaints about him from anonymous, nonexistent students. Darius was certain that he'd been discarding good teaching ratings and penciling in bad ones about him. And worst of all, he'd been dangling tenure in front of him for years, only to put it off with one excuse or another.

The Czar was the only one in the department who didn't teach or do research and had some nebulous doctorate in education. But the dean was his brother-in-law and the provost his childhood friend, along with many top bureaucrats in the Ministry of Education, all of whom belonged to the same patriotic, faintly antisemitic, misogynistic, homophobic political organizations. He'd been ensconced as chair for thirty years. The only way he was leaving was feetfirst.

"Did she say yes? Is she coming? Let me see . . ." Paulius came in and leaned over his shoulder, crowding him, trying to decipher the writing on the screen. "Not very friendly, is she?" He grinned, shaking his head. "Just as well, then."

"What do you mean? What's 'just as well'?"

"Well, there's no way you can give her what she demands, so that's that."

Darius looked at his friend, puzzled. "Why not?"

"Are you serious? She wants you to swear to her that she will have complete freedom to say anything she wants!"

Darius shrugged. "So? We are in the EU now, are we not? Putin is far away."

"Forget Putin. We have our own dictators. And this program isn't just something we are doing inside the university. We are involving high school kids, the municipality, the mayors . . ."

"Okay, but isn't this exactly what we've been fighting for, Paulius? As a country? This kind of independence and freedom to explore, to debate? A little dose of controversy never hurt anyone." Darius smiled, already envisioning the debacle, the excitement, the raised voices, the interest . . .

"Oh ho! Hurt? Talk about a massacre! What they will do to *you*. To our department . . . to the Czar . . ."

"They can kill you, but they can't eat you." Darius grinned.

"You are so-o-o-o naive. Everyone in the university is sworn to 'cultivate . . . creative, dignified, morally responsible, public-spirited educational activities.'"

"Where is *that* from?"

"Republic of Lithuania Law on Higher Education and Research, 30 April 2009, Number XI-242."

"And this you know by heart?" He was incredulous.

"You had better learn it, too, my friend."

"What else does it say?"

He did a quick search on his iPhone. "If a higher educational institution . . . has violated the requirements laid down by the legal acts of the Republic of Lithuania regulating conducting of studies and carrying out of activities related thereto, the Minister of Education and Science may suspend the authorization to conduct studies or to carry out activities related thereto for a certain period of time, taking account of the type of the established violations; the Ministry of Education and Science shall notify the Register of

Legal Entities about an adopted decision to revoke or to suspend the authorization to conduct studies or activities related to studies."

Darius didn't say anything, staring at the screen. "I'm not telling her what to say, and I also have no intention of reading it in advance. Period," he said stubbornly.

"Why would you give her that leeway, considering her reputation? Don't be stupid. You are taking a real risk here. This could screw you up unbelievably. Remember what happened to Rūta Vanagaitė."

"That was her stupid publishing house."

"Everyone in the country sided with them! Everyone thought they were being very patriotic! If you think the university will be kinder to you than her publishing house was to her, you're delusional. Come to think of it, do you think *your* publishing house will be any less patriotic or stupid?"

"What do my novels have to do with this conference about the Jews?"

"And Rūta wrote about the problems of middle-aged women! But when she started exploring and publicizing what happened to Lithuania's Jews during WWII, her publisher dropped her like a hot potato. And not like you, she was very well-connected. All the politicians were her friends. She was the toast of the town. Once."

Darius swallowed hard. The vision of all his success, modest as it was, circling the drain was terrifying. He clenched his jaw. "Listen, Paulius, from what I know about the Survivors' Campaign and Milia Gottstein-Lasker, they speak hard truths, not lies. And no one has the right to punish me, or the university, for speaking the truth. Otherwise, what's the point?"

Paulius said nothing, shaking his head. After all they had suffered under brutal Communist regimes, no one treasured their freedom more than Lithuanians. But the vestiges of the education and the norms they had imbibed for decades from the

Communists had left its poisonous residue behind, instilling the fear of grasping freedom with both hands, as well as the tendency to use Communist tactics in solving their problems, especially repetition of "the big lie." That, he realized, was the tactic now in play among the country's hard-liners when it came to dealing with the historical problem of Lithuanian-Nazi collaboration and the murder of the country's Jews. He sighed. "Well, all right, then. Maybe I will join you for that karaoke thing Friday night since your time on earth is clearly limited."

"You are a good man, Paulius my friend."

"Just don't involve me in this conference."

"Wait, you're getting off the boat?!"

"I never got on!"

"You promised you'd help!"

"That was before you decided to go kamikaze. I thought you forgot all about it."

Darius leaned back, resting his head on the back of his hands and putting his feet up on his desk.

"That's the other problem."

"There are worse things than having invited Lithuania's public enemy number one to lead your conference?"

"Do you really think she's number one?"

"Look at you grinning like that's a compliment. You're an idiot."

"Wait, now it's suddenly 'your conference'? What happened to 'our conference'?"

"Milia Gottstein-Lasker and her uncensored keynote speech. That's what happened. Besides, you never specifically asked me to do anything."

"That's the other thing, as you read, she's demanding a complete itinerary before she commits. I haven't got one. Not yet, anyhow."

Paulius's mouth dropped open. "You don't know what you're planning to do?"

"Of course . . . well . . . not exactly. I have the general outlines, but nothing really specific for every one of the locations. We're planning to do this all over the country, remember?"

"Good luck! I'm getting a stomachache just thinking about it."

"No, that's those greasy pies you keep eating at the student cafeteria. Please, Paulius. I'm counting on you."

"Talk specifics."

"Well, for one thing, make some suggestions and then go over all the plans with me."

He shook his head incredulously. "I can't believe it's all still up in the air! You don't have much time, you know."

"Six months. It's enough."

"Not at the rate you're going!" Paulius threaded his fingers harshly through Darius's thinning dark hair.

Darius slapped them away. "No pulling out hair! Not at our age! Be grateful for what you've got left."

"Thanks so much for worrying about me. Now if you'd only worry about yourself a little more."

Darius looked at him intently. "Are you in or out?"

He shrugged. "How could I abandon you now? It would be like leaving a baby out in the snow."

Darius got up quickly and grabbed Paulius by his muscular, boyish shoulder, pulling him in for a short, manly hug. "You won't regret this."

"I already regret it."

"By next week at the latest, I'll have figured it all out, you'll see. I just have to go over my notes. Then you can give me your wise advice . . ."

"Which you'll ignore . . ."

". . . and keep me out of trouble."

"Impossible."

"Don't worry."

"One of us has to." Paulius gave one last headshake, then closed the door softly behind him.

When Darius was alone again, he sank back down in front of the computer, staring at Milia's letter. It *was* a bit hostile, he thought. Then sighed. Jews. They insisted on clinging on to this stereotype of collective guilt that encompassed his entire country! Interestingly, though, no public official in Israel had ever accused the entire Lithuanian nation or demanded any apologies, nor had the head of the Lithuanian Jewish Community.

After independence, the first stage had been to idealize pre-Communist, prewar history.

Only now had an open debate begun on what had happened to Lithuanian Jews. It was a devastating topic all over the Baltics. People found it difficult if not impossible to directly confront the sinister chapters in their wartime history. But it was Lithuania that was advancing on this issue at the slowest pace of all. He remembered the words of Irena Veisaitė at the Stockholm International Forum in 2000: "Attitudes and judgments change slowly. But the process of building bridges has begun. Dialogue and mutual understanding require time and goodwill on both sides."

Maybe he should write Ms. Gottstein-Lasker exactly that! If she didn't like it and didn't come, his life would be far easier, he admitted to himself. But it was the coward's way out. No, he really wanted her attendance. In fact, the very nature of the conference he envisioned *depended* on her being there to set it apart from the useless memorials that usually comprised these undertakings year after year.

It wasn't just the agenda of these conferences that made them irrelevant, but the fact that Lithuania was constantly saying all the right things, only to contradict them by their actions. For example, the Road of Memory 1941–2021, marking the eightieth anniversary of the Holocaust in Lithuania, had done everything right: partnerships with the March of the Living, widespread memorials at killing sites all over the country; a mission statement that said boldly:

"The main goal is to achieve a natural universal understanding that the Holocaust was a great tragedy not only for Jews but also for all Lithuanians. During these tragic events we have lost our phenomenal intellectual, cultural, political, and economic potential." Alas, if only the project hadn't been sponsored by the notorious International Commission for the Evaluation of the Crimes of the Nazi and Soviet Occupation Regimes in Lithuania!

Nicknamed the Red-Brown Commission, it was the chief cheerleader of the double genocide theory, whose aim was to downgrade and trivialize the Holocaust, asserting that Lithuanians had had it just as tough under the Communists! It was just one of a number of well-funded government agencies, including the Genocide and Resistance Research Center and the Genocide Museum, that had been tasked with "fixing" the very problematic history of Lithuanian pro-Nazi participation in the Holocaust.

The head of the commission, also responsible for education at one of Lithuania's "Tolerance Centers," even contended that Lithuania's Holocaust problems stemmed from propaganda by people like Dr. Efraim Zuroff, whom he mocked as a little-known, unimportant personality even in Israel, ignoring Lithuania's 2010 legalization of public swastikas; Genocide Center personnel and members of parliament joining neo-Nazi parades; a "Genocide Museum" that won't mention the Holocaust; the campaign to glorify the LAF and other Nazi henchmen; and the 2010 law passed by the parliament that effectively criminalizes the view that the Holocaust was actually the genocide that occurred in Lithuania. Those things, not Zuroff, might have something to do with Lithuanian's Holocaust "problems."

If that wasn't offensive enough, the commission head had also labeled a Vilnius Holocaust survivor and eyewitness a liar for questioning the veracity of the heroic tale of a Lithuanian family who had supposedly not only dug an underground bunker with their own hands, but also tended for two years to the Jews hidden there, thus saving forty-three Jewish lives, a tale as fabulous as any in the Arabian Nights. When asked to verify this tale by naming the Jews thus saved, the originator of the story, the deputy director of the commission and coordinator for educational projects, had a sudden, inexplicable lapse of memory.

It was always one step forward and two steps back.

No, this was not going to happen to him! He was going to go around the country—his beloved country that had suffered so much under so many horrible oppressive regimes—and he was going to lay everything on the line, the bad, the unforgivable, the good, the praiseworthy . . . And for those who claimed that there was nothing good that could be said about Lithuanians, then or now, he was going to reveal his own personal history, his grandparents' life-imperiling heroic act in saving the Kensky family. With any luck, perhaps some Kensky descendant would even join him. He leaned back, closing his eyes, imagining sharing the stage with these Jews, a child, a grandchild, maybe even a great-grandchild, alive and well and prospering because of what *his* family had done to shield them! He and they would stand before the world and embrace—Lithuanian and Jew—without pretense and without obfuscation. The event would not sanitize or hide the horrific dimensions of Lithuanian participation, but neither would it minimize all the good that had been done, the personal, individual sacrifices made by simple, good people, like those who had saved Getele, during that nightmarish time.

With that in his back pocket, he wasn't afraid of anything Ms. Milia Gottstein-Lasker would spring on him! When it came to that, he also had a few surprises up his sleeve that she'd be forced to deal with publicly! And then all his critics and naysaying friends would have to admit he'd pulled off quite a coup. Maybe his book sales would even go up! And finally, and most importantly, the country he loved would be given some good press for a change. And the process of building bridges would finally have begun in earnest.

He looked over his notes, then turned his attention to the boxes, opening one and spreading its contents on his desk, getting ready for a long, long day.

EIGHT

HE SCRUBBED UP for yet another lifesaving intervention into the body of a human being who until now had lived thoughtlessly and carelessly with little concern for the length of his existence, fully expecting—no doubt—to be saved by the decades of honed skills and hard work of people like himself. As he thrust his hands into the surgical gloves held out for him by his nurse, the stretchy material hugging his skin, his mind was already fully focused on doing just that. The surgical plan had been decided weeks before, taking into consideration everything known about the patient that might go wrong.

Dr. Julius Lasker was, as usual, full of self-confidence. He had learned his profession tiny procedure by tiny procedure, stitch by stitch, every new element a painstaking lesson added to his knowledge over many years until his skills had finally become automatic. By the time he reached the anesthetized patient, he had already mapped out in his mind how it would begin—the first cut, and then the next—keeping track of where he was and where he wanted to go and all the pitfalls he might encounter on the way. He was fierce in his focus, much like a world-class athlete facing the track, or the water, or the ball, fully engaged in creating the optimum conditions for prolonging the existence of the damaged body that lay prone before him.

While he gave absolutely no thought at all to his personal life, what did concern him was getting an itch, or having to sneeze (just exhale, it takes air in the lungs to sneeze!), or having his glasses fog up, or sweating into the wound . . . And most of all, he hoped and prayed that his best would be good enough.

At the end of the operation, he felt drained, but also exhilarated. Everything had gone well. As always, no matter how exhausted he was, he remembered to thank the anesthetist, his scrub nurse, and the people handling the technical equipment. He was also quick to acknowledge a suggestion the nurse had made, which was a good one.

"Is the patient okay?" he asked the anesthetist.

"Fine. He'll be up in two hours."

He looked at the patient, taking a quick inventory of his neurological vitals. Only after ascertaining that everything looked good did he leave the operating theater to wash up and meet the anxious family members pacing outside.

"Everything went as well as it could," he told the careworn middle-aged woman who had brought two twentysomethings with her, probably the kids. They all looked at him like he was a deity. The woman sighed and reached for his hands, wanting to kiss them.

He smiled back, shaking his head. "Not necessary. But you have to keep him well. No more kebabs!" He wagged his finger at her with mock displeasure, an old-fashioned patriarchal display that would have sent millennials howling for his blood if someone had recorded him and posted it on TikTok.

The woman thanked him, clasping her hands together, while the younger family members smiled and hugged one another.

He stopped at his office to write up his operating theater notes, his orders, and a medication schedule, calling in the nurse and the resident who would be there overnight to fully explain his instructions and to answer any questions. After a final visit with the patient, he finally went off to change into his street clothes and get ready to go home.

Only when he had left the revolving doors of the hospital spinning behind him did he give himself permission to think about the comedic farce that his personal life had turned into. His wife, his mistress, and her husband. *How very Noël Coward*, he thought, grimacing.

He was a neat man, an organized man, who enjoyed the flow of a day not interrupted by sudden unexpected crises or drama, so common in the life of a top surgeon.

While he had come to terms with the inevitable intrusion of such events in his professional life, he found that with the years, he had even less tolerance for them in his personal life. The current imbroglio in his marriage was absolutely intolerable.

He was guilty, he admitted to himself. Thoroughly and absolutely. Yes, everything he now stood accused of, he had done. And what's more, he had enjoyed it. And tough luck to anyone who found that disgusting or wrong. A person was allowed some joy in his life, he thought bitterly. It wasn't all duty. And for whatever reason, this woman had brought him happiness.

He thought about his wife, about Milia.

They had met at the extravagant Tel Aviv penthouse of his uncle during a fundraiser for the Survivors' Campaign. Uncle Shimon Klein, who once renovated kitchens, had not only become a builder, but also had the foresight and initiative to bypass the Tel Aviv seafront lots everyone else was bidding on and to concentrate instead on little parcels of land available in the less desirable, far-out suburbs. In the beginning, his fellow builders actually laughed at him. But when he constructed one after another high-rise where modestly priced apartments sold like jelly doughnuts on Chanukah, they thought again. Perhaps people didn't want to live in these apartments, but they were happy to invest their money in them as a hedge against inflation or a place for children to live when they grew up and got married.

Shimon's gamble paid off spectacularly; he was now one of the richest men in the country. And there was nothing he enjoyed more than being generous to those people and institutions he cared about, which included his old brother-in-arms Marius Gottstein and his organization, the Survivors' Campaign.

Like Milia's grandfather, Shimon Klein had also been a veteran of the Brigade. They had fought side by side through Italy to the end of the war, two Palestinian Jews who knew that their alliance with the British was going to be brief. While they and the British had both been fighting the Nazis, their loyalty had been fierce. But once the war had been decided and the British started hauling survivors off leaky ships headed for the Jewish homeland, blockading Israeli ports, and using armed escorts to force people just out of Auschwitz into intolerable barbed-wire holding camps in Cyprus, all to please their new oil-rich Arab friends, the ties speedily unraveled. Marius and Shimon often related to their children how they and the rest of the Brigade had become convinced that the British would never willingly leave the land that they'd been mandated to turn into a Jewish homeland but were instead hell-bent on using it to serve their own interests. If Palestine was ever to take in the thousands of Jews who had survived Hitler or been thrown out, penniless, from their homes all over the Arab lands that had been their home for centuries, then the British and their army, now standing shoulder to shoulder with the rabid Arab enemy, would have to be ousted, by force of arms if necessary. In the end, they'd been able to create a situation in which the British and their army found it just too costly in terms of lives and negative press to fight on. Together, they'd won that war, too.

Julius had been an intern in his last year of medical school when he accepted his uncle's invitation for the evening charity soiree. As soon as he entered, his attention had been drawn to a slim, pretty, dark-haired girl standing all by herself looking out the window at the sea.

With his usual confidence, he'd approached her with a drink from the bar.

"Thirsty?"

Her lovely blue-green eyes, rimmed by black, impossibly thick lashes, had stared out at him with curiosity and bit of disdain he'd found as unfamiliar as it was unnerving.

"And you are . . . who?" she asked almost rudely.

"Shimon's my uncle."

"Ah, yes. I know all about you. Julius, right?"

The yentas had been pestering her mother for months about Shimon's nephew Julius, the doctor, whom she just absolutely, positively *had* to meet. They had sent her photos and asked for ones of herself to send back. She had ignored them. He, too, had probably been pressured to speak to her now by the same indefatigable group, she thought, annoyed.

"Yes, Julius. Is that a good thing?" he asked her, his confidence waning.

"Is what a good thing?"

"That you know all about me?"

"Medicine," she said abruptly, not answering his question. "Why?"

He was taken aback. No other woman had ever asked him that. Usually, they just swooned at his feet, their eyes growing larger and larger, as they attempted to find favor. And why not? He knew he was attractive—tall, dark, and appealingly athletic with a strong build and wide shoulders from years of swimming for exercise every morning. And he was *going to be a doctor.*

"Why the skepticism?" he answered, with a grin he hoped was disarming.

"Well, I just wanted to know if it was 'my son the doctor' or another reason you took up medicine."

"I actually think I'll be good at it, saving lives. Someone has to do it. Why not me?"

"Why?"

"Why what?"

"Why do you think you'll be good at it?"

He was silent for a few moments. "Well, I spent high school training as an EMT with Magen David Adom, and I saw many situations where a few minutes of skill could save families from being devastated and destroyed. You know what happens to somebody who loses a child? To women who lose their husbands? To men who lose their wives? To a child who loses a parent?" He could see her eyes lose their sternness and soften.

"Yes," she said almost in a whisper, looking down.

It was then he remembered who her grandfather was, and what she was trying to do for survivors and their children.

Suddenly, she looked up at him, almost kindly. "I'm impressed. And believe me, I don't impress easily."

"Why is that?" he asked her, amused at the contrast between her quick recovery, her implacability (pretended or real? he wondered), and the petite softness of her lovely young face and body. She was trying so hard to be tough. He wondered why. Usually, women tried to be the opposite around him. She had obviously not been to "finishing school," as well as having a mother who'd failed to adequately impress upon her the rules of attracting a husband.

"My grandfather—"

"Yes," he said, cutting her short. "I know all about him."

"So, you know, then. About the work of the Campaign?"

"I've heard some things."

"Well, when you grow up hearing about how human beings can behave worse than animals toward one another, you sometimes find it difficult to imagine that real altruism and kindness can exist in the same species."

"That can't be true!"

"Oh, I promise you, it is."

"He must have come across many good stories, too. No?"

She thought about it. "Yes, many people did unbelievably selfless things to save others. I guess we just tend to focus on the negative."

"You don't mean 'we,' do you?"

She blushed, breaking into an embarrassed smile. "No," she admitted. "I suppose *I* tend to focus on the negative. I'm already a bit jaded, if you must know."

"My, my. And you look like such a sweet, innocent little thing!"

She grinned at him. "Oh, I assure you, I'm absolutely none of those things."

That was the way it began.

He soon discovered she was speaking the truth. Despite her size, there was nothing "little" about her. In any room, she had a huge presence the moment she opened her mouth and the weight of her knowledge and determination was revealed. She had a fierce intelligence, and a bruising sense of humor that took him a long time to get used to. But it grew on him, especially since most of the girls he went out with behaved like handmaidens, or like giggling schoolgirls. He loved the challenge of their relationship, and how it kept him on his toes. And at a certain point, he loved her, too.

He walked to his car and got inside, sitting behind the wheel but making no move to start the engine.

Had she ever really loved him? Or did she accept his proposal because he was a "catch" and she was a twenty-two-year-old doctoral candidate who worked part-time in the Survivors' Campaign and had no time to look for a better prospect? Did she settle for him so people would leave her alone and she could go back in peace to pursue her real love? Because even if she didn't know it and never admitted it, the only thing in this world that Milia Gottstein truly loved and gave all her attention to was her work; even her children had to share her. Hitler's victims were her real family, and she was in a constant, relentless war with their enemies, living and dead.

That insight had come to him during one of their many marriage counseling sessions, from an overweight psychologist with a big black kippah on his balding head. He had been shocked at how accurately that summed up the relationship between them. Her work was her lover. She betrayed him and the family every chance she got to be with him, to give him all her focused, loving attention.

They had been married twenty-five years when he finally realized that he'd had enough. For the first decade, his own work and then the children had kept him from noticing too much.

He was also dedicated to his work, which, like hers, wasn't just a job but an avocation. But then somewhere along the way, toward the end of the second decade, he realized that he was lonely most of the time. He was bored, too. How much Holocaust can a person live with?

He wanted to be done with it, to leave it in the past, where it belonged. To move forward. To let someone else take up the burden. He had more time now that the kids were grown and he had reached the pinnacle of his career, his skills and his experience having earned him the place in his profession he'd always craved. Now he wanted something else in life. Something more. Now he wanted someone who would bat her eyelashes at him and treat him like a rock star; who would drop everything to be with him the moment he asked her.

And that wasn't Milia.

He sighed, punched in the car code, then put his key into the ignition. Where was it all going to end? He thought about Haviva. She was so much fun to be with. Lighthearted, and yes, okay, light-headed. She was always amused about something. And she always had a new restaurant she wanted to try, or some new play that was opening she wanted to see, or some fabulous plan for a vacation in Tuscany, Provence, or the Virgin Islands she was in the middle of investigating. And yes, she always looked great, and the sex was as vigorous and satisfying as it was forbidden. In short, she knew exactly when to bat her eyelashes.

Was it going to end in marriage? Did he want it to? Did he want to divorce Milia and start all over again with someone who wasn't fit to lick her boots but who made him happy, at least short-term? He really didn't know. He needed more time to think about it. That phone call, however, had sped up the urgency of coming to a decision. Being banned from his home was beginning to annoy him. He needed clean clothes. He needed his own bed. He needed to talk to his wife, to Milia. Impulsively, instead of heading toward his hotel, he made a left toward the Carmel Tunnels and the road to Zichron.

NINE

MILIA WAITED FOR the footsteps, the opening of the front door, and then the turn of the key in the lock of her office door. Only when she was sure Shoshana was gone for the day did she allow herself a long sigh. She leaned back, exhausted.

It had been more than a week since she and Julius had spoken. He had made no move either to demand to be let back into the house, or to explain himself. He had made no move to come home.

All week, she had been leaving home ridiculously early in the morning, telling herself it was easier to find parking at the train station, only to drive all the way into Tel Aviv. And then the day just melted away, until the sun went down and it was dark again. She had been staying later and later each night, dreading the return to their big, gorgeous empty house; their big, luxurious empty bed, which more and more had taken on the impersonal atmosphere of a five-star hotel you'd grown tired of, longing for the more modest embrace of the comforts of home.

Not that she was looking forward to the inevitable, ugly confrontation. What could she say without sounding like some pathetic character in a soap opera—the wronged woman, the female equivalent of the cuckold? She tried to think of some scenario in which she would have the upper hand, some exchange that would leave her—at the very least—feeling morally superior. But she honestly couldn't imagine it.

Throughout their marriage, Julius had shown himself to be a considerate, patient man whose feathers didn't ruffle often, and even when they did, he had never descended into overwrought drama. Only twice had she seen what his absolute fury looked like: on the phone with a panicked resident who had given a patient the wrong dosage of medication, requiring immediate intubation, and in the emergency room with fifteen-year-old Karin and her boyfriend after the boyfriend managed to smash himself, his motorcycle, and their daughter into a parked car at night during a downpour. To top it off, neither of them had been wearing helmets. Karin broke her arm. The boyfriend, both legs. In both instances, Julius's voice had reached decibels of which she had not known him capable.

She herself was quite a screamer. She raised her voice when things weren't going her way at work, at misbehaving children, at newscasters making inane remarks, and at the unseen authors of books or articles with whom she vehemently disagreed. And just when she felt overwhelmed.

Even though 99 percent of the time her vehemence was not directed at him, it was something Julius absolutely couldn't stand. "Lower your voice!" he would hiss at her with quiet fury, especially if they were in a public place and others might overhear. He had a true anathema of displays of emotion in front of strangers, of "making a spectacle" of yourself. She, on the other hand, couldn't have cared less what others thought of her or what she had to say.

But what, if anything, could be said now, in any tone of voice, that could suture the wound between them, pulling them together so that healing would have a fighting chance to begin? She tried to imagine such a scene: He, crestfallen, too embarrassed to look her in the eye. A mumbled "I'm so sorry, it will never happen again! Please, please forgive me. I just want our life back." And then maybe a "I don't know what came over me. I was such a jerk, a fool, an imbecile." And certainly: "She means nothing to me: it's you I love and have always loved." And for good measure, some really pointed insults at Haviva. Something along the lines of "She's such a shallow person, so silly. Not at all like you, my darling wife, of whom I am so incredibly proud." She mused on it, turning it over in her mind like an omelet she was frying to see if it was cooked to the exact doneness she preferred.

Then, suddenly, she gave up. What difference did it make if she was happy with this fictional scenario? The likelihood of it actually becoming reality was nonexistent. For one thing, nothing about it sounded remotely like Julius, who hardly ever said he was sorry about anything, even if he was in the wrong; he always assumed that eventually she'd get over it. However demeaning she found this quality in him, particularly since she herself was quick to apologize, she had long ago accepted it as part of their life together.

But this time it was different. If she was to retain a shred of self-respect, he had to say the words in order for her to take him back.

And what if, true to form, he wouldn't?

So let him stay away waiting "for her to get over it," she thought bitterly. He should live so long! In the worst-case scenario, there would be no grand exit, no slamming of doors and vicious accusations, just a sad, dribbling away of their lives together, one more day added to one more day in which they had no contact, until they were notified of the date on which to meet at the Rabbinical Court for him to throw her religious divorce, her *get*, at her, which was the way it was done in Israel. It wasn't a metaphor; the husband physically threw the divorce agreement at his wife, who had to catch it. That was actually religious law, one more addition to her long list of humiliations.

Yet given the circumstances, wouldn't it be better that way? A quick, unconditional parting in which he agreed to release her from her marriage vows, and in which they both agreed that there was no hope at all for reconciliation, *shalom bayit*?

How she wished she could agree with that sensible and likely outcome! But just the thought of it made her sick to her stomach. After so many years, he was such an integral part of her life, such a major—and yes, beloved—part. Few people on the planet understood her the way he did. Who else, for example, would immediately understand the depth of her anguish over the readings of a thermometer in the mouth of a ninety-year-old former SS guard she had been tracking for two decades, which could thwart, perhaps forever, the final chance to make him stand trial for his vicious crimes? Julius was, in all ways, her partner, which was more important than his being her lover, or even her husband. Without him, she would be all alone. At least, this is what she had always told herself.

In many ways, he was just like her. They were both ambitious, both focused on goals that were, each in its own way, altruistic, even holy. They respected each other's work and gave each other the gift of time to pursue it: she never complained about the endless hours he spent at the hospital and clinic, about long-planned vacations canceled at the last minute because of the medical emergencies of strangers, and he, in turn, allowed her to fly off to the ends of the earth at a moment's notice when the opportunities arose to finally bring Nazi scum to justice. So there had been a housekeeper and a nanny on those occasions. No one expected Julius to wash dishes or change diapers. But even so, not many men would agree to such a life.

How ironic, then, that the break between them should come just now, when this lifelong partnership was the least demanding it had ever been, both of them less pressured to prove themselves, the kids grown up, and the house practically running itself with twice weekly outside help?

She suddenly caught her breath. Yes!! That was it! Maybe he didn't need a partner anymore. Maybe now what he wanted was a lover.

Could that be true? She considered it. Over the last few years, he had taken less and less interest in her work, going so far as to actually avoid conversations about anything to do with the Holocaust. She'd never looked into that too deeply, always ready to assume that it was just the moment that had been inopportune; that he was tired, or depressed over a case, or simply not in the right mood. Now she wondered if his lack of interest—repulsion?—had been a clue to some deeper change in him that she'd willfully overlooked out of laziness, or embarrassment, or simply to avoid confrontation.

Well, whether she liked it or not, there was going to be confrontation now. The battle lines had been drawn. For the first time since she'd gotten that phone call, she looked past her own fury and wounded pride, wondering if what he had done had made him happy, if it had been worth it. She wondered, too, if he was still the man she had married, the one she had always loved, or if that person had ceased to exist except in her imagination. Worse, she wondered if he had ever existed, or if it had all been a good dream that was now exposed as a decades-old fraud she had willingly bought into. The idea struck her like an unexpected punch in the stomach. She doubled over, hugging herself, wondering how she was going to survive.

It was just at that moment that the computer dinged, announcing a new email.

It was, she saw, from Darius Vidas.

Dear Dr. Gottstein-Lasker,

Please forgive how long it has taken for me to get back to you. Your request to give a lecture that will be unread and uncensored stirred up quite a hornet's nest of controversy here. But I have finally discussed your requests with my colleagues and am happy to say that we can accommodate your wishes. Our university, as well as our Lithuanian institutions, which have suffered in the past from the heavy hand of partisan censorship, are freedom loving in the extreme.

As for the itinerary, I am attaching what we have so far, which you will see is not complete. But I suggest that instead of being dismayed or allowing this to deter you, you'll consider it an opportunity to share your own input, and to thus become an important participant in shaping the form and scope our conference will take.

At this point, however, because of time constraints, I must ask you to send us immediately a firm commitment to be our keynote speaker in Vilnius, and elsewhere as our itinerary specifies. We await your answer with hope.

Sincerely,
Dr. Darius Vidas, Chairman

She opened the itinerary file and stared at it. It was filled with to-be-decideds.

Opportunity for her own input! What a joke. But they'd agreed about the noncensored speech. Maybe that was good enough. A rare opportunity to reveal before young people, and in full view of the Lithuanian media, the carefully suppressed truth of the extent of Lithuanian collaboration with the Nazis and the critical part the average Lithuanian had played in perpetrating the Final Solution on their own Jewish communities. As for her own "input," she had the perfect suggestion, as long as she pitched it carefully enough that they wouldn't catch on to just how lethal it would be to all of that country's obfuscations and double-talk. And by the time they did, it would be too late.

All hell would break loose. She couldn't even imagine the consequences, both for herself and for Darius Vidas. It was almost as if she was laying a trap for him. But once again, as had happened so many times in the life of Milia Gottstein, she felt the ends justified the means and that her obligations were to a higher calling.

TEN

THE FIRST TIME Milia Gottstein understood there was something special about her family was when she was sitting in her mother's lap in the big easy chair and suddenly her grandfather appeared on the television set.

"Ima, Zaydie!" she had shouted, pointing, astonished.

Her mother patted her head. "It's all right. Your grandfather is a very important man and people want to know what he thinks, so he is telling them."

"Thinks about what?" She saw her parents exchange secret glances over her head, sending messages she could not decipher. She took it as an insult, as if they were making fun of her, and began to sob wildly.

"Hey, little one! What's wrong?" Her grandmother came rushing into the room, snatching her out of her mother's arms and cradling her in her big, cushiony embrace.

Wordlessly, she pointed at the screen.

"That's why you're crying?" she asked incredulously, trying not to laugh.

Milia jumped down, running to her room, diving under the pillows.

Her father knocked softly on the door.

"Go away!"

He came in and sat down on the bed. "Milia, darling, do you want to know why your grandfather is on television?"

Slowly, she slid her head out of the envelope of bedclothes and nodded, wiping a face wet with tears and snot with the back of her hand. He laughed, peeling a clean tissue from a package in his pocket and gently wiping her clean.

"Blow," he commanded, holding the tissue over her nose. She complied. "Now, no more crying, not for such a silly reason? Promise?"

She nodded, moving closer to him on the bed. "Tell me, Aba."

He took a deep breath. "There was a time when the Jewish people didn't have their own land, when they lived among the gentiles. And there came a time when a very evil ruler came to power and wanted to kill all the Jews . . ."

To her childish ears, this sounded like the beginning of so many Jewish stories. "Pharaoh? Haman?" she asked.

He smiled sadly, shaking his head. How many times had this story repeated itself throughout Jewish history! "Yes . . . no . . . not exactly. His name was Hitler, and he wasn't from Egypt or Persia, but from Germany. And then we didn't have a Moses or a Mordechai and Esther to save us," he said grimly.

"So who saved us?" she asked, looking up at him innocently, startled by the pained expression that suddenly crumpled his features, giving him a look she had never seen before. It was almost as if he wanted to cry, she thought, alarmed, regretting her question.

For what seemed like forever to her, he said nothing. But then he suddenly began again. "For a long time, no one. And then Hitler made war on other nations, strong nations, who were able to fight back, and who finally won. But they didn't fight for the Jews; they fought for themselves and their own people. Even when the war against these other nations was clearly lost, Hitler and Germany kept fighting their private war against the Jews. And when it was finally over, a new war began that only the Jews themselves could win. Your Zaydie and his friends fought like the Maccabees, first against the Germans, and then against the British, who wouldn't let the Jewish people leave the countries that had made war against them to live safely in their homeland, Eretz Yisrael. We won that war, too, which is why we now live in our own country, the land of Israel, the land God gave us.

"But even though those wars are over, our Torah tells us never to forget what was done to us. Twenty years ago, the Jewish people found and brought to justice one of our biggest enemies, a German Nazi who organized these terrible things against us. His name was Adolf Eichmann. He was brought back to Israel and had to answer for what he'd done. And just like Haman, he was hanged."

She smiled, relieved. It was a familiar ending, read aloud in the synagogue every Purim as she and all her friends vociferously swung their noisemakers to drown out each mention of the villain's name until he and his ten sons were swinging from the fifty-cubit-high gallows he'd built for Mordechai, his Jewish nemesis.

"Your grandfather is on television now because he knows about the things Eichmann did and the people he hurt. People are asking him questions and he is answering them so that we understand better what happened and can make sure it never happens again. You are going to be seeing him on television a lot now, and hearing his voice on the radio and seeing his photograph in the newspapers. You should be very proud."

She nodded slowly, trying to get her head around this startling idea, the idea that Zaydie, *her Zaydie*, who belonged only to her and to her siblings and parents, was somehow also known to many other people, strangers she had never met and had no knowledge of, people who thought about him and wanted to listen to him. And if this was true, then strangers, people she had never met and didn't know, might know all about *her* as well. It was a thrilling idea, almost as wonderful as it was terrifying, like being surrounded by figures in a misty fog whose faces you couldn't see but who could somehow see you. He was special, her Zaydie. He was a hero. But did that mean she was also special? And if she wasn't, did that mean she had to *try* to be? And that was a frightening thought, because she had no idea how to be a hero.

She got up and went back into the living room. Sitting on her grandmother's ample lap, she watched her Zaydie on the little screen. She didn't understand anything that was being said, or the terrible pictures that intermittently flashed across the screen, sometimes blocked out by the two soft palms her grandmother slipped over Milia's eyes.

She wasn't surprised people wanted to listen to him. There was something commanding in her grandfather's deep baritone, something impressive and noteworthy that made people around him stand at attention. She felt the faint stirrings of jealousy that she now had to share him with the whole world. Still, she found comfort in the idea that the stories he was now telling these strangers were nothing like the stories he told her in their very private time together.

The story she loved most was "The Story of the Family." Whenever she could, she asked to hear it again, never tiring of the narrative, which was more powerful and wondrous than any fairy tale.

"Once upon a time, hundreds of years ago, our family lived in a tiny town in Lithuania where all the Jews had little wooden houses with farms attached. They had cows and chickens and ducks, and apple trees. In the summers, they would swim in Lake Mastis, where the water was clean and refreshingly cold. My father, your great-grandfather, was a rich man with a very big house and so much land you couldn't see the end of it. He sold wheat and barley and rode into the deep, dark forests he owned with his horses and his workmen, cutting down his own trees and selling them for timber. And every Friday night, the whole family would come to your great-grandfather's house and sit around a big table filled with delicious food and cakes and challah bread and wine and talk and laugh and eat, all the aunts and uncles and cousins. There were so many of us, so many small children and babies." And each time he came to this part, he would stop for a moment and wipe a tear from his eye. One of the aunts, he would tell her, was his favorite sister, whose name was Milia. "And so when you were born, I asked your parents to name you Milia, too, because I loved my sister so much."

"Do I look like her?"

Her grandfather, instead of looking at her, would look over her head at someplace far away.

"Zaydie?" she would call him softly, until his eyes refocused, and he saw her once more.

And then would come this part, her favorite part: he would smile and turn his attention back to her and shake his head no. "She was not like you at all, *maideleh*," he would say as he stroked her head. "She had very light blond hair and dark blue eyes. But she was very pretty, just like you."

That part always made her happy.

"What else?" she'd urge him on, not wanting him to stop.

"In the center of the town, there was a great synagogue, called a *beit midrash*, and a yeshiva, the Telzh Yeshiva, with hundreds of boys from all over the world who came to learn with the famous rabbis. The students would rent rooms from the townspeople, who would give them a place to sleep and food. And all over the world, everyone had heard of this yeshiva, where the rabbis and students were extremely learned, and where only the very brightest and best yeshiva boys from all over the world were allowed to learn."

"Did you learn there, too, Zaydie?"

He shook his head and laughed. "My father wanted me to, but I didn't."

"Why not?"

"Because I loved to be outside. I loved the smell of the earth, and the animals and the trees and flowers and plants. The boys in yeshiva had very white hands that they couldn't get dirty because they might soil the pages of the holy books they pored over day and night. And . . . and . . . I wanted dirty hands, hands filled with soil, and leaves, and new wheat."

"Did you get punished?"

"Oh my, yes! All the time. I would run away from the rabbis, taking my horse into the forests for a ride or helping the laborers with the harvests. And when I came home, I would get a whipping."

"But you didn't stop?"

He shrugged. "I didn't mind getting hit by my father. The rebbe hit a lot harder," he'd chuckle.

"And then what happened?"

This part of the story was the only part that was different each time, always veering off in a new direction. Sometimes he spoke about his friends in the Zionist youth groups, and sometimes about how he loved math and wanted to be an engineer, or the big fight with his parents and, afterward, how he had run away for the final time.

"It was the last time I ever saw them. Any of them," he would say, sighing. "And then I was sorry about the fight, about running away." He would always crouch down and hold her close, looking seriously into her eyes. "You must *never* fight with your parents, with your family. You must *never* run away. A family must always stay together and help one another." And then she knew, even without looking at him, that his eyes would be sparkling with tears.

She knew that there must be more to this story, but she never pressed him. And now, with her father's revelation of the new

Haman and what he had done to the Jewish people, listening to her grandfather as the terrible pictures flashed by on the screen, the dawning of a new, nightmarish knowledge blossomed inside her, a poisonous plant that she realized she could not, and would not, ever uproot.

Instinctively she understood that all this was the continuation of the story, why he had never seen his family again. That it had to do with her namesake, her grandfather's pretty young sister of the white-blond hair and deep blue eyes, the Milia who had lived in that wooden house and had swum in that lake during hot, carefree summers, its cold, crystal clear waters making her tender flesh rise in goose bumps; the Milia whose sweet young voice had joined in Sabbath songs around the big table, part of a large, happy family. The Milia she had never met, and would never meet, as long as she lived on this earth.

* * *

To be the child of someone famous, or their grandchild, is a double-edged sword, Milia often thought. On the one hand, you enjoy the acclaim, the recognition on the faces of your teachers, your doctor, your friends' parents, your friends.

"My mother says that your grandfather was a hero in the War of Independence, and that he saved many lives." "My sister did a school project on the Brigade and found a picture of your grandfather. You must be so proud!"

On the other hand, there was this: Itamar, her youth group leader in the scouts, always pointing her out to everyone, telling them how proud they should be to have her among them. "You must try to be a leader," he exhorted her privately, believing he was motivating her instead of stoking the fires of inadequacy that always flamed within her. "People look up to your family."

You could never do anything wrong, because it wasn't Milia

who would be disgraced but the whole Gottstein clan. Whatever mistake she made, it would be "the granddaughter of Marius Gottstein" who had made it, and the shame would spill over, tainting all that was most precious to her.

Sometimes, she fantasized about escape, about buying an airline ticket to a new country that had very few Jews, and even fewer people to whom the name Gottstein meant anything. She tried it once, as a senior in high school, entering an exchange program with a school in Hong Kong. She spent a blissful time completely free of any outside expectations in a place that was far removed from anything she had ever known.

It was there she realized her fantasy also had its drawbacks. To her surprise, she found she missed the automatic recognition, the clannish support of her own kind. Meeting students who had no idea who she was, and only a vague idea about the Holocaust in general, was a shock to her. Even worse was confronting fellow students who automatically sided with the Palestinians because, as a very sincere and intelligent boy from Sri Lanka explained to her one afternoon during a tour of the Chinese market, "They were the native people of the area and the Jews stole their land." She barely controlled the urge to punch him and call him an idiot.

But what else was she supposed to do? Give him a catch-up lesson on two thousand years of Jewish history? Tell him about the Kingdom of David, which predated Mohammed by over a thousand years? Explain the very name Palestine came from the Romans, who were invaders and "occupiers" who destroyed the Jewish Temple on the Temple Mount, exiling the Jewish inhabitants to what turned out to be thousands of years of diaspora horrors—pogroms, blood libels, and genocidal wars? Go argue with these ignoramuses! Besides, their minds were already made up, she realized. It was confusing, wearying, and ultimately infuriating.

She had come back home gladly, thinking that the saying "Be careful what you wish for" was absolutely true. Never again did she take for granted growing up in her own land with people who shared her history and customs and religion, people with whom she shared a consensus about the meaning of current events and modern life. Israel was home, and she was proud of what her family had contributed to make that possible.

Still, she struggled incessantly with her grandfather's legacy. Her entire college years had been an attempt to carve out her own life, to separate herself from his achievements, to create accomplishments that could truly be called her own. The years studying English literature had almost felt like a vacation. Imagine, earning a degree by reading all the books she loved and would probably be reading anyway! And the work itself, the criticism, the papers on the love poetry of John Donne, or D. H. Lawrence's strange fixation with Mexican gods, felt pure, without emotional overtones.

Getting married, getting her doctorate, had allowed her to hide in full sight. Few people who met her connected the university instructor in English literature Milia Gottstein-Lasker to Marius Gottstein's granddaughter. And, honestly, she was happy about that. After her grandfather's death, with the reins of the Survivors' Campaign fully in her father's hands, she felt so liberated that she even allowed herself to participate in events honoring her grandfather's legacy, events in which she would expose herself to the prying eyes of people who viewed her simply as an appendage of no intrinsic value, her only accomplishment in having been born, an offspring of the great man they so admired.

All that changed abruptly once her father died and she was forced to fit her feet into the shoes both had left behind. She found that once she was presenting herself not as an appendage, but as a successor, the person who had taken on the mantle of responsibility for an enterprise in which the soul of her people was intrinsically and passionately entwined, the honeymoon was over. The vicious comparisons, the winks about nepotism, the misogynistic comments couched in phrases like "such heavy responsibilities placed on such slim girlish shoulders" never stopped.

Ironically, the onslaught had made it easier for her to firmly establish herself in the position she had never wanted, and never dreamed of being. The first thing she decided to do was to stop reading articles about herself. She let Julius read them and then asked for a summary, a thumbs-up or thumbs-down. In either case, she put them into a folder and filed them away.

"Why not read the good ones?" her husband asked her, puzzled.

"Because I have no idea who the person is who wrote it. So why should I allow myself to be swayed in my work by someone I don't know who may or may not be an idiot? And the good articles may be just as wrong as the bad ones. Besides, I'm doing the best I can do at this time in my life. Maybe tomorrow or next week, or next year, I'll be smarter or more experienced and do a better job. There might even be someone out there who could do a better job than I'm doing. But right now, this work has been given to me. I'm stuck with it and I'm doing the absolute best I can do at this moment."

This became her mantra, seeing her through some absolutely vicious criticism, most of which came from Holocaust deniers or obfuscators or secret fans of the Third Reich. But not only. She was raked over the coals by fellow Jews for not winning enough high-profile cases, or not finding as many old Nazis in hiding as they thought she should be able to find. There were also some Jews who thought everything the Campaign was trying to do was an absolute waste of time and effort and money; who thought Jews should just file it all away in some neat folder, in some metal file cabinet in some obscure office and concentrate on making "peace with the Palestinians." And then there were the ones who complained that she was "grandstanding, looking for personal publicity, wallowing in fame . . ."

She did her best to ignore them all, repeating her mantra until she herself began to believe it. But there were times when she wondered if the personal sacrifice was too great.

Like anyone involved in a public cause that took up their time and often destroyed their relationships and peace of mind, she wondered if she was a fool to sacrifice so much. She had no doubt she would never get any credit. That would all go to the organization and—rightly, in her opinion—to the man who had founded it.

What was important, ultimately, was the work. She wanted to do great things, not for the public, or for the world, but for that girl with white-blond hair and dark blue eyes who had been about to begin her life, to find love, to start a family, to learn a profession, and instead had been buried along with all her loved ones, all the Jews of her entire town, in an unmarked grave after suffering what no young girl should ever suffer.

Someone had to pay for that, whether the currency was shame, disgrace, or cold, hard cash. The perpetrators, who considered themselves safe now because their lives had gone on so long in such comfortable and honorable obscurity, or because they were already dead, had to be exposed. Their families, their birthplaces, their countrymen, had to be troubled by the inconvenient reemergence of those brutal facts, which, like gravestones rising up after heavy rains on the verdant lawns of the parks refashioned above them, refused to stay hidden. That was her job, to see that they would never be set free of their past, and that their children, grandchildren, and nation would never stop paying the unredeemed bond of their guilt.

It was a job and a responsibility that she had never sought and did not want. It had weighed her life down with implacable obligations and had distanced her from her husband and children.

She looked down at her hands, which, despite the careful application of numerous expensive creams, already seemed like those of an old woman she did not know. This would be her life, she thought. And if that were true, she had nothing to fear. The worst had already happened.

She went to her computer and began the message to the unfortunate Dr. Vidas, who had been cast in this scenario as the villain or the unsuspecting buffoon. She already felt sorry for him.

When she had read her answer over for the third time, she felt not exactly satisfied, but confident that it was the very best she could do given the circumstances. It was firm but not hostile. Clear but not too pushy. She was sure it would be a relief to him after all he must have heard about her. In any case, her eyes were closing and she still had a long drive ahead of her.

When she finally opened her front gate, the light drizzle she had left behind in Tel Aviv had turned into a sudden downpour, the way it did in Zichron, where it went from nothing to a flood in two minutes. It was cold, too, she thought, regretting not turning on the heating system when she'd heard the forecast that morning. Now it would take at least an hour to banish the winter chill.

But when she opened the front door, she saw the furnace had been lit, and the room was already warm. "Julius?" she called out softly. But there was no reply. And then she spotted it, a small blue envelope over the mantel.

Dear Milia,

I came home hoping to find you ready to talk to me, but instead, you weren't here at all. I don't know what that means, and I don't want to guess (maybe you also have some surprises you haven't shared with me?). In any case, instead of waiting to find out, I've taken my clothes and will be renting an apartment near the hospital. I don't know if Haviva will join me. That's up to her. In any case, I've

*done you the favor of turning on the heat. The house was freezing.
I don't know why you still don't know how to work the thing. It's
very simple, really. When you decide you are interested in an adult
conversation, please let me know. You have my cell number, and
I know you aren't shy to use it, even when the house isn't burning
down.*

Julius

She crushed the letter in her cold, wet hand. He had been
here, and she had been at work struggling with the wording of an
email to some stranger in Lithuania. He was right about the heating system. It scared her. When you turned it on to let in the oil
after it had been shut down for some time, you never really knew
how much oil was flowing in. If it wasn't enough, it wouldn't light.
And if it was too much, the flame went shooting up like a sudden
bonfire, terrifying her. She had always let him do it. How thrilled
he must have been to have had something so handy to throw in
her face to remind her of how inadequate and helpless she really
was, she thought bitterly. After all that had happened, this was
all he had to say for himself? *What a pompous ass*, she thought, the
longing she had been feeling for him vanishing like smoke. She
opened the heater and threw the letter into the climbing red and
blue flame. Then she just stood there, letting herself enjoy the
warmth as she watched it burn.

Eleven

Darius Vidas was exultant. He walked quickly down the hall, opening the door to Paulius's office only to remember that his friend was teaching class until four. This fact almost caused him physical pain, so anxious was he to share his good news with someone. Too restless to go back to his office, he decided to take a walk over to Old Town.

Everything was falling into place, he thought with joy. The mayors had accepted. The school principals were on board. And now, finally, he had gotten a positive reply from Milia Gottstein-Lasker. She would come! He wasn't worried about what she was going to say. Her participation would be enough to give this conference prominence and garner media attention.

He walked briskly through the old, cobblestoned streets, pulling his warm wool scarf—blue cashmere, Karolina's birthday gift from Paris—around his neck like a caress.

Here he was on Žydų Street, or the Street of the Jews, which had once been the beating heart of the Jerusalem of Lithuania, as the Lithuanian tourist industry eagerly pointed out in their advertisements to lure American Jews. Once, it had even been the center of European Jewish culture, home of the Mitnagdim, those

Lithuanian Jews who had fought the Hasidic movement tooth and nail for supremacy, appalled by their lax study habits, preference for drinking and dancing, and easy relinquishment of responsibility for their religious behavior to "holy men" or "wonder workers." There was no shortcut to holiness, the Mitnagdim taught, which lay in meticulous study of the sacred texts, and the use of reason. The Litvaks, as they were known, were such marvelous people! And to think, his country had been their birthplace.

How often he mourned that nothing remained. How he would have loved to walk through the magnificent seventeenth-century Renaissance-Baroque structure that was the Great Synagogue of Vilna. It had been a national treasure. Or to have wandered through the labyrinthine *shulhoyf* that had grown up around it, containing all that was needed for a rich Jewish life: twelve smaller synagogues, the community board, the Burial Society, the *kloyz*—or study houses—for male adults. There had been so many of them: the Old Kloyz named Shiv'ah Kru'im Kloyz, the New Kloyz of Yesod, and the famous *kloyz* of the head of the Mitnagdim, Rabbi Eliyahu ben Shlomo Zalman, known as the Vilna Gaon. It had also housed the community's ritual baths as well as the communal bathhouse, a public lavatory, a communal well, kosher meat stalls, and the famous Strashun Library. Despite their conflicts, Hasidim had also built their synagogues there: the Koidanover Hasidim, as well as the Lubavitch Hasidim.

It had been a historical treasure, three hundred years of magnificent achievements. Brutal, ignorant Nazi scum had simply burned it all down. The Soviets, some of them of the same mentality, filled with the same poisonous Jew hatred, had completed the destruction, pulling down whatever remained in the 1950s. Afterward, they'd covered half the area with an ugly, Soviet-style elementary school, which still imposed itself on the area's innocent children. He shook his head at the criminal waste, the stupidity, the incalculable loss.

And if that wasn't enough, they'd also destroyed the old Šnipiškes Jewish cemetery on the right bank of the Neris River and used tombstones from the new cemetery in Užupis for paving stones. Only the third Jewish cemetery in Šeškinė—his old neighborhood, started in 1941—remained.

While it was true that in the early 1990s memorial monuments and plaques had been placed on sites and buildings connected to the Jewish history of the city, they came nowhere near compensating the loss. Out of a hundred synagogues in Vilnius, only eight buildings had survived, of which only Taharat Ha-Kodesh (the Choral) Synagogue still functioned as a house of worship to the tiny remnant of the Jewish community that still existed in Vilnius.

How ironic, then, that after finally regaining their hard-won independence and longed-for freedoms from these heavy-booted foreign marauders bent on erasing the city's heritage, they themselves were now willingly choosing to follow in their footsteps! Only recently there had been widespread enthusiasm for a plan to build an elaborate convention center over the remains of the Old Jewish Cemetery. Luckily, the vociferous worldwide outcry that had greeted this decision had prompted the mayor to wisely suggest an alternative location. Of course, this sensible and sensitive decision had been met with a vicious backlash with antisemitic overtones.

He knew that people like Professor Dovid Katz called conferences like the one he was planning "quisling and useful Jewish idiot" conferences. There was some truth to that, he had to admit. But it was exactly what he wanted most to avoid.

It wasn't enough to talk about the "good old days" when the Jews had lived and been part of them. They had to talk about how that ended. The time had come for a frank discussion about the 1930s, the time that preceded the Nazis; about how the Lithuanian Businessmen's Association had urged government restrictions on Jews, boycotts of Jewish businesses. How Lithuanian clergymen like Stasys Yla told everyone who would listen Jews wanted to rule the world and could achieve it best through Communism. How the Tautininkai party adopted Nazi ideology and race theory, calling minorities "incompatible foreign matter in the body of the nation." How the newspaper *Lithuania's Echo* had advocated for separate beaches for Jews. And worst of all, the vicious, unfounded lie that it was "Jewish Communists" who were responsible for the brutal Soviet occupation of their homeland when the sad, ignominious truth was that it was Lithuanian politicians who'd capitulated to Russian demands, allowing their tanks to roll across the borders in 1940 without a single shot being fired. This was not because of the Jews, or the handful of Jewish Communists, who were powerless.

Now it was popular to forget that, to blame it all on the few Jews who were Communists who had welcomed them. To forget that such Jews were an anomaly, the vast majority of Jews being conservative, deeply religious villagers who strongly supported Lithuanian independence and who had no reason to want a Russian takeover. Why, the Russians were even bigger Jew haters than the Lithuanians! The first time they'd taken over, they'd deported thousands of Jews to Russia, where they'd died like flies because of starvation and disease.

This lie was first formulated by Lithuanian "patriots" who'd swallowed the Nazis' poisonous mixture of racial superiority and Jewish conspiracy theories. How easy it was to blame the Communist deportations of Lithuanians on the "Bolshevik-Jewish regime" instead of on the Lithuanian politicians who had rolled over and let the Russians invade and conquer.

Lithuanians devoured these scurrilous propaganda leaflets, swallowing every lie like it was a piece of delicious pie. Of course, after that, it was child's play to get them to rally to the cry of "Take up arms and free Lithuania from the Jewish yoke."

When Germany invaded the Soviet Union in 1941, the local population was already primed to annihilate not only retreating Russians, but every last Jew they could lay their hands on. And why waste the young Jewish women, even little girls? Why not rape them first and then murder them? Why waste bullets on the babies when smashing their heads into walls and trees served the same purpose? Better yet, throw them alive into pits and cover them with earth and let them cry themselves to death . . . And then there was all that loot! Why not move into the Jewish houses, parcel out Jewish silverware, take the warm coats and dresses off the backs of Jewish women as they stood by open pits and give them to your wives and sweethearts? After all, the Jews would not be needing them.

For Lithuanians, the German invasion had meant freedom from Soviet oppression; for the Jews, it had meant the Final Solution. Was it any wonder, then, that Jews with any guts took up arms and did their best to protect themselves from Lithuanians fashioning themselves variously as "police," "partisans," "resistance fighters," or "white armbanders," who were savagely murdering, raping, and looting their families? Whatever they pretended to be, many of the Lithuanians were working hand in hand with the Einsatzgruppen, the mobile Nazi killing units.

But Lithuanians couldn't bear to hear any accusations against their precious partisans, no matter how true. After all, hadn't they fought bravely and died in battles against the Communists? Hadn't they been tortured in KGB prisons and executed for their love of country? And while it was true that many of them had died to make Lithuania free, and the good things a person does stand separately from his misdeeds, neither canceling the other out, common sense decreed that no matter what else they had done, one could simply not honor people who in addition to being freedom fighters had also been rapists, murderers, and thieves.

Maybe this was part of the reason why so many Lithuanians were fleeing the country. It was so hard to face the complicated truth of the country's past, so difficult to delineate where the fine lines of responsibility began and ended. But certain facts were indisputable. In this very spot, the Great Vilnius Ghetto had been created on September 6, 1941, housing almost thirty thousand Jews. The so-called little ghetto, into which an additional eleven thousand Jews were crammed, only lasted months until all were killed. And by September 23, 1943, almost all the remaining Jews of Vilnius had been trucked out to the forest in Ponary. Here was the main gate. Those who entered had no hope of exiting alive. His fellow Lithuanians had seen to that.

He remembered the descriptions of the ghetto by Gregory Szur in *Notes from the Vilna Ghetto, 1941–44*, comparing the two ghettos to ant colonies, describing how every day the Jews would get up at first daylight, lining up in disciplined rows to work the hardest jobs in factories, building sites, and German army camps cutting peat, laying train tracks, and moving heavy items in enormous warehouses. Each had been given a *schien*, or a work certificate, which they guarded zealously, believing it would spare their lives. Often, Lithuanian guards would tear this precious document to pieces on a whim, sending workers to prison. The Germans were terrible, of course, enjoying their power to humiliate and degrade the helpless, trapped Jews, beating those who didn't take off their hats and bow to their captors fast enough.

And most of the time, the work itself was simply a form of torture: men forced to run up a hill carrying timber on their backs so that they could be beaten when, exhausted, they fell; women forced to collect horse manure with their bare hands, to clean army barrack floors and windows with the dresses they wore, or to be harnessed to heavy wagons, which they dragged from place to place, afraid to protest lest they lose their certificates, which in the end were another cruel joke. The *schien* saved no one.

He looked up. There it was, the memorial plaque, two pieces of gray granite depicting the outlines of the ghetto and stating the bare facts. It seemed almost grudging. Of course, it had been defaced with a swastika almost immediately after going up. They'd cleaned it up. No one stopping here and reading it would have any idea how much the Jews of his city had been made to suffer before being murdered by their Lithuanian neighbors working alongside the relatively few Nazi soldiers dispatched from the Russian front. The Nazis could not have done it alone.

With our own hands, he thought, trembling, *we killed some of our most educated and talented people, and this tragedy continues to wreak havoc, leaving behind a stagnating country, rotting for want of opportunity.*

If we want Lithuania to thrive, we need to educate our citizens about the terrible mistakes that were made. We need to be able to face the past, the way the Germans have, and turn a new page. Look how Germany was thriving! Tourism, industry, cooperation with Israeli companies, trade! Why, over two hundred thousand Jews and Israelis now lived and worked in Germany, helping that country to prosper! Why can't we simply do that, say what happened, say we are sorry, pay reparations, honor the mass graves? We need to stop creating fake heroes out of thieving-rapist-murderer-Nazi wannabes; we need to stop creating excuses for them, stop hiding their ugly flaws and appalling moral failings.

Anyone who can convince our country of that, who can set the ball rolling, would be a real Lithuanian hero! Milia, Dovid Katz, Silvia Foti, Rūta Vanagaitė, Grant Gochin, Efraim Zuroff, and yes, me, Darius Vidas! If we succeed in achieving that, we, all of us, will deserve to have statues of ourselves put up everywhere and streets and towns and schools named after us, because we are the only hope that Lithuanians have of finally freeing themselves from their ugly past and striding forward to a future worth living.

He looked around at his city. How many times had it been invaded, destroyed, and oppressed? Its existence was a triumph over the Nazis, over the Soviets, who had both done their best to erase it and remake it in their own image. They had not succeeded. It was still Vilnius, Vilna, Vilne, Wilno, Yerushalayim de-Lita (Jerusalem of Lithuania). It belonged to him and to all the many and diverse peoples who had ever lived there and called it their birthplace and their home. He loved it deeply, wholeheartedly, and passionately. He wanted only the best for it. But Lithuanians still did not comprehend the true nature of the gift that was their birthright, the heritage hidden among the ruins. They had not yet learned to preserve and defend the diverse reminders of all who had lived here, and everything of value they'd left behind, reminders of all they, as Lithuanians, had achieved and had suffered. Why was that?

All over Europe these terrible things had been done. In Paris, they had been done, Jews forced together in a stadium without food or water for days, then shipped off and murdered.

French police had participated, sometimes rounding up their own neighbors. The French, no less than the Lithuanians, had collaborated with the Nazis, befriended them, went out on dates with them, dined with them, listened to opera with them. Yet a black cloud did not hang over Paris. No one hated the French for what they had done under Nazi rule. There were two different attitudes for the same crime. Why was that? Because the French were more stylish? Or simply better liars?

We Lithuanians are not good liars, he thought. *We are so clumsy, so transparent. So stupid. We put up statues to the perpetrators and collaborators. We refuse to condemn them, refuse to put them on trial, or participate in their prosecution. Instead, we embrace them openly.* He shook his head. Why? Why turn Noreika, who was a monster who facilitated the death of thousands under the cruelest possible conditions, into a saint and hero? *His own granddaughter* refused to be part of the elaborate excuses they had found for him. And instead of applauding her amazing courage, they were doing their best to discredit her.

Wherever you looked in the city, the Jews seemed to whisper through that black cloud, right into your ear, demanding to be heard.

We must get rid of the whispers, the black cloud, or at least make a hole in it to let the sun shine through. We must stop defending the indefensible, tell our children the truth.

He thought of the stirring events in the most recent Holocaust remembrance program the Road of Memory, where participants had marched to over two hundred mass murder sites to pay tribute to the innocent victims and to demand greater attention be paid to the maintenance of all known mass graves of Holocaust victims.

It was good. It was part of the answer. But it wasn't enough.

In his own program, he would try to build on this, but in a more personal way. Not Holocaust mass graves, but the words of the individual victims. There was that book of YIVO contest entries. And of course the uplifting story of his own family's heroism.

He had written to Yad Vashem in Jerusalem with the particulars, but so far he had not received an answer as to the whereabouts of the Kenskys. But with the positive reply from Milia, he felt lucky. It was all falling into place. He felt so hopeful that this conference would be a momentous turning point in Lithuania's long fight to clear its name and to prove to those haters that they were no different from any other European, dedicated to diversity and against all forms of racism and xenophobia.

This was his chance to prove it in front of the world.

TWELVE

MILIA WOKE UP in the morning feeling sick. Her nose was stuffed and her throat scratchy. She wondered if she'd caught Covid, especially with all the sneaky new variations going around the world making life miserable for everyone, particularly those like herself who had trusted that vaccinations and masks were impregnable armor, and that only lesser beings too silly and incompetent to take care of themselves were now at risk.

The thought terrified her. She inhaled some nose drops, which gave her a moment of relief and clarity.

She didn't want to get any sicker, to need help. To need a doctor. To need Julius.

She picked up the phone and called Gilad. He didn't pick up. But then, he never did. She knew it was his policy to ignore all incoming calls and to call back if and when he found it convenient. She prayed he would find her convenient.

The phone rang two minutes later.

"Hi, Mom. What's up?"

"Gilad! I'm so happy you called me back."

There was a silent pause.

"Not that you wouldn't, don't . . ." she sputtered, lost.

"Mom, Mom, calm down. It's okay. I'm not accusing you of anything. What's wrong?"

That was a question! *Ask me what's right*, she wanted to shout into the phone. She took a deep, calming breath. Don't over-whelm him. Don't convince him *not* to call you back the next time. "I don't feel well. I'm obsessing over Covid."

He was immediately all concern. "Do you have a fever? What does Dad say?"

Oh my God! She hadn't told any of the children, she sud-denly remembered, moving out of her brain fog into a moment of clarity. She cleared her scratchy throat, making it hurt even worse. "Your father and I . . . we are having some problems."

"What kind of problems?"

She made an impulsive decision to rip off the Band-Aid.

"He's having an affair with Haviva and he's moved out."

The was a moment of absolute silence.

"Haviva, as in Nadav and Haviva, your good friends?"

"Yes."

He was quiet for a moment and then he said, in his best ther-apist manner, "I see."

She was devastated. If only he had used an expletive! Even an explosive and satisfying "What?!?!?" would have satisfied her. She wanted that, needed it. At least from her children. They needed to side with her unequivocally.

"Is there anything I can do to help, Mom?"

"No, I'm sorry I'm calling to bother you. You are probably very busy . . ." She felt herself tear up with an anguish of disap-pointment.

"Now you're punishing me for not giving you what you want. I'm sorry, but I'm not planning on taking sides here. I love you both, you know that. But maybe what you both need is profes-sional counseling."

Right. That was the answer to everything that ails you these days. A hundred-dollar-an-hour *professional* who will accept credit cards or cash, but no personal checks, as payment for doing what your family and friends are *supposed* to do out of love: listen, empathize, and offer kind advice.

"Mom?"

"We are way beyond that. Nadav called me. That's how I found out. Your father showed up at the house when I was at work and took all his clothes. He left me a nasty note."

There was silence. "This is against my better judgment, but do you want me to talk to him?"

No. I want a hit man to beat him to a bloody pulp and throw his carcass into the sea, she thought, furious. *I want Haviva to be stripped naked and paraded through the Machane Yehuda marketplace at high noon wearing a sign around her neck that says "Whore."*

"No, of course not. This is between the two of us. I guess I called because I just needed to hear a friendly voice . . ." *that would take my side, reassure me that I'm not dying of Covid, offer to come visit and make me hot tea . . . act like a loving son.*

"Well, I sympathize with you. This must be very hard, all of it together, the shock about Dad and your friend Haviva, feeling ill in the middle of a pandemic . . ." He paused. "*Do* you have fever?"

"No. At least, not yet. But I feel ill. And I've been invited to speak in Lithuania."

"You're not going, right?"

"Why shouldn't I?"

"You can't be serious! They've always been so horrible to you there. All those Twitters and WhatsApps they send out defaming you and your work . . ."

"But the people who invited me are really appreciative of what I do. It's sort of a golden opportunity."

"Don't give them an answer until you are feeling better and your head clears."

"My head is perfectly clear. I'm going," she said with a sudden vehement conviction that at the moment she did not feel about anything else. In fact, she was already half regretting the email she'd sent out to Vidas. "I didn't call to ask your advice or permission," she added with unnecessary harshness, immediately regretting it. "Oh, I'm sorry. I didn't mean that, Gilad. It was uncalled for . . . I'm just not . . ."

"Stop," he interrupted her. "You don't need to apologize. I'm sorry if the reaction you've gotten from me has hurt your feelings."

She shook her head. He saw right through her. He always did.

"But I care about you—and about Aba—and I'm happy to help in any way I can. Do you want me to come by? I have work until five, but then I can be at your place. It will take about three hours."

He lived so far away, in the Negev. The thought of forcing him to make that drive, almost three hours each way, was unthinkable. "No, I guess I just wanted to catch up with you and let you know what's happening. I'm going to be fine, don't worry. Two aspirin and a large cup of tea . . ."

"Take the damn Covid test."

"Yes, of course," she agreed, considering it for the first time. So much progress in the world, and that's all they could come up with, a stick up your nose practically into your brain? "As for your father, that will work itself out. It always has. And Lithuania is not until June . . ."

"Well, call me when you get the results. And if you want to talk over the situation with Aba, I'm always here. Please call me if you need *anything*."

Even though she knew she would not be calling him again for *anything*, and he would not be coming over anytime soon, she was still comforted by his voice on the phone; that there was someone who knew the truth about what she was going through and cared—well, more or less—was also something.

When she hung up, she took out the gadget she'd purchased recently, along with all the other terrified Israelis, which let you point and shoot at your forehead to get your temperature. Thirty-six point five. Was that normal? Or a low fever? Her usual temperature was thirty-six. Although sometimes it went up a bit. It was a long way from outright fever. Maybe it was nothing, just a little sniffle. Nowadays, people were terrified of any kind of illness, imagining it was just the beginning of an onslaught that would lead in a straight line to coma and death. Not a good situation for people like herself who were slight hypochondriacs to begin with.

Still, she felt unsatisfied, as if she'd sat down to lunch only to be served a tiny, unappetizing portion that left her hungry. She tried to think of who else she could call. The only person she really wanted to talk to, of course, was Julius. Her heart felt suddenly heavy, a sense of despair settling over her like cold, black lava dust from an old volcanic eruption.

Impulsively, she dialed her daughter-in-law.

"Renee, it's Milia. I hope I'm not bothering you."

There was something about the lively redhead whom her eldest son had had the good sense to marry that she had always adored. Maybe because Renee didn't hold it against her that she had been less than thrilled when Amir suddenly got engaged instead of going to Columbia University in New York to finish his MBA. She'd been shocked, more than anything, worried it would hold her son back. The opposite had been true. They'd traveled to New York together and Renee had helped the capricious Amir, who might not have finished if she hadn't been there to support him. But it wasn't only that. Her connection with her daughter-in-law went way beyond her connection to her son.

Renee was a talented artist in her own right who was passionate about her craft and didn't let anything interfere with it. She was perfectly okay with the house being upside-down when she was in the middle of working. There was none of that "stop-everything-and-clean-up-my-mother-in-law-is-coming-over." Milia admired that so much. "Everything is going to be dust eventually! So what does it matter?" Renee would say cheerfully, refusing to be embarrassed when the sink was full of unwashed dishes and the floor a carpet of toys. Renee always told you the truth, even when it would have been so much more expedient to lie. That took a bit of getting used to, but once Milia did, she adored her for it. Gradually, she had taken to calling Renee when she wanted an honest opinion about things that troubled her.

"Renee? Got a minute?"

Forty minutes later, after she'd taken the Covid test and gotten a negative, she parked her car and headed toward the Nina Café in Tel Aviv's trendy Neve Tzedek neighborhood. She looked around the usually bustling coffeehouse, which was still nearly full despite Covid-related restrictions.

"Milia, over here!" she suddenly heard behind her. She pivoted. Renee's satiny, shoulder-length red hair took her breath away. *Such a beautiful girl*, she thought once again, wondering at Amir's amazing luck. He was not exactly a ladies' man, at least not that she had ever noticed.

And still, here he was with this gorgeous, talented, intelligent, kind woman. She made herself a mental note to remind him to thank God every day for his good fortune.

"Renee." She walked over slowly. "I just got a negative on Covid. Can I hug you?"

Renee laughed but put her arms up. "You should be worried about getting it from me. After all, it's the kids who are spreading it. They're not vaccinated like the rest of us."

"I'm not worried," Milia insisted, reaching out and hugging her, then kissing her on both cheeks, French-style. "Thank you so much for making time to see me. I hope I'm not taking you away from your work."

"You are, but so what? This is more important," Renee said frankly. "I'm so happy you called, but it's not like you. Are you all right?"

She shrugged. "Actually, no."

Renee reached out and took her hand. "Let's get the best coffee and an almond croissant. That for sure will make things better."

It did. Only after picking up the last crumbs with a wetted forefinger did Milia blurt out, "Julius has left me."

Renee gasped. "I can't believe it! He'll regret it."

She loved this girl.

"Is it like, official?"

Milia nodded. "Last night. He came home while I was still at work and emptied out the closets."

"Where is he now?"

She shrugged. "With her. Probably."

Renee's mouth fell open. "There's a 'her'?"

"Haviva Melnick."

Renee shook her head. "It makes no sense! I've met the woman. She's so . . . so . . . ordinary."

"I guess that's a plus if you're married to someone who goes around the world looking to put octogenarians in jail."

"Who spends her life trying to get justice for victims who can't fight for themselves," Renee corrected her vehemently.

Milia took her hand gratefully. "I guess I wanted to talk to you because . . ." Milia hesitated, afraid to offend.

"Because I went through a divorce. Hey, it's perfectly fine, Milia. I just don't know if my experience will help you at all. I was very young when I got married the first time, barely twenty, and my ex was much older, someone I'd met in the art world. He dazzled me for a while. He seemed to know everyone worth knowing. He had showings of his work to which famous people came. He was encouraging to me, in the beginning. It took me a while to notice that the people he 'knew' were just strangers being polite to him when he approached them, and that his showings hardly ever sold anything and the galleries who put them on were people who knew his father, who was a banker. As for the encouragement, that ended pretty quickly, as soon as I started winning awards and having showings of my own. I guess there came a certain point when I had to stop lying to myself about what a great relationship we had."

Milia looked up. "When did that happen?"

"Well, I had just had my first big showing at a major gallery, and all these flowers were being delivered to me from people I knew, and they were lined up in vases at the entrance. And then my friend Abigail said, 'Which one is your husband Mark's?' Well, none of them, as a matter of fact! So I said, 'Mark doesn't need to send me flowers. Every single day he shows me how much he loves me and how proud he is.' And as soon as I'd said it, I realized it was a total lie. Mark never told me he was proud of me. The opposite. He kept telling me that I shouldn't have a showing because I wasn't good enough, that I should wait five or six years and he would 'tutor' me. And he never showed me any love at all, except for sex, which, as we women both know, isn't the same thing at all."

Milia nodded.

"Well, that was the moment I knew I was going to leave him. And as soon as the option opened up in my mind, I felt such a flood of pure relief! I could do that, never see him again, not go home with him, not listen to a word he said. The joy of that option filled me with so much light I started smiling and didn't stop the entire night. Everyone thought it was because of the success of the show. But it wasn't. It was because I realized I could get rid of Mark."

Milia stirred her coffee, making designs from the foam. She stared into the cup like it was some kind of Rorschach test. *What am I looking for?* she wondered. "You're right, Renee. It's not the same. I've been married to my husband for many years. He's my partner, my helper, my best friend."

"Still?" Renee inquired gently.

Milia thought about it. He *had* been those things. In the past. But it hadn't been like that for years now. At first, she had been too busy to notice, and honestly, she had more important things on her mind, like her work, which never let up. She hadn't allowed herself to miss him, to miss the "us" they used to be, resigning herself to the inevitability of changes that age brings to relationships. It had never occurred to her that he was distancing himself because he'd found someone else.

"I don't know what to do," she sighed.

Renee squeezed her hand kindly. "Why do you have to *do* anything? Is he demanding a divorce?"

"No," she realized.

"Then"—Renee made a dismissive wave—"just leave it."

"Really?"

"You know, the chances are, the more you leave him alone to do what he thinks he wants, without standing in his way, the more likely he is to come to his senses. Julius is a brilliant man. I can't see him long-term with someone like Haviva. Once the novelty wears off, he'll be bored out of his mind."

"Maybe not. She's good with men; she knows how to flatter them, how to make them laugh."

"That's okay when everything is going well, but the moment a man like Julius needs a real partner, she's not going to be enough. Knowing what kind of a man he is, I think he'll figure that out pretty quickly."

"You think so?" Milia said, looking into her eyes, wondering if that would be a good thing or a bad thing. The thought of even being in the same room with Julius at the moment made her feel sick, let alone the idea of getting back together.

Her daughter-in-law nodded sagely.

"You know, I have no idea if that's even true, but thank you so much for saying it, Renee."

At this, her daughter-in-law rose, came over to her, crouched down, and looked up as she held both of Milia's hands. "You are such an admirable woman, Milia. You're a national treasure. You deserve better."

Milia rose, helping her up, and the two women embraced like people outside an ICU ward where someone they both loved was on life support.

Milia's smartwatch buzzed. "It's my office. I have to take this."

"And I'll have to pick up the kids soon."

"Renee, thank you."

"I hope I've helped. You mean so much to me."

"And you to me, my dear Renee! You can't imagine how much you've helped me. Thank you!"

"Do you want me to clue Amir in?"

Milia hesitated, but then thought, *Why not?* It would be one less burden on her shoulders. "Yes, please. But tell him that no decisions have been reached yet."

Renee eyed her curiously. "Is that the truth?"

Milia nodded, then sighed. "Unfortunately."

Renee laughed, opening her purse and taking out her wallet.

"Put it away. I'll take care of it."

"Thanks. I'm going to run. And Milia, if you need me, please . . ."

"You see you're the first one I called."

"Really?"

"No, actually the second. I called Gilad first."

She smiled. "The therapist."

"He was no good whatsoever."

"Therapists can be tricky."

"I prefer nonprofessionals when it comes to commonsense advice."

Her watch buzzed again.

She dialed her office, watching the flaming-red hair disappear through the door. She felt comforted. Renee had said all the right things to soothe her battered ego and broken heart. She even allowed herself the thought that perhaps what she'd said was possibly even true when it came to her husband and his mistress.

Julius did have a very low boredom threshold. Maybe he *would* come to his senses, seeing through the peroxided hair, the fatuous giggling, the bouncy breasts, and the still-slim waist. He would notice the wrinkles and hidden pockets of flab. More, he would see into the empty head and weak character and ordinariness. He would get tired of the one-sided conversations about nothing. But by then, she suddenly thought with a bit of astonishment, perhaps he'd find that it was just too late.

THIRTEEN

DARIUS SAT WITH his mother in the small living room of her old, comfy but ugly apartment in Grigiškės. On the wall facing the sofa was the inevitable crucifix next to Lithuania's coat of arms—Christ rubbing shoulders with Vytis, Lithuania's knight in shining armor, their togetherness symbolizing what he and all Lithuanians imbibed during childhood. Also all that was wrong with the country, Darius thought, shaking his head. Still, having been raised in a devout Catholic home as well as a very patriotic one, both symbols tugged at his heart.

"So why don't you eat something? I made borscht," his mother, Regina, said in that aggrieved tone that she had become so fond of lately, using it to complain about everything from the Eurovision song contest to the price of cucumbers and salami.

"I will have a bowl, but not now. First I have to ask you something."

She sat down across from him in the elaborate chair she'd recently reupholstered in a garish gold velvet. Smoothing down her damp apron, she laid her weathered hands calmly in her lap and waited.

"It's about the Jews Grandfather saved," he said.

She shrugged, annoyed. "I already told you everything I know. It was so long ago. I was only a child . . ."

"I'm sorry to bother you again, Mamytė, but it's really important."

"What could be so important that happened so long ago?"

"That necklace . . . do you still have it?"

"Of course. I would never sell it. But let me tell you, I'm sure it's worth a pretty penny. But it was given to me by my mother, who treasured it." She suddenly looked up at him, her eyes narrowing in suspicion. "Don't tell me you have another woman and you want to marry her and give her the necklace?"

He laughed. "No. Your precious necklace is safe. I just want to see it again."

She shrugged, standing up and going into her bedroom. "Bring me a chair, will you?" she called out to him.

He grabbed one of the kitchen stools. "Don't you have a proper step stool? You can kill yourself climbing up on this, Mamytė!"

"Don't worry about me. I'm used to it."

Reluctantly, he gave her a hand climbing up, all the while holding it steady with his other hand, sure this was going to end up in the emergency room. What would he tell his father? Buy her a proper stepladder and bring it already, he exhorted himself, watching in horror as she reached unsteadily up to the top shelf of her closet and fumbled with the lock on her small metal safe.

She climbed down carefully clutching a square jeweler's box of blue velvet tied with strings of faded gold ribbons. When she no longer had to balance, she laid it reverently in both outstretched palms, like an offering.

He reached for it, but she backed away. "Since Bobutė died and left it to me, I don't let anyone touch it. Be patient. I'll open it for you."

She laid it down on the coffee table, carefully undoing the many elaborately tied ribbons and slowly pulling back the lid.

Although he had seen it before, it still took his breath away. White gold leaves set with tiny pearls rose out of a golden vase at whose center a stunning blue emerald gleamed, encircled by sparkling pavé diamonds and larger matching pearls.

"It's beautiful, Mamytė."

She nodded. "So beautiful I'm afraid to wear it."

"Can you tell me the story again, about how your father came to have it?"

"I don't know anything more than I told you the last time."

"Please, Mamytė."

She sat down, placing the velvet box in her lap. "I'll tell you what I told you last time you asked: Your grandfather said that a Jewish factory owner came to him at the beginning of that terrible war. Grandfather had just been made the mayor of J—. It was the worst of all times, my mother told me, when bombs were dropping on the city and the center of town began to burn.

"Then guns started firing. There was so much shooting you couldn't even figure out where it was coming from! The next day, the Germans came in their cars and tanks. The former mayor, Tolushys, had been shot by the Russians when they left because he was a patriot and had put overturned cars and trucks in their path. Your grandfather was recruited by the partisans to take over as mayor, even though he was still very young— only twenty-two or twenty-three—and working as a baker in the next town over. He always said he'd joined the partisans in order to help people. He and his friends wanted to protect people's property, make some law and order. He saw the Germans were robbing the Jews, taking over their houses and businesses. But what could he do? He was just one man." She sighed, squeezing the fabric of her dress with nervous hands. "This Kensky, who ran the Shus Shirt Factory and had also just started a candy factory, was a very smart and respectable man. Kensky begged your grandfather to help him. He brought his young wife and three small children to your grandfather's office and told him, 'They are throwing us out of our home! Everyone is being sent to the ghetto in Žagarė. We have heard they mean to harm all the Jews. Can't you hide our family?' Let me tell you, this was a very dangerous proposition—your grandfather could have been shot like Tolushys! But being such a good and devout Christian, your grandfather couldn't just turn them away. He hid them in a secret alcove just above his office in city hall. He risked his life to bring them food and warm clothing. Imagine it! The Germans were in and out of that building every day! He hid them there until the war was over. Then, Mr. Kensky said he had relatives in America, in Danver—"

"Denver."

"Maybe. Anyway, he wrote to them, to his American relatives, asking them to help him get American visas. Your grandfather remembered mailing the letters. He even paid for the postage stamps, which weren't cheap! But it worked. The Kenskys' American relatives arranged for the visas and paid for the boat tickets. The Kenskys were so grateful for everything your grandfather had done for them that before they left, they insisted he take this necklace as a parting gift for saving their lives."

Darius nodded. Yes, it was the same story he had heard as a child. "Do you remember their names?"

"I told you! Kensky."

"First names? The wife's name? The children's names and ages . . . ?"

"I think it was Emil and Beyle, and the children were Itele, who was five, Henokh, three, and a baby. Ruchele."

"You think, or you know?"

"It's what I remember being told," she replied irritably. "You want a notarized guarantee? I was young at the time, and now my memory is not the best . . . Why are you getting all upset anyhow? What does any of this matter now?"

He tried to hide his frustration. "Because I am trying to find them."

She widened her eyes in astonishment. "The Kenskys?"

He nodded.

"Why?"

"Because I want to show our people and our country that not all Lithuanians were gold-digging murderers who hunted and robbed their Jewish neighbors. I want to show that there were also good people who helped, like grandfather. I'd like this Jewish family to visit us, to tell people about what happened, how they were saved."

She shook her head, clutching her fingers in distress and alarm. "Darius. Leave it alone!"

He was shocked. "What do you mean?"

"Just what I said. Leave them be! You don't want them to come back here and tell everything they know, believe me."

"What do they know, and more important, what do *you* know, Mamytė? Tell me!"

But her lips were sealed. She merely continued shaking her head, looking down at the sparkling jewels to make sure they were settled securely back in their blue velvet case, before closing it and tying the many faded gold ribbons securely.

"Who else can I talk to about this, Mamytė? What other relatives might remember more?"

"It's a mistake, I'm telling you . . ."

"Please! I'm going to do it, to find out. I have all the papers. I'm going through the KGB files. Please help me."

She sighed. "Well, I see I'm wasting my breath. You won't listen. As usual," she huffed. "There aren't too many of our relatives left alive, if you must know . . ." Seeing his disappointment, she relented. "There is your great-aunt Emilija Balchunus—your grandfather's youngest sister—and her daughter, Daiva Melis, and another cousin, Marijus Norbut, and his children, Ricardas, Goca, and Edita. But I don't know how much they would know."

"Well, are you sure there is no one else from the family?"

She hesitated. "Well, there is one, but we aren't in touch. They fell out with the family so many years ago. No one talks to them."

"What happened?"

"You know, one of those silly family arguments that gets all blown up and then it's World War Three. I never heard the details. Something that happened during the war, I was told. They were peasants, very poor farmers. No education, living out in the boondocks."

His mother had always been a snob. "Who is this?"

"I think his name is Ramunos Jonaitis. He's the only one from that branch of the family left. He lives in some tiny village. I don't even have an address or phone number for him."

"Please, Mamytė, give me what you've got."

Reluctantly, she went to the old-fashioned wall unit she had inherited from her mother, a monstrosity in carved oak that had been stained a revolting shade of dark brown, the kind people on DIY videos were always painting over. Why they bothered, he couldn't fathom. Even after DIY, most of these salvaged pieces remained massively ugly, except now they were blue, or ivory, or mint green.

She opened one of the drawers and took out an old address book. Licking her finger, she began turning pages. "Here. Emilija is still in Kaunas, and Daiva and her family live nearby. But Marijus is in Telšiai."

He let out a groan. It was the other side of the country.

"You could call him on the phone."

He certainly intended to start with that. "What is he doing all the way out there anyway?"

"There is a small farm he inherited. He's retired now, so he went to live 'off the land' as the hippies like to call it."

"And exactly how are we related?"

"Marijus was your grandfather's cousin's son."

"And what about this black sheep? This Jonaitis? Where does he live?"

"I'm not sure . . . but also far away from the city, I think. That part of the family was always very poor."

"It's not a crime, Mamytė!"

She arched her brows. "It's no great honor, either."

"Well, give me the address book and I'll copy out the addresses and phone numbers."

She handed it to him reluctantly. "Darius, don't pester them. No one likes to talk about the war years. And they are old and probably not so healthy. Promise me!"

"I will be on my best behavior, Mamytė. But tell me, aren't you even curious? This was a heroic deed Grandfather did. It should be acknowledged, written about . . ."

"Listen, boy, I'm *telling* you it's not something the family liked to talk about."

Her attitude intrigued and disturbed him, piquing his curiosity. Far from discouraging him, it only made him want to look into the matter more.

So he took out a notebook and started looking up the contact information for his relatives, struggling to decipher his mother's handwriting. There it was, Ramunos Jonaitis, and an address in some place out in the middle of nowhere near the Latvian border! Distracted, he didn't notice when she disappeared back into her bedroom with the blue box.

He jumped up. "Don't stand up on that chair yourself, I'm coming!"

"It's done," she called back to him. "You see, I'm not dead," she added dryly as she rejoined him.

"I'll get you a step stool this week. But until then, please, Mamytė, promise me! No more acrobatics on swaying chairs!" He was already slipping his notebook back into his bag and putting on his coat.

"What? Already? You didn't even touch the borscht! And what about your papa?"

"Where is he?"

"He went to visit his friends in the park."

"Then who knows when he'll be back. I'm sorry, Mamytė, but I'm very busy. You know I'm arranging a conference, right?"

"What is this going to be about, your conference?"

"About what happened to the Jews during the war. The Holocaust."

Again, her lips tightened. "Darius, I'm warning you. Leave it alone."

He leaned in and kissed her. "Don't worry so much. I'm not going to get into any trouble."

"That's what you always say!"

He grinned and waved. But as he made it to his car, he felt troubled. That necklace. Who would willingly part with something like that?

He felt a chill down his back.

* * *

"You just missed your son."

"What? He didn't tell us he was coming. Why didn't you make him wait for me?"

"Like you can make Darius do something. Besides, he said he was in a rush."

"What did you talk about?"

"Nothing."

He made a face. "Nothing? No wonder he ran off so fast."

"He didn't want to talk. He wanted to see the necklace."

"When are you going to get rid of that thing?"

"You always want to get your hands on the money. But I told you, it is my inheritance. It doesn't belong to you; you have no say."

He scoffed. "It didn't belong to your grandparents, either."

"What do you mean?"

He looked up at the wall and the large framed photo of his father-in-law in uniform, darkly handsome, his narrow face unsmiling as he peered into the camera. "Too bad you never asked your precious Bobute."

"I did, and she told me," she huffed, getting red in the face now.

He arched his brows. "Yes, I bet she did. All about your kindly *senelis*, the saintly Tadas Vidas. The hero. The partisan. The mayor of J—."

"You always had a grudge against him."

"Why do you say that?"

"You can't stand that I come from a family of heroes! That my *senelis* had a street named after him, and a school. You're jealous because your own family did nothing."

"It's true. My father wasn't a heroic 'partisan.' He was just a good, decent human being. A true Christian."

"A big nothing."

"And yours, from what I heard, was none of those things. Even the school was about to change its mind about using his name, until your mother got some government official to pressure them. When are you going to tell your son the truth?"

"I told him the truth!"

"You know Darius applied to Yad Vashem in Jerusalem to have him recognized as a Righteous Among the Nations? They will investigate."

"I told him to leave it alone!" She shook her head, alarmed. "He just won't listen."

"He's going to find out."

"There's nothing to find out," she said stiffly, firmly setting her jaw.

* * *

When Darius got back to his office, the phone had seven messages and did not stop ringing. He kicked himself. He should never have spoken to that reporter about the conference! It was still months away, and look what one measly item in the newspaper revealing that Milia Gottstein-Lasker would be giving the keynote address had done! If this was the result of the mere mention of her name, he was afraid to think what her actual uncensored speech would do!

He spent the afternoon trying to calm down school principals, his nefarious department head, representatives of various government agencies concerned with the Holocaust and one very, very unhappy woman from the Genocide and Resistance Research Center who demanded information he didn't have about the exact contents of Milia Gottstein-Lasker's speech.

"It is a conference about reconciliation and forgiveness. She knows that. From what she has told me, it will be in that spirit." He paused, listening to the determined and extremely agitated voice on the other side of the conversation while mentally scrambling for some plausible response, which at the moment eluded him.

How much easier his life would be if he could simply tell the truth, he thought. If he could just say, *I would be happy to give you a copy of her speech if I had one, which I don't.* But since that unfortunate little fact had to be hidden at all costs from all his interlocutors, he had no choice but to hem and haw and act dumb. Finally, when all else failed to appease, he said, "I understand your legitimate concerns, but I'm not at liberty to divulge the exact contents of what she's going to say—you do understand, I hope? I *assure* you that everything is going to be *just fine.* More than that. A triumph. Lithuania will finally get some very good press for a change."

Everyone was willing to accept that, except the vociferous

and determined little man from the Ministry of Foreign Affairs who refused to be fobbed off.

"Conferences can be shut down, you know. In the public interest," he threatened.

"Shall I share that information with our conference partners from the European Union? I think they'd be surprised. After all, we joined the EU as a democracy. Thank God we are no longer slaves of the KGB. We cherish our freedoms, do we not, my dear friend?"

"You are walking on a tight rope with no net beneath you, Dr. Vidas," he sneered, not fooled for a second. "I hope you'll remember that."

"What chance do I have to forget, since you seem so intent on reminding me?"

There was a short pause. "I look forward to attending. As do others from the Center for Quality Assessment in Higher Education and the Ministry of Foreign Affairs."

Darius swallowed hard. "How delightful to know we will be so well attended by such important people with such busy schedules."

"Not too busy to listen carefully to every word of Dr. Gottstein-Lasker's speech," he said with a hint of threat. "Perhaps you would both be our dinner guests before, or after?"

"I think she will need to rest the evening before the conference," he said, thinking fast. As for after, who knew if the invitation would still be valid? "But speaking for myself, I'd be delighted to join you. As for Dr. Gottstein-Lasker, I suggest you consider extending your invitation directly to her *after* hearing what she has to say."

The call ended abruptly, but not hostilely, Darius tried to convince himself.

He spent the rest of the afternoon and evening going over the itinerary, and tying up loose ends, like hotel reservations and travel schedules. Finally satisfied, he decided to take a long, hot bath just to clear his head.

He poured in some bath salts someone had brought back as a gift from Turkey. He had no idea what the point of the stuff was. It didn't make any bubbles, which would at least have been a distraction. His nerves, he finally realized, were shot. He tried not to let the what-ifs take over. But as night fell, he became positively jittery with foreboding.

Maybe Paulius had been right. The head of his department wasn't thrilled with him on many levels, but he had so far avoided giving him actual grounds to fire him. This conference going down in flames would immediately change all that.

He tried to put himself in Milia's place. Yes, there were many problems she had been attempting to solve over the years concerning Lithuania's official portrayal of the country's behavior during the Holocaust. But she was a respected professional. Wouldn't it be in her best interest and, especially, in the interest of her organization to achieve some concrete results, rather than blowing up the conference with ill-advised rhetoric that would be chalked up to an ungracious attempt at revenge?

True, but it depended on how angry she was, how she was treated, and what she honestly believed could be accomplished. It was up to him to convince her that his attempts were sincere, a departure from all the infuriating official positions she had encountered over the years. That, in any case, was the truth. It also wouldn't hurt for there to be some chemistry between them. He went to sleep in a fog of dread.

But when he awoke the next morning, he was inexplicably filled with excitement. After all these years of walking in place and marking time, he was finally on track to do something really important, something that had meaning for him and for his country. He showered and dressed quickly, anxious to make some phone calls and to begin diving through those closed cartons taking up half his office. He was eager, hopeful, the dread in the pit of his stomach having shrunk to manageable proportions.

Fourteen

SHE WAITED FOR Julius to call her. Weeks went by. Finally, he texted her asking when they could talk. When she saw it, a stab of pain ripped through her insides. After everything they'd been to each other over the years; all those nights walking the floor at two in the morning with babies screaming from colic; wiping away tears of pride at graduation ceremonies; toasting each other's successes and mourning each other's defeats, this was all she got, all she deserved, an SMS? Really? He didn't even have the decency to call and speak to her personally? To ask how she was doing? How had it come to this?

Oddly, although the pain she felt was intense, it was already not as bad as it had been at the beginning. You can get used to anything, she thought, wondering at the resiliency (or was it stupidity?) of the human species. So she answered him with a text. Why not? It was impossible to go on the way they were. It couldn't hurt to explore where Julius's brilliant mind was wandering these days. What were his plans? Where was Haviva in all of this? She had to know. She *deserved* to know.

She chose the restaurant of the local winery, always one of their favorite places. Outdoor wooden tables under a pergola embroidered with tangled grapevines. And the food! All freshly cooked from ingredients out of the winery gardens, the bread and cakes created by their own bakers, taken out of their own ovens, whose delicious scent infused the air the entire meal. The restaurant made their own ice cream, too, and imported a brand of Belgian chocolate that was hard to find anywhere else in the country and was heaven on earth. But most of all, the wines! The rosés, and the full-bodied reds, and the sparkling whites.

Too bad it's going to be a wake, not a wedding, she reminded herself, putting her finger on a mental Delete button. But however horrible the circumstances, why deprive herself of a delicious meal and a lovely glass of wine? She'd let Julius pay the bill.

* * *

The day before they were scheduled to meet, the children began calling her, each of them with their own agenda.

"You can't be angry at him, Ima," Amir told her. "He's out of his frigging mind! He's pitiable! Confused! I tried to talk some sense into him, but it seems that he isn't interested."

"What did he say?" she asked anxiously.

"He says he doesn't know how long he's going to live, and it's time for him to have some happiness in his life."

She felt her stomach turn. "And she, Haviva, makes him happy? Is that it?"

"He's deluding himself! She's just a distraction. I think he looks in the mirror and sees his hair turning gray, and he's panicking. That's all it is. It's well-documented."

"And therefore, what? I should put up with this disgusting situation? I should feel *sorry* for him?"

There was a beat. "I don't know, Ima. Maybe. You've been together so long."

She took a deep breath, held it, then let it go. "Listen, my dear son, my beloved, I realize you are just trying to help, but know this: I'm not prepared to be his punching bag, for any reason, most particularly some lame psychobabble theory. As you may have noticed, your mother is also not getting any younger."

"Of course, of course, I agree. It's inexcusable." Amir sighed, embarrassed to be in this position, firmly wedged between two people he loved, trying to be the referee. But he could see now there was no point. Renee had warned him not to get involved. Why hadn't he listened to her? "Well, then tell me how I *can* help you, Ima. I'll do whatever you want."

"You know what you can do? You can bring yourself and Renee and the munchkins over for Shabbat. Sit and drink wine with me and your lovely wife, whom I adore. How about that?"

"Maybe you want to come to us?"

She thought about the busy streets around the big apartment building where they lived. Even though their apartment had a spacious, comfortable layout, with plenty of room for guests, she always felt like she was in the way when she was there, invading someone's bedroom, intruding on their privacy as a family.

"No, it's better if you come to me. The house feels so empty all the time. It would be a big help."

"Of course!" Amir promised, feeling relieved. "Just tell me when."

"Next week?"

"That would be great. The kids will be thrilled. They love your new house."

"It's not so new anymore! But yes, I know they do. I'll let them pick the carrots and lettuce, which are ripening now." She smiled at the thought of puttering around her garden with the two little girls, their shiny faces full of happiness at shoving their hands into the dirt. It always seemed like magic to them that things their parents bought in the supermarket actually sprouted up from the earth. "Has your father seen them lately?" she asked abruptly, the thought just occurring to her.

He hesitated. "Yes. He came last Shabbat."

So, it was only her he was boycotting and planning to get rid of, not the children and grandchildren. They still interested him. "I'm happy to hear it."

"You don't sound happy."

"Well, it's not a happy situation, is it, my dear son?"

With that the conversation basically came to a close.

The next to call had been Karin, who was more or less hysterical and ready to murder Haviva.

"It's not just Haviva's fault, you know, Karin. If it hadn't been her, it would have been someone else."

"What are you saying?! You're not furious at her?! She was supposed to be your friend! All those years . . ."

"Only five," she murmured, almost to herself.

Karin pretended not to hear. "All those dinners, vacations . . . They slept over at your house, for goodness' sake. This is bullshit!"

"Don't swear," Milia admonished her mildly, recognizing what state she was in, one she herself had only recently exited. Now she was less angry and vengeful than simply sad and hurt.

"So, I'm not taking his calls. Sorry. He can't behave that way, treat my mother that way, and expect to come waltzing in here to play with his grandchild. No way."

"I appreciate your loyalty, Karin, but I don't want you to be alienated from your father, or for Tal not to see his grandfather."

Karin was shocked. "It's not up to you!"

"It is if you're doing it out of loyalty to me. All I'm saying is that it isn't necessary, that's all. I don't care."

"I have to say, I'm surprised, Ima. I thought you'd be happy to hear this. I understand he was at Amir's for the weekend. I let Amir have a piece of my mind. Idiot."

So this was what impending divorce brought: not only dissolving the personal bonds between two people, but contaminating all the familial bonds. Father and child. Father and grandchild. Brother and sister. Mother and child. The permutations were endless, all of them going up in smoke on the altar of the selfish urge for more, better, different. All for the sake of that devil's dance Julius had started, and now everyone was joining, uprooting decades of firm roots planted with so much effort and toil in fertile, loving soil that had produced such a beautiful, flourishing family tree. All those gossamer threads created by myriad interactions over the years, binding them to one another, that had formed strong, coiled roots, were now under attack, in danger of unraveling. Of everything Julius had done, this was the most unforgivable, she thought. It was the worst betrayal imaginable, endangering everything they had built together over a lifetime that was most precious to her. For the very first time since that phone call from Haviva's stupid husband, she felt herself despise Julius.

The last phone call was from Gilad. "How are you, Ima?" he asked kindly.

"Not good, honey."

"What's happening?"

"Everything's falling apart. Your sister is angry at your brother and furious at your father. I feel the whole family is under attack. I don't know what to do."

"First of all, stop taking responsibility for something that you didn't start and can't control."

She exhaled slowly. Her wise son.

"Are you going to speak to Aba?" he asked.

"Yes. We have a meeting set up for tomorrow at the winery."

"What's the agenda?"

"I don't know. We haven't talked at all since this happened."

"So it's good it's in a public place. It will help keep you both restrained."

She hadn't thought of that. Maybe the winery *wasn't* such a good idea after all. "I want to know where we stand. What's the next step. He hasn't made that at all clear."

"What would *you* like the next step to be, Ima?"

Leave it to Gilad to come up with the $64,000 question. What indeed!

"I have no idea. I've been waiting, hoping I guess, that it would blow over and we could get back to normal. But the more time passes, the more things happen, the less that seems possible."

"But if it *was* a possibility, would you embrace it?"

How could she even begin to answer such a question? "I . . . I . . . don't know anymore. At first I was praying that your father would just come to me and apologize and say it was a mistake and that it would never happen again. I thought I had an answer in the case of that scenario," she said with a sad smile. "But now, after all that's happened . . . ?"

"What's happened?"

"All the bad blood that this has created among you kids. Karin is furious at Amir for having Aba over for Shabbat. I can't forgive your father for that."

"Why do you hold him responsible for the way Karin treats Amir, or Amir treats Karin? Those two have always had issues."

"But this time, it's your father who's created the issue. He's responsible for it all, Gilad. He deserves no mercy."

"Ima, everyone deserves mercy. Even death-row prisoners. So certainly Aba."

Well, they had produced these three marvelous children together. You had to give Julius credit for that. He'd provided half the DNA and half the input in their upbringing, after all. Despite her heartache, she was overwhelmed with love for each of them as each in their own way tried to navigate these treacherous waters, and in so doing revealed the goodness of their hearts, their love and compassion, and true concern. She felt tears come to her eyes.

"I won't bite his head off, Gilad, if that's what's worrying you. I'll listen respectfully to what he has to say."

"That's really good of you, Ima. I know this can't be easy for you. It's a shocking situation. It takes great wisdom and courage to figure out a way to handle it that's not demeaning to either of you."

Wisdom and courage, she thought, wondering if she had either in amounts sufficient to pull this off.

The day dawned, sunny and mild, a sudden welcome respite from the sodden, gray winter days that had preceded it. She stood on her porch looking out toward the sliver of sea visible through the trees. Then she checked her freesia bulbs and the tiny cherry tomatoes on her vines. All they needed was a solid week of sun to ripen and sweeten. She closed her eyes, raising her face to the warming rays, which felt like kind, warm fingers caressing her skin. Perhaps that was all she and Julius needed as well.

She showered, taking special care to use her favorite perfumed soaps, rinsing out her hair with an especially fragrant conditioner. She was almost ashamed of herself for bothering. Still, it felt like a compulsion. To smell great, to look great. *And the reason?* she asked herself bluntly. *To show him what he's missing so that when you tell him you want a divorce he shrivels and dies? Or to tempt him to forget why he left in the first place?*

Milia, she asked herself, *do you want him back?*

Many things went through her mind as she continued dressing. When she put on her bra and panties, she thought of him reaching out for her, naked, as they lay side by side, desire pulsing through them; the practiced way in which he knew how to bring her pleasure, each touch a revelation that made her see herself in a new light as a sexual being. He was the only one who had ever brought out that part of her, introduced her to *that* Milia, the woman who was flesh and blood and desire and physical instincts. No one knew that Milia but Julius, who had helped to create her.

She flipped the hangers in her closet, searching for something to wear, something for *that* Milia to wear. She stopped when her fingers touched the silk of her favorite blue dress. It was a wrap dress that fit her like a glove, chiseling in fine relief her petite, womanly form. With its low neck, revealing a hint of cleavage, and its figure-hugging silhouette, the dress was not something she wore on any occasion in which she was conducting official business. She couldn't even remember now why she'd purchased such a dress. And then it suddenly came to her: formal nights on their Caribbean cruise in celebration of their twenty-fifth wedding anniversary.

She'd actually gotten Julius to dance! And then the ship photographers had taken photos of them. She still had them somewhere. It had been only five years ago. Even if everything else had gone to hell in that time, the dress, she saw with satisfaction and no small sense of irony, still fit her perfectly.

She took extra care applying her makeup: the tiny hint of blue eye shadow on her lids that brought out the striking color of her blue-green eyes, startling against the whiteness of her skin and those abundant dark lashes that had never needed mascara. A little blush made her whole face shimmer with summer light. And that was it. She brushed her long, mostly dark hair, with its attractive highlights of silver, curling it at the edges and gathering it back with a clip.

Turning her head this way and that in the mirror, she decided to discard the clip, freeing her hair to flow down her back.

When she looked into the mirror at what she had done, the answer to her question became as clear as day. *Yes, I do want him back. Desperately*, she finally admitted to herself. But it was not up to her, now, was it?

* * *

She drove down to the winery and parked her car under a tree in a far corner where it wouldn't easily be seen. She didn't get out, waiting until she saw him arrive in his blue Honda. She imagined walking toward him from a few meters away, letting him take her in before they entered the restaurant. She wondered what he would say to her, and what would not need to be said, his face saying it for him as he looked her over with the old appreciation and passion that she had always drawn from him. She missed him so much, she thought, wondering how this conversation was going to go. What would he say? Would he apologize right off the bat? No, that wasn't Julius's style. He didn't like making mistakes, and admitting them was ten times worse. It had something to do with the God complex most surgeons suffered from, as well as the highly developed guilt complex of people in his profession, a job in which even small, casual mistakes sometimes had life-or-death consequences.

Well, she could live without an apology. She could be the bigger person, that much she knew she had in her. And so, with or without an apology, where would the conversation go next? Would they talk about Haviva, about his feelings for her? That would be hard to bear. But it was better to know, wasn't it, than not to know how deep this thing went? But maybe she could steer the conversation over to safer territory.

What she really wanted to talk to him about, she realized, was why he was suddenly unhappy. Where was this coming from? What had she not noticed, done wrong? What could she do to make it right? That would be essential, useful, purposeful.

But what if he didn't want to talk about that? What if he only wanted to talk about getting a divorce? What if he was really and truly done?

In that case, she thought, it would be a very short lunch. Perhaps she should order wine and drink it first, before the food came. And she shouldn't order the fish, which took forever for them to prepare and serve. Maybe she wouldn't have enough time for the fish . . .

She saw his car drive in past her. She rolled down her window, staring. It wasn't possible. Really?!

She couldn't believe her eyes.

He had brought her with him. Haviva.

They got out of the car together. They were holding hands.

Milia sat back, her breath short, her heart racing until she thought she would pass out.

This, she thought, was the last straw. It was so wildly inappropriate, so gratuitously cruel, an act of such inconsiderate, boorish selfishness that it could never be forgiven. It was an obscene act of which the Julius she knew would have been incapable.

She took out her cell phone and texted him: *"Have a nice lunch with Haviva. And then have a nice life. You and I will meet at my lawyer's office. Don't bring her with you or my demands will double. Until then, we have nothing to discuss."* She pressed Send. She could just make out his taking out his phone and looking down at it as she put her key into the ignition and pulled out, racing toward home.

FIFTEEN

HE COULDN'T PUT it off any longer, Darius thought, slamming the notebooks back into the cardboard boxes. All this dry academic stuff wasn't giving him the real picture of a living human being. If he wanted to figure out his grandfather, he needed to visit the town where he had been mayor, walk into the city hall, sit in that secret room that had been the scene of his family's heroism and pride. He needed to talk to the older people who still lived there who might remember something and give him more than the vapid old framed portraits hanging on his parents' walls, all the flaws camouflaged. He wanted to hear about a person, not a symbol. Someone with strengths and flaws. A human being.

But Šiauliai! What a road trip! Did he have time for it now? It was a good three-hour drive without any bathroom stops or snack binges, and J—, the village where his grandfather had been mayor during the war, was another forty-five minutes farther on from there, on probably terrible roads. And what if he got there and couldn't figure out where anything was?

"Call your great-aunt Emilija. She knows everything there is to know," his mother advised him when he shared his plan.

"Do you think she'd agree to come with me?"

"Don't you dare even ask her! She's much too old. And with this virus, it's not safe. But maybe she can get one of her children or grandchildren to come with you. Emilija would bring her children to J— every summer. I'm sure her daughter, Daiva, would remember."

"Well, okay. I'll try."

It took three phone calls, two of which were not answered at all even after waiting patiently as it rang and rang and rang. On the third attempt, someone actually picked up.

"Auntie Emilija? Is that you? It's Darius. Vidas. Your great-nephew."

There was a long silence, and then another voice came on.

"Who is this?" it demanded.

His eyebrows shot up. "Cousin Darius Vidas. From Vilnius."

"Oh, Cousin Darius, sorry! Some very aggressive telemarketer has been pestering Mama. They keep selling her things she doesn't need. Her hearing isn't wonderful, either, and she's always forgetting to wear her hearing aid. How are you, Cousin?"

"Who am I talking to?" Darius asked politely, a bit taken aback.

"Why, it's your cousin. Daiva."

He exhaled. "Daiva! Good to hear your voice. It has been so long."

"Yes, especially now when we are all hibernating like little bears because of this Covid. Are you well? How are your parents? Vilnius?"

"Good, good. Listen, Daiva, I'm calling because I'm doing some research on a book about my grandfather Tadas and I was thinking about driving up to J— to look at where he worked during the war."

"Oh, that's a long drive! Sounds like a lot of work."

"It is. But it's also very interesting. The truth is, I need a tour guide for this trip. Can you spare the time?"

She hesitated. "Listen, I'd really like to help you, Cousin. But, well, the thing is, I don't want to use up my vacation days from work. And it's also a *really* long drive. I'm not such a good driver, especially on these wintry roads."

"I understand," he said a bit forlornly.

"You're disappointed. I'm sorry. But I'll tell you what. If you can pick me up at Mama's, and we can do it on a Saturday, then stay over one night and explore all day Sunday, I'll come. The drive up and back is too much for a one-day trip anyhow."

"No problem! I'd be happy to pick you up. And I'll make reservations in J— at a hotel and I'll pay for everything!"

"Wow, how can I say no to that? Very generous, but you don't have to bribe me. I'd be happy to do it and pay my own way."

"Don't worry. I'll get the university to pay."

"In that case, I happily give in. But leave yourself some time to come up and talk to Mama about your grandfather. Her mind sometimes wanders a bit, but you'd be surprised how clear the past is to her, more than the present! It's strange. It will be nice to go back to J—. I haven't been there for years. We used to go up all the time in the summers to visit your grandpa, Uncle Tadas."

"So you're familiar with the place?"

"Sure! They have all these nature reserves. It's a beautiful area in the summer, so much to explore. And Uncle Tadas was always so kind to us kids. I'll be happy to show you around. Just too bad the weather is so cold."

"Maybe it will warm up by the weekend."

"No chance."

"Okay, see you soon, Cousin Daiva. And thank you!"

* * *

The weekend dawned, sunny and so cold that the remnants of the recent snowfall simply solidified into pure, hazardous ice all over the roads. Driving was going to be even more fun than he'd imagined, Darius thought grimly. He had a big breakfast, then poured the leftover coffee into a thermos, which he put into a holder near the steering wheel. It wasn't like there'd be little roadside diners along the way, like in American movies. He'd planned the trip out this way: Drive to Kaunas and visit with Emilija and collect Daiva; then drive for about an hour and a half, stopping in Panevėžys for lunch, then straight on to Šiauliai, with bathroom and snack breaks at the mall. Then the final drive to J— and hotel check-in. Although it would probably be dark by the time he got there, he still planned to explore a little before dinner. He wasn't worried. There would still be all day Sunday to explore. With Daiva's help, it might prove phenomenal. Already he could feel excitement bubbling inside him.

He plugged in his iPhone to the car speakers, then connected to his playlist. With no one to please but himself until he picked up Daiva, and thus no one to cringe at or make fun of his choices, he found that his oldest playlist was still his favorite. Foje and especially Antis—those punk rock young architects. He loved Algirdas Kaušpėdas's ironic, anti-Soviet lyrics. Darius found himself singing along shamelessly to "Zombiai," glad there were no witnesses. He followed that with Bix, and then the heavy metal band Katedra.

By the time he turned off to Kaunas, his head was swimming and he felt like he was going deaf. He parked the car outside the address, an old apartment building on the outskirts of town. Even though there was an elevator, considering the condition of the building, he thought it prudent to walk up the three flights instead. All he needed was to waste hours stuck between floors waiting for rescue!

He knocked, then waited. And waited. Suddenly he heard footsteps on the stairs behind him. He looked down.

"Cousin Daiva?" he asked. She was a woman in her sixties,

salt-and-pepper haired, rotund, with bright blue eyes and pink cheeks. She was lugging a small suitcase.

"Darius!" She put out her arms and hugged him in a motherly way. "Sorry I'm late."

"No, actually I'm a bit early."

She tilted her head, looking at him searchingly. "You knocked and she didn't answer, so you were worried, right?"

He grinned, then shrugged.

She shook her head, then took out a key and opened the door.

"Mama, it's me. Cousin Darius is here to see you. Remember?"

He followed behind her, pausing respectfully to remove his shoes before stepping over the threshold.

It was a tiny apartment, no more than forty square meters, with large overstuffed red chairs and a garish oversized couch covered with an old bedspread, which made the room seem even smaller. How strange that he had never been here before, he thought. He had so few relatives, and yet they only met when absolutely necessary, during weddings and funerals.

Daiva disappeared into the bedroom. Soon he overheard the low tones of a heated discussion. Was his appearance unexpected or perhaps even unwelcome? This surprised him.

Maybe his family weren't particularly close, but neither were they on the outs with one another for any reason, at least as far as he could recall. But he wasn't the expert in family dynamics; that was his mother's realm, and wasn't it she who'd suggested he call?

Daiva reappeared, her arm entwined with that of an elderly woman in her eighties who was more than a little overweight, with very short hair and big glasses that magnified her blue eyes.

"This is Cousin Darius, Kotryna's boy," Daiva informed her, squeezing her hand encouragingly. "You remember, right, Mama?"

At the words *Kotryna's boy*, the older woman suddenly broke out into a charming smile, reaching up to pinch his cheek. "Little Darius," she murmured. "So tall! Always such a smart kid. And a real troublemaker."

"Mama!"

Darius laughed. "I guess her memory is just fine."

Daiva gently steered her mother to the sofa, helping her to sit down.

"So, Teta Emiljia, it is good to see you. How are you feeling?" he ventured awkwardly.

"Oh, same as always, I suppose. I'm not dead yet, but one foot has definitely entered the grave."

He smiled uncertainly.

"Darius and I are going to J—. To see where your brother, Tadas, was the mayor during the war."

Her eyebrows rose up to a sharp point. "To J—?" She shook her head vehemently. "Bad idea. Why?"

"Because he is writing a book about Uncle Tadas. He is doing research. Why is it a bad idea, Mama?"

The old woman didn't reply, reaching out and grabbing Darius's arm. "You don't want to know," she told him.

Daiva seemed shocked. "Why not? Uncle Tadas was a hero! There is a street and a school named after him, Mama."

The old woman shook her head and closed her eyes. "They say many things about him."

"Who, Mama? Who says many things? And what do they say?"

"The Jews," she said, the words like an overfull mouth of food, leaving her unable to speak as she chewed on it.

"Please, Teta. What do they say?" Darius asked her, shocked.

She gestured to him to come closer, whispering in his ear: "That he was a Jew killer."

He leaned back, flabbergasted. She had obviously lost her marbles, so there was no reason to be upset, he told himself. Still.

He took a deep breath. "No, Teta. He *saved* Jews. A whole family. The Kenskys," he told her patiently.

"Darius," she murmured. "I remember when you were born. Everyone was so worried about you because you came out ass first with the cord around your neck. But Kotryna had a doctor, not just a midwife. Such a pretty woman, your mother! The most beautiful girl in the village. No one had doctors in those years. But she had money to pay. My brother, Tadas, always made sure of that, even though that husband of hers earned so little . . ."

"Mama, that is Darius's father you are talking about . . ."

Emilija glared at her daughter. "I know what I'm talking about."

"It's all right. My father would be the first to agree he never earned much."

"So ask yourself, Darius," the old woman continued, her eyes narrowing shrewdly, "from where did Tadas, your grandfather, suddenly have money?"

He swallowed. "I don't know, Teta. You tell me."

She smiled a bit cynically. "You are a professor, right? You should find out."

"I don't know what's gotten into her, Darius. I'm so sorry. Maybe it's this new medication she's on for her arthritis or—"

"I'm not hallucinating, Daiva. I'm telling him the truth. But it's not so nice to hear. He wants to write a book about a hero. A hero," she scoffed. "Where was he when *I* needed money to buy a decent place to live?" She closed her eyes and seemed to doze off.

Daiva tiptoed out of the room and brought back a blanket, which Daiva wrapped around her mother.

"I think we should go," she mouthed soundlessly, pointing to the door.

"Will she be all right on her own?"

"She's got a day nurse coming in fifteen minutes. She'll be fine."

They quietly put on their shoes and walked down the stairs, Darius insisting on carrying the suitcase.

"Are you all right, Cousin?"

"Fine. But it was a shock."

"I'm sure she's just confused. After all, people have looked into all of this. They don't name streets and schools after just anyone."

"So you're not surprised? You've heard this before?"

"My mother has some kind of secret grudge against her brother. Only a psychiatrist could tell you why. Brains change when they get old. They develop obsessions and false memories."

He had no idea if that was true, but the thought comforted him. Surely, the incoherent ramblings of an old woman were not a reason to get upset and change his plans.

"Shall I put on some music, Cousin Daiva?"

"An excellent suggestion!"

He switched over to his classical collection. As the strains of Sibelius's *Finlandia* filled the car, the music seemed a perfect score for the wintry scenes passing before him: the dark, snow-covered pine and birch forests, parting at intervals to allow the flash of steely blue, half-frozen rivers and lakes. Despite the cold, the plowed fields already hinted at the golden sway of rye and wheat and barley that would come in the spring. Such a flat and fertile land! Land of the rain, they called it, and it was, with all the blessings that rain brought.

Daiva's phone rang. She answered it and began a long conversation, obviously with one of her kids, which released him from making conversation.

He thought about the landscape. Anyone who had been out of the country couldn't help but contrast the empty roads, the sparse farms and factory buildings with places where the countryside fermented with industrial and agrarian activities and ever more numerous housing estates sprouting like mushrooms all over the place. The picturesque countryside of his homeland simply underscored the lack of economic activity that plagued the country, revealing a stagnant economy.

He thought about Karolina. No wonder so many of the country's most promising young people were leaving, one way or the other. The country also had one of the highest suicide rates in the world. It was just not producing enough well-paying jobs, enough opportunities, for the young. More and more people flocked to the cities—the only places educated Lithuanians wanted to live. Outside the centers of population, there was nothing much to do. People lived meagerly, the old, the unskilled, the uneducated, surviving on scraps, or government handouts.

He blamed the Communists. Their ironfisted and wrong-headed policies had played havoc with the country's well-being, collectivism destroying flourishing small farms only to produce collectives that had failed miserably and were eventually abandoned. Now they lay strewn across the landscape like wounds, he thought bitterly.

Daiva hung up. "My daughter. Boyfriend trouble."

He smiled knowingly, commiserating. "Are you hungry? I thought we'd stop in Panevėžys and get something to eat."

"Well, I don't know. I brought sandwiches. But by the time we get there, I'm sure I could certainly use a pit stop."

"Of course!" He smacked his forehead. "Should I try to find something closer?"

"No, I'm fine so far."

"So, how are you, Cousin? Your husband? The kids?

"*Šlove Dievui!* Praise God!"

"What kind of work do you do?"

"I'm a hospital administrator. I was a nurse, but I was promoted," she said proudly.

"And your husband? Sorry, I forgot his name."

"Gintaras. But we are separated."

"Oh, sorry. I didn't know."

"It's okay. Better this way. The children are grown. I basically threw him out because I got tired of paying his pub bills. It's a good life now! I have money saved. I go on vacations whenever I have vacation time. Which is why I hate to waste it. I'm going to Greece this summer."

"Sounds good."

"On a cruise," she added, her eyes gleaming. "With my boyfriend."

This was already too much information. He cleared his throat. "I really appreciate you giving up your weekend. It's so kind of you. I just was afraid of going to J— and getting lost."

"Don't worry. I remember it all so clearly. We spent whole summers there with Grandfather and Grandmother and Uncle Tadas. What fun we had!"

"Daiva, do you have any idea why your mother would say such things?"

She cleared her throat uncomfortably. "Well, you know, Darius, what she said isn't exactly a secret. There were many complaints when the school was named after your grandfather Tadas."

"I didn't know this! I remember coming to the naming ceremony, but that's all."

"My mother told me it was almost called off."

"But why?"

"Rumors. You know the Jews, so many of them were Communists. Uncle Tadas was a partisan, the mayor of the town during the war. All kinds of things were said about partisans by the Communists after the war. They wanted to blacken the name of patriotic Lithuanians who had resisted the Soviet occupation. So they made up stories to discredit them."

He nodded. It made sense. Still a residue of discomfort washed over him.

"I guess I will just have to do my research," he said.

"So you're going to look into it?" She sounded uneasy.

He turned to look briefly at her suddenly unhappy face. "Of course. I'm interested in knowing the truth."

She said nothing, looking out the window.

They drove the rest of the way to Panevėžys in silence. He pulled into the shopping center and parked. She went searching for a bathroom while he went looking for some pizza, which he found at Charlie's. It was actually not bad at all, he thought, wolfing down his third slice, and washing it all down with Diet Cokes until even his iron stomach registered a weak protest.

When he started driving again, it was with renewed enthusiasm. It wouldn't be long now, he thought, feeling a bit of excitement at actually being able to answer so many questions that had plagued him over the years about his family history.

"Ah, look there, another stork!" Daiva pointed.

Suddenly, they were everywhere, he realized, on the roadside, resting on top of telephone poles, their huge nests a wonder. How strange. He had no recollection of ever seeing these creatures even though they were Lithuania's national bird. It stood to reason that he had come across them numerous times over the years when traveling in this part of the country. And then he suddenly realized that he had never been in this area before. Unlike Daiva, his own parents hadn't taken him to visit Grandfather Tadas in J—. He had always accepted that as a fact of life, but now he began to realize how strange that was. After all, Daiva had been going there her whole life. He'd have to discuss it with Mamytė when he came back from the trip, he thought.

They stopped off briefly in Šiauliai, a large city, before continuing on country roads to J—.

"Be careful of the ice," Daiva warned him every time the little car meandered dangerously on the frozen road. Fortunately, it was empty enough to make their slipping and sliding more annoying than dangerous.

By the time they entered the city, it was nearly dusk. In another hour it would be as dark as night, he thought. "Let's check in, then go out before we lose the light completely. We can unpack later if that's all right with you, Daiva."

She nodded, already tired and longing for a hot shower. "No problem. This is your show, Cousin."

The Hotel and Guest House, as it grandly called itself, was really the only place to stay in town. It was centrally located, and had good reviews for its breakfast and cleanliness, although the customers grumbled about the less than helpful staff. Darius hoped registration would go quickly. He was in a rush. The desk clerk, a sullen young woman who looked them over suspiciously, was finally placated when he told her they were work colleagues and needed separate rooms. It wasn't a lie.

"Meet you out front in ten minutes?" he asked Daiva hopefully.

She nodded, scurrying away, dragging her suitcase behind her.

"Do you need help with it?" Darius belatedly called after her, but she waved him away.

She reappeared twenty minutes later, having changed into brown slacks and sturdy walking shoes.

"Where do you suggest we start?"

"Well, let's go to Old Town. All the things you are interested in are there, no?"

"I suppose," he answered.

It was a short ride. The area was run-down, but looked authentically preserved, as if no one in town had the time, money, or inclination to change anything since the end of World War II. "That's where your grandfather, Uncle Tadas, lived," Daiva said, pointing to an old house with a gabled roof and large, pitched windows. "And two blocks away is where he worked. I remember it well because it was painted blue."

"The municipality building?"

"I don't know if they called it that then. When your grandfather showed it to me, he called it the mayor's office. It was a large, two-story wooden house. His office was upstairs, and the Gestapo had their offices on the ground floor."

He felt his stomach lurch. "The Nazis used the same building?"

"That's what he said."

Darius hurried down the street. And there it was: a large, old wooden house, which had obviously not been touched since the 1940s. The outside walls were still painted blue, but badly faded and chipped. The signs indicated it was a clothing store.

They walked inside, activating a small bell that brought a young woman to the counter.

She smiled welcomingly. "Can I help you?"

Daiva's eye had already been caught by some little sweaters, size six months, embroidered with Disney characters.

"*Labas*," Darius greeted her politely.

The saleswoman smiled again, moving over to Daiva. "What size are you looking for?"

"Well, size six months, and size two. My grandchildren," she said warmly.

"Excuse me, but is there another floor to this building? My grandfather used to be mayor here, and he told us his offices were upstairs."

She looked at him without expression, nodding. "My mother mentioned something. We use the upstairs for storage. But you're welcome to go up there." She pointed to a winding staircase hidden behind some racks.

"Thank you so much!"

"Do you need me?" Daiva asked him, reluctantly tearing her attention away from the adorable merchandise.

"No, that's fine. You keep shopping."

He walked quickly over to the stairs, climbing up two steps at a time. At the top was an area with high ceilings and large windows, and space enough for perhaps a desk and chair and maybe some file cabinets, he thought. But it was basically one open room. There was no bathroom or kitchen he noticed. Anyone coming up here would see the entire space.

He went around the room, examining the floorboards and the walls carefully, looking for the slightest indication that something had been taken down, or that it had been renovated. He looked out the window. It had a clear view of the street, now bright in lamplight, which meant anyone outside would probably be able to see whatever was going on inside. And if it was true, as his grandfather had said, that the downstairs had been full of Nazis . . .

Darius sat down on one of the boxes, a frisson of fear running through him. The secret room. The Kenskys' hiding place. Where was it? Was this the wrong address? Or, was it, perhaps, the correct address, and Emil, Beyle, Itele, Henokh, and little Ruchele had never found a hiding place at all?

SIXTEEN

Six months later

As Milia strapped herself into the airline seat, she wondered once again how she had gotten herself into this mess. Wizz Air! A super discount flight! Even Vidas had been apologetic. "It's the quickest flight from Tel Aviv," he'd explained. "Really, it has nothing to do with the cost. We would have gladly got you onto first class with Lufthansa, but the flight is three times as long . . ."

She leaned back, closing her eyes, hoping against hope for the miracle of sleep, even though from long experience she knew it was impossible. Even if you didn't have a child drumming into the back of your seat, or a stranger leaning aggressively into your space, or flight attendants alerting you every two seconds about safety, offering fattening snacks, or hawking useless overpriced merchandise, the engine noise alone would still destroy any possibility of dozing off.

Morning flights were torture, she thought. They were really middle-of-the-night flights, chasing you out of the house at 2:00 a.m. so you could reach the airport three hours before takeoff.

This, in effect, meant you couldn't go to sleep at all. She shifted in her aisle seat, grateful at least for that. But given the sardine-class accommodations, it would mean being intimately connected to the whims of the bladders of her two seatmates. But getting up for them was still preferable to being trapped at the window and having to rely on them to let her out.

She looked over the two still-empty seats beside her. What were the chances no one would show up for them? she mused, daydreaming about the joy of appropriation, about stretching out in a modified fetal position, a pillow under her head and the thin, better-than-nothing blanket dispelling the chill. She did not get very far when a "pardon me" in Hebrew destroyed her reverie. She looked up. It was a woman about her age, she guessed, maybe a bit older, who stood there with a cheerful smile on her face.

Reluctantly, she got up and moved out of the way, letting her unwelcome seatmate squeeze past to the window. At least the middle seat was still empty, she thought, holding on to her last flicker of hope. The flight didn't look very crowded, perhaps it might stay that way? It would be a small mercy.

From the corner of her eye, she saw her seat partner drop a large handbag on the middle seat, already marking her territory.

"Please feel free to put down your own things, too," the woman said, noticing her stare.

Her Hebrew was unaccented, Milia noticed, very Tel Aviv suburbs, Holon, or Bat Yam. She was no doubt one of those medical technicians, a person who squeezed your boobs to hell during mammograms; or maybe she assisted in colonoscopies, Milia thought with strange relish. Someone who invaded private spaces and thought they were doing you a favor.

She bided her time, waiting for everyone to find their seat, almost holding her breath. The middle seat remained empty. She allowed herself a small sigh of relief but did not get her hopes up.

There was always that late arrival who kept everyone waiting because they couldn't be bothered to get up in time, or just had to make one more unnecessary purchase in the duty-free.

But as the cabin doors slid closed, and the flight attendants began the ritual march down the aisles to check the closure of the overhead compartments, she finally allowed herself to lift her briefcase off the floor where it was cramping her feet and to place it next to her on the middle seat.

"Vacation?" her seatmate asked brightly.

She shook her head slightly with an inward groan. Oh no! A chatty one!

"Business," she answered politely, but curtly.

"In Vilnius? Are you buying, selling?"

She exhaled, giving in. "Actually, I'm attending a conference."

"How interesting! What's it about?"

"The Holocaust," she said reluctantly.

That word, once spoken, once heard, evoked so many different responses in people, she'd found. Gentiles usually nodded, then lapsed into a respectful, troubled silence. But with Jews, it varied much more widely, depending entirely upon their personal history. If there was a survivor in the family, this was the time they'd haul them out for her inspection. Those most distantly involved often showed interest, even admiration for her work. But then you also got the opposite response, the ones for whom it just erased the casual, friendly smile on their faces, turning them hostile. This woman, she saw, was one of those.

"Why," she said, "can't they just leave that alone already?"

Tired as she was, Milia felt the rage bubble up from her stomach, a visceral fury. "And what are *you* planning to do in Vilnius?" she asked the woman, almost sweetly.

The smile returned to her face. "I'm on a heritage tour! I'm meeting other relatives there from all over the world. My Israeli relatives all took an earlier flight. We've been planning this for such a long time! We are all going to visit the village where our great-grandparents once lived. We've arranged a Lithuanian tour guide who speaks several languages." She was delighted, enthusiastic.

"What's the name of the village?"

"Jurbarkas!"

Milia closed her eyes and shook her head. "And what do you know about it?"

"Well, not much. I know it was close to the German border, on the right bank of the Nieman River. There was another village on the left bank. Our great-great-grandfather owned a boat, apparently. Our family immigrated before the war. It was a very Zionist town."

"Well, when you get there, I'd like to give you a few pointers of what to look for."

The woman sat up eagerly.

"Don't look for the synagogue, or the study house, or the kosher butcher. German troops invaded on June twenty-second, 1941, but they just marched through, chasing the Russians. There were only two Germans in the whole town during this time: the commandant and his deputy. A week later, hundreds of Lithuanians from the town and surrounding villages, calling themselves 'partisans' and wearing self-made armbands, gathered the Jewish men in the synagogue. They made them carry out a Jew holding a Torah scroll on the plank used for carrying coffins. He and the scroll were drowned in the lovely nearby river. Then the rest were told to drown each other. The next day, they pried all the mezuzahs off the doorposts, and made the Jews bring their Torah scrolls, holy books, and prayer shawls, which were dumped together in the synagogue courtyard. They forced them to unroll the scrolls and then jumped up and down on them. In the morning, they forced the Jews to tear down the walls of the synagogue, the study house, and the Jewish slaughterhouse, and transport the lumber to Lithuanian peasants. On the Sabbath, the Jews were forced to take the heap of holy objects to the banks of the river and burn them. They forced the women out of their houses to clean up the streets. One woman was put in a wheelbarrow and mercilessly beaten by the Lithuanians. When she spotted a German officer, who had been standing by the river taking pictures, she begged him to shoot her. He said he couldn't because the authority over the Jews had been given to the Lithuanians."

The woman leaned back in her seat and closed her eyes briefly. "And then?"

"The 'partisans' worked the Jews every day for about three weeks. Then one day they told the men to take the day off and go home. 'Partisans' then went house to house, rounding them up— the doctors, the dentist, the lawyer, the optometrist, the kosher slaughterer, the cantor, and the rabbi, about five hundred and fifty men. When the women returned from work, they couldn't find anyone."

The woman's face had lost its color.

Milia paused. "Shall I go on?"

"Please."

"Rumors circulated. Then Lithuanians began boasting that the men had been taken to the Jewish cemetery, forced to dig graves and kill each other with their shovels . . ."

The woman leaned back, blinking. "And the women?"

"First the 'partisans' took the old, the sick, those without families. The next day the women left behind found a pile of crutches and canes and some earrings with part of the ears still attached."

The woman let out a small gasp.

"Finally, when they got tired of torturing the Jews, they went house to house, took everyone to the forest, and shot them there. They brought all the clothing of the murdered Jews to the house where they'd been kept prisoners. Then the Lithuanians partied all Friday night."

"But how can we know this," the woman protested, "if everyone was killed?"

"Because a girl, Khane Goldman, was an eyewitness and testified after the war about what happened in Jurbarkas. She had been standing at the edge of a pit, watching the women mercilessly beaten, forced to throw their small children alive into open graves before being shot themselves when a Lithuanian she knew told her to run. She survived by bribing a Lithuanian peasant who knew her to hide her. She said that during the murders and lootings, she didn't see a single German. Just Lithuanians. You might want to remember that when you go shopping for souvenirs on your 'vacation.'"

The woman turned away, looking out the window. For the entire journey, she didn't say anything, didn't ask to use the bathroom, didn't eat her meal.

Milia's anger drained out of her, replaced by guilt. What had been the point of that? The woman was going to meet her family. They had the vacation of a lifetime planned, and here she was opening up a Pandora's box of horrific Holocaust memorabilia no one wanted to know, not even the descendants of the victims.

She had read a book by Shalom Auslander in which a couple buys a house and finds Anne Frank living in the attic. It was an outrageous book that made you laugh until you cried, then made you feel guilty for finding any humor at all in the situation. But the more she thought about it as a metaphor—which she was certain the author intended—the more brilliant it seemed to her. Wasn't every Jew living with Anne Frank in the attic, an inconvenient but unavoidable part of their lives since the Holocaust? Wasn't there some part of every Jew that wondered if it had happened once, could it happen again? The very slogan "never again" was like a child daring the monsters in the dark to pounce, a false bravado, a way of admitting the fear by pretending to conquer it. How many books had she read about second-generation Jews—children and grandchildren—struggling with that legacy? She'd recently gotten a Facebook post from a Jewish young man who had visited Auschwitz in January and decided to take off his coat and shoes to test how long he could endure the cold. "Not a minute!" he declared.

That was so typical! No one could imagine surviving what the survivors had gone through. All of us, herself included, were certain that we would have died immediately. In his book, Auslander's character hilariously asks his suburban neighbors, if the time should come, could he hide in their home? Wasn't that also typical? Wasn't there a little part of Jews—even in the most assimilated, the ones about to disappear altogether into nondenominational Americans, British, or French—that wondered who of their gentile neighbors would risk their lives to shelter them, and who would happily dial up the Gestapo to exchange them for a new pair of shoes or a bowl of oatmeal?

Part of the support Milia knew organizations like her grandfather's received from Jews was because in hunting down Nazi perpetrators, Jews were shoring up the wall that kept murderous antisemitism at bay. By finding the old Nazis and bringing them to trial, there was a certain message to the new Nazis waiting patiently in the wings. The more relentless the search, the harsher the prosecution and calumny, the more complete the cooperation of the legal system in seeking to punish them, the safer Jews could feel in their own towns and their own skins today.

Places like Lithuania, which not only refused to prosecute and punish, but even denied the guilt of proven perpetrators, were the most frightening of all. They had to be made an example of, not only because the voices of the victims needed expression, but because the silence of the authorities was terrifying to every Jew.

Lithuania, which was so delighted to call Vilnius "the Jerusalem of the North" for tourist purposes, lulling innocent but uninformed Jews like her seatmate to spend their tourist dollars there, was an egregious practitioner of Holocaust deception and distortion. While she felt sorry for having ruined this woman's vacation plans, had she kept her mouth shut, she wouldn't have been doing her job.

Sometimes, though, Milia couldn't help hating the inevitable outcome of sharing such revelations: the fury, the sadness, the helplessness. People *should* be allowed to live their lives in peace, she thought. Honestly, the idea of "leaving it alone already" had come to her more than once. She considered this her most dangerous weakness. With all her determination, she battled against it.

Whenever she got on a plane that took her from the precious Land of Israel, that bastion of Jewish confidence and power, to visit the lands of the diaspora with their ugly history and endless pits of murdered Jewish corpses; whenever she had to do battle with the descendants of the murderers and the bystanders who were still in denial, it felt like a debilitating expenditure of her strength and will.

They didn't want to know.

They didn't want to care.

They didn't want to punish.

They didn't even feel sorry.

They were indifferent.

And here she came knocking on their lovely European antique wooden doors with the polished brass handles, persona non grata, bringing up everything they wanted to forget. She knew she bothered them, showering them with embarrassing, shameful facts that threatened their self-image as modern European liberals, enlightened and good, people who held virtuous, ritualized memorials to the Holocaust dead. They were annoyed. They couldn't understand what more she—the Jews—could want from them?

It fell to her to explain to them how all their ceremonies were tailored to meet the needs of the guilty, not the victims or their descendants. By portraying what had happened as a product of the times, based on the delusions of a madman, they managed to neatly leech blame from the average local citizens who had willingly held the guns, rounded up and guarded the prisoners, or simply turned their backs so that the victims could not escape their deaths. It certainly did not hold to account the citizens who had stood by, clapped, and laughed at the sadistic tortures of their neighbors as if they were watching a circus; people who happily dressed themselves and their children in clothing still warm from the backs of murder victims, allowing them to continue telling each other and their descendants, "It was unfortunate. But what more could our families have done?"

She, with her overloaded shopping cart full to the brim with statistics and incidents and facts, was happy to inform them, handing out blame like a devilish Santa Claus. You couldn't expect them to like it. But for many, she knew, it went further than that. They found her dangerous.

They felt an urgency to silence her, and if not, then to ridicule or contradict her. What never occurred to any of them was just how easily she, and the Jews, could be appeased and made to shut up and go away. After all, what was being asked of them? That they acknowledge the sins committed? That they try to punish the guilty? That they feel true regret? That they sincerely apologize and give back the stolen loot? And finally, that they undergo an honest transformation so that in the same circumstances, they would act differently? The proof would be simple: rooting out the endemic antisemitism in their societies, including the demonization of the Jewish State. Setting up true memorial plaques and honoring the mass graves. Educating their children to the embarrassing truth of their country's history. That was it. Ridiculously small, all things considered.

Lithuania refused to do any of those things. And until it did, it shouldn't be allowed to become an honorable part of the "new" Europe. And certainly *not* a Jewish tourist attraction. Capable as it was of a repeat performance, it needed to remain a Jewish nightmare epitomizing the monster that, on behalf of her people, Milia had chosen to battle.

She took a deep breath, remembering the sense of disaster that had gripped her that morning as she stared into her eyes, shakily putting on her eyeliner. Honestly, Lithuania was the last place on earth she wanted to be right now. The country scared her. Maybe if she had been a six-foot, two-inch, broad-shouldered man like Dr. Efraim Zuroff she might have been able to wave off the possibilities of being threatened—even physically accosted— by furious Lithuanians after giving her presentation. But as a petite woman, all she had was her moral authority to keep her safe. And perhaps her hosts.

She thought about Dr. Vidas, Darius, and the extraordinary letter he had sent her a few days before.

Dear Milia,

As we go into the final preparations for our events, I must share with you some extremely distressing information.

The Genocide and Resistance Research Center of Lithuania has declared Jonas Noreika a "rescuer" of Jews. They are basing this on a single testimony given forty years after the Holocaust in a Chicago courtroom by Father Jonas Borevičius, a Lithuanian priest. His testimony wasn't even about Noreika. It was solicited to defend Antanas Virkutis, warden of the Šiauliai prison in Lithuania from 1941 to 1943, who was fighting attempts of the American government to take away his US citizenship. As we both know, during those years, Jews were murdered wantonly and publicly. Jewish property that wasn't destroyed was brazenly stolen, even auctioned in "town festivals" after slaughter sprees. There was no possibility that anyone could have been unaware of what was happening, and Borevičius testified he had lived in the very center of the town of Šiauliai. Yet his testimony denies it all!

I think the timing of this declaration has to do with the translation and publication of Silvia Foti's book in Lithuanian this year. I am so sorry. Please know that I am on your side, on Silvia's side. Both of you are very brave women. It is my privilege to support you.

But I thought it was my responsibility to let you know that this is what you will be facing when you arrive. I promise you, we will face it together.

With sincere best wishes,
Darius

Over the last few weeks, they had written to each other almost daily. He had an excellent command of English. And he was funny, and kind, and truly accommodating. There would, no doubt, be repercussions for him as well when she pursued her agenda.

As for the Genocide and Resistance Research Center of Lithuania, according to the information published by the Simon Wiesenthal Center in Jerusalem and Vilnius-based scholar Dr. Dovid Katz's Defending History blog, it had been established by the Lithuanian government for the sole purpose of creating a pleasing fiction to replace the ugly truth that 1 to 2 percent of the Lithuanian population had killed Jews during the Holocaust and only 0.04 percent had been involved in rescue attempts, not to mention the multitude who had participated in the looting.

With the backing of the government, the Research Center was intent on disproving these clear facts and promoting the false narrative that Lithuanians had not been perpetrators, but victims of the Soviets, victims of the Nazis. That Lithuanians who had mercilessly murdered and looted their neighbors had actually been "resistance fighters" and "heroes." That the victims were not blameless bystanders but Communist ideologues who had aided the Soviet oppressors—all two hundred thousand plus—including the little girls and boys and six-month-old babies and high school girls raped before they were shot. The Research Center and the government were willing to allow that perhaps a handful of Lithuanians might have been "bad apples," but certainly not the numbers she was talking about. Facts did not dissuade them. All incriminating evidence was easily rejected or reinterpreted. Period. End of story. That a member of NATO and the European Union was using its power, its government, and its national courts to back such blatant Holocaust revisionism was horrifying.

She closed her eyes, envisioning a black monster wave rising in the distance and coming right at her. It made her feel small and helpless and foolish for even attempting to withstand its power. But this was her legacy, the work that had been handed over to her.

How inadequate I am, she thought. But she could only do her best. One day at a time. She had no doubt that all her efforts would be met with forceful attempts to silence and ruin her. It wouldn't be difficult. Thanks to Julius—who had already started the process—it would be so easy to finish her off now.

SEVENTEEN

AFTER MONTHS OF planning, it was finally happening. He checked his computer. She was on the plane. Right on time, no delays. He rubbed his hands together, wondering what he should wear. He looked through his wardrobe. Not a suit, too formal. A brown tweed sports jacket? The one with the elbow patches? Yes! And a pair of brown corduroy pants, recently dry-cleaned.

Leather boots, or sports shoes? Leather, definitely.

When he finished dressing, he washed his face and combed his still-wet hair, noticing the pinkness of his scalp as it peeked through his part with shocking new prominence. The gray, once camouflaged, also seemed more visible. But it was still as unruly as ever. He looked more like an aging California surfer than a college professor. He ran his fingers through the blond tangles once more, then gave up.

This wasn't a Tinder date. It was a serious, perhaps even fateful, attempt at righting some historical wrongs and allowing the long pent-up hostilities between Lithuanians and Jews to air out. More than ever, he felt that it was necessary for the country's progress and modernization.

Whatever the stiff old-timers—entrenched in government

ministries and holding important posts in the academic world of his country—believed, he was convinced that Lithuania's success in the world depended upon its willingness to give up long-held and intransigent positions of denial and obfuscation when it came to what had truly happened in the country starting on June 22, 1941.

Even though it was a very short ride to the airport, he got there early. The vision of Milia Gottstein-Lasker lost and defenseless among milling crowds of Lithuanian strangers who might accidentally jostle her, or say something inadvertently rude to her, sent goose bumps up and down his spine. That was all he needed! It would be the first nail in the coffin of his attempt to create a new era of cooperation and mutual respect.

He found parking easily. After all, with Covid, no one was traveling these days, and anyway, Vilnius wasn't exactly high on the list of the world's vacation hotspots, although in his opinion his beloved city had much to offer that was unique. It also had good hotels and restaurants rich with the local cuisine.

He had booked her into the very comfortable Radisson Blu Royal Astorija Hotel, which was considered a huge splurge by his partners. But after that cheapo flight, he felt it was the least he could do. Besides, it was only for a few nights. He had thought it best to pamper her before their cross-country odyssey together visiting the towns and villages that even now were awash with excitement at the unusual events that under normal circumstances passed them by in favor of more substantial population centers. They would return in a week to Vilnius, and the Radisson, for the final presentation at city hall, which was a one-minute walk from the hotel (he tried not to think "good for a quick getaway").

He had to admit to himself that he was worried. While Lithuanians on the whole were polite and kind and friendly to visitors, they definitely had a sore spot when it came to being accused of historical crimes given the terrible injustices committed against them, especially during the Soviet occupation. Sagas of family members whose small farms and businesses had been expropriated and given to others according to Communist ideology; who had been imprisoned and executed for displaying defiance; and worst of all, the thousands exiled to Siberia according to Stalin's mad plan to subdue resistance in the Baltics and populate Siberia as far north as the Arctic Circle, were still sharp in the nation's collective memory. Thousands of Lithuanians had died during this horrifying episode, from cold, starvation, and brutalization, the majority vulnerable women, children, and the elderly. Even after thirty years of independence, these unforgivable injustices were still sharp in the minds and hearts of the nation.

March 11, 1990, Lithuanian Independence Day, was not only a day of rejoicing but also of bitter remembrance. Nothing upset Lithuanians more than having aspersions cast upon their gospel of blameless victimhood. Inconvenient but proven facts pointing out active Lithuanian collaboration with both the Communist occupiers as well as the Nazis made them see red. They became incensed and irrational. It was a point of honor. Not knowing what Milia planned to say, there was no way to estimate how the participants would react. All these things looping endlessly through his mind in the last few days had made it impossible for him to fall asleep. He was exhausted.

He looked at the arrivals board. The plane was on time, which meant it was due to land in ten minutes. He estimated it would take a half hour before she got through customs and collected her luggage, enough time for him to order some espresso and one or two *spurgos*—local doughnuts without the holes—to which he was addicted but did his best to avoid owing to their catastrophic effect on his midriff. They arrived drowned in powdered sugar, but alas, a bit soggy. He wolfed them down anyway, hardly tasting them as he glanced nervously at his watch. His hand trembled. *My nerves are shot,* he realized, wondering once again if any of this was worth it. He went to the restroom and looked at himself in the mirror. There were dark circles under his bright blue eyes, and veins of red within the whites. His hair was, if possible, even more unruly.

He relieved himself, then checked twice if he had closed the zipper all the way. That's all he needed! Tucking in his already neatly tucked-in shirt once more, he closed the last button on his jacket, then went into the terminal to stand guard at the arrivals hall. Only standing there and looking at others did he realize that he should have brought a sign with her name on it to hold up. *How were they going to find each other?* he thought with sudden panic. He had seen a photo of her, of course, and she of him. But from his Tinder dates, he knew how inaccurate these things were.

There it was again! Tinder dates! *What is going through your mind, my friend?* He lowered his head and shook it, ashamed. *Just because she is a woman? Just because I am a man? Really?* Was he really on such a low level as a human being that that was all he could focus on? Then he realized the most ridiculous part of it all: they were both wearing masks!

* * *

The landing was a bit bumpy, nothing like the way Israeli pilots on El Al gently rolled into Tel Aviv, she thought. But no airline anywhere had commercial pilots like that, all trained in combat by the Israeli Air Force, familiar with flying through enemy airspace. Landing a plane without having to dodge antiaircraft fire must be child's play for them.

She waited until it looked as if the people ahead of her had taken down their luggage so that she wouldn't be blocking the aisle when she got up. Her seatmate, she saw, was already standing, waiting patiently for her to move out of the way, but obviously too intimidated to make a peep.

She felt sorry once again that she had been the one to disabuse her of her fantasy fun heritage tour. But it had to be done. "I hope you enjoy being with your family and you find what you are looking for," she said by way of apology.

The woman merely nodded, her eyes desolate.

She remembered the airport vaguely from the last time she'd been there. Hardly anything had changed. After customs, she headed toward the luggage carousels, touching her handbag for reassurance. Everything was in there: her passports, her wallet, and most importantly her phone. The phone was her lifeline, containing everything from the address of her hotel, Dr. Vidas's phone number, to an app that would translate from Lithuanian into English. It even held a digital copy of her speech, in case the written one nightmarishly vanished. She shuddered to think of anything happening to it. Of course, it was all backed up on her computer, but this was so much more convenient to carry around.

She took out her phone, waiting for it to connect to the local carrier. Its battery was very low, and unlike most modern airports, run-down Vilnius had few recharging outlets. As an experienced traveler, she never left home without a fully operational battery recharger. She plugged it in gratefully, then placed them both snugly into her purse, all the while keeping a protective hand on the strap of her cross-body handbag so that anyone inclined to attempt a smash and grab would have to haul her along with them.

It wasn't paranoia. Once, in the crowded Paris metro, she had been holding on to a center pole when someone began to crowd her. She'd tried moving away and he'd very politely murmured "*excusez-moi*" and then "*pardon*" right up to the moment he'd forcefully put a hand over hers, then grabbed her purse strap, fleeing out of the door when the train stopped. She hadn't let go, and the purse had swung back to her just before the doors closed. And he'd looked so young and fashionable! So Parisian!

Over the years, she had honed her strategies to meet every contingency. Still, it seemed unlikely to her she would need them as she looked over the very European crowd of travelers who surrounded her. Everything about them said average, normal, liberal, law-abiding European, who enjoyed wearing designer this or that and indecently body-hugging Kardashian-style clothes. She could just as well have landed in Charles de Gaulle or Berlin Brandenburg.

Maybe people all over the world were becoming interchangeable, she thought, everyone united, the entire population of the planet frighteningly homogenized, differences plucked out by status seeking, ridicule, and bullying. And where, then, did that leave her, a person determined to remind everyone of their individual past and their cultural and historical inheritance?

Her suitcase looked like she felt when it passed her on the carousel, tired and a bit battered. She grabbed it, relieved that at least that potential disaster could be crossed off her mental list, along with how she would solve the problem of not having any clothes or makeup when addressing a crowd as keynote speaker. That, too, had happened to her: a short flight in which she had taken only a roll-on, hanging the clothes she needed in a garment bag. Only at the airport had she remembered the garment bag was still hanging in her closet. After going through an interval of pure panic, where insane ideas rollicked through her head, she finally accepted that there was nothing to be done. There was no time to go home and come back, and the flight would land with only an hour to spare, of which thirty minutes would be spent traveling to her hotel and then the venue. She'd looked down at what she was traveling in: a pair of old black slacks, a green sweater that had seen better days, and beat-up trainers. She had no choice but to get up onstage like that. While she at least had her makeup bag, she doubted the power of mascara and a touch of lipstick would improve the deplorable situation. When she arrived, she wondered whether or not to apologize and explain. But that would only call attention to the situation. She decided not to bring it up unless someone else did. To her astonishment, no one even noticed! When she scanned the crowd from the podium, she realized why: most of them were dressed similarly, or even worse. This forever changed her attitude about what constituted a disaster on speaking tours. As long as you showed up and were breathing and could speak, nothing else mattered.

She followed the crowd out of the terminal, only briefly glancing toward those awaiting loved ones at the arrivals gate, briefly scanning the placards held up by taxi drivers. Her name wasn't written anywhere.

She was just about to head out toward the taxi stands, when she heard someone call her name. She looked up. He was very tall and very blond, with piercing blue eyes, every inch of him shouting "Aryan." She recoiled, speechless.

"I'm so sorry if I startled you. But are you, by any chance, Dr. Milia Gottstein-Lasker?" Darius asked hesitantly.

"Dr. Vidas?"

"Yes." He smiled, relieved. "With the mask, I wasn't certain. But then I saw that Israeli flag sticker on your suitcase and took a chance."

She looked down at her roll-on, surprised. She didn't usually allow herself to travel to Europe with anything that might attract unwelcome attention from the growing hordes of antisemites now populating what was once safe territory. She had no idea where the sticker came from.

He watched in discomfort as she pulled it off and put it in her pocket without comment. "I am here to take you to your hotel.

I hope the flight was all right, aside from being sardine class. Again, my apologies."

"It was fine," she lied, tired of being the bearer of bad tidings. "I didn't expect you to pick me up. How kind of you!"

"It was the least I could do after subjecting you to that flight. Besides, I would just have worried the whole time. I'm so very happy you're here! Can I help you with your luggage?"

"That would be great!" she told him, meaning it. "I'm dead tired. I got up really early. I'm sure you're in the same boat. I expect you still have a million things to take care of for the conference?"

He did. "Not at all! It's a privilege to escort you. We, all of us, are so grateful that you agreed to come. I'm sure it wasn't a simple decision. You haven't always been on the best of terms with our country."

His honesty was disarming. She laughed. "Well, that's certainly true. But I'm hoping for a breakthrough this time around."

He smiled, his stomach churning. What did she mean by that? *A breakthrough.* Like smashing through a door with a sledgehammer? "I . . . am . . . hoping nothing breaks."

She looked at him more closely. The red flash of embarrassment was already climbing up his long, white neck, touching his cheeks outside the mask. My goodness! He was terrified of her! Well, maybe that was a good thing, she told herself, deeply amused. "I promise you if I do, I won't make you clean it up. Besides, the noise and activity will keep everyone awake instead of snoring into their paper cups of bad coffee."

Now he smiled, trying and failing to feel relieved. It was just a figure of speech, right? An English idiom. She certainly didn't look dangerous. Five two, maybe three, petite with long dark hair tinged with gray and large, alert blue-green eyes, she looked like a very efficient and determined lawyer on her way to court, he thought. Certainly someone you'd want on your side if you were the accused.

Only as they walked through the exit toward the car park did the truth dawn on him: *We are all the accused, and she is not on our side.*

As they got into the car together, he began to wonder if he shouldn't have sent one of his teaching assistants to pick her up. But then, it was a very short ride, only about fifteen minutes. Surely he could hold up his end of a conversation without offending her for fifteen minutes, no?

"I want you to know, I am fully vaccinated. Besides that, I actually caught Covid last year," he said, closing the door.

"Ohh. How bad was it?"

"I was as sick as I've ever been. I even needed oxygen at some point. It was a nasty, nasty experience. But I wasn't intubated. And as you can see, I've fully recovered."

"I'm also fully vaccinated. Israelis have even been given the option of a fourth booster, which I took."

"So I guess, for this short ride, we can dispense with the masks?" he asked her anxiously, curiously hopeful to see her face at last.

She felt the same way about seeing him. They peeled their masks off, then stared at each other shyly.

"I think I would have recognized you from your photos," she told him. He had a strong, Slavic face, fair skin, blond stubble, a determined chin, high cheekbones, and a straight nose. His eyes were startlingly blue. His mouth, rather thin, was curled now in a self-deprecating smile. It was an attractive, appealing face, she thought, a bit taken aback.

"And I you," he gallantly reciprocated, although he wasn't at all sure. The photos he had seen were all from conferences or press releases, the hair short, fixed and sprayed, the eyes hidden behind large glasses. In person, the eyes were large, widely spaced, gracefully feline; the eyelashes amazingly long. Her complexion seemed almost olive, or was that the strong Mediterranean sun? Her lips were plump, and her teeth strong, even, and white. It was a pretty face, even with such a standoffish, reserved expression. Not hostile exactly, but certainly not welcoming. *Correct* would be the word he would use to describe it.

He extended his hand. "Pleasure to meet you."

His hand was large and warm. When he let go, she found herself secretly flexing and unflexing her fingers to remove the sensation, which lasted the entire ride.

"Tell me about the conference," she said, closing her seat belt and leaning back.

"Well, starting tomorrow, we are booked into six small towns across the country. We return to Vilnius for the main conference at city hall, for which we've had an avalanche of RSVPs. We expect a very nice turnout. In fact, the media and various government institutions are still bombarding me for tickets. I think all Lithuanian major media will be represented, as well as the foreign press. We will be well covered."

"That's good to hear. Dr. Vi—"

"Please, Darius. And what should I call you, Dr. Gottstein-Lasker?"

"Milia is fine," she said, actually not sure. Milia sounded uncomfortably familiar, intimate even. But on the other hand, that long, hyphenated name of hers was a mouthful and he had given her permission to use his first name. It seemed churlish, insulting even, not to reciprocate.

"About how long do you think your talk will run?" he asked, his tone neutral as he maneuvered around the touchy subject of what she was planning to say, and then out of his parking space.

"I'm sure you're hoping not too long." She smiled impishly.

He gave her a quick, alarmed glance, noticed the smile, and relaxed. "You are being very naughty." He shook his finger.

"Why are you so scared? You, after all, invited me!"

Might as well tell her the truth. "Well, Milia, there have been some people who have given me a very hard time with that decision. Mostly from within the university, but also certain very aggressive government employees."

"Yes, like the Genocide Center, right?"

He nodded.

"Look, Darius, I might as well tell you the truth. I feel that your country has a long road to travel toward making peace with the Jewish people over what occurred here. Conferences like these are only worthwhile if they force people to confront all the things that have been festering for so long. It's like infected tissue. It has to be cut away for the body to heal. That operation isn't a pleasant or easy one. It is also quite painful. But there is no noninvasive or pleasant way around it, I'm afraid."

He nodded, feeling a bit sick. Even though, deep down, he felt the same way, he knew many others did not, preferring the present Band-Aid—anything—that would cover the ugly problems so they wouldn't have to be faced. "I completely agree with you, Milia. But I beg you to take into consideration that not everyone here is mature enough to welcome such an opportunity."

"Then it's time for all of them to grow up," she said curtly.

They traveled in silence for a moment. He cleared his throat. "You know, my grandparents hid Jews during the war. A whole family. In a secret room in city hall. My grandfather was the mayor of the town when the Nazis invaded."

She looked up sharply. "Really?"

He nodded. "I actually have been trying to get in touch with the Jewish family he helped. I was hoping to fly them over to be part of the conference."

"Have you been able to find them?"

He shook his head. "Not yet. But I have some new information from my mother, so I'm going to get in touch with some of my contacts again. Maybe this time . . ."

"Well, if you give me the names of the Jews, the name of the town, and the name of your grandfather, I have many contacts who would be happy to help you."

He cleared his throat. "Certainly! That would be great. Just . . . right now . . . both of us have our hands full. But of course, I'd be deeply grateful," he murmured.

His reluctance was not lost on her. Nor on him.

"So, can you give me a rundown of the trip we'll be taking, where we are going first, and what will happen there?"

He gave her a sharp glance. "You got the itinerary, no?"

"Yes, of course. I'm just wondering what to expect and how long you'd like me to speak."

"Well, our plan is to meet up with small-town officials and students at an assembly at the local high school, and then, perhaps, we might head out to the memorial sites—"

"Killing fields . . . ," she murmured softly.

He glanced at her, uncomfortably. "Well, yes. But in some places that wouldn't be possible."

"Why not?"

"Well, we'd need electricity for the sound system, and a place for people to sit."

"I see. Sorry for the interruption. Go on."

"We've asked the mayors to say something, and one of the students will be talking about the Holocaust. This will be followed by a reading from Ken Krimstein's book *When I Grow Up*, which is a bestseller here in Lithuania. I thought reading the essay of a teenage Jewish boy or girl, high school kids their age, talking about their hopes for the future, right before the Holocaust, would be meaningful to them."

"Yes, of course. I agree. And then what?"

"Well, we thought you could say a few words."

"How few?"

"No, I mean . . . that you could speak, something appropriate to the occasion."

"And you would translate into Lithuanian?"

"Yes. Would that be all right?"

"Perfect. But I insist it be an accurate translation. I'm going to be recording it."

He was hurt. "Why would you doubt me?"

Now it was her turn to be embarrassed. Was it that obvious? "I don't want to be censored."

"Why would I do that?"

She could think of many reasons, but somehow it felt discourteous to distrust him. Besides, what choice did she have? This was his country and his show. She only hoped she wasn't going to regret the moment she got off that plane.

Eighteen

"Can I offer to take you to dinner?" Darius asked shyly.

"Listen, and don't take this in the wrong way . . ."

He stiffened.

"No, really, it's very kind of you, and I'd love to take you up on it, but I've been up since two a.m. and I'm about ready to fall off my feet. I'm just dying for a hot shower and an early night. I'll call up room service for a salad or something. But I look forward to a rain check."

He smiled, relaxing. He felt instinctively that she was telling him the truth. "I know, these early morning flights are a killer. I'll just park and go inside with you just to make sure they've got your reservation, and to help you with your luggage."

"Thanks so much, Darius." So nice to have a man fluttering around her, helping her, she thought, ashamed of herself. It had been a while.

The desk clerk was very friendly, and Darius made sure it all went smoothly.

When she got her keys, she put out her hand to him. He shook it. "Have a good night's sleep and I'll see you in the morning."

"Are we leaving early?" She seemed alarmed.

"No, not until eleven. You'll have plenty of time for a leisurely breakfast." Was *that* the problem? He paused for a beat, hoping she would invite him to join her for breakfast. She didn't.

"Well, I'll let you get some rest. And once again, thank you so much for coming. Ah, do you need help getting that to your room?" he asked, pointing to her rather large suitcase. "Shall I take it up for you?"

But just then a bellhop came by and wheeled it away. "I guess not." She smiled, relieved and yet a bit disappointed, too, she realized, chagrined. "Thanks, Darius. See you tomorrow at eleven."

She hurried away, feeling a blush climbing up her cheek. His presence, she realized, disturbed her, taking away her peace of mind. The reason for that was not as uncomplicated as it should have been, she scolded herself.

The hotel was really very nice, she admitted, trying to distract herself. She remembered it from decades past, when she'd stayed there with her father. She was curious to explore, to note the changes, but her weariness overtook her. She barely had time to shower and brush her teeth before literally falling into bed and into a deep sleep.

She awoke around 3:00 a.m. with a bit of a headache and a growling stomach. Room service had probably closed down for the night—this was, after all, the Baltics. She went to the minibar and took out a Diet Coke and a candy bar. From her bag, she still had a box of kosher cookies, and a bag of rugelach from her favorite bakery. She tried putting on the television. It had cable, but it was all in Lithuanian except for CNN, which she had been boycotting ever since the Second Intifada, when it seemed to her that CNN had blatantly taken the side of the terrorists to promote their new CNN Arabic channel.

Restless, she put on her computer and looked up the speech she had written for the high school students in Raseiniai. She leaned back against the tufted headboard, trying to get comfortable. But it was no use. You couldn't feel comfortable with a text like that in front of you. By the time she had finished, she felt the tears falling down her cheeks. She dried them with the heel of her hand. You could never get used to some things, no matter how many times you read about them. If you were human, that is.

She closed the file and saved it, opening up her email. *The usual, the usual, the usual,* she thought, scanning the myriad messages, stopping only when she came across one from Gilad. "Good luck slaying the dragons, Ima!" he wrote with his characteristic sensitivity. He had remembered where she was, and how difficult it was going to be for her. *What a great kid!* she thought. He had always given her the most trouble growing up, dancing to a different tune only he could hear. She and Julius had both been at a loss to direct him. Swans raising a duck, she thought, remembering how she and Julius used to laugh about it. There had been so much laughter in their lives, despite everything.

She thought about her speech. It was going to infuriate many, many people. It might even shut down Darius's whole tour. But that was just too bad. She wasn't here as Dr. Vidas's friend. She was here to push her own agenda. She had never pretended otherwise. But now, having met the man, who had been so kind and hospitable, she felt a niggling doubt. She didn't want to hurt him personally or get him into any trouble. But there was nothing else she could do without being a hypocrite and a coward. There was no way to soft-pedal this information, which the young people of this country needed and *deserved* to hear, information that was deliberately being withheld from them in the hope that they would never learn the truth. Even now, those responsible were being canonized as the country's heroes, the people its current leaders wanted young people to look up to and imitate. What a horror!

If Lithuania was to raise a better generation, one incapable of the kind of atrocities that had been committed in the past, these youngsters had to be educated and forewarned. If their own leaders and teachers refused to do it, it must come to them from the outside. She'd be doing them an enormous favor, she told herself. *Just don't expect flowers and a thank-you card*, she thought cynically. She yawned, crawling back under the covers and falling asleep once again.

* * *

Her wake-up call shoved her out of a strange dream about a young boy who was arguing with her, trying to make a point. She could see his face clearly. He wore an old-fashioned suit with short pants, and one of those poor-boy caps Lithuanian beggars were fond of. His arm was bandaged, and he was barefoot. His face was very expressive as he spoke to her, but she couldn't understand a word he was saying. Was it that she couldn't hear him? Or was he speaking in a language she didn't know? Just as she was trying to decide, the telephone rang, startling her awake.

For a moment, she forgot where she was, the residue of the disturbing dream confusing her. She took a few deep breaths as she slowly came back into the present.

The idea of a quick breakfast and the long car journey to their first stop filled her with a sudden fright. To be together in the car for such a long time with a man she hardly knew, a Lithuanian! What would they talk about? He seemed friendly enough, but afterward, when it became clear to him what road she was traveling in her speech . . . he would not be friendly at all, and then they would still have the entire week ahead of them, hours and hours as they traveled from place to place. It was a nightmare in the making.

It was insane to have agreed to all this, she thought, pushing herself into a sitting position. She wondered once again where her brain had been during the entire correspondence with Dr. Vidas. No doubt her troubles with Julius had interfered with her good judgment, the longing to put some distance between herself and her situation dominating her thoughts. Israel had never before seemed like such a tiny country. Everywhere she went, everyone she spoke to seemed surprisingly well informed about their shattered marital status: friends, colleagues, and people she barely knew at all. Everyone wanted to express sympathy, commiserate, or to simply gossip while pretending to sympathize and commiserate. However good their acting skills, their eyes gave them away: pitying eyes, appraising eyes, shrewd eyes that bore into her, mining for truth, or, failing that, at least for fragments of useful new information that would impress and astonish their friends.

Well, it was just too bad for them. She had no intention of fulfilling their fantasies of buddyhood. She was closemouthed to everyone, even her children, admitting only that her relationship with her husband was "in transition," and that it was "only natural" considering how long they had been married. But privately, she raged against the humiliation and heartbreak Julius was putting her through.

After their failed lunch date, their contact had been minimal. He continued to pay their mortgage, gas, and electric bills. He even once called her asking if she wanted him to order more heating oil for the furnace, which she curtly declined, getting Amir to show her how to measure how much oil was left in the tank, and getting a neighbor to recommend a supplier. It was a silly assertion of independence, she realized, more trouble than it was worth, but still important. How did that line in the Donna Summer song go? *"Did you think I'd lay down and die?"*

Well, the "lay down" part wasn't happening. Which was probably why she'd accepted the conference invitation and gotten on that flight. Not that she hadn't come perilously close to crumbling, to *wanting* to "lay down and die." But things had changed, she realized.

Her self-confidence had come back to her in a slow, steady stream, filling her with the kind of strength she had learned about from conversations with survivors. That dark, empty void had begun to fill again with light as she transformed the trauma of Julius's abandonment into a lesson in self-love, fulfilling the difficult tasks meted out to her.

Just writing that speech, just imagining delivering it in front of a jeering, hostile crowd, channeling the words of those incredible survivors who had fought so hard to live in order to pass on the truth of what had happened to them had given her back her sense of purpose and worth.

Her spirit was linked to the spirits of all those brave women who had used every ounce of their intelligence to preserve their lives and thus their memories in order to pass them on. She was their partner, her arms metaphorically linked through theirs, comrades with the same goal. Being abandoned by her husband no longer felt like the worst thing that had ever happened to her. In fact, she honestly couldn't imagine going back to the way things had been, having to apologize for talking about her work, having to devote the time and energy it required. Julius never apologized for his dedication to his work. Why should she?

But would she tell him to "*go, get out the door*" if he came back? That she still didn't know.

So far, Julius had still done nothing formal. No letters from lawyers had arrived, no threatening phone calls or demands about their jointly owned property. He seemed to have simply moved on and left everything behind him intact, replacing it. Sometimes she thought that was kind of him and she was lucky, and sometimes it enraged her. He had thrown everything away, like so much garbage, the whole life they had built up and shared over decades. And she was either on the top or the bottom of that pile of discards, depending upon how you looked at it.

The phone calls from Haviva's husband had continued for a while, until she'd finally just told him, "Look, Nadav, Haviva is your problem, not mine. I couldn't care less about either of you. Deal with it!"

That had been the last time she'd heard from him.

As far as Haviva was concerned, that wasn't exactly true. She did care, but only insofar as wanting the woman to suffer. While it would have made her feel less petty to pretend in retrospect that Haviva had betrayed a great and intimate friendship, Milia had to admit to herself—rather reluctantly—that it wasn't true. They had never been more than dinner companions trying out new restaurants together. Their time together wasn't even something she'd particularly enjoyed, finding the pair of them—Nadav and Haviva—a bit grating. They were either trying to convince you—or themselves—that their son, who had married in his early forties and was now, three years later, already in the throes of a bitter divorce and custody battle, was a misunderstood genius and his wife a shrew, while simultaneously demanding you recognize just how superior their life choices were to your own. They were always full of advice about how you could achieve the levels of success they themselves enjoyed, imparting the names of therapists, interior decorators, fabric stores, stock picks, and vacation spots that would "seriously change your life."

She hadn't wanted her life changed. But now, it seemed, Haviva had accomplished just that all by herself, single-handedly turning Milia's life upside down in the most decisive way of all. Thanks to her, Milia's life would never be the same.

What was the end goal going to be? she wondered. Nothing was stopping Julius from opening a file in the Rabbinical Court or the Family Court for a divorce at any given moment. He didn't need to discuss it with her or get her agreement. In Israel, women were seriously disadvantaged in this area.

She could, of course, also file, but ultimately he would still have to agree to divorce her. Nothing could go forward without that. Often, the rabbis were key factors in keeping a reluctant couple together, refusing to agree to a divorce on the grounds that the marriage still had hope.

The term used was *shalom bayit*, or *family peace*, which was another way of saying: try harder. It was frightening that in a modern country like Israel, aging religious zealots could stick their noses into your life choices. It was like living in Iran.

She would have a better chance of a favorable settlement if she started the proceedings herself in the secular Family Court, shutting down Julius's ability to go to the Rabbinical Court, which was known to give men a much better settlement. It was the sensible thing to do, her good friends had advised her. But she needed to do it fast.

She had so far resisted that option, telling herself—and her friends—that there was no point in starting these formalities until she knew what Julius really wanted. Did he want to marry Haviva? Did he want to get rid of her, his wife of so many years? It wasn't at all clear to her, seeing as all this had come out of the blue and they had not once really sat down to discuss it. She didn't have more than some vague clues as to her husband's motivations, his unhappiness.

When she tried to figure it out, the best she could do was connect Julius's unhappiness to her constant traveling. But his absences from home were just as bad when it came to that. All those emergency operations that interrupted their lives; all those weeklong conferences on the other side of the world. Her shoulders slumped. What was the difference *why* he had left? He was gone. His side of the bed was empty, his closet cleaned out.

This image strangely gave her new energy. Whatever had happened between them, it had a certain finality that in its way was comforting. *Off with the old and on with the new*, she told herself bravely, faking it until she could actually feel that way without imploding. She picked up the room service menu with determination.

Even though she strictly kept the kosher laws, there was always something you could eat wherever you went. Cornflakes and milk, for example. Fresh fruit, or a vegetarian salad. Coffee or tea. Some of those cookies she had eaten at 3:00 a.m.

After she'd placed her breakfast order, she stepped into the shower again. She'd read that air travel dehydrated you, and your skin loved the moisture. The hot water felt like a gift to her body, which was chilled even though it was spring and the hotel was generous with heat. It was the sleeping alone, she thought, soaping herself generously just to feel a warm hand on her cold body, the waking up alone, always being conscious of the lack of something to encompass and warm you, leaving you bereft of familiar comforts and, most of all, boundaries. Rolling over in bed, you never came up against a solid, bracing wall to keep you from falling into the abyss.

How strange! She had been on dozens and dozens of business trips all by herself since taking over her father's work. Julius seldom, if ever, joined her. So what was so different now? she asked herself, drying off with the large, fluffy hotel towels. Perhaps the idea that this wasn't just temporary, that she had nothing different waiting for her when she went home.

A new life, she thought forlornly. *A life I never planned for, a life I don't want.*

She wrapped the huge, thick hotel bathrobe around her and put her wet hair in a towel turban.

There was a sudden knock on the door. "Room service," a voice called out.

"Just a minute!"

She threw on some fresh clothes, then opened the door

barefoot. The cart rattled over the threshold, comfortingly full of fresh fruits and berries and a hot pot of her favorite tea.

She tipped the smiling bellboy, who was neither tall nor blond, she noticed. Just a normal, brown-haired kid trying to pay for college or a new car. She had to stop seeing enemies everywhere. She had to stop thinking in clichés.

There is something about room service, she thought, that is so delightful! Even though the food is pretty ordinary, just being served everything on trays with silver covers and stiffly ironed linen napkins made you feel rich and pampered. She decided to take some time off from her worries, promising herself not to think about Julius more than five minutes a day. *Pick a time,* she ordered herself, suspicious of her ability to keep this resolution. She determinedly set her watch to beep at 9:30 p.m. That was it. Each night at that time, she would give herself permission to use five minutes to ponder Julius and her marriage. Not a second more. He didn't deserve it. And she had better things to do, after all.

When she was done eating, she curled up on the couch, taking out her speech for the high school students in Raseiniai, their first stop, and reading it over once again.

NINETEEN

THE PHONE RANG at a quarter to eleven. *Right on time,* Milia thought to herself a bit grimly, picking it up. "Darius? I'll be down in a few minutes. Thanks."

People always envied her many trips abroad, thinking they were exotic vacations. They weren't. They were marathons of sleepless nights, packing and unpacking of suitcases, checking under beds and all over bathrooms and closets for anything she might have left behind, a scrutiny that somehow never prevented her from leaving things behind. Usually, the inevitable lost items were cheap and replaceable. But now she checked her briefcase for her computer, her cell phone, and the printed backup copy of her speech, all of which were indispensable. Satisfied that no imminent disaster was looming in that direction at least, she wheeled her two suitcases out the door to the elevator.

He stood waiting for her by the front desk: tall, athletic, blond. A man in a good suit with flashing electric blue eyes above his face mask as he turned to her. She suddenly felt a weakness not related to jet lag.

"Sleep well?" he asked, relieving her of her large suitcase, then motioning for her to hand him the small one as well. She relinquished them both gratefully.

"Yes, thank you. The room was very nice."

"I'm happy. I thought you'd like it," he said animatedly, as if they were friends on a joint vacation they'd been planning for months. While the latter was true, was the former? This was hardly a vacation, Milia thought, and they were hardly friends, although not exactly enemies.

Time would tell, she supposed, thinking of the words of her speech and reminding herself once again that their relationship was not important; that whatever it was, it was going to be sacrificed on the altar of a higher cause. There was nothing to be done.

Still, dishonesty was not in Milia Gottstein-Lasker's bones. And this relationship between them—so convivial and considerate—was all a lie, even if the lie had not yet been discovered.

Every friendly body movement, every polite gesture she made toward Darius Vidas, held within it an implicit deception. She followed him to the car, glad her mask made it unnecessary for her to smile, something that would only compound her crimes.

He sensed her reserve. "Are you sure you're okay?" he asked with sudden concern.

"Please, Darius, don't worry. I promise you I'm fine," she murmured, climbing into the passenger seat. Even if she'd entertained the possibility of putting some distance between them, the back seat—crowded with books, papers, and what looked like sound equipment—would have made it impossible. Besides, it would have been too overtly hostile to treat him as her chauffeur.

He backed expertly into traffic. "I'm heading toward the A2, which is a modern four-lane highway. It's an easy, straight drive to Raseiniai."

"How long do you think it will take?"

"About two hours, depending on how many stops we make."

She nodded, betraying nothing. *Two hours!* she thought, appalled. Was she going to have to make conversation? What could they possibly talk about? It was like being trapped in a broken elevator with a neighbor who had repeatedly ignored your requests to stop using the hallways to store his bicycles.

"I guess we can unmask ourselves, if that's okay with you. Is it?"

"Yes, please." She found the face mask torturous, making it hard to breathe and fogging her reading glasses. She removed it, taking a deep breath.

"Shall I put on some music?" he offered politely, beginning to sense that driving her from place to place on his own was a plan fraught with dangers to which he had not given sufficient consideration. But it was too late now.

She brightened. "Music! That's a splendid idea! What did you have in mind?"

"Well, I've got my iPhone and Spotify playlists. But I doubt you'd want to hear them."

"Why not?"

He grinned sheepishly. "It's Lithuanian rock and heavy metal bands from the eighties . . ."

"Oh, right." She smiled. "Hmm, don't think so. What else do you have?"

"I've got a classical playlist, Chopin . . ."

"Nocturne in E-flat Major?"

"Opus nine, number two, yes."

"I adore that, but it might put me to sleep, given my present state."

"Quite understandable. Well, what about Brahms, Hungarian Dance number five in G Minor . . . ?"

"That's certainly not a lullaby! Well, okay. And do you have Pachelbel's Canon?"

"Of course. But if I might make a suggestion?"

She looked at him alertly.

"Are you familiar with Khachaturian? His *Masquerade Waltz* from *Spartacus?*"

She gave him her first genuine smile. "You know, the first time I heard that was in the ballroom scene from the movie version of *War and Peace*. There is something slightly off-kilter about it, almost like a dance scene in one of those strange Tim Burton movies where he gives a sinister gloss to Christmas and weddings . . ."

Darius laughed. "I know exactly what you mean! It's the way the music suddenly goes off in a minor key when you were expecting Strauss happy hour."

"Precisely! I love it!"

"Here. Can you just scroll down and find it?"

As he handed her his iPhone, their hands brushed against each other. They both recoiled, pretending it hadn't happened. She found the music quickly, handing it back to him carefully.

"Can you just plug it in on the dashboard and press Play?"

"Of course."

The music filled the car. There was something deeply romantic about it, but dark, also, with all those cymbals clashing almost violently and the minor notes taking you off the polished dance floor to someplace frantic and confusing, not at all where timid, standardized social dances usually went. It was, she thought, urgently passionate, almost frightening in its blatant insistence on destroying the fiction that what was going on between a man and a woman was simply a polite, choreographed turn around the dance floor amid dozens of other couples.

She found herself almost breathless. Luckily, it was soon replaced by another song on the list, Mozart's Piano Sonata no. 16 in C Major, which was in comparison steady and reliable and almost childishly innocent, with its repetitions, and then the brilliant variations on the theme at which Mozart excelled. There was nothing even vaguely personal in it, she thought, as she exhaled.

And then, suddenly, the next song came on: "O Mio Babbino Caro," but sung in such an ethereal way that it sounded like angels singing. When the exquisite soprano voice reached the high notes and rested, she found tears streaming down her cheeks. Embarrassed, she laughed, wiping them away. But his eyes too were wet.

"I've heard this so many times, but never like this. Who is that singing?"

"Amira Willighagen. She's all grown up now, but she gave this concert when she was nine years old on some talent show in Denmark."

"A child singing such a passionate love song . . ."

"I saw a video of this concert. The entire audience was weeping."

"Once, I actually looked up the lyrics. It's a young woman pleading with her father to allow her to marry her handsome lover and threatening to throw herself into the Arno if he refuses."

He smiled. "Ah. But I don't think anyone really needs to know the words to understand the feeling in the music, do you?"

"That's true. The music itself evokes such pathos. Can we listen to it again?"

"Sure, just press Replay."

As soon as she did, she knew it was a mistake. The music and the girl's voice touched something raw within her. The tears started up again, and this time, they wouldn't stop. She reached for his phone, frantically trying to turn the music off.

"I'm so . . . sorry . . . I don't know . . . I've never . . ." She gasped, mortified.

It was everything. Julius. Lithuania. Her speech. Facing a crowd of Lithuanians in Raseiniai, which had been the setting for so many horrors, none of which had lain under the dust of history long enough to become bloodless or desiccated, she thought. They still throbbed with an evil life of their own, crimes no Lithuanian had ever owned up to or even admitted.

He opened up the glove compartment and handed her a tissue, which she took gratefully, careful this time not to touch him.

"I might as well tell you the truth. I'm in the middle of a separation from my husband. I guess it's finally gotten to me," she admitted.

"That's tough. I've been there."

"Really?"

"Yes, but it was years ago. She found someone she liked better. But you know what? It turned out fine. We are both happier this way."

She wiped her eyes and blew her nose, staring at him. "Did you remarry?"

He laughed. "Not on your life."

"But isn't it . . . lonely?"

He cocked his head, thinking about it. "Maybe. Sometimes. But not lonely enough to do something stupid like getting stuck in another relationship that will make me miserable."

"But you're not celibate, are you?"

"Hardly." He laughed, a bit embarrassed at the turn the conversation had taken.

"So, you go out with women, but you are vigilant about protecting your heart, yes?"

That was a good description that fit him to a T, he thought appreciatively. "Something like that. You know once you've raised the kids, it isn't so urgent anymore, having a partner."

"I'm not so sure about that."

"I'm free to travel as much as I like, and stay out as late as I like, and waste my hard-earned money without anyone complaining or trying to reform me . . ."

"Yes, of course," she sighed, feeling a bit bored by the clichés.

"You don't sound convinced."

"Because none of it is believable. I'm sure *you* don't believe a word you're saying."

He began to protest.

She held up her hand. "Unless a person is a complete narcissist, who doesn't hate being alone? I know I do. Before, even when I was traveling, I had someone to call, to share my day with. Someone I cared about." She suddenly started feeling uncomfortable. "I'm sorry. This has gotten very personal."

"I don't mind," he assured her with alacrity. If the truth were to be told, this sudden turn in the conversation was exhilarating to him. He was finally cracking open the hard shell that encased the implacable Milia Gottstein-Lasker, public enemy number two of the Lithuanian people.

She noted his interest with mortification, kicking herself, and hurried to change the subject. "So, tell me a little about this school we are going to."

"The President Jonas Žemaitis Gymnasium."

"Who is it named after?"

"One of our country's most famous partisans . . ."

She felt her heart sink at the words: a Lithuanian partisan . . .

He could read her face. He shook his head. "I know what you are thinking, but you'd be wrong. He wasn't one of *those* partisans, the white armbanders, the Nazi collaborators."

She couldn't believe her ears. A Lithuanian actually admitting that at least some of their "saintly" partisans were also Nazi collaborators! It was the first time in her life she had heard such an admission from a Lithuanian, most of whom insisted on treating them all as martyrs and freedom fighters. The murderers of women and children of Raseiniai! That in itself had made the trip worth it.

"Žemaitis became active only after the Nazis were defeated," he went on, oblivious to her profound amazement. "In 1949, Žemaitis founded the Union of Lithuanian Freedom Fighters and worked to continue partisan resistance to Soviet occupation. In December 1951, he was betrayed, and a gas grenade was tossed into the bunker where he was hiding. He suffered a cerebral hemorrhage. He was arrested and sent to Moscow, where he was tried in a closed session and sentenced to death by firing squad. The Soviets executed him, cremated his body, and scattered the ashes in a common grave with other Soviet victims. He had actually been a student in the gymnasium in Raseiniai. And a legitimate national hero," he concluded passionately.

Milia listened. Yes, there were so many things she still did not know about these people, especially the man sitting next to her. "Thank you for explaining that to me. I admit, when I hear the word 'partisan' as related to Lithuania, all I hear is a euphemism for the filthy murderers and rapists of my people."

He looked at her, shocked at her venom.

"Let me ask you something, Darius. Are you happy with the current state of your beloved country?"

"What do you mean?"

"I mean, look at your economy, at your tourism, at the exodus of your young people."

"Actually . . ."

She didn't bother to wait for his answer. "Did you know that Lithuanian Jews were given a special name by other Jews?"

"Yes. They were called Litvaks."

She nodded, impressed. "Do you also know that they were the crème de la crème of the Jewish people—sharp-witted, intelligent, learned, creative? They were a treasure for your country and your people. These 'partisans' whom you honor, name streets and schools after, put up statues and plaques to commemorate, destroyed Lithuania's present and its future by killing off one of your country's most precious and important human resources—scholars, doctors, lawyers, entrepreneurs, small factory owners.

They destroyed your country. So why aren't you Lithuanians angry? Why do you try to hide and ignore what they did to *you*, never mind to the Jewish people? You should be furious. You should be only too happy to put every one of them still left alive in their wheelchairs with their pacemakers on public trial, then let them rot in jail until they die."

He was silent. He had thought these very things himself. But it was different to have it thrown in his face by a hostile stranger. It put his back up. "Milia, you have to understand, Stalin decided to break the Baltics with terror. He grabbed tens of thousands of innocent families, mostly women and children and old people, right out of their beds in their pajamas, giving them twenty minutes to pack and stuck them on cattle cars without food or water and transported them to Siberia. Russian soldiers stood guard over them, beating them up and killing them if they tried to escape. They threw the corpses of children and the old off the trains at every stop. They were imprisoned for years in hellish places with no food . . ."

"And that was an unspeakable crime. But what did that have to do with the Lithuanian Jews?"

"Don't you see? The Jews welcomed the Russians. And for us Lithuanians, they were the murderers and exilers of our people. We welcomed the Nazis as liberators from the Stalinists."

"Can you honestly blame any Lithuanian Jew who opposed the Nazis roaring into their hometown?"

"Of course not! But . . ."

"Besides, some things did get better for Jews under the Soviets. Some local anti-Jewish legislation was overturned. Jews could get civil service jobs that had been previously closed to them. Given their choices, it's true that some Jews preferred socialism. But they were in the minority. Still, Lithuanians accepted the Nazi propaganda that Jews controlled the Soviet Union and wanted to take over the world."

"Taking those government jobs was seen as Jewish collaboration with the Communists."

"How convenient for the Lithuanians to overlook how many
Lithuanian nationals were only too happy to collaborate with
Soviet authorities! Besides, what did the deportations have to do
with the Jews?"

"It was widely believed that the Communist Jews helped to
draw up the lists of those Lithuanians who were to be deported.
There was a lot of anger and resentment toward the Jews because
of it. I'm not saying it was right. I'm just saying this is how it
happened."

Her mouth fell open. "Maybe it was *Lithuanian collaborators*
who drew up the lists, the ones who rose high in the ranks of *your*
government when the Communists were in power?"

"You know, when the war was over for the West in 1945, it
was just beginning for us Lithuanians. In some places, more ethnic Lithuanians died after V-E Day than during the entire war!
We remember those days as the 'pokaris,' which literally means
'postwar.' But for us the term doesn't recall a time of peace, but
a violent struggle. After Germany was defeated, the guerilla war
here against the Soviets resulted in thirty to forty thousand civilian and combatant deaths, while mass deportations and other
repressive measures affected another one hundred and thirty
thousand. And it wasn't just us. Estonia also had thousands of
deaths under the Soviets."

"Thirty to forty thousand, you say? And Jewish civilian
deaths under the partisan armbander patriots was in the hundreds of thousands. Repressive measures? Do you have any idea
what these 'partisans' did to Jewish women and children?" she
fumed. "If you had a hard time with the Soviets, I'd say you had
it coming."

He shook his head. "We will not get anywhere by measuring
one atrocity against another."

It was her turn to be silent. "No," she agreed. "We won't."

"Both of our peoples were under the rule of monsters."

"But my people never *became* monsters. Yours did."

"It was the times. It is inexplicable what happened. There were never any pogroms in Lithuania. Jews lived as equals, side by side. Jews flourished here, their culture, literature, scholarship. You yourself just said so! The Litvaks led the entire Jewish world!"

"But they were never fully accepted here. Even before the Nazis, your jealous businessmen wanted them ousted from their jobs, wouldn't let them join your guilds. There was jealousy, covetousness. Your church was part of that. Your antisemitic priests who, instead of inculcating their flocks with so-called Christian values, filled them with race hatred."

"Now you've gone completely overboard," he shouted.

"Oh, have I? Just compare what happened here to what happened in Bulgaria, which wasn't invaded; it was an *ally* of the Nazis. And yet when Eichmann came in demanding his pounds of Jewish flesh and their king gave in, the Bulgarian people refused to put their Jewish neighbors into the cattle cars, refused to deport them. Even when the Jews were rounded up and put into the courtyard of a school and the trucks stood by ready to begin their journey to the death camps, it didn't happen. They were all allowed to go home. Even their belongings weren't touched. And do you know why? Because the *priests* refused to allow it. They ordered all the church bells to ring nonstop. Metropolitan Kirill, a bishop of the Bulgarian Orthodox Church who later became its patriarch, and three hundred of his congregants stood in front of a train that was to transport fifteen hundred Jews from Plovdiv, Bulgaria's second largest city, saying he would not allow it to leave, even though armed SS officers surrounded them. Kirill sent a telegram to the Bishop of Sofia, Metropolitan Stephan, who said he would lie on the train tracks. He influenced forty-two members of Parliament to fire off a letter of protest to the

Bulgarian king. The deportations were stopped. The Jews of Bulgaria were saved by their neighbors. That is *their* national character. They gave their people one legacy, and your 'partisans' have given them another."

He felt tears come to his eyes. There was nothing he could say, no defense he could offer.

It was all true. His own daughter refused to live in the country of her birth. Yes, he was angry. Angry, and sick, and tired of covering up crimes he had inherited and was stamped with, like a birth defect.

"The Kenskys."

"What?"

"The Kenskys. Emil and Beyle and Itele, Henokh, and baby Ruchele. I want to know what happened to them. What my grandfather did as mayor of J—. Please find out."

She nodded, surprised. "My people," she whispered.

"'My people.' What do you mean when you say that, Milia? Are you talking about *your* people, the *Jewish* people, or about *your* people, the Litvaks, the Jews of Lithuania?"

"I think either one would be valid, Darius. We Jews are an extended family, a tribe. When you harm a Jew anywhere in the world, we don't care under which flag it happens, we unite to encircle our own. But in this particular case, I was referring to my Lithuanian family; my grandparents, my aunts, uncles, and cousins, who were descended from Jews who had lived here for centuries. They were killed by the other kind of partisan, not the heroic freedom lovers like your Žemaitis, but the butcher's boy and the farmers who tied pieces of torn, old sheets around their arms and declared themselves in charge of Lithuanian Jews; the 'partisans' who decided to do the Nazis' work for them—and to solve the problem of retribution by simply murdering every Jew they could get their hands on. There was nothing 'heroic' or 'freedom-loving' about it."

She watched his face carefully, waiting for him to protest, to deny, to obfuscate and find excuses. But he didn't. He simply let her speak, his face registering pain and shame and sorrow. "Tell me about them," he said softly.

"About who?"

"Them, your Lithuanian Jewish family. Where did they live?"

"They lived in Telzh. They were descended from great rabbis. They were very pious, very learned. But my grandfather didn't want to be a rabbi. He wanted to be an engineer. So he ran away to Poland and enrolled in the University of Warsaw, where he did very well, until in 1938 he and all the other Jewish students were expelled. That's when he came to Israel. There, he had no problem getting into a university. But he had left his family behind. That he hadn't . . . couldn't . . . save them, tortured him until the day he died. He returned to Europe with the Jewish Brigade to fight. But by then it was too late."

"But you, and your parents, were born in Israel. You are all Israelis, aren't you?"

"If you go back far enough, the word 'Jew' comes from the tribe of Judah, which makes every Jew a descendant of the natives of the land of Israel. Jews didn't leave there of their own accord. They were expelled by invading Roman legions led by Hadrian in 136 CE. That's when Jews scattered all over the world. Some places they reached through the Roman slave markets; others they escaped to of their own accord. The Jews of Lithuania date back to the Jews of Babylonia, who came to Russia, and the Khazars, who were widely believed to have converted to Judaism and were expelled in 969 by the Russian Orthodox Church. They came as traders, prisoners of war, and individuals. Your King Gediminas welcomed the Jews, and all peoples who could build the country and make it prosper. At that time, Lithuania stretched from the Baltic Sea to the Black Sea, a huge empire. The Jews were spared the horrors of the Crusades, and were not blamed for the Black

Plague, probably because Lithuanians were pagans, the last Europeans to embrace Christianity. The more Christian people become, the more heartless they became toward my people. That's just a fact."

He clutched the steering wheel. As a Catholic, even though quite lapsed, this was difficult to hear. The truth was, this was news to him. But he had nothing to say that might counter it.

"Shall I go on?"

"Please."

"When Gediminas's grandson married a devout Catholic Polish princess, all that changed. The fanatical clergy controlling Poland began to spread through Lithuania. Prince Vytautas, the grandson's cousin, had a castle near Kaunas. He demanded autonomy for Lithuania, and somehow managed to achieve it. He settled Jews, Karaites—a Jewish breakaway sect—in Vilnius. This was in 1392. Subsequent kings were very generous to the Jews, affording them rights and religious freedoms that they did not enjoy elsewhere in Europe. Eventually, of course, all that changed."

He was surprised. "Why 'of course'?"

"Well, if you must know, it's because the Church made it a priority to show the world how miserable the unconverted were, and the most blatant unconverted were, of course, the Jews, who refused to accept the story of the Jewish family whose virgin mother gave birth to God's son. Jews are unrelenting monotheists. God can't have a son."

"Well, we are also monotheists. The Trinity is one of the mysteries of our faith."

"Sorry. It's a little too mysterious for us Jews. We prefer our one God, without a wife and child."

He smiled, shaking his head. "Okay, but that's simplistic."

"I'm sure it is. But please don't enlighten me. Jews are notoriously bad-natured when it comes to being lectured about the virtues of the Christian religion, much of which was unabashedly culturally appropriated from us Jews anyway."

"Fair enough. So by 'of course' you meant that the persecution of Jews was led by the Church and was inevitable?"

"Yes. There was a constant struggle between the reasonable, decent rulers who viewed the skilled, clever, hardworking Jews as an asset who brought wealth and education to their countries, and the religious fanatics who were willing to cut off their nose to spite their face. So the benevolent duke or king or other ruler who had welcomed Jews was always going to be outvoted by the fanatics who wanted to irrationally expel and murder them. That in a nutshell is European Jewish history. Lithuania was no different."

"But we never had the pogroms the Jews suffered in Europe and especially Russia."

"That's true. Which is why Jews prospered in this country for hundreds of years and helped Lithuania to prosper as well. They made leather goods, and opened clothing and candy factories. They were sober, and hardworking, and educated. But it didn't matter. Eventually, the Lithuanians demanded to slaughter them for committing the most unforgivable crime of all."

"Which was?"

"That they succeeded. That they had good, happy, prosperous lives. That they were learned and pious, instead of ignorant, drunken brutes. And that's when jealousy was added to the old Christian hatred. The combination of those two elements was lethal."

"But why then? Why in 1941?"

"Because they were given permission by Hitler, and they saw how the Germans were treating Jews, and how they got away with it. The German invasion was their chance. Even before the Nazis set foot in the country, the Lithuanians started murdering their Jewish neighbors because they felt they could. It was a joyous orgy of rape, murder, and robbery. They killed so many Jews with such malice that even the Germans were sometimes appalled."

He was incensed. "Very one-sided, don't you think?"

"Okay, defend your country. I'm willing to listen."

"These partisans who put on the white bands and did the killings were the scum of the earth. Many Lithuanians opposed them and tried to save their Jewish neighbors."

"If only. But statistics don't lie. In a country of two and a half million, only nine hundred and fifteen Lithuanians have been recognized by Yad Vashem as having rescued Jews. That's zero point zero four percent of the population. There were less than a thousand Germans in Lithuania when almost the entire Jewish population was massacred. It's called the Holocaust by Bullets. Some say that the ease in which the Lithuanians murdered their Jewish neighbors in 1941 gave the Germans the idea for the Final Solution, which only became German policy at the Wannsee Conference in 1942. Before that, the Jews were rounded up and put in ghettoes. After Wannsee, the mass murders began. Lithuania can take moral responsibility for that as well."

"You are taking it too far! It's not fair . . . ," he protested angrily.

"Perhaps. But what happened to my family here doesn't incline me to fairness."

They sat in silence for a while, looking out the car windows at the view. There was very little to see from the highway. Forests, scrub, an occasional clump of houses, road signs.

Suddenly, he pulled over to the side of the road.

"What?"

"Let's take a walk, shall we?"

"What, now?"

He ran his fingers through his hair, which had been recently cut and neatly combed, allowing the curls to reclaim their natural territory.

She shrugged, wondering if he had any sinister plans for her. After all, it was pretty deserted . . . Then she began to feel silly, even cowardly. She took off her seat belt, put on her sweater, and stepped out of the vehicle.

"Masks?" she asked him.

"Please, let's not! It's just the two of us and we *are* outdoors . . ."

It made sense. He walked slowly through the grass, finding a winding path that led down to a river. It was beautiful weather. The slanting rays of the sun through the treetops touched his hair, making it glint with gold and silver.

"Look, we better have this out right now, right at the beginning. Do you hold me personally responsible for what happened to your family here during the war?"

The question took her breath away. It was not an easy thing to answer. Of course, one part of her—the rational part, the educated, liberal part—couldn't possibly blame a person who was not yet born for crimes committed by his ancestors. But another part of her—the emotional, irrational part—felt the descendants of such people were "bad seeds." That Jew hatred was in their genes, or if not their genes, in their upbringing and education. That it was simply dormant at the moment, waiting to burst forth at the first opportunity.

"What's your answer, Milia? Do you hate me?"

"Of course I don't hate you!" she said, looking over the tall, handsome, cultured European, the liberal organizer of well-meaning Holocaust education projects; the do-gooder, who at least recognized what had actually happened in his country and who was the first one she'd ever heard admit that some Lithuanian partisans had been Nazi collaborators and scum of the earth. "Listen, in all the time I have been working to get the government and people of Lithuania to admit what happened here, you are the first one I've come across who seems aware of the magnitude of the crimes committed here and wants to do something real in terms of reconciliation. That's the only reason I decided to come. I trust you. I like you," she told him, hoping it was true, but not completely sure.

He turned to her, staring at her face. So much passion in such a small person! She seemed almost childlike, and vulnerable, but her words were like daggers. He had no shield against them. "That means a great deal to me. I was born into this mess. And believe me, I have read all the books coming out now, the Zuroff-Vanagaitė book, the Silvia Foti book, even the book by Grant Gochin, who hates everything Lithuanian with a passion. I understand the facts. But there is nothing I can do about them. The past is beyond our ability to change. All I can do is try to make amends. I am *trying*, Milia. Do you believe me?"

She searched his kind face, made wretched now by the strength of his attempt to appease her, to get her to accept his sincerity.

She nodded noncommittally.

"So tell me, honestly, is it possible to make amends? Or is it a lost cause? Is the hatred between our peoples so deep, so ingrained, that all this"—he waved his hand—"is a waste of time?"

"I don't know," she finally whispered, shaking her head. "Maybe it is a waste of time."

"So do you want to turn the car around and call the whole thing off? I'll get you a flight out tonight."

She stared at him. Then she saw it, a sunbeam glinting off the moisture in his eyes as two tears fell down his cheeks. She felt a sudden sense of deep shame. From the beginning, he had come to her with an open heart, while hers had been resolutely locked against him, against this whole enterprise.

"No. I don't want that."

"So, what is it that you do want, Milia?"

She was a Jew, a descendant of Holocaust victims and survivors, people who had been marked for extermination and left to suffer the unspeakable amid a suddenly uncivilized world whose humanity, developed slowly over centuries through religion and education, had abruptly and inexplicably disappeared overnight. But she herself had not suffered. She had been born into freedom and prosperity, and most of all, her own country, her generation turning back the clock, making Jerusalem the capital of the Jewish people once more. Her position was one of strength, she told herself. She could now take her rightful place among other good, civilized people of the world, reaching across age-old barriers to heal old wounds, to create a new world, a better world. With people like Darius on the other side of the divide, it suddenly seemed possible.

"What I want," she said slowly, "is to change the world so that what happened then can never happen again."

"That's what I want, too," he said. "Exactly that."

"Are there enough of us to matter?"

"What?"

"Enough people like us on both sides of the divide, people who admit what happened in all its truth, people of goodwill, who care desperately enough, to create that new world?"

"I don't know," he admitted. "But if there aren't, we need to create them. That is what we are doing now, Milia, you and I, attempting to create that new world by transforming both our people, one by one by one."

"What transformation would you like us Jews to make?" she asked levelly.

"To remember that the perpetrators are dead. Not to live in the past. To recognize a friend when he comes to you with open arms," he said, opening his arms wide.

She backed away, wondering if it was in her, wondering if she could trust him. Then, slowly, and to her own astonishment, she saw her hand reach out to him. He met her halfway, grasping it in both his own.

TWENTY

THEY MADE A quick stop to check into the nondescript hotel where they would be spending the night, changing their clothes before setting out again to their first engagement. Twenty minutes later, they could already see the flags in the distance, waving energetically from the decorated high school courtyard, Lithuanian flags mingled with yellow, green, and red banners that gave the area a festive look.

As they neared the school, Milia rolled down her window. The building was a three-story modern complex, white and beige, with a large outdoor gathering place. It looked like high schools everywhere. As they pulled in and parked, she heard the happy chattering and buzz of excitement that came anytime and anywhere teenagers were let out of class for any reason.

Students were already being led to the rows of chairs that had been set up before the raised platform.

She looked at them. Young people, so similar to their counterparts in Tel Aviv, or London, or New York—the young girls lithe and heartbreakingly pretty, with long, straight hair held back by stylish headbands or barrettes; the boys in white shirts, sweaters, or jackets.

Obviously, great effort had been expended to create a respectful anticipation for this occasion, and students had been instructed to dress accordingly. They were young, healthy, happy.

Milia felt butterflies in her stomach. She clutched the bag that held her speech. And this program, this commemoration in honor of the victims of the Holocaust, was a worthy project, done with the best of intentions, she thought, glancing at Darius's glowing, expectant face. He had worked so hard for so long to bring it all together. The nagging thought she could not escape returned to her now: Why do this to them? To *him*? Why ruin this perfectly lovely summer day and taint all the efforts that had been invested, sending them away with this terrible, life-changing information instead of the feel-good vibe of reconciliation Darius wanted? After her speech, they would never think of their own town, or their own parents and grandparents, in the same youthful, innocent way. And it would be her doing. Something in her wanted to back away before it was too late.

Darius parked the car, then went around and opened the door for her. For a moment, she couldn't move.

"Everything all right?" he asked anxiously for the umpteenth time.

"I have some things I'm planning to say . . . but it isn't easy for me," she confessed.

Her honesty surprised and touched him, but also caused some anxiety. If she was having second thoughts, what *exactly* was in that speech of hers, anyway? he wondered. It must be pretty bad. But how bad? he worried, plowing his hand nervously through his hair. "Just keep in mind our goal. We are trying to help them become better people, more sensitive and educated. *Creating a new world*, remember? If what you have to say will do that, then it's all right, Milia. It's why I invited you."

* * *

She sighed. If only it were so clear-cut; if only she could be absolutely sure her efforts *would* make them better people, and not totally screwed-up, resentful adults, feeling forced to justify the crimes of their country and relatives by distorting, denying, and excusing them, the way their grandparents and parents had. There was no guarantee. But you had to try, didn't you? Otherwise, there was no hope at all. She got out of the car and shut the door behind her. Darius started emptying out the back seat.

"Can I help you carry your equipment?"

"No, absolutely not. I'll get some of these kids to help me." He wandered off, returning a few minutes later with a tall, blond boy with the build of a budding Arnold Schwarzenegger who wore khaki pants and a camouflage shirt inscribed with an insignia.

"What does his shirt say?" she asked Darius.

"It's the insignia of the Young Shooters of the Gymnasium Club," he told her.

She stood stock-still. "The what?! This school has a club called Young Shooters?!"

"Yes, many of the schools have these clubs. They are following in the footsteps of the freedom fighters who fought for Lithuania's independence . . ."

"Don't tell me. Following in the footsteps of the 'partisans' . . ."

His face turned a bright red. He shook his head slowly. "Oh, it's . . . not what . . . you think, Milia! It's like a rifle club, for sharpshooters. The kids are all doing this on computer games. It's very popular."

"And so the town and school think it's a great idea to channel this love of online shooting into actual rifles and bullets. How charming!"

He shook his head. "You don't understand."

She took a deep, furious breath. "Oh, believe me. I do." Of all the extracurricular activities and clubs to set up for young people in a place with a history like Raseiniai! She didn't know whether to laugh or weep. She could feel the recent rapprochement with Darius melting like wax under her boiling outrage.

"I know it sounds strange, but please, Milia! Don't jump to conclusions and say anything you might regret," he begged her.

"Oh, don't worry. I promise you I definitely won't say anything *I* might regret."

He somehow didn't like the sound of that. But there was no time to talk. The school principal was already coming over to them, shaking hands.

Darius set up the sound system, and then the principal invited both him and Milia to join him onstage behind the lectern.

After singing the national anthem on a stage adorned with the tricolors of Lithuania and the flags of the Raseiniai municipality and the EU, they were joined by Raseiniai's mayor and two of the city's distinguished-looking, white-haired elders. There was also a short man in a dark suit, who was introduced as the EU representative for the educational programs heavily funded at the school.

First the principal stood up and took the microphone. It gave a long, shrieking whine, eliciting snickers and laughter.

"*Nurimti, nurimti*," the principal said, his hands gesturing for calm.

"What did he just say?" Milia whispered to Darius.

"He just told them to 'settle down.'"

She sat back, listening to words she didn't understand, clapping when everyone else clapped, smiling when everyone else smiled, all the while her heart dropping inside her as heavy as a stone. The small, suave EU representative made a short speech in English with emphatic hand gestures, extolling the EU tolerance education programs being funded in Raseiniai and elsewhere and praising Darius and the other conference organizers. "We believe this is a big step forward for your country and its youth." Polite applause followed, none more enthusiastic than from the principal and the teachers.

Darius was next. He handed her the text of his speech translated into English so she could follow along.

He stood before the microphone. "Welcome, students. I am Dr.
Darius Vidas of the Department of Philosophy and Cultural Studies at Algirdas University and one of the organizers of this program. We are very grateful that your principal and your teachers
agreed to participate in our Holocaust commemoration project,
To Walk in Their Shoes. This assembly comes after many sessions
in which you and your teachers discussed the history of Lithuania
and the role of Jewish communities in that history. In those sessions, you learned about the customs, traditions, and important
members of that Jewish community. In this assembly, we would
like to speak about the lives of Jewish teenagers—high school students like yourselves—so that you may 'Walk in Their Shoes.'

"In 1932, YIVO, the Yiddish Scientific Institute for Jewish
Research, housed in Vilnius, decided to hold a contest. They invited Jewish young people living in the Yiddish-speaking world
between the ages of thirteen and twenty-one to send in essays
about their lives, and offered a one-hundred-fifty-zloty prize for
the best one—a lot of money in those days! They warned them
not to embellish the truth by inventing incidents, or by using
overblown language. They told them not to think that only those
with amazing stories could enter, or that small, everyday things
weren't important enough to write about. They also suggested
some topics: You and Your Family, the War Years, Teachers,
Schools, Boyfriends, Girlfriends. Because they didn't want the
writers to be embarrassed or afraid to write the truth, they invented a system where they could enter the contest anonymously
yet still get their prize money. From the beginning of the compe-
tition until the Nazis took over, more than seven hundred entries
were made. Each of them was read and judged by YIVO staff.
The date of the grand prize announcement was September first,
1939, the day the Nazis invaded Poland. So the prize ceremony

never took place. But all the contest entries were saved and stored in YIVO's library in Vilnius. On June twenty-fourth, 1941, the Nazis conquered Vilnius. They went straight to the YIVO offices to steal all their priceless material, which the Gestapo wanted for their museum: the Institute for the Experience of the Jewish Question, which they planned to build after the war when they believed the Jewish people would be extinct, and only their 'museum' would remain to explain who Jews were and why they had to be annihilated. To keep this precious material out of Nazi hands, some forty YIVO librarians calling themselves the Paper Brigade defied the Gestapo and risked their lives to hide as much material as they could around the Vilna Ghetto, including these essays.

"Only eight of these brave men and women survived the war. They returned to Vilnius after the Nazi defeat and gathered all the hidden materials together and created the Vilnius Jewish Museum. But five years later, in 1949, when the State of Israel sided with the West against Stalin, that despicable dictator ordered the entire contents of the Museum destroyed.

"Then another hero appeared, a Lithuanian librarian, Antanas Ulpis, who risked his life to rescue these contest entries and one hundred eighty thousand pages of other YIVO materials, hiding them from the KGB in the organ pipes and confessionals of St. George's Church. There they slept until 2017, only discovered during a final clean-out of the building.

"We will now call up your fellow students, who will read the newly discovered words of these young people, so hopeful for their future, a future no one could have imagined."

Milia was familiar with this story. She thought it very clever of Darius to have incorporated it into his program. But as student after student came up, reading the sometimes moving, sometimes funny stories of teenagers in the throes of unrequited love, failure to get into the colleges of their choice, dealing with dysfunctional families, and experiencing their parents' divorces, stories that could not help but endear them to these listeners, eliciting their sympathy, identification, and interest, she thought once again, as she had back in Israel when deciding what she would say, that her speech should take up where the feel-good essays left off.

And when the last one had finished, Darius got up once again, introducing her. She heard him say her name, the words *Israeli* and *the Survivors' Campaign*. He also made it clear that they had hired a translator who would be translating the speech into Lithuanian for them.

Milia got to her feet and approached the podium, adjusting the microphone, which from experience she knew would be much too high for her. She smiled and nodded at the translator, a young, pretty Lithuanian woman wearing lots of red lipstick and high-heeled shoes. They shook hands and agreed upon how often she should pause. Then she looked out into the sea of curious, hopeful, smart-alecky faces, and cleared her throat, taking off her mask.

"Hello. I'm sure we were all very moved by these wonderful stories. As you probably realize by now, the young Jews of Lithuania in 1939 were pretty much like you, filled with dreams, lusts, ambitions, problems. They had crushes on pretty girls but were too shy to approach them, they had to help mediate between warring parents, and they had dreams of being writers and movie stars."

She took a deep breath. "But the most important part of their story, you haven't yet been told. It has been kept a secret from you, by your parents, your government, your teachers." She paused, waiting for the translator to catch up. She saw the audience turn toward one another, nervous giggles going down the rows, the older boys knitting their brows, teachers wide-eyed. She glanced at Darius. Was that panic she detected in his eyes?

"I would like to tell you what happened here in your hometown, in Raseiniai, starting on Sunday, June twenty-second, 1941. We have this information because Dvoyre Lazarsky, whose maiden name was Yankelevitsch, lived in your town. She went to school here and completed six grades of gymnasium. She was a milliner and made beautiful hats. After the war, she told her story to Leyb Koniuchowsky, a Lithuanian Jew and himself a survivor, who went from camp to camp interviewing other survivors about their experiences. It is a story you have never heard before, because no one wants you to know. What I will read to you now is Dvoyre's first-person testimony to Leyb, in her own words, of what happened here." Again she looked at Darius. He gave her a curt nod of agreement even as a nervous buzz went through the audience like a wave among students and teachers. Milia ignored it, avoiding Darius's eyes.

On that morning, the people of our town looked out their windows and saw refugees running towards Raseiniai from towns closer to the border with Germany. They came on carts, on trucks, and by foot. They told us that war had broken out between Hitler's Germany and the Soviet Union. The Soviet authorities told us to leave the city because Hitler was going to bomb the town. Everyone ran away, and the town was heavily bombed the very next day. Me and my husband, Yakov, my parents and my brother, Leybl, had all run away to a nearby village. From there, we saw Raseiniai burning. My cousin Frida Praz, who didn't know the situation, arrived in Raseiniai from Taurage that Sunday morning and found the town burning. Many of the houses had been destroyed, mostly Jewish houses.

Almost immediately, even before the Germans entered the town, armed Lithuanians calling themselves "partisans" and waving Lithuanian flags came prepared to welcome the German army with joy, and to shoot at the backs of retreating Red Army soldiers.

Again, a mild rustle of nervousness swept through the audience at this unflattering description of the partisans.

*On Tuesday, the Germans entered Raseiniai. Soon Jewish
women began returning to their homes to check out how things were.
The men waited, but soon joined them. Because so many homes had
been destroyed, several families squeezed together in the few remaining houses, as well as in the barns, stalls, and yards on Vilnius and
Nemakshtsiai Streets.*

There was a slight hum of recognition as the streets were
named.

*My father-in-law was robbed by civilian Lithuanians. When
he protested, they said: "Before it used to be yours, and now all of
it is ours."*

Now the whispers grew louder, angrier. She saw one of the
teachers get up and walk out. She waited for Darius to approach the
podium, to regretfully tell her to stop. But to her surprise, he made
no move. She hurried to continue before he changed his mind.

*Soon people who had lived peacefully alongside their Jewish
neighbors for hundreds of years told them to hand over their possessions. Some of them did it "morally," pretending to be friendly.
They suggested that the Jews hide their more valuable goods with
them so that no one could steal them. In exchange they promised to
bring them food and hide them when the time came.*

*The mayor of Raseiniai at that time was Jodko. He had been
mayor for three years. Before the war, he had been a liberal man, and
the local Jews used to vote for him. His assistant was a Lithuanian
German from Raseiniai named Ernst Schmit. The police force in
town was recruited from those who had been policemen during President Smetona's rule, and from the "partisans" who had shot at the
retreating Russians. These "policemen" forced every Jew from age*

fifteen to work. The "partisans" bullied and abused them. They got
no wages, and no food for their work.

Now a general ruckus broke out, young men standing up and shouting belligerently, including the teenager from the Shooters Club who had helped Darius with his equipment. Darius stood up and went to her side. She steeled herself, waiting for him to express his fury at her for ruining all his plans, alienating the audience, and undoing all the good he had tried to do. She wondered what she would be able to say in her defense except that letting them hear the truth for the first time may not have been on his agenda, but it was in hers. She had betrayed him, but not her work.

Darius said nothing to her. Instead, he addressed the audience with a shout of "*Nurimti, nurimti.*" One or two of the most boisterous students were led away by teachers. As they left, they flung hostile epithets at Milia over their shoulders. Darius, his face wan but determined, simply nodded to her to continue, then calmly took his seat behind her.

She felt a sense of shock at his unconditional support, which she had not expected and which, she thought, she did not deserve given the underhanded way she had injected this material into the program, *his* program. Almost in spite of herself, she felt an unexpected and growing sense of gratitude toward him, which instead of making her want to stop, encouraged her to continue. Because of him, she now had a chance to make a real difference. It was a once-in-a-lifetime opportunity and he had provided it. She had an obligation not to squander it.

One day when the Jews were assembled in the marketplace be-
fore going out to work, the "partisans" selected the religious Jews,
with beards, and made them dance, fall, crawl on their bellies, run,

and fall again and again, while the townspeople watched. Some Christian women wept to see it, but many laughed.

The audience grew silent and tense.

New regulations were passed. Jews were not allowed to walk on the sidewalks; they could not go out at all except at specific times; they had to put on a white patch. The Jews bowed their heads and waited for it to pass, wishing each other courage.

Six weeks later, Jews heard from their non-Jewish neighbors that a camp was going to be created for them. Not far from Raseiniai, there was a storage building used by the priests that people called the "monastery." It had farm machinery and a barracks that the Russians had used for their soldiers. Jews were forced to clean it out and repair it. They never dreamed they were preparing a jail for themselves.

One morning, all the Jews were woken up and ordered to the yard of the town church. Each one was registered and then allowed to go home. This frightened us even more, because we didn't know what the next day would bring. People couldn't sleep after that.

Early the next morning announcements were made that every Jewish man between fifteen and forty-five, and every Jewish woman between sixteen and forty-five had to move into the camp. You were allowed to take two sheets and a pillow, three sets of underwear, and a coffee cup. You had one day to do this.

We went, with packs on our backs, on foot. We wept as we left our homes, our heads bowed. It was heartbreaking to say goodbye. We kissed and hugged our families. Even Lithuanians wept with us, and accompanied us to the ghetto, but they didn't forget to remind us to leave our valuables with them "until after the war."

The camp had only one entrance and exit, and was surrounded with barbed wire. The men and women were separated. Two people from Raseiniai were appointed commandants: Norbutas for women, and Grigelevitsius for the men. Both were from the "partisans."

I entered the camp with my cousin Frida. On Saturday and Sunday, everyone was given time off. Early on Saturday morning, July 26, 1941, all of the men and women were told to hand over their gold, silver, money, and watches. Those who didn't would be shot. Everyone gave almost everything they had. That Saturday, my brother, Leybl, didn't come home. On Sunday, he came home and told us his watch had been taken, too, the watch I had given him as a present. He was very depressed. On Monday at about three o'clock, I saw my brother on a truck with other men being driven back early from work, which usually ended at six, to the camp. I never saw him again. Later, we were reassured that some of the men had been taken to work outside of town. They gave us letters in Yiddish that they said the men had written asking for clothes and food.

Only slowly did we find out the truth.

That night, I personally saw truckloads of happy, singing "partisans" coming back from the forest. On Tuesday, Fradl Lazarsky, Frida's cousin, walked into the forest following the road the trucks had taken. On the way, she met a peasant woman who told her that she had seen everything. She described how a truckful of armed "partisans" singing Lithuanian songs had guarded the selected men as they were driven on foot down the Jurbarkas Road; how some of the prisoners had been made to undress beside graves already dug, how some were shot, but how most were beaten to death with military shovels.

And now a general outcry went up from the audience. She saw several teachers standing up, waving their hands in protest, and certain rows of students being led out of the assembly and into the building. Darius approached the principal. She saw a heated discussion until he brought over the EU representative, who spoke emphatically and angrily. The principal shrugged in defeat and approached the microphone.

"*Nurimti, nurimti,*" he said, this time half-heartedly, his hands once again gesturing for calm. Whatever else he said, he did in a raised voice. One by one Milia saw the students led back into their seats by their teachers who, sullen and furious, joined them. Milia waited for quiet, then continued.

All those hundreds of men were dead in a pit in the forest, the woman told Fradl. She said that seeing it, hearing the cries, made her sick. When Fradl came back and told us this, some refused to believe it. They said she had lost her mind. But others knew she was telling the truth and that there was nothing we could do to save ourselves. My dear brother was gone.

One of the teachers suddenly stood up, waving his hands in protest. He faced the audience, speaking loudly and underlining his words with emphatic gestures, then turned his back and walked out. She heard intermittent applause from some of the students, who snickered as they looked up at her.

Milia watched the teacher go, his tall frame erect, his back straight and proud. He was supposed to be an educator, bringing truth and enlightenment to these kids, she thought bitterly. Instead, he had chosen to betray his calling, becoming a symbol for everything that was wrong with this country. It took everything she had to retain a calm professionalism when inside she was shaking with rage. But as she looked over at Darius, he smiled encouragingly, gesturing her to continue. It was exactly what she needed to strengthen her resolve.

When almost everyone in the camp had been killed, the murderers began taking the rest: the elderly, the sick, the women with small children. Those too old or sick to walk were loaded into wagons and driven to Zhuvelishkiai and there they were shot. We watched the "partisans" roaming the streets and waited to be taken. No one was certain of his life anymore. People simply waited fearfully for death.

On the morning of August 26, 1941, all the Jews left in Raseiniai were ordered to leave and go to Biliūnai, eight kilometers away, no later than 1:00 p.m. the next day. I received a letter from my husband, who was hiding with his Lithuanian friend Vasilersky. He wrote: "If you decide to go to Biliūnai, I will join you there." I didn't know what to do. To let my mother go there alone? To leave my sick father in the hospital alone? Or to risk the life of my husband to accompany my mother to what I imagined was a ghetto where we could live together? I went to ask my father's advice. He was a very wise man and understood my dilemma. "If Biliūnai is a place you can live, you'll be able to return to visit me. But if it is a place where people will be killed, then why should you risk your life and your husband's? You won't be able to save me or your mother anyway. Go to your husband!" He made me promise I would obey him. I helped my mother pack her things, and with a broken heart, I accompanied her to Biliūnai but didn't enter. It was there my mother died. My father was taken from his hospital bed and shot.

From my hiding place, I got word to my husband to join me in hiding. But on the way, he was betrayed by peasants and caught by "partisans," who jailed him and his badly beaten sister and eventually shot them.

Again, a low rumble of protesting voices filled the square. She ignored it.

When I heard this, I wanted to die. I even tried to get poison from a doctor. Soon my hiding place became unsafe, and so I went elsewhere.

She saw the principal lean over and whisper angrily to Darius, who shook his head and leaned back. She hurried to finish, knowing her time was limited.

Before the camp was emptied, a young woman, Frida Miller, decided to run away.

Norbutas, the women's commandant, who she knew for years, offered to help save her. But what she understood was that he was offering to use her before shooting her.

The low buzz now became outraged cries. The principal stood up, his face a stern mask.

Quiet again ensued. Milia didn't dare to look in Darius's direction.

So instead of showing up to the planned meeting with Norbutas, she ran away with her cousin Shifre. Dressed like Lithuanian peasant girls and holding flowers, they climbed into the cart of a kind Lithuanian peasant woman named Michalina Janushkevitiene, who picked them up in a wagon and took them to her home in the village of Pashaltonis. The Janushkevitiene family were Polish. They were among the Righteous gentiles of that time. They sacrificed themselves for those two girls who had run away.

Other women also tried to escape that day, three days after the 350 men had been shot. The "partisans" were still celebrating and drunk. They caught the escaped women hiding in the grainfields and bushes and threw them back into camp. That night, the "partisans" raped them, and the next day they were shot.

Now there was a riot. Teachers stood and waved their fists at Milia, at their principal, at Darius and the EU representative. The principal stood up, turning to Darius and the EU representative, shrugging helplessly. "There is nothing I can do. I'm sorry."

"Tell them whoever wishes to go may go. But for those who wish to stay and hear the rest of the story, I and the translator will continue."

At this, the translator gave her a cold, hard stare, turned her back, and walked off the stage.

So that was it, Milia thought. *The end of my speech. And I ruined Darius's program for nothing.* For the most important things she needed to say were still to come.

Darius stared at the audience. In a moment, they could easily turn into a lynch mob, he thought. Many had removed their masks, and their faces—teachers and students—were ugly with menace and fury. He glanced at Milia. She was so small, such a graceful, petite woman, almost childlike in the space she inhabited. And yet as she stood there defiantly facing the crowd, not a flicker of fear was visible in her face or her stance. She made no move to leave, or hide, or back down. He felt a sudden, almost overwhelming sense of admiration for her. He had never met anyone like her, certainly not a woman.

She was the embodiment of everything he as a Lithuanian had been taught to respect and admire in the heroes that his country had chosen, holding them up to him and his generation as the ideal to be emulated; heroic figures who had unwaveringly faced down ruthless suppressors of truth and freedom, fearlessly ready to make any sacrifice to protect and advance all they held dear. Some of those heroes, he had discovered of late, had been frauds, unworthy of admiration. But she, Milia, was the real thing.

Something surprising and rare filled his cynical heart as he looked at her standing there facing down the ugliness. Darius got up and walked toward the podium.

Now he will take his revenge, she thought, watching him advance. *He will deny all I've said. Throw me off the stage. Save his precious conference and his reputation.* And who could blame him? His excellent, carefully thought-out program had turned into a debacle, and it was all her fault. Because she had wanted more than easy, maudlin sympathy. She had wanted to be the voice of the dead whose mouths had been filled with Lithuanian soil in the nearby forests; to shout out their truth, their story, to these young people, forcing them to confront the terrible facts about the part their own town, their own families, and their own country had played in cutting short these innocent dreams. She wanted to confront them to accept that knowledge, that reality, and to deal with it.

She had done her best, and yet she felt sorry it had to end this way. There was an important story she needed to tell them that might change the atmosphere, something she would now never get to say. She began to fold up her speech. To her surprise, she felt Darius cover her hand with his own.

"Don't. Continue."

"But my translator . . ."

"I will translate for you," he said.

Milia looked into his eyes. They were sad, alarmed, angry, but most of all, resolved. And there was something else there, too, that touched her deeply, burning with an intensity she could hardly bear to look at. Admiration.

"Are you sure?" she asked him.

He nodded sharply. "Go on."

"Thank you," she whispered, almost overwhelmed with gratitude. "But tell the audience whoever wants to leave should leave, but for those who stay I will continue." He nodded, conveying this to the principal, who made the announcement.

Milia watched as half the students and many of the teachers turned their backs and left, returning to their classrooms. But to her surprise, about half remained.

"Darius, please thank them for staying."

He did so.

She cleared her throat.

On Thursday, August 28, a group of "partisans" came to where the Jews were gathered. They were singing. They were armed. They took the women and children and the few men still alive to pits that had already been prepared days before the order to come to Biliūnai had been issued. The pits were nearby, although no one knew exactly where. There, they shot every Jew. The next day, sick Jews were brought from the municipal hospital directly to the pits, where all of them were slaughtered.

Milia waited for the translation, her eyes scanning the audience. Some of them were openly weeping. She swallowed hard, steeling herself.

The murderers divided up the clothing of the murdered Jews. The less expensive items they distributed for free or sold at auction. The expensive items, the "partisans" kept for themselves. On those two days, August 27 and 28, 1941, the Jewish community of Raseiniai was erased from the earth.

She paused for a moment, reaching for the glass of water that had been poured for her before she began speaking. She could see in the upturned faces every emotion she had felt herself in reading this story, and the many others recorded by Koniuchowsky in the almost six hundred pages of his remarkable and devastating book, *The Lithuanian Slaughter of Its Jews.*

Shifre joined me in Kaunas. Cousin Frida continued living on the farm with the Polish family. She obtained Aryan documents. She did everything to help: milking cows, feeding cattle, doing housework, and kitchen work. The other workers did not suspect she was Jewish, and from them she learned that the vast majority of Lithuanians were happy that the Jews had been annihilated. The most intelligent and educated among them thought that it was not necessary to slaughter the Jews, but as long as the process had begun, no witnesses should remain alive or else the Lithuanians would pay dearly. She did not see any sympathy on the part of anyone for the Jews whose lives had been taken. But everyone feared they would be held responsible if the Germans lost the war.

More than once, Frida found herself in danger when bands of "partisans," whose motto at the time was "Look for hidden Jews, Red "partisans," and moonshiners," showed up at the farm as she was out working in the fields. Michalina would laugh at them and say sarcastically: "You are looking for Jews, here?! You won't find any." And the "partisans" would reply: "We've shot them all. There aren't any left." At such times, Frida kept her head down so no one would see the terror in her face. Often, her coworkers would tell her about Jews who had been found hiding and shot. She was afraid her heart would burst. Once, Frida was invited to a birthday party where a "partisan," Jonaitis, was also a guest. All around her, people started acting out how Jews walk, how Jews talk. Frida also had to laugh, trying to hide the tears in her eyes. Jonaitis then described how he and two other "partisans" had picked up a Jewish couple with a small child. The child had fine shoes on its feet, Jonaitis said, describing how he took off the shoes from the little boy's feet. The ground was frozen. And the child first stood on one foot and then on the other. "Mama, I'm cold," the child said. The mother hid her eyes and told her child: "It's nothing. Soon we will be warm."

"They spoke perfect Lithuanian. Just like us," Jonaitis said. "We shot all three. I never had any pity on the Jews, but I can't forget that child's words."

Milia paused, hearing a sound coming from the audience in waves. It was the sound of weeping. She saw rows of young people and their teachers sobbing openly, wiping their eyes and embracing one another. It was the child, the shoes, she thought. The heartless cruelty of inflicting pain for no reason. It was somehow worse than the subsequent murder of that same child.

Frida was forced to listen and say nothing. She did her best to avoid the company of Lithuanians in order to remain alive and someday tell the world about what had been done to the Jews of Raseiniai. This hope gave her strength and courage to fight for her young life.

She paused.

Frida convinced her saintly savior to take in and hide her cousins Dvoyre and Shifre who were hiding in Kaunas. In the spring of 1944, the Red Army quickly grew closer to Raseiniai, but did not advance to free them until August, when they were finally liberated.

Milia folded her speech. "Everything I have just read you was related in person by Frida Praz and Dvoyre Lazarsky to Leyb Koniuchowsky. It is signed and dated July thirtieth, 1947, and cosigned by the head of the Jewish committee in the Zeilsheim Refugee Camp, S. Meldung, where they were after the war. It was translated from the Yiddish by Dr. Jonathan Boyarin, August third, 1988, and signed by him. While I have shortened it, and rephrased some of the words, I have not altered the testimony, which remains absolutely true. I invite any who doubt this to read pages seventy to eighty-two of *The Lithuanian Slaughter of Its Jews* for themselves. This is the truth. It should not be forgotten. I have tried to be their voice. I thank you for staying to listen. I thank you for your tears."

She waited for Darius to translate, but he said nothing. She turned to him, surprised. Then she noticed his face. He was devastated, tears pouring down his cheeks, his throat choked. With great effort, he translated her final words. She reached out, squeezing his hand gratefully.

Just as she turned to take her seat for the orderly conclusion of the program, she heard a cacophony of car horns fill the air. She looked out toward the road to where a long convoy of vehicles and motorcycles were quickly making their way to the school complex.

The principal got up and whispered something to Darius.

"We have to leave. Now!" he told her, gripping her hand firmly and rushing her down the steps to the car.

"But . . . the sound equipment!" she sputtered. "And we didn't say goodbye!"

"Please, Milia. Get into the car!"

Shocked by the urgency of his tone, she slid in beside him. He backed away, swiftly heading for the exit, passing the cars streaming toward the school in the opposite direction. They had almost reached the end of the convoy when someone must have recognized them. People rolled down their windows, shouting and waving their fists. Then one of the motorcycles pulled out of line, turning around to follow them. The driver had a shaved head and tattoos. His face was contorted with hate as he aimed the vehicle in their direction. They braced themselves for the impact, but at the last moment, it veered away. Soon they heard the sirens of the police cars, realizing why they had been spared.

Darius stepped on the gas, pulling onto the highway, speeding away from Raseiniai as fast as he could go.

TWENTY-ONE

THEY DROVE ON in silence, the only sound that of their tires and other cars whizzing down the paved road.

"Darius, where are we going?"

He sighed, looking straight ahead. "Are you all right?"

"You keep asking me that."

"But . . . now you see why."

"I'm shaken, I admit it. But glad as well."

He looked at her, astonished. "Glad?"

She nodded. "It was one of the most rewarding experiences I've ever had in all my years."

"I'm . . . I don't know what to say! Half your audience got up and left! The town was . . . is . . . in an uproar! One of the kids must have called his parents . . ."

"Oh, so that's the source of the caravan of cars."

"No doubt. And that skinhead on the motorcycle . . . Let me tell you, *I* was terrified."

"Were you? But they're your people. Surely, they wouldn't have harmed you."

"What makes you so sure?"

She paused, wondering, then growing doubtful. "But nothing

happened to us. And didn't you see the faces of those kids that stayed behind? How they listened! How they wept! It was life-changing for them. It really gives me hope. So, where is our next stop?"

He stared at her. "You can't be serious? You are willing to go on? Even after that experience?"

"It was the first time I really felt I got through to Lithuania's young people; that I bypassed all the politicians and officials and designated Holocaust obfuscators and apologists. I was able to speak to their hearts, to tell them the truth."

"They were ready to lynch you and me both, Milia."

She looked at him, smiling. "Only half, but you didn't let that happen, did you, Darius? You kept your word, you stepped up and translated for me. Why?"

"Because I'm just as insane as you are."

"Oh, I'd say a little bit more, because you realized what was going to happen when I started speaking about the 'partisans' in Raseiniai, and I didn't, not really."

"So, you would *really* do this again, put yourself in danger, again?"

"Why not? This is what I do. It's the only way to change the world, one young person at a time, one teacher at a time, one principal at a time."

He shook his head, his eyes softening. "You are either a naive fool, or the most wonderful person I ever met."

"That pretty much sums up how I feel about you, too, Professor Vidas."

"Darius. I don't have tenure, and at this rate probably never will. About me there is no question. I'm definitely a naive fool. As soon as word gets back to the university, all hell is going to break loose."

"Why should it get back to them? It was just a little gathering at some high school in the boondocks. You didn't invite the press, did you?"

He gave it some thought. "No, I don't think so. They are invited for the finale in Vilnius where you are giving the keynote address at the end of the week."

"So how will anyone find out?"

He began to feel a little more hopeful. This was true. Maybe it was just a storm in a teacup.

He hesitated. "Listen, Milia, do you have something similar planned for our next stop in Tauragė?"

She nodded. "But if you think it's too much, I'll change it. Edit out some of the worst parts." Maybe it hadn't been appropriate to speak to high schoolers about sexual assaults.

But before he could answer, his phone rang. He watched it for a few moments, not answering, letting the sound fill the car with ominous foreboding. Then he pulled over to the side of the road.

"What's happened? Why are we stopping?"

"I have to take this. Hello?"

She watched his handsome face, so mobile and expressive, as he listened, his eyes narrowing, his lips stretching into a firm, tight line, his jaw flinching. While she couldn't understand what he was saying, his tone was unmistakably firm and convincing, summoning up all his charm and powers of persuasion, until he suddenly went silent. She heard him grunt, then close down the phone.

"What?"

"That was the principal of our next school, in Tauragė. He was cancelling."

"Can he do that? What about the EU—your partner? Isn't the Tauragė school also getting EU funding?"

"Apparently he has discussed it with the EU representative, and considering what happened in Raseiniai, they both agreed it might pose a physical danger to the student body to continue."

"I can't believe that! Half the students and teachers *chose* to stay behind; they listened *willingly*. This was an amazing breakthrough in Lithuanian Holocaust distortion. Don't they realize that? No one got hurt!"

"You're wrong about that. This was extremely damaging to the Lithuanian government, particularly to the people determined to push the double genocide theory and portray Lithuanians as victims and partisans as heroes. You will put them out of business if you go from town to town reading these testimonies to young people. They will have to take down all their plaques and statues honoring their Nazi collaborators and murderers . . . ," he said with feeling.

"You really are on my side, aren't you, Darius?" She spoke softly, taken aback.

He raised his eyebrows. "Did you ever doubt that?"

Of course she had, she thought, with a growing sense of shame. She had assumed all kinds of things about him because of his ethnicity and nationality, just as the people she had been fighting against all her life assumed things about her because she was a Jew and an Israeli.

"Is there anything we can do to change his mind?"

He shrugged. "It's his job that's on the line, don't you see?"

"They would *fire* him?"

He nodded. "In a minute. You don't know how powerful these people are."

"Wait a moment. Then you are saying the principal of the Raseiniai school is in danger of being fired as well?"

"Absolutely. And so am I."

She turned to him sharply. "What are you talking about?"

"You really don't know, do you? They can cancel the conference. I'm sure the principal in Raseiniai is scrambling to distance himself from everything that went on even as we speak. He's probably busy calling every other principal on our schedule to warn them about what might happen and advising them to cancel."

"Surely, they wouldn't do that! At least, not every single one of them."

"Oh, most surely, they would. Why not? It's the safe way out. And don't think that will be the end of it, either," he said ominously.

"What do you mean?"

"There will be personal consequences. For me."

"Such as?"

He shook his head. "I don't even want to think about it."

A sudden shiver of regret went up her spine. She had hurt this man. She could not even estimate how deep and wide the damage would go to his life and his work. A sharp, painful prick of guilt and remorse stabbed her suddenly. She thought of apologizing, but she couldn't do that, either, not in good conscience. She straightened her back. Because she wasn't sorry. No. She had only done her job. It was this country, she thought with sudden clarity, *his country*, and the people in it, who were at fault; people who refused to accept the truth and were ready to do violence to anyone who disabused them of their distortions and lies.

And yet . . .

She studied Darius, who was hunkered down over his phone, reading his email messages, looking worried. This was a real person, a kind person, with a good heart and good motives. And she had upended his life for the most selfish of reasons. It didn't matter that it was for a good cause. It was, in a way, despicable to have harmed him when he had only ever been kind, helpful, and respectful to her.

"Maybe I should call them personally. I'll accept complete responsibility. I could offer to drop out. We—"

His phone rang again. He picked it up. "Paulius?" he asked. But it wasn't his friend. He stared open-mouthed at the screen and the video someone had just sent him.

"What is it? What's happening?" she asked nervously.

"Please, just give me a moment, Milia," he begged, never taking his eyes off the video.

She looked surreptitiously over his shoulder at his screen. It was a video of what had just happened: her speaking, him translating, and the students and teachers shouting and waving their fists.

"How many hits has it gotten?" she asked.

"It's already up to five hundred," he told her dully. The parents had seen it, the other principals had seen it. By tomorrow, he guessed, it would go viral. And what would happen after that, he thought, was not a guess. It was inevitable. Everyone in Lithuania would see it: the head of his department, the government officials from the Genocide Center who were already out for his blood, and, last but not least, his publishing house.

"Darius, I'm so sorry if this will cause you any trouble. But I couldn't be more pleased! This means that everyone will hear this testimony. Perhaps, in other places in Lithuania, they will finally be open to hearing the truth about what went on in their own communities. This could be the beginning of true change, true reconciliation. And I owe it all to you."

He nodded absently, thinking about the home he loved, his well-paying cushy job at the university, his book contract, and the friendly relations with the media that until now had been sympathetic and nurturing to his career. In a few hours it would all be over as he became Lithuanian public enemy number three.

He thought of Rūta Vanagaitė, one of Lithuania's most popular authors, who had had the country at her feet until she cowrote that book with Dr. Efraim Zuroff. How quickly all her important friends and political contacts had turned on her! He'd even heard she had been forced to leave the country.

Was that his future as well? If worse came to worse, he would have no way to support himself. He would have to sell his apartment—his fantastic apartment that he had worked so long and so hard to buy and furnish—find some low-level teaching job, try and fail to get another publisher. His life as he knew it would be over.

Now it was her turn to ask him if he was all right.

"I don't know. Maybe not," he said.

Impulsively she reached out for him, squeezing his shoulder. He turned to look at her, covering her hand with his own. And then, before either of them had a chance to catch their breath, he took her in his arms and kissed her.

TWENTY-TWO

THEY WERE SHY and awkward with each other as they returned silently to their hotel, hurriedly packing, hoping not to run into any more skinheads with murderous intentions, or outraged parents. The hotel clerk seemed as cordial as when they'd checked in, which gave Darius hope that perhaps he was simply being paranoid. But just as they'd climbed into the car and locked the doors, someone came running up to them and smashed eggs on their windshield. It was the brawny high school student who'd helped him with the sound equipment, he realized, the one from the Young Shooters Club.

Milia gave a short gasp, then hissed through clenched teeth, "Just drive!"

He stepped on the gas.

"I'm going to call the police," she said, taking out her phone.

"Don't bother. They won't come."

"Then I'll call the Israeli ambassador."

He sighed. More headlines. Just what he needed. "Listen, let's just see if anyone follows us first. But he's just a kid. I think he's done. Let's just get out of here."

No one followed them, she saw, looking out the back window the whole time. She finally turned around. "I think we are okay."

He took her hand and squeezed it gently. "We are fine. Don't be frightened. I'll protect you."

"Thank you, Darius," she said softly, wondering what was going to happen now. They were in free fall, parachuting into uncharted personal territory. "What's the plan?"

"Well, for starters, let's find a gas station and clean the windshield before it dries."

She grinned, nodding. "Of course." The fate of their lives, of this project, would just have to wait.

Darius pulled into a gas station, then parked, walking inside to talk to the attendant. They came out together, the man pointing to a water hose. Milia could see him looking over at the car, shaking his head and grinning, saying something to Darius, who answered him. The man grimaced, shaking his head once more before heading back inside.

Darius moved the car closer to the hose.

"He seemed to think it was funny. What did he say to you?"

"'Little vandals,' he called whoever did it. He asked me what I did to make someone so angry."

"What did you tell him?"

He exhaled. "I said I got his sister pregnant and wouldn't marry her. That shut him up."

She rolled her eyes. "You're a man who courts disaster."

"Yes." He nodded. "We are a perfect match."

"Oh, um, about that. We really . . . need to talk . . . discuss . . . it's . . . ," she mumbled, having no idea what she was trying to say.

Did she want to discuss her incendiary presentation that had them fleeing? Or that kiss? Which was more shocking? He had a feeling that they might not agree. "We will. We will talk . . . about that . . . about everything. I promise," he reassured her, wiping down the windshield. *Yes*, he told himself, scrubbing. *Let's deal with one disaster at a time, shall we, Darius?*

Once they were on the road again, she waited before posing the question again, not wanting to be a nag. "Sorry, I don't mean to pester you, but in which direction are we headed now, Darius?" she asked brightly, like a good sport on a difficult hike.

"Honestly, I don't know. I need to make a few phone calls, get a few answers first. Why don't we head for a restaurant and talk over dinner?"

Dinner. In some out-of-the-way Lithuanian restaurant serving local cuisine, heavy on the pork, she thought, shivering. "Well, it will have to be vegetarian. I only eat kosher food."

He laughed. "Not much chance of that outside Vilnius. I'm sorry. I didn't mean to laugh, it's just that you really don't know where you are, do you?"

"Apparently not," she admitted, feeling foolish. "Well, what about a fish restaurant, then? If it's a kosher fish and they prepare it a certain way, I can eat it."

"Then we should head toward the sea." His eyes suddenly lit up. "I know an amazing place, a charming little fishing village, right near our most beautiful national park in the Curonian Spit. It's called Nida."

"How long will it take to get there?"

"It's a bit of a drive."

"How long?"

"Two and a half hours. But it's a beautiful day, and the weather is supposed to hold up the rest of the week. And since we have nothing else scheduled . . ."

"Listen, Darius. I . . . if the event is over, maybe I should just change my ticket and fly home early," she ventured reluctantly. For reasons she felt uncomfortable exploring, she didn't really want to go yet.

He sighed. "Yes, you could do that. But what I'm hoping is

that even if all the high schools cancel—which isn't definite—we could still salvage the main event in Vilnius at the end of the week where you are the keynote speaker."

"Is that still on?" She was surprised. "I just assumed . . ."

"Well, the high schools can say: 'It's too much for the children.' But they can't say that about the closing event, which is for adults. All the media have already accepted invitations to be there. It will be embarrassing for everyone if we cancel. It would be a real opportunity to have a global impact despite what's happened in the small regional areas."

"And you are telling me that it's still on?"

He shrugged. "So far I haven't heard anything to the contrary. But that's one of the phone calls I want to make."

"And if we go to Nida—" She smiled to herself.

"What's funny?"

"That word. 'Needa.'"

"It's pronounced *ni-da*."

"Okay. That helps, because in Hebrew a 'needa' is a menstruating woman."

"Oh." He grinned. "Nida means 'fluent' in Old Prussian. It was first mentioned in 1385 in documents by the Teutonic Knights who ruled over it. It's located near the highest dune in the National Park of the Curonian Spit. The town was moved a few times to its present location to keep it from being buried by sand drifts, which happened to other towns along the coast when too many trees were cut down. Artists and writers flocked there— expressionists who were fond of drawing the dunes and the animal life—they even founded a colony there. In 1929 Thomas Mann paid a visit. He loved the area so much he built a summer house there on a hill overlooking the lagoon, dark wood with lovely blue shutters. The locals made fun of it, calling it Uncle Tom's Cabin. Don't ask me why! He wrote part of his novel *Joseph and His Brothers* there. Of course, when the Nazis took over, he fled. Hermann

Göring confiscated it and turned it into a recreation home for Luftwaffe officers."

"Of course. What else?" She grimaced.

"Now it's a museum. The scenery is spectacular. And I think we could both use some time off to get our energy back. At least, I know I could." He glanced at her hopefully, his eyes questioning.

"I could definitely use a rest," she admitted, even as nagging doubts plagued her. What was she doing?! Going off on vacation to a hotel with a handsome man, a Lithuanian? A gentile! And she was, after all, still a married woman. If anyone ever found out—her kids! Julius! The supporters of the Survivors' Campaign! How could she possibly explain herself?

On the other hand, if she insisted on going home immediately, she might miss out on an important opportunity to deliver her keynote address in front of the international press at the end of the week, which in the scheme of things was much more important than the little speech she had given to teenagers in Raseiniai, she told herself. But was that really the reason she wanted to stay? She searched her heart for the answer.

It wasn't absolutely clear to her. She had no doubt that what had happened in Raseiniai at the gymnasium was an important breakthrough. And she had no doubt that without this man's help and support, it could not have been accomplished. But that kiss? Where had that come from? Was it gratitude? Was it a way of making amends for getting him into hot water, which he surely was? Was it a way of sticking it to Julius, having her revenge? Or was there something more there that she couldn't even bear to admit to herself?

For her as a Jewish Israeli woman, a descendant of survivors, brought up in a traditional home where Biblical laws were honored, holidays celebrated, and the primacy of the clan never questioned, the rule was simple: you didn't date gentile men. You certainly didn't fall in love with them. And as a child of survivors, how could you possibly have any feeling other than antipathy and loathing for a child of perpetrators—never mind all his talk about his family being Righteous gentiles. Everyone in Lithuania claimed that, but only a few hundred had ever been recognized by Yad Vashem.

He was the embodiment of the sexual taboo: an (most probably, although certainly not verified) uncircumcised Catholic Lithuanian whose extended family had perhaps collaborated with the Nazis and murdered Jews. And yet that kiss . . . There was no use pretending it was he who had kissed her. Facts were facts, and she was a person used to looking unpleasant facts in the face and dealing with them. She knew quite well that the kiss had been absolutely mutual and it would never have happened if she hadn't physically reached out to him first. Worse, she wasn't sorry. She was thrilled. It made her feel—after all the blows and humiliations she had suffered over the last few months—like a desirable woman again, instead of some aging castoff soon to be relegated to that asexual refuse pile where no one looked at you as a man or a woman, but simply as an old person whose sex was irrelevant.

Still, why him? She didn't understand it. It went against everything she believed in, her entire upbringing. It made absolutely no sense at all that she was falling in love with Dr. Darius Vidas.

She studied him: the unruly blond curls, the fair skin, the light blue linen shirt stretched over his strong, tanned arms and broad shoulders, the electric blue eyes. Was it simply lust? Because that would be shameful, she thought, embarrassed. But then something else woke up inside her and shouted: *Why is Julius allowed to feel lust? Haviva allowed to steal my husband because of her lust? While I have to pretend I'm above all that? Well, news flash, darling. You're not. You also want to live! You also want to feel, to experience! To be a woman! It's not too late for you, because it wasn't too late for them. If* it was simply lust, then why not just go for it? Wouldn't that be wonderful, at her age!

But then something else occurred to her. Maybe that was all it was on his part, too. How would she feel if this were simply some cheap little fling for him? Or worse, the unthinkable: simply a way of getting back at her, at Jews, for making things difficult for him and his beloved country? Because one thing she knew for sure. Darius Vidas loved his country. He was a patriot. He had only helped her because he honestly believed it was better for his country to recognize what they had done to the Jews, to understand that it had made the country he loved a poorer, weaker place. Murdering them was like cutting off your own right leg, leaving you to limp through life without hope of recovery.

This is what you *believe*, she told herself. *But does he?*

"Look, we really need to talk, Darius. Let's stop somewhere, anywhere, soon. I'll get a salad, and you can make your phone calls. Let's talk about where we are, Darius, and where we are going."

* * *

About a half hour later they pulled into a charming roadside inn with adorable wooden trellises and baskets of hanging dwarf petunias and peonies.

"Are you sure?" he asked her doubtfully, unimpressed by the décor. "I'm not familiar with the food here."

"Well, it doesn't make any difference to me. I can only eat a raw salad, without dressing, in any case. But if you think *you* wouldn't enjoy the food, I can wait until we get to Klaipėda."

"No, not at all. I'm sure it will be fine."

He ordered drinks, a kind of sweetish malt beer sans alcohol and sparkling water. Then he spoke at length with the waitress. "Are you sure you don't want any dressing on your salad?"

"Just some olive oil and lemon juice, please."

He conveyed this to the waitress, then ordered a few entrees for himself with names she would never remember.

When the food arrived, she picked at her salad without appetite, all the while ogling the dishes in front of him. "And what is that?" she asked, pointing hungrily and enviously to all kinds of lovely stuffed vegetables and pies. "What kind of filling do they have? Not pork, is it?"

"If I say yes, are you going to get up and go screaming out of here?" He grinned devilishly. "Actually, it's spinach, cheese curd, and rice. And this," he said, lifting a little bowl attractively garnished with parsley, "is fried bread."

"It looks wonderful," she said sincerely, reluctantly spearing a tomato and something green and chewing on it without appetite.

He shook his head, pointing at her salad. "It can't be easy, especially when you are on the road."

"What can't be easy?"

"Sticking faithfully to all those rigid Jewish dietary laws."

She shrugged. "People used to sacrifice their firstborn in order to worship their deities. All that's being asked of me is to eat salad instead of meat. Not a tragedy. Probably healthier in the long run."

"I suppose," he said, unconvinced. "But half the fun of traveling is tasting the local cuisine. You never get to do that, do you? Can't you get, like, some kind of dispensation?"

She laughed. "In order for a rabbi to issue a *heter* it would have to be a matter of life or death. Our rule is that you can break the rules in order to live another day to keep all God's commandments."

"So, I suppose what we are doing, our relationship, won't get a *heter*, either, will it?" he whispered, reaching out to her.

She reached back, holding his hand and shaking her head as she looked into his eyes. "What's happening?"

He shrugged, his thumb caressing her knuckles. "Damned if I know!"

They sat there, not saying anything, because there was nothing to say. They both knew it was forbidden—to her because of her religious beliefs and tribal affiliation, and to him because of his ethnic identity and patriotic loyalties. Both of them realized that it was something they couldn't talk through. In fact, the more they voiced their feelings and fears over their situation, the more aware they would both become of all that stood between them. It was better, he thought, to say nothing at all.

"To change the subject," she said, reading his mind as she gently took back her hand, "don't you think it's time for you to make those phone calls and find out how much trouble you and your conference are in?"

The gentle, dreamy smile on his face suddenly tightened into a frown. "I suppose so," he agreed, sighing as he reluctantly took out his phone and dialed.

She heard him use every tone of voice imaginable: he pleaded, threatened, cajoled, and finally thanked whoever he was speaking to, so by the end of the conversation he almost seemed cheerful. He didn't pause to give her an update, but went directly on to his next call. Here, too, his voice began politely and gradually changed. But this conversation had less nuance, she realized. He was polite, and resigned, throughout.

"One more," he mouthed to her apologetically as he dialed again. She made out the first word: Paulius. He was speaking to his friend. Of all the calls he had made, this one went on the longest, and was by far the most fraught, she thought. At one point he even stood up, speaking in a raised tone that was just short of shouting. But by the time it was over, he was sitting again, buttering a roll, laughing. Finally, he hung up.

"Shall we order dessert? Cake for me, fruit for you?"

"First tell me what just happened."

"I spoke to my partner in the EU. Well, you'll be surprised to learn he thought your speech was perfect. His exact words were: 'It's about time.'"

A burden seemed to slough off her shoulders. "Wow. I didn't expect that!"

"Honestly, neither did I. But of course there is nothing either he or I can do to force the other principals to hold assemblies. And they are well within their rights. So we compromised. We are going to insist they go on with the program, with the students reading the YIVO contest entries, and the EU representative attending and making a speech where he'll suggest that the students look into what happened to those teenagers during the war. We'll make it into a kind of a project, sort of our own variation on the YIVO formula, with the EU giving out prizes for the best follow-up."

"That's an amazingly good idea! Tell the EU representative that he can give out my name and the email of the Survivors' Campaign to the students and that we will be happy to help them with their research."

"That's very generous of you! But you risk being inundated."

"I wouldn't mind at all. We get these kinds of questions from young people all the time. I consider answering them one of the most important aspects of our work, the educational side."

He hesitated. "Would you do that for me?"

She looked at him without understanding.

"Would you really help me research my grandfather and the Kensky family, who supposedly survived the war thanks to my grandfather's help?"

She noted his language, surprised. "*Supposedly?* But I thought you'd already researched that, no?"

"I tried. I went down there to J—, the town where he was mayor, and to the town hall, where he supposedly hid the family. But . . . I . . . couldn't find any hiding place in the building. The whole story seems implausible. But I don't want to jump to conclusions. Perhaps I got it wrong, or my parents did."

"Darius, don't ask me to help you unless you are prepared to deal with whatever I find. Maybe it would be better not to know."

He took her hand urgently in his. "No, Milia. I want to know the truth. I have to."

She exhaled. "All right. Give me whatever information you have and I'll forward it to some of my contacts in Yad Vashem. Now, tell me about your phone calls."

"According to my friend Paulius, the university is livid about the video. He thinks for sure they are planning on giving me trouble."

"What for? What possible excuse can they come up with?"

"They can say that you are not a historian and that what you read to the high school students was simply a Jewish folktale, hearsay, with no historical basis, and that I, as a historian, had a responsibility to tell the students this before or after your speech."

"None of that is true! This wasn't a folktale, but eyewitness testimony, which was notarized and confirmed."

"You don't have to convince me. But facts mean nothing to these people, except as an opportunity to twist them. They have the power to silence me and denounce me, and that's exactly what they'll do."

"I'm so sorry. But maybe you can fight it. Surely there are also good people in your department, in the government."

"I guess we'll soon find out." He shrugged, grim. "And . . ." He hesitated. "My publishing house is trying to get in touch with me."

"Oh, no. Not your books, too!"

"I think I can fight that more easily. I have a contract. I'll sue if they dare take a single one of my books off the shelves of the bookstores."

"And the bookstores themselves?"

"That's a little trickier. I can't force them to keep selling my books. I have no legal connection with them."

"What were you yelling about to your friend Paulius?"

"Yelling? Oh, you mean when I got up. He told me that the newspaper where my son Jurgis works is giving him a hard time."

She was shocked. "That's horrible."

"That's what we—and everyone else in the country trying to fight for change, for truth—are dealing with. I'm prepared for it."

Her heart sank. It was one thing to put yourself on the line, but quite another when your enemies went after your children. She had no idea what she would do in such a situation.

"So, what do you think we should do?"

"Milia, we can't give in! We can't let them cancel the final meeting or your keynote speech!"

"Aren't you afraid my keynote speech will dig the hole you are already in even deeper?"

"Are you going to tell the truth?"

"Absolutely. And nothing but."

"Then I don't care. Say whatever you want. It's not about me, remember that. It's about them. The Litvaks. The people who we, in our stupidity and malice and cruelty, murdered and whose desecrated bodies lie in the deep, dark earth, cursing our forests and rivers, our towns and villages. We can never be free of that curse until we admit what happened and honor their memory with our tears and our regret. Until each mass grave is treated the way we Lithuanians treat the graves of our parents and grandparents."

She was deeply touched. She had not thought it possible to find a partner and ally among those she had always considered the enemy. This was a whole new world, she thought. "I believe my speech will help you advance your cause," she said. "It is also mine."

"Thank you."

"But it's five days away. What do we do until then?"

"I have some ideas. First, let's spend a day or two in Nida. We both deserve that. And I want you to see another side of my country. Not just mass graves and murderous skinheads."

"Fair enough. And then?"

"Let's go to pay our respects to our ancestors. I will go with you to Telzh, where your family lived, and then we will go visit my cousin, who lives nearby. Perhaps there are people there who are still alive who will remember what happened to our families, and they can fill in some of the missing blanks for us."

It was all unexpected, spontaneous. It went against the grain of the cool, meticulous planning that had always been the mainstay of her life, even as a child. The children and grandchildren of survivors didn't like surprises. They liked to know where they were going, and with whom, and when they would be coming back.

But when Julius left her, all that changed. It was an adventitious disaster, like a tsunami.

She'd felt tossed away, belittled, shattered. There was nothing left to do but try to pick up the pieces and put them back together in some new kind of order, producing someone she herself could respect. This new person, she realized, was less rigid, less unforgiving, more open to new ideas, new behavior. At least, she was trying to be. And she would, whatever happened, be proud of herself for that.

She nodded, threading her fingers through his. "I'm ready for an adventure."

TWENTY-THREE

JULIUS OPENED THE door of his new house—a lavish rental in the best area of Haifa, high above the cliffs, overlooking the sea. "Haviva?" he called. But there was no answer. *Great. Just bloody great,* he thought, shaking his head and heading for the liquor cabinet. It was part of a ridiculously expensive custom-made wall unit constructed entirely of dark African blackwood—the most expensive wood in the world—and ran the entire length of one wall in the living room. The owners of the place had more money than taste, he thought. Everything that they'd put into this house—a place they apparently had no intention of ever living in—was over-the-top. Ugly, too. It was like the lobby of an overpriced hotel furnished to impress the wide-eyed peasants, to convince them they were getting their money's worth when they spent thousands for a two-night stay. Haviva had gone with the agent and picked it out. Her enthusiasm still knew no bounds. She had even hinted that the agent was sure that the owners would be willing to sell it to them completely furnished (as if that was a plus . . .) "at a price."

He could just imagine what those idiots thought their house was worth. What difference did it make? He was never going to be that customer, he thought, pouring himself a large glass of gin, then adding some tonic, a few ice cubes from the built-in refrigerator unit, and a twist of lime. The ice tinkled prettily as he clutched the glass in his hand, heading for the long, dark green Italian leather couch, which he also hated, the leather sticking to the backs of his thighs in the heat. He kicked off his shoes, stretching out his long torso until only his head was raised and the cold, moist glass made rings on the fabric of his blue shirt where it rested just above his stomach. He took long sips, then finally just gulped it down whole.

He closed his eyes, trying to erase his day from his mind, his heart, and his fingers.

He had done organ harvests before: people in their eighties who had died peacefully in their sleep surrounded by loved ones, their organ donation cards securely placed in their wallets. It was not a problem. Mostly, he felt grateful to be the conduit through which the generous and lifesaving gift of one generation, no longer in need of it, passed life and health on to the living who were in desperate need.

But today that wasn't what happened.

It was a little girl, barely three, who had fallen off a slide in nursery school and fatally banged her head. She had a soft, heartbreakingly lovely little face, eyes of sea blue with lovely long lashes that swept her now-pale cheeks, and a delicate rosebud mouth. Her golden curls fell to her soft little shoulders, and her pudgy hands lay softly beside her as if she were merely sleeping. Except for a gash on the top of her head, barely visible, there wasn't a mark on her.

Her distraught parents had made the heroic decision to keep every part of her alive they could by distributing those of her organs that could be of help to others. Her corneas would help a blind person see. Her little heart would enable a sick, bedridden child to get up and play and live a long, happy life. Her kidneys would replace dialysis machines, and her skin would help burn victims regain their looks and their humanity. But the work of harvesting all those human parts, the horror of cutting into the flesh, the eyes, the organs, of this lovely baby girl, had been left to him. The first cut had been almost unbearable.

When he was done, he'd felt close to collapse. He just wanted to sit somewhere with his arms around someone he loved and hold them close, pouring out his heart, someone who would understand. Someone who looked the horrors of the world in the face every day and refused to blink. Someone like Milia.

He got up and went back to the liquor cabinet. This time he fixed himself a tall glass, which he filled with ice cubes and then drowned in the most expensive amber liquid of the finest scotch he owned. He took a long gulp and sighed, finally feeling something in the place had actually been worth the money.

Soon, his mind would blur, he told himself. The images, before and after, would dissolve like snow in the sun, petering away and leaving no trace. But until then . . .

Impulsively, he picked up the phone and called his . . . what? She wasn't his ex. Not yet. It rang and rang and rang until the answering machine picked up. He put it down, then redialed, this time calling his daughter, Karin.

It had been months since he'd spoken to Milia or the daughter he adored, a separation that suddenly felt unbearable. While the other kids had voiced their dismay in no uncertain terms, Karin had cut him off completely after one furious and expletive-filled final call. He wondered if he was in for another earsplitting diatribe, or if she'd simply hang up. But it didn't matter. He suddenly needed to hear her voice.

"Shalom," she answered. "Enough already! Why are you crying?" he heard her say to what he assumed was his grandchild Tal, who was screaming bloody murder in the background.

"It's me. Aba. What's wrong with the munchkin?"

"Aba." Her voice was as cold as the glass in his hand.

"What's wrong with Tal?" he repeated anxiously.

"If you must know, he wants to eat something I don't want him to eat."

"Too much sugar?"

"No." She sighed. "He wants to eat a package of sanitary napkins he found in my bathroom. He is very unhappy I interrupted his feast."

He grinned, relieved. "I won't bother you, then. I just wanted to ask you if you know where your mother is these days."

There was a short pause. "She left for Lithuania a few days ago."

"Lithuania! Yes, right. Have you heard from her?"

"She sent all of us a message on the family's WhatsApp account that said she'd arrived safely. You used to be on it, no? Oh right, *I took you off when you left our wonderful mother for that brainless nincompoop*."

"Please, Karin . . ."

"Okay. I'll stop. Why do you need to speak to her? Is it something urgent?"

"No, no," he answered hastily, swallowing the rebuke, glad it wasn't worse and she hadn't hung up. "I just wanted to talk to her, that's all."

"Where's Haviva?" she asked pointedly.

"Not home right now." He wasn't annoyed with his daughter. It was a valid question, one he was asking himself.

She seemed to soften at this. "Do you want Mom's cell number in Lithuania?"

He thought about it. He did, but his pride wouldn't allow it. They had been talking through lawyers for months, ever since he stupidly gave in to Haviva's insistence to be brought along to the meeting he had set up with Milia before getting lawyers involved. He should have realized that the minute Milia saw Haviva she'd refuse to get out of the car.

"Does this mean there is trouble in paradise?" Karin asked archly.

"You know I can't talk to you about these things, Karin."

"Hmm, yeah, well, you are all alone and I'm the only show in town at the moment. Maybe I can help, Aba."

Could she? His lovely girl? His daughter who had also once been a tiny dynamo climbing up slides and whizzing down with her golden curls flying in the wind, her lovely blue eyes alight with the joy and glee that only a small child feels so deeply in motion, in pushing the envelope of their physical prowess? Luckily, his grandson was screaming even louder now. "I don't think so, but thanks, Karin."

"Well, let me just say this, then: you shouldn't have brought your mistress along the last time you arranged to meet Mom. You know, Mom got all dressed up. She was looking forward to seeing you. Hoping you could work things out. And there you were with that . . ."

He was shocked. "How do you know that?"

"Because she came over to see me afterward. She looked lovely, but so sad. I know this is not what she wants."

Was that true? He suddenly wondered what dress she'd worn, and how she'd done her hair—tied back, or loose over her shoulders the way he had always liked it. Had she been looking forward to seeing him? Even after what he'd pulled on her? His heart filled with a sudden glimmer of optimism.

"I have to go. Tal's in full meltdown. But I'm glad you called."

"Are you?" he asked hopefully.

Hearing his voice, so unsure, so unlike the confident, arrogant man she knew as her-father-the-surgeon, she suddenly felt sorry for him. He'd been an idiot, and now he was paying the price.

"Yes. But I have to go."

"That's okay, honey. But . . . but . . . listen. Be careful when he's in the playground, okay? Those slides . . ."

"Okay, Aba, I'm hanging up now. But . . . call again. And come over to see Tal. He misses you."

He felt the tears needling his eyes. "Sure. Bye, sweetie."

He sat there, the room growing dark, the alcohol finally beginning to do its job.

* * *

"Well, look who's home early! Today of all days!"

He opened his eyes, trying to focus. Whose voice was that? Was Milia home? No, not Milia. She was . . . away . . . Lithuania. He felt confused.

Haviva sat down next him. Her hair was a bright new shade of yellow, like those taxicabs in Manhattan, he thought. And what was that on her feet?

"What are you staring at, Julius?"

He pointed to her toes.

She opened her mouth and peals of laughter bounced off the walls and ceiling. It was the thing that had so attracted him to her, and now he found himself wincing. "I had a mani-pedi. They put you into paper slippers to separate your toes so the nail polish doesn't smear," she pattered on. "Men are so clueless."

Yes, her toes, too, were a strange color, bright orange, or was that red? She'd paid for someone to hover over her and paint them that color. He swallowed hard.

"You like?" She held her foot up to him, twisting it coquettishly right and left for his inspection.

"Please, Haviva, cut it out. I've had a hard day."

She put her foot down peevishly, offended, sitting up straight. "Well, that's no reason to take it out on me," she said, waiting for an apology, he realized. *Let her wait,* he thought. Then he thought better of it. "Listen, I'm tired. I had to harvest organs from a baby who fell off a slide. A beautiful little girl . . . ," he began.

She grimaced. "Oh, please. I can't listen to stories like that! Why don't we just get ready to go?"

"To go?"

"You haven't forgotten, have you? The Jacobs invited us over. They are going to teach us how to play bridge. They are champion players, you know."

"How do we know these people?"

"Oh, you don't. But I met them on a cruise two years ago. They are a lot of fun, and they live in this mansion in Caesarea. She just had it redone. I'm dying to see what it looks like."

"I'm not going anywhere tonight, Haviva."

Her jaw hung loose. It was most unattractive, he thought. Made her look older. Old . . .

"Why not? That's rude. And I was so looking forward to it." She pouted. "Besides, this is just what you need to take your mind off your work," she wheedled. "It'll be good for you."

He shook his head. "Why don't *you* go, Haviva?"

She hesitated. He could just see the little wheels turning around in her head as she calibrated what it would cost her to have a good time versus staying by his side to nurse him through what she had taken to calling his "black dog" moods. It didn't take her long. "Well, if you're sure you don't want to come. Maybe it's better you have some time to yourself," she said, inspecting her nails and her toes. They both had her approval, he saw from Haviva's pleased expression, which was more than he could say about himself.

"Do you want me to make you dinner before I go? An omelet or a salad?" she offered, half-heartedly, he saw.

"No, I can manage," he said stiffly.

"Oh, don't be like that! There is no reason for both of us to be miserable."

That was certainly true, he thought, feeling a bit of sympathy for her.

He'd never had any illusions about her intelligence, her education, or her empathy. She was a good-time girl. He'd always loved that about her, the way she surrounded herself with fun and laughter. Perhaps it was the alcohol clouding his vision or giving him a new perspective.

Because from where he sat, she seemed like a doppelgänger for that billionaire's ex, the frowsy blonde in her furs and jewels trailing around with younger men. Not charming and fun-loving, but stupid and shallow, flashy and tasteless.

"Well, I'm going up to take a shower," she called over her shoulder.

By the time she came down, dressed to the nines, he was curled up on the couch fast asleep. Annoyed, she found a blanket and covered him, then tiptoed out the door.

TWENTY-FOUR

"WHY DON'T I plug in my iPhone this time, and you can listen to *my* music?" she suggested.

"Plug away!" He nodded, smiling.

She found her playlists, then worked to put them into some kind of hierarchy. The first were the songs she had played on long trips with her family; next the songs she listened to when she was alone, jogging along the Mediterranean shore close to home; and lastly, the Hebrew music she wanted to introduce him to.

"Here goes!"

There was "Stayin' Alive," to which neither knew the lyrics, so they just hummed along, miming dance moves with their arms; "Get Lucky"; and "Fame": "*Give me time, I'll make you forget the rest,*" Darius declared.

She laughed, blushing.

The car sped down the roads edged by lovely rivers, endless forests, and pretty wooden houses. For a moment, Milia almost forgot where she was. It could have been anywhere in the Europe of an older era, unblemished by rapid industrialization: still, lovely, and green.

And then the Beach Boys were singing: *And wouldn't it be nice to live together, in the kind of world where we belong?*

They laughed like two teenagers.

And then came Gloria Gaynor's anthem to the scorned woman, "I Will Survive."

It was startling how accurately the lyrics described her feelings: the fear of living alone, the anger and resentment. He reached out and took her hand, searching her face and wondering if this fearless woman, public enemy number two, was close to crumbling.

"How bad has it been?" he asked her sympathetically.

"The worst," she sighed, shaking her head. "We've been married such a long time. And . . . I thought . . . at least, for me, I was . . . happy."

"And so there was no warning at all? That's strange."

"It was more than strange. It was unfathomable. And the woman was someone we knew, a friend, part of a couple we spent time with socially."

"Ugly." He shook his head. "The betrayal part." Justyna had at least had the decency to find a stranger.

She nodded. "I can't understand the woman. How could she do something like that? Okay, you can argue that immorality is relative. But selfishness, unkindness, deceitfulness? That's not up for debate. What do they tell themselves at the end of the day?"

"I know what you mean," he murmured, keeping his eyes on the road even as his mind wandered back to the terrible time when his own marriage had fallen apart. "But for myself, it really wasn't such a trauma. I think my ex and I both knew we were just going through the motions. We hadn't seen eye to eye for a very long time."

"What did you argue about?"

"She thought I wasn't ambitious enough; that I should do

more to ingratiate myself with my fat, insipid department head. But I wasn't willing to condemn myself to years of poring through KGB files just to prove how abused my country was in order to excuse certain 'patriots' their unforgivable excesses. You know, in the end, maybe she was right about me. I don't have a gram of that kind of ambition."

"I think it's admirable that you weren't willing to give up your intellectual freedom and kowtow to your bosses."

"Maybe. Admirable and foolish," he said, thinking of the cool shade of his tiny private backyard and the little table covered with blue and green mosaic tiles where he loved to drink his coffee on warm summer mornings. How he would miss that when he had to sell and move back into a *khrushchyovka*.

She composed herself. "You know, Darius, in the middle of all that, I wasn't sure I could even make this trip."

"I'm glad you did."

She looked into his eyes. "Are you? It's brought an avalanche of trouble down on your head."

"I'm always digging out from under something." He grinned. "That's the way I like it. Otherwise, life is boring. But what about you? Are *you* glad you came?"

She had come so close to crumbling, she thought, to wanting to *"lay down and die."* But because of this journey, things were beginning to change. Standing in front of that hostile, jeering crowd, channeling the words of those eyewitnesses who had fought so hard to survive in order to pass on the truth of what had happened to them and their loved ones, had given her back her sense of worth and purpose. She sensed the kind of strength in herself she had learned about from survivors, a resilience that suddenly fills the dark, empty void inside you with light. If she could only succeed in transforming the trauma of Julius's abandonment into a lesson in self-love as she accomplished the difficult tasks meted out to her, she would not only survive, but flourish. With or without Julius, she tried to believe she had her own place in the world, an important place that only she could fill. And with or without him, she had to believe she wasn't alone.

She was connected to the spirits of all those brave men and women who had stared into the eyes of ultimate evil without being degraded or diminished, leaving behind their priceless legacy. She was blessed and proud to be their partner, to be allowed to lend them her voice, to link her arms with theirs through time.

"Yes, I'm glad I came. For so many reasons. Being on my own suddenly doesn't feel like the worst thing in the world anymore."

"But if he turns up, would you tell him *'go, get out the door, you're not welcome anymore'*?"

She shrugged. "I honestly don't know."

"It's cumulative, you know."

"What?"

"Studying about crimes against humanity, absorbing the pain of others until you don't have any space left inside you that isn't tainted by it. For years, I studied about the crimes committed against Lithuanians by the Soviets and then the Nazis. The forced migrations to Siberia. The looting of businesses. The imprisonments and executions. It gets to you. Sometimes, you even forget it happened to someone else and not yourself."

She was astonished at his words, which mirrored so precisely her own struggles. The pain and humiliation that she'd only ever read about sometimes became so vivid she felt she'd experienced them personally. Her compensation and that which kept her sane was her ability to use this connectedness to bring those long dead into the living world again, standing in the way of those who wanted nothing more than for the dead to stay buried and silent, their mouths filled with earth, their testimonies lost to time. At this exact moment, her playlist sang out:

"No more talk of darkness,
Forget these wide-eyed fears;
I'm here, nothing can harm you,
My words will warm and calm you."

It was Andrew Lloyd Webber's "All I Ask of You" from *The Phantom of the Opera*.

They looked at each other, startled by the amazing coincidence of lyrics that had insinuated themselves into their conversation with such perfect timing. He sang along:

"Let me be your freedom,
Let daylight dry your tears;
I'm here, with you, beside you,
To guard you and to guide you."

She turned to him, mouthing the words:

"Say you love me every waking moment
Turn my head with talk of summertime.
Say you need me with you now and always;
Promise me that all you say is true,
That's all I ask of you."

They were both silent, listening to the words, the music.

He thought of the story of that little boy standing on the icy winter ground without his shoes as his mother looked on helplessly. He knew he would never in his life forget that image. Milia had come across stories like this her entire adult life, thousands of them. He couldn't even imagine being immersed in such a life, in such darkness. And for some reason, maybe because the little boy was a Litvak and the murderer who'd made him suffer a Lithuanian partisan, Darius felt some kind of responsibility and shame. Of course, that was absurd! It had all happened long before he was born. But hey, go argue with gut feelings! And so he raised his voice in song, using someone else's words.

Neither were young enough or naive enough to think that singing love songs was going to wash away the suspicion and wariness that stood between them. Enemies do not become friends overnight, they knew, especially when past wrongs were not merely personal, but based upon an entire culture and belief system that had expressed itself in crimes so gargantuan they could never be forgiven.

It was easy to understand her wariness. She was a Jew, inviolable in her righteous wrath against unbelievable human outrages committed against her people for centuries. But he, too, was part of a people who had suffered and been wronged. Yet strangers who had never set foot in his country, or been personally harmed by his people, still refused to forgive in the name of long-dead ancestors. They declared his people—long dead themselves and thus unable to defend themselves—despicable criminals. And so the living on each side would continue to hate each other as long as victims and perpetrators lay buried in the same dark earth, justice evading them both.

But the question now facing Darius and Milia was a far different one. If justice and reconciliation were impossible on a national level, was that also true on a personal level? Or could each of them remove, pincerlike, one single individual from that entire dark collective that comprised "the enemy" and love them? Could it be done? Or was that, too, an impossibility, a toxic affront to all those whose memory they—as patriots and descendants— had been designated to honor and protect?

They did not yet know, but they needed to find out.

* * *

The road to Nida was long. They were exhausted physically and emotionally by the time they reached the New Ferry on Nemuno Street in Klaipėda. The ferry to Nida, the only one that took cars, ran only several times a day. To their incredible luck, it was just pulling in as they arrived. They took it as a good omen as they waited in line for boarding.

When the ferry pulled away from the dock, they left the car and climbed up to the top deck. The Baltic Sea, a dark gray mass, stretched out calmly before them. "It's called the Scandinavian Mediterranean," Darius told her. "It's very long and quite shallow, surrounded by more countries than you can count."

"Count them," she teased him.

He wagged a finger at her, smiling. "Okay." He held out his hand and bent his fingers at each name: "Denmark, Sweden, Finland, Russia, Estonia, Latvia, Lithuania, Poland, and Germany."

"Bravo!" she clapped. "What are those birds?" She pointed upward.

"Seagulls, herons, cormorants," he improvised with a laugh. He hadn't a clue. "I have a confession to make," he said.

"Okay, I'm steeling myself," she murmured in mock terror.

"I've . . . actually . . . never been here before."

She looked at him, mouth open, eyes wide. "But you said it was so beautiful! And I thought you were going to be my tour guide!"

"I've seen pictures, doesn't that count? And I know the language, so even if we get lost I can always ask."

"Then you are a unique version of the male species," she said, shaking her head. "So then I'm curious. Why did you pick Nida?"

"Because it's as far away from Lithuania as you can get without actually leaving the country."

"That bad?"

"Worse."

"But no one is following us."

"You never know," he said morosely.

Now she was beginning to worry. "Are we in danger?"

"No! Of course not! If that were the case, I'd have taken you to the airport and insisted you leave. It's just that . . . I don't want to run into anyone I know."

She leaned her back against the ship railing, her elbows akimbo resting on the cool metal.

She studied him. "What are you running away from, Darius?"

"The mainland. Lithuania. With all its mass graves, and lying government agencies, and mad patriots rewriting our history." And people who might have seen the video and not approved, or some colleague from his department who wanted to gloat about how much trouble he was in, or some functionary from the Red-Brown Commission sent to search him out to browbeat him into submission.

"I can't imagine feeling that way about your own country. Even in the worst of times, for example during the Intifada in 2001 and 2002, when public buses were being blown up by Hamas terrorists, and people were getting slaughtered in coffeehouses, pizza parlors, bar mitzvahs, and discotheques, I still never felt like distancing myself from Israel."

"Because you had nothing to be ashamed of. You and your people were the targeted victims."

She nodded, agreeing. "That's true, even if the mainstream media is determined to find us the guilty ones. Like CNN. You know, I was in Jerusalem during the Intifada, and I saw with my own eyes how the terror attacks were reported as 'flashpoints' and suicide bombers were counted as 'victims' in terror attacks. At that time, CNN was trying to set up CNN Arabic to compete with Al Jazeera. They reported the news the way the Arab world wanted it reported."

How did they get on this subject? he wondered, regretting it. There was no way out of this labyrinth. He accepted his ignorance on these subjects and her superior knowledge as a native—even though this was something she would *never* do for him when it came to Lithuanian current events. He could press the point, he thought, and get into a fight in which they would both end up bloodied and furious and neither would win. Or he could simply change the subject.

"Tell me about your kids," he asked her, gratified to see an immediate change in her face as her expression went from fury to pleasure.

"Amir is my firstborn. He's in high tech, working on a billion-dollar exit." She smiled.

"I hear Israelis are good at that," he said with a laugh.

"Very. He's married to an artist. Renee. She's a lovely girl. One of my very best friends," she said, realizing it was true. "I absolutely treasure her."

"You are putting all those mother-in-law jokes to shame."

"Right? So strange how people think there has to be antagonism between a woman and her son's wife. They are both women, both mothers, and they both love the same people. My granddaughters are adorable, just like their mom."

"And Dad? No?"

She exhaled. "He's never home, so thank God their mother has her studio in the house and she is always there. Of course, the little ones believe themselves to be very artistic, and the house is always a big, fun-filled, creative mess. I just love being there."

"Again, another cliché destroyed about mother-in-laws' insistence on housekeeping."

"Clichés are for people who, instead of living, recycle other people's opinions and experiences about life."

"I agree. But I still think your Renee is lucky to have you."

"We are fortunate to have each other," she corrected him.

264 | NAOMI RAGEN

"And the rest of your kids?"

"My daughter, Karin. She's in medical school, along with her husband. They have one child, a son. His name is Tal."

"How are they managing—both being in medical school at the same time?"

"Not great." She smiled, shaking her head. "I wish I could help her out more. She could really use me to babysit, cook, clean . . . all the things good mothers do for their young, busy, married daughters. But they live very far away, in the South, Be'er Sheva. And I am in the Tel Aviv–Haifa area. But even if I lived nearby, I don't think I'd be much help. I'm not really a very good grandmother. I'm not retired, and so most of the time I'm working. I come over to visit, of course, and play with Tal, but I can't pick him up from school if his parents are running late or cook dinner and bring it over."

"Well, if that's your criterion, I'm a pretty bad grandfather, too. Actually, I think it's highly overrated, this whole let's-drop-our-kids-off-at-our-parents' lifestyle. I think people should raise their own children and not expect their parents, who have worked hard all their lives bringing *them* up, to give up their lives to be at their children's and grandchildren's beck and call once they are old. Believe me, our kids aren't going to do that for their own children."

"Maybe because we are setting a bad example?"

"Yes, we are setting an example, but it's a good one. Would you want your kids to drop everything in the interesting lives they've worked so hard to create for themselves when they reach our age, just to become the unpaid help?"

She'd never thought about it that way. It was just assumed when a person got older that they had nothing much going on in their lives and were *just thrilled* to be called upon whenever and for whatever reason their children and grandchildren saw fit. "That's true," she admitted.

He nodded. "Absolutely! I also adore my grandson, Matas, but two hours is all I can take at a time."

"How old is he?"

"Matas is two. Terrible two. I hope his parents survive to give him a sibling. Right now, it's touch and go."

She laughed. "I know what you mean. Sometimes taking care of them at that age verges on cruel and unusual punishment. Good thing there is no such thing as 'emancipating' yourself from your kids! Age two would produce an epidemic."

"You've got a third child, right? A boy."

How did he know that? She looked at him, surprised.

"Ah, I looked you up online," he said, a bit embarrassed.

"Okay. To be expected. There are no secrets anymore. We can use Google Maps to find someone's front door, and Facebook to see who his friends are, and Instagram to check his lifestyle," she said solemnly. "Why were you so interested?"

Was he in trouble? "Honestly, I had been warned against inviting you by numerous people. They said you'd be a mouthpiece for Putin's anti-Lithuanian propaganda. That you'd ruin my conference and destroy the reputation of my country."

"Except for being Putin's mouthpiece, they were all pretty much on the mark, wouldn't you say?"

He shook his head vigorously. "I don't think you hate Lithuania. I think you hate what Lithuanians did to your people. And rightfully so. I also don't think you ruined my conference."

"Well, what would you call it, then? We basically had to change the whole agenda, and you got yourself thrown off the speakers roster."

"The purpose of my conference wasn't for me to stick to a certain format, or for me to be front and center getting maximum exposure. The purpose was to open the door to understanding and reconciliation. When I think about the faces of those high school kids when they heard for the very first time what the people of their own town did to their neighbors, I am filled with hope for the future of my country. There was horror in their eyes, and anguish in their hearts. I can't see *them* putting up plaques to murderers."

"You're right. I saw it, too. It's the beginning of real change here."

"Even I, who have researched this subject thoroughly, could never have imagined that story about that little boy and his shoes." He shook his head. "The malice, the cruelty . . . so much needs to be atoned for. It will take a thousand years."

"I don't agree with you about that."

"About what?"

"About forgiveness taking a thousand years. Jews love to forgive. It's in our Torah, and in our DNA. We love to forget everything that was done to us the minute the perpetrators ask sincere forgiveness. Just look at how many Jewish Israelis are living in Berlin! Ten thousand moved to Berlin over the past decade alone! All you have to do is convince us people are sincere and understand what really happened. Once the Lithuanian people recognize the truth, the decent ones will feel true sorrow, like those high school kids did. And that will be enough for most of us."

"Really? I would never have understood that in a million years." He mulled over her words, studying the sea. "This is the reason inviting you was the best idea of this whole conference. No matter what happens, I won't regret it."

"I really hope you don't get into too much trouble, Darius. It would hurt me terribly to think I was the cause."

"Whatever happens, the responsibility is mine. I signed up for this." He put an arm around her shoulders and pulled her close. "You are an amazing woman."

"And you are a very special man," she told him sincerely, loving the feel of his body next to hers, the cool sea breeze on her face, and the sound of the birds following the ferry as they circled and dived. She took two steps sideways out of his embrace.

He dropped his arm. "I hope I haven't offended you."

"No, not at all. It's just that . . ."

"You don't have to say anything, Milia. I understand."

"It's all pretty new to me. I married my first boyfriend and never left. I don't know how to do this."

"You'd be surprised how it will come back to you. It's like dancing the tango. Once you've done it, the steps feel natural."

"Do you know how to tango?"

He nodded. "I learned on a trip to Argentina. Took three lessons and boom! There I was having the time of my life."

She had been to Argentina numerous times for work, but it had never once occurred to her to learn the national dance.

"Show me," she said. "Come on."

"What, right here, now?"

"Why not?"

"Okay. Wait, I even have some music." He took out his phone and scrolled through his playlist. He raised the volume and put the phone back in his pocket. He beckoned her.

"Wait, you can't be serious! I can't . . . I have no . . . ," she protested as he put an arm around her waist and took her hand in his.

"Just follow my lead. When I go forward you go back."

A crowd was gathering, she saw, embarrassed, but since she had started this whole thing, she couldn't very well beg off, now, could she? Besides, she was enjoying it. She'd always wanted to learn how to dance, but it was hard to do without a willing partner, and Julius—along with many other serious, career-driven men who had been in the Israeli army—thought the whole floating around the dance floor was ridiculous.

Darius was explaining the dance steps to her, twirling her around, showing her some things she could do to make it more complicated. It was a very macho dance, she realized, the men aggressively leading and the women content to mirror their steps.

But then the women had the chance to do some very sexy things, he explained to her, like rubbing her leg against the man's.

"Whoa! This is where I get off. Sorry."

People applauded, and he bowed.

"Would you like something to drink?" he asked considerately.

"That would be wonderful."

She found a place to sit, leaning back, her face raised to the sun. She closed her eyes. He was fun, she thought. Her life was so very serious, so heavy. Maybe Julius had felt the same way. Maybe Haviva also knew how to tango.

"Here, it's cold." He handed her a brown liquid. "It's malt beer. Unfortunately not alcoholic."

She tasted it cautiously, but it was actually excellent. "We've got something similar in Israel. People used to tell me to drink it when I was nursing. They said it was good for the milk."

"Ah, such romantic connotations! I really know how to woo a woman!" he mocked himself.

Hearing him say that was so strange, she thought. So flirtatious and young. So flattering.

"You never told me about your children."

"Ah, yes. The *berniukas*." He hesitated.

She looked at him curiously. "Have I said something wrong?"

He shook his head. "It's just that I don't see them very often. My eldest, Domantas, is in the PhD program in Gothenburg. He's got a gorgeous blond Swedish girlfriend. It doesn't look like he'll be coming home anytime soon."

"I see. And the others?"

"My other son, Jurgis, graduated from a local university. He's working as a journalist." *If they don't fire him*, he thought. "And then there is my darling Karolina, who took off after the gymnasium for a summer trip to Paris. That was four years ago."

"Oh, my." She could see now why the topic was uncomfortable for him. "Is she in school there?"

He sighed. "No. She's working as a bartender."

They sat there silently, listening to the steady hum of the boat's engine as they plowed through the quiet waters. "That's hard, Darius."

He nodded. "There is nothing I can do. She won't come back. She says there is nothing here for her."

"But her education . . . She could get a better job if she got a degree."

"She says she's happy bartending. I'm frightened for her. She's so young." *So beautiful,* he thought. *So heartbreakingly beautiful.*

She heard the anguish in his tone. Gone was the flirtatious tango dancer, the flamboyant conference organizer. Beneath it all was this wretched father longing to save his little girl and helpless to do it. She had no advice to offer.

"Someone once told me that you educate them as best you can, but by the time they hit eighteen, you have to sit back and let them make their own choices."

"Like we have another option," he muttered.

They lapsed once again into silence.

"Does she . . . Is she . . . happy?"

"She says she is, but who knows. Every night I go to bed expecting someone from the embassy to wake me up at two in the morning with terrible news."

"Oh, Darius. How awful for you. I'm so sorry." She reached over and took his hand in hers.

He looked up at her. Her face was filled with compassion.

"You have another son, right?"

"Yes. He's a psychologist. He's almost thirty. Also struggling to find his place in the world. He's out in some tiny settlement surrounded by terrorists. I'm also terrified about getting that phone call."

"It never stops, the worry, the desire to help make things good for them. We are tied to them forever."

"But it's all right to take a little vacation from worrying about them every once in a while, don't you think?"

"Oh, I don't know about that. What will they do without our worrying?"

"Shrivel up? Snort cocaine and swallow fentanyl?"

"Cross the street without looking both ways?"

"Worse, they'll forget to wear their sweaters and boots . . ."

They laughed.

"We're both hopeless," she said.

"Speak for yourself," he objected with mock outrage. "I take a vacation from worrying about my kids every single day . . . between three and four a.m."

"Just about right," she said, smiling. She was still holding his hand as land suddenly veered into view.

"Look." She pointed. A long strip of beach gradually drew closer. Milia suddenly filled with excitement. An adventure, she thought, with someone who cared about her and found her attractive and interesting. Someone who thought what she was trying to do was admirable and important. It had been so long since she'd had that kind of companionship. Too long. Why had she never realized that? Why had she never demanded more from her marriage, from Julius? She wove her fingers through his, excited and eager to see what would happen next.

TWENTY-FIVE

THEY DROVE OFF the ferry feeling a sense of freedom. No-where to go and nothing to do. *What fun!* Darius thought. He glanced at Milia, wondering if she felt the same way, or if she was already regretting the frivolousness of the situation in which she now found herself. She was a distinguished person with a rare work ethic, he thought, a bit intimidated. She was, after all, famous all over the world. And what was he? Some ordinary academic in a third-rate Baltic backwater university. He was honored she had agreed to spend time with him, anxious for her approval, and for her to have a good time, to see another side of his country after having been exposed all these years to only the worst moments in its history.

"Are you hungry?" he asked her.

She was, but not for the lettuce leaves that were practically the only thing she could eat. "I can wait," she murmured, look-ing over the landscape.

"Well, I'm hungry," he said. "So let's stop at a restaurant first and then check in to the hotel."

They drove through the pine forests, the car filled with the smell of the sea. "Here it is. Fisheria," he said. It was a pretty place, she thought, whitewashed with charming blue shutters, decorated with all manner of nautical objects. The service was quick and friendly. They even provided a menu in English. To her surprise, it looked like there were a few things she could actually eat. While she knew she should just order salmon wrapped in tinfoil, she couldn't bear the idea. They didn't seem to have shrimp or lobster on the menu, which would make the pans and cooking utensils unkosher, so she took a leap and ordered something from the menu.

"I'll take the Atlantic salmon with gooseberries, spring onions, pears, and hazelnuts," she told the girl in English, pointing to the menu.

"I'll take the fish soup, and then the cod with potatoes, leeks, hemp seeds, and cream," Darius said in Lithuanian.

They sat there, enjoying the calm, the scent of the sea, after their boisterous and confusing day. They had started out practically as strangers, with more than a small dose of hostility, he thought. But now, sitting across from her, he felt as if he had known her for a long time.

Their voices were low and measured as they exchanged pleasantries in the fading afternoon light. A young waitress with long blond braids smiled at them, lighting the tall blue candle in the center of their table. Its faint light lent a mysterious glow to the room, washing away Milia's wrinkles and highlighting the shadows beneath her high cheekbones and the sweep of her long, thick lashes. She looked so youthful, he thought. So lovely.

"You look like a girl," he said impulsively.

She looked at him, torn. He was such an attractive man, a little Brad Pitt, a little Mads Mikkelsen. She'd always imagined Wehrmacht pilots must look like that, not to mention SS officers, that Germanic-Nordic physique and coloring so beloved by Hitler. In the past, that look had always aroused so much irrational fear and loathing in her. Now she wondered if she had always been attracted to it, but simply too ashamed to admit it. Had she spent her whole life bullied and imprisoned by clichés because of the fear of public condemnation, of her family's shocked disapproval? And if that were true, then how abysmally circumscribed a life it had been! So much fell into that category, she realized. Whole peoples and whole nations you had to avoid and despise to prove your loyalty; hatreds and resentments you needed to keep close to your heart forever, never missing an opportunity to express them when the occasion arose, anything else being disloyal to the martyred dead.

It was exhausting. Hating took so much energy, while opening your heart took almost none at all. There, a smile, and it was done, she thought, smiling at him.

For the first time in her life, she wondered about the state of her heart. Was it really necessary to allow hatred and suspicion to be her guiding lights until the day she died? Would it not be better to spread happiness and joy? Would it not be better to love?

Besides, had Darius not shown himself to be a kind man, a good man? How he looked was irrelevant, an accident of birth, the collusion of factors over which he had no control. He was formed this way, a baby in the womb of his mother, product of his parents' genes. Over that he had had no choice. But as an adult, he had rejected the toxic teachings of his family and his community; he had had the courage not only to find his way to the truth, but to take on the same enemies she had fought all her life. Did that not need to be acknowledged? If the child born to your enemies made the large, improbable leap to be your friend, should he be rejected simply because you could not get over your own prejudices? And if so, where did that leave the world, the future? Nothing could ever change. Old hatreds could never be replaced by new loves and real understanding. She squeezed the hand he offered her, pressing it against her cheek.

"I think," she said softly, "that you should ask for the check."

The drive to the hotel took ten minutes. Just as they were leaving the car, her phone rang.

It was Karin. "I have to take this. Why don't you go ahead, I'll be there in a minute?"

He pressed her hand and nodded.

"Is everything all right?" she asked her daughter.

"Well, it depends on your point of view," Karin answered.

"What is that supposed to mean?"

"It means Aba has left Haviva and moved in with me. He says leaving you was the biggest mistake of his life. He wants you back."

She took the phone away from her ear and held it against her thumping heart.

"Ima?"

"Yes, I heard you."

"So, what do you think?"

"I think I need some time to process this. I can't . . . keep up with your father's sudden impulses. It's giving me whiplash."

"I understand. I have to say this, though. You know I was the one angriest with him. I boycotted him for months. Last night, he just showed up at my door. We had a heart-to-heart. I was very harsh with him, completely unforgiving. But in the end, I really believe he's learned his lesson. He needs you. His life is falling apart. He realizes Haviva was just a mistake made out of some desperate need to have an easier life. But now he realizes she's a selfish, shallow, materialistic woman looking for a meal ticket."

So good-time Haviva was not enjoying his medical horror stories, or his late nights, or his sudden emergency calls during weekends and holidays, and she couldn't keep up the pretense, Milia thought cynically. How very sad for him, for them both, she thought with heavy sarcasm. She was just about to tell Karin this when she thought better of it. Why put her daughter in the middle? "Listen, Karin, I appreciate that you're trying to mediate, but it's not a healthy situation. I don't want you involved. If your father has something to say to me, tell him we will talk when I get back."

"He says he wasn't running away from you, just the Holocaust. That it's hard to live with."

"Unfortunately, I *have* to live with it. So it's a package deal," she answered more sharply than she intended. She took a deep, calming breath. None of this was her daughter's fault. "As I said, your father and I need to talk when I get back."

"When will that be?"

"I'll be here another week."

"How's it going?"

"Oh, that's also a question that deserves a long, detailed answer! I guess you could say that there have been some surprises."

"Good or bad?"

"Both, as a matter of fact."

"Are you okay?"

"I'm actually better than okay."

There was a moment of silence on the other end of the phone.

"Where are you now?"

"I'm in the Curonian Spit National Park."

"What are you doing *there*? Are you giving a lecture?"

"No, it's actually not part of the program. It's more rest and relaxation."

Now her daughter's voice took on a suspicious edge. "And who are you with?"

"I'm with the head of the conference, Dr. Vidas . . . and . . . ," she suddenly improvised, "the others."

She heard Karin exhale. "Well, okay, have a good time. I'll tell Aba you are willing to talk to him as soon as you get back."

"You do that, honey. And thanks for caring. You are a good daughter to us both. Love you. Kiss the baby for me."

She ended the call. Her arms felt suddenly stiff as she held the phone, as if she'd been in some marathon exercise session lifting weights. Julius was miserable. Just what she'd been hoping would happen! Then why did she suddenly feel it wasn't a victory, but a burden for her to carry?

Darius opened the lobby door and looked at her questioningly. "Everything all right, Milia?"

"Couldn't be better," she told him, troubled.

He beckoned her, smiling.

She walked toward him feeling all her senses suddenly acutely alive, her body strong and young and full of desire. Karin and Julius, Tel Aviv, and Haifa suddenly seemed far away.

TWENTY-SIX

THEY SAT IN the car waiting to board the ferry that would take them back to the mainland. Darius looked across at Milia, studying her face as she checked the calls on her phone.

They had been together now for two days, he thought, exploring the sand dunes, spending time at wild Nida beach, renting bikes and cycling through the beautiful scenery to the Vecekrugo Dune and the little fishing village of Preila. He'd bought her an amber necklace in the local museum and gift shop, and she got him the same beautifully colored wind chime she'd purchased for herself. It was a normal holiday, he considered, rubbing his knuckles thoughtfully along his strong chin. Except . . . except for the nights.

"But why?" he'd ask, beg. "Don't you want to?"

But she'd just shaken her head. "I know European culture has a different approach to adultery, but in my religion, it's the ultimate sin. Like murder."

"But he left you. He's been living with another woman all this time."

She shrugged. "It's like eating kosher food. It's not modern, and it's very inconvenient. And sometimes, I look at something that isn't kosher, and I know it would be absolutely delicious. But there is nothing to be done. This is my culture and my history and my beliefs. It's who *I* am. Other people's sins don't absolve me from my own."

Even that word—*sin*—put him on edge. It was so anachronistic, straight out of some medieval religious text. Of course, certain backward religions today were still big on sin, but their followers were primitive. It didn't suit the image of Milia he'd formed at all. He just couldn't understand what was holding her back, any more than he could fathom why he himself wanted to go forward with an eagerness bordering on recklessness.

He was not, after all, a hormonally challenged teenage boy. For the most part, his lusts had been well under control and expended reasonably among mature, intelligent, consenting adult women whose company he enjoyed. Then why this . . . passion?

Was it—the terrible but undeniable thought occurred to him— the primitive desire to vanquish the enemy? The satisfaction of seducing his most difficult conquest, making someone who hated you love you instead? He blushed at the very idea. No, no! It had nothing to do with that, he told himself. He wanted her because he adored her and admired her and was deeply attracted to her physically. But also, he had to admit to himself—and it was painful— proof that he had been absolved of the sins of his fathers and countrymen. Here again, those primitive words! Sin, absolution. Did he need absolution? Perhaps not, but he wanted it anyway. Not for personal crimes. But for those of his family. That necklace . . . No matter how liberal and modern you were, there was still a rock-hard foundation that delineated what human decency required. There were still acts that were abhorrent and sinful.

"There it is!" Milia said, pointing at the harbor as the faint outline of the incoming ferry appeared at the horizon.

He took her hand and kissed it. "Are you glad you came?"

She turned her body to him, her hands lifting his blond curls, caressing the back of his neck. She pulled him toward her, kissing him full on the mouth. "I am." She nodded.

He felt his whole being resonate to her touch. For the present, this would have to be enough for him, he thought. But only for the time being. He wasn't done trying, hoping, needing.

It was the first boat out, and so they reached shore at a reasonable time. And now they were off to Telzh. Milia had insisted on it.

"It's a short drive, a little over an hour," he told her. "We Lithuanians call it Telšiai. It's also called the Town of Seven Hills and the Bear Capital. Statues of bears are all over the place. Some of us call it bear pollution." He laughed. "They say that if you rub the nose of the Samogitian Legend bear, your dreams will come true."

She looked up, as if suddenly awakened from a dream, and not a good one. The trip back to Telzh had been one she'd avoided for as long as she could remember. It was the bedrock of her primal nightmares. And now Darius was chattering on like some airhead tour guide.

"Legend?" she asked politely.

"Sort of like the wolf legend about Rome's founding. The legend has it that Samogitians were raised by bears. From their reputation, you can imagine it's not just a story."

"What do you mean?"

"Samogitia has always been a separate republic. The people there are fiercely independent, stubborn, and combative, or so they say. They are part of Lithuania, yet not part. They've preserved their language and culture for hundreds of years. They were the last Europeans to convert to Christianity, and pagan altars can still be found on the hill forts there to this day."

"Raised by bears . . ." She shook her head. Sounded about right.

"Why are you shaking your head?"

"Please, Darius, just leave it!" she said sharply.

He was taken aback, insulted even. He lapsed into a cautious silence.

She saw this, relenting. It wasn't his fault. "Let me tell you something about *my* people who lived in Telzh. They came in the fifteenth century and were nearly half the population of the city. They weren't combative. They weren't raised by bears. Most of the local Jews were simple people, craftsmen, and peddlers, but at the heart of the Jewish Telzh were religious educational institutions that were the pride and joy of the entire Jewish world. There was a special Jewish girls' school founded in 1865 by the Jewish enlightenment poet Yehuda Leib Gordon, who was a rare feminist, and most important, the Great Yeshiva of Telzh founded in 1880 with four hundred students, the best of the best, from all over the world." She paused meaningfully. "These were deeply religious scholars who had absolutely no use for the godless Communists, who, when they returned in 1940, nationalized all the Jewish businesses and closed down all the Jewish educational institutions, including the Great Yeshiva of Telzh. After that, Jews believed no one could possibly accuse them of having Communist sympathies, let alone being Communists themselves. So they thought they didn't have to worry when the Germans invaded on Thursday, June twenty-sixth, 1941. Very few even tried to flee with the retreating Russian army, and those that did were turned back at the Latvian border. But even before that, your 'partisans' with the white armbands showed up and started lording it over them, treating them like Red Army conscripts! As if Jews had somehow colluded with the Russians and had it coming."

"Why do you call them *my* partisans?" he said, hurt. "Because I'm a Lithuanian? Are we really back to square one, Milia?"

She shook her head, trying to clear it, reaching out for him. He took her hand.

"I'm sorry, Darius. This is very hard for me."

He nodded. "I understand."

He didn't. Not really, she thought. Because what had happened in this lovely, bucolic place was unimaginable to any normal person. Yet could he bear to hear yet another horror story that began with "the partisans with the white armbands"?

They drove through the city until they reached the shores of the lake. It was beautiful, with fishing boats, bicycle paths, cafeterias. A lovely place to take your family on Sunday for a picnic, if you didn't know. That was the problem with most of Lithuania, she thought. Not a lake, nor forest, nor city, nor village had been spared the bloodletting, the horror stories. The whole country was like a lovely woman sitting in jail for cutting off her husband's head. Once you knew her history, the beauty faded and disappeared. The silent, tortured cries of the butchered hung in the air like smog, she thought, shivering.

"Shall we park?" he asked solicitously.

It wasn't lost on her that there was something in his manner reminiscent of the way healthy people talked to those with terminal illnesses. Perhaps there was even some truth to that, she thought, unoffended.

They strolled along the banks of the river. "Let's find someplace to sit, shall we?" she suggested.

He smiled, relaxing. "Sure. What about on that bench near the bear? You can rub its nose and have all your dreams come true." But she was in no mood for jokes, he saw, as she reached into her bag and took out a manila envelope.

"When my father wanted me to take over the Survivors' Campaign, I was absolutely opposed. Just the idea of being involved in this kind of work . . . Well, at the time I was pretty sure it wasn't for me. And then he handed me this."

She held out a few typed pages that had been stapled together.

He looked at it warily. "What is it?"

"The story of my Lithuanian family here in Telzh, my

great-grandparents, great-uncles, great-aunts, and cousins. One of them was a fourteen-year-old girl named Milia. My namesake." She inhaled, but stopped short of taking a deep breath, as if her lungs were suddenly too small to contain it. She exhaled emphatically, the way people do when they are trying to make a point, although what that point could be escaped them both. "And when I finished reading this, I knew I was going to quit my job at the university and take over from my father."

He looked at the bedraggled pages clutched in her hand. "Have you ever regretted it?"

She shook her head. "It was a privilege. I like to think that everything I have done since then has harkened back to what is written here."

"In what way?"

"Every Nazi and collaborator I ever brought to trial; every story of every victim I brought to light. Every piece of property I helped get restored to its rightful owner." She shook the pages in her hand. "It was all for them. To honor them, to be their voice. To be the wrench in the wheels of every attempt to bury Holocaust victims in unmarked graves and move on. As long as I lived, I was going to make sure that didn't happen. You can't understand anything about me, Darius, until you hear what is written in these pages." She held them out to him. "Darius, I need to share this with you."

He settled back, not sure how to respond. Honestly, he felt like fleeing. Instead, he lowered his head and clasped his hands between his knees. "Go on."

"On June twenty-seventh, 1941, a Friday, the 'partisans,' armed to the teeth, drove all the Jewish men, women, and children out of their homes in Telzh. A woman named Malke Gilis was one of them. She was a wife and mother and one of the very few Jews who survived. This document contains her notarized testimony and that of her cousin Khana Peltz as they shared it with Leyb Koniuchowsky, the same person who took the testimony we read to the students in Raseiniai."

"Who was he, this Leyb?"

"An engineer from Kovno. He escaped the ghetto and survived because a farmer took him in. After the war, he went wandering from one displaced persons camp to another, interviewing Lithuanian survivors. He was meticulous in having the testimonies notarized and verified. I guess he knew there would be denial. He tried to get them published but got rejection letter after rejection letter. No one cared."

"That must have broken his heart," Darius whispered.

"I'm sure it did. But he guarded the pages and eventually some of them were published in Yiddish—one hundred and twenty-one testimonies describing every town and village across Lithuania where wholesale slaughter took place, wiping out the Litvaks. My father had the testimony about Telzh translated into Hebrew for me. Shall I translate it into English for you?"

"Please."

"*Two 'partisans' . . .*"

"Baltaraiščiai," he interrupted her. "White arm stripers, or armbanders they were called by others. They called *themselves* 'partisans.'"

"All your officials and the media call them that, too! The holy 'partisans'," she said bitterly.

Two "partisans" and a German came to my house. They didn't give me or my husband, Leyb, time to get dressed, chasing us, our two small children, and my mother, Sheva, out of the house. We, and all the other Jews, were forbidden to lock our doors as we left. As we passed through the town, our Lithuanian neighbors stood on the sidewalks laughing and pointing, throwing wood, barbed wire, and stones at us. Along the way, one of the "partisans" bashed my mother on her back with a rifle butt because she wasn't walking fast enough for him.

"That's terrible," he whispered, shaking his head.

She raised her eyebrows. He had no idea what was coming, she thought, almost pitying him. *"The 'partisans' told the Germans that the Jews had shot at the German army."*

"What?! That's ridiculous. They weren't even armed. They were grandmothers and yeshiva boys . . ."

"I don't know why"—she stopped herself from saying *your Lithuanians*—"they felt they needed to invent an excuse."

"Because they were ashamed of themselves?" he offered.

"Not enough to stop," she replied pointedly, then sighed, trying to remind herself once again he was her friend, her colleague, a man she cared for, not one of her enemies. But it was hard. He was so big, and so blond, so . . . Lithuanian. She couldn't help but imagine him with the white armband banging down the door of her family as they cowered in their homes in this very place.

"Malke Gilis described the scene that Friday at the lake."

We were surrounded by machine-gun wielding "partisans" under the direction of the Germans. We were certain we would all be killed or drowned in the lake. We kissed each other goodbye. Women fainted, and the children cried in terror, clinging to their parents as the "partisans" aimed their machine guns, threatening to shoot.

Very quietly, the head of the great yeshiva, Rabbi Bloch, whispered to us to say our final confessions. He tried to comfort us, telling us not to be afraid, to be proud that we were dying for the sanctification of God's name. Who knows if he helped? We were very religious people. We were kept there until noon when they separated the men from the women and children who were sent home. Those who begged to remain together with their husbands and sons and fathers were beaten just for asking.

When we women returned, we found our homes ransacked, the windows and doors shattered. There was nothing . . . nothing. No food. No clothes. No bedding. Nothing to cook and no utensils to cook with. Everything had been stolen. You can imagine what kind of night we had, especially not knowing what had happened to our men. The next morning, Saturday, the "partisans" were back with their machine guns. Again we were driven out of our homes, this time into the forest at Rainiai.

She put the pages down and looked at him.

"I sometimes try to imagine how that must been for my family, my great-grandparents—Rabbi Leibel and Rivka—my great-aunts and great-uncles and cousins, especially my name-sake, Milia. She was only fourteen. A pretty, sheltered teenager from a loving family." Her voice broke.

He put an arm around her. "Come, sit closer to me."

They sat there, looking at the men in their fishing boats, at the people picnicking and riding bikes.

"Let me bring you something to drink."

He walked away, coming back with beer, soft drinks, and some bottled water.

"I wasn't sure what you'd want . . ."

She smiled, taking the water and gulping it down. "Thanks." She sat there silently, breathing deeply. "I'm sorry. I know how difficult this is to listen to."

"I'll tell you what's difficult. Imagining you reading this for the first time. It must have broken your young heart."

She nodded. "I imagine her often, little Milia, walking into the forest, hungry, thirsty, tired, not knowing if she would ever see her father or grandfather or brothers again. It was a long walk, about four kilometers. But when they got there, they found the men, so it must have been a relief.

The Rainiai compound was owned by a famous Lithuanian opera singer, Kipras Petrauskas. There were thousands of people and no shelter, so the "partisans" and Germans forced everyone to crowd into cattle stalls filled with manure. They made us sleep there.

He shook his head helplessly.

The next day, we Jews began to organize ourselves. We made a place to sleep over the filth. We took over the military kitchen used by the Soviets. But there was nothing to cook except for rye meal. Later everyone got one hundred grams of black bread and twenty grams of butter and a few potatoes. Ten days later, the men were taken out to "work."

Apparently, before they retreated, Lithuanian Communists and the NKVD emptied the local jail. They took seventy-two locals arrested for belonging to "anti-state parties" or for being rich farmers or intellectuals, tortured and killed them, burying them in pits in the Rainiai forest. Now the Lithuanians decided to make us Jews pay for this Soviet crime.

Milia threaded her fingers together and brought them to her mouth. "I don't even know how to tell you what happened next." She shook her head. "That's always the problem with the crimes of these beasts. Your mind and mouth feel polluted just thinking or speaking about them."

He nodded, taking a sip of beer, then thought better of it, putting down the bottle.

"*They, the Lithuanians, spread ridiculous rumors that the Jews were somehow responsible for the death of these Lithuanian prisoners. They chose thirty Jewish men and forced them to dig up the corpses with their bare hands. They . . .*" She shook her head, sickened. "Darius, they made them kiss and lick the corpses with their tongues! Perhaps my great-grandfather, my great-uncles, my cousins . . ."

He felt his eyes sting with tears as he went rigid with disgust.

These Jews were forced to transport the corpses to a Christian cemetery, and dig a pit and rebury them. And all the while, they were mercilessly beaten, until every single one became a cripple or an invalid. Their arms, their feet, their sides swelled with bruises. Peasants came from all over to attend the funeral. There was a huge parade. And the Jews were made to sit on their knees in the center of town, so everyone could mock and abuse them, as if they, and not the Communists, had committed these murders.

After that, we were regularly taken from the compound to do the hardest, dirtiest work.

We were given nothing to eat. We were made to walk to work on our knees, four kilometers, imagine!

The commandant of the camp was a Lithuanian named Platakys. All of the guards at the camp were Lithuanians, not Germans. When we Jews had been in the compound for twelve days, the Germans and "partisans" asked to see Moti Levin, director of the Jewish national bank, and several prominent merchants. They were told that the Jews had to surrender all their valuables, gold, silver, jewels, and cash. They were allowed to keep only 1,000 rubles per family. They told us the money "would be stored safely in the Lithuanian state bank until the situation calmed down." If anyone considered refusing or stashing their valuables in a hiding place, they were warned that their entire family would be shot. Some did anyway, afraid they would starve if they had no money, because we were not being fed. Several days later, the Germans and "partisans" entered the compound and collected everything, driving off with it in trucks.

Most of us were left with nothing, no way to buy food. A few days later, the compound was visited by high school and college boys and girls accompanied by the "partisans" who demanded our wallets, shoes, umbrellas . . . They even took baby carriages, throwing the little ones to the ground. This was on Monday, July 14, 1941.

That same day, the Germans and "partisans" arrived at the

compound on motorcycles. The Germans ordered the Jewish men to clear away the farm equipment from the yard and to leave a wide, open space. Then they led everyone—men, women, and children— into the yard. The Lithuanians and Germans searched through the barns to make sure no one was hiding. The sick and the elderly were also driven into the yard. It they couldn't walk, they were carried. The women and children under fourteen were then driven back into the barns, and the doors were locked. All of the men remained. They were told to get into a circle. Lithuanians with spiked sticks and whips stood in the center and forced them to run in a circle. Everyone, without exception, was beaten. This went on for hours. And each time a German whistled, they were to fall to the ground and when they got up, they were beaten on the head and their sides. Several soon fell dead. They called it the Demon's Dance.

"Velniu shokis," Darius whispered to himself, his eyes shut in pain and disgust.

Many Lithuanians had come from the town to watch. They acted as if they were at a show, or a circus . . .

"Or a Roman colosseum . . ."

"Yes, exactly. Except these were not slaves. These were their neighbors, half the population of their town, people they had lived with all of their lives."

Afterward, the men—unrecognizable with cracked heads, missing teeth, bleeding and crippled—were sent back into the barns. You can imagine how their families received them! The women did their best to bandage them, but some were so damaged, their own wives didn't recognize them.

But the worst was still ahead. That evening, they chose eighty young men and gave them spades, telling them they were being taken to work. The Jews in the barns heard the shots ring out in the forest but it never occurred to them that it had anything to do with the young men who had been taken away. The next day, July 15, at one p.m., Lithuanian men came to the Jews with their rifles aimed and ordered another twenty-four young men "to go to work." A short time later, shooting was heard. But even then, we Jews refused to make the connection. It was only with the third group taken that people realized that not a single one who had "left for work" had returned.

The men started to look for hiding places and refused to report. But then the "partisans" announced that if anyone didn't report, their women and children would be killed. So the men came out of hiding, wanting to protect their families. Another forty were taken away and shot. This group included Leyb Gilis.

Darius looked up sharply.

"Her husband?"

Milia nodded.

For some reason, this shocked him profoundly. The teller of this tale had experienced such tragedy, and yet she had had the courage not only to survive but to bear witness.

That same day they took away all the rabbis from the Telzh Yeshiva and all their students—the pride of the Jewish world. Many had already had their beards cut or torn off during the Demon's Dance, but some prominent, long-bearded rabbis remained. At the pits Rabbi Zalmen Bloch told everyone to die proudly for the glory of God's name, repenting all the sins that the Jews had committed over many years. Someone else, a Revisionist named Iske Bloch—no relative—told the murderers that "you are sprinkling the trees with our blood, but the floors will be washed with your blood in revenge." They cut him to pieces with knives and tore out the rabbis' beards—including the flesh—before they shot them all.

The slaughter continued, group by group, with each group forced to shovel earth over the corpses of those who had preceded them. Except that sometimes they weren't dead, just injured. Some recounted that they had been forced to bury their sons and fathers alive, even as they begged them for help.

Her hands trembled.

"Milia . . ."

She shook her head. "No. You have to hear it all. Until the end."

He nodded, gripping his hands together tensely in his lap and staring down at them.

At the exact moment when one of the last groups were all stripped to their underwear waiting to be shot, a powerful storm suddenly descended out of nowhere, with thunder and lightning and rain. This seemed to frighten our captors, as if suddenly they remembered there was a God in heaven watching them. Instead of shooting the men, they sent them back to the barns. The storm continued for hours. It looked like the guards began to have real misgivings. The men who had been temporarily spared at the last minute sat like lumps of clay. For most, this three-hour reprieve was the most terrifying thing they had ever experienced in their lives, knowing as they did what awaited them, and feeling helpless to save themselves because the barn was locked and surrounded by armed guards. Besides, the men were physically and emotionally exhausted—all of them had broken bones and torn muscles. Perhaps, too, having been so close to death, they'd given up. Still, when the rain cleared up and the men were forced to return to the pit, a few somehow managed to hide in the hay. The rest were shot. Altogether, over 5,000 Jewish men from Telzh and neighboring towns were killed that day. Jewish men who had not been brought to the compound and had been living and working for the peasants in town were now brought back, and taken to the barns. These men didn't want to live anymore. They were hopeless. They, too, were shot.

The last group of men to die had no one to bury them. So the Lithuanians poured lime over the bodies, including the wounded, who screamed in agony . . .

"Milia, please!"

"I'm sorry. I understand you. I felt the same way, I also begged my father to let me stop reading. Do you know what he told me?"

Darius shook his head.

"He said: 'It's the very least we can do for them. To at least know what they suffered, how they were treated, and the crimes committed against them.'"

He raised his hands in defeat. "He's right. Go on."

After the men were dead, two SS men and the "partisans" looted us women, taking anything that was left—our money, shoes, wallets, fur coats . . . I had 17,000 rubles left. I hid it. And when they left, I burned it. Before they went, the SS man stood before the women with a long knife in his hand. He told them, "Nothing will happen to you and your children. But you will never see your men again." Later that day all the possessions of the men that had only sentimental value were brought from the pits and laid out next to the camp command post. We women were ordered to go out and take those things that had belonged to our murdered fathers and husbands and sons. We found photographs of ourselves and our families, we recognized our husbands' underwear and socks. And each thing we found was a dagger to our hearts. I think the murderers did this simply to amuse themselves with the sadistic pleasure of watching us poor women as we recognized our loved ones were gone forever. But this was only the beginning of what they had planned for us helpless women.

"Oh God!" Darius moaned.

Every night as we women slept, the "partisans" who had mur-
dered our men would creep into the barns holding knives and flash-
lights, frightening us and dragging some of us away to be raped in
the forest.

"Beasts . . . ," he murmured, wanting to crawl away and hide
himself, like a wounded animal.

"Darius . . . You didn't do these things. You weren't even
born."

"But these are . . ."

"Yes. Your people."

"My people," he repeated, thinking of what she had said to
him that had so offended him at the time: *Your people became mon-*
sters. She had been right about that, too.

On Friday, July 18, I and my mother, Sheva, and Lea Kopel
went off to see the death pits ourselves. They were only a hundred me-
ters from the camp, but still we risked death in doing this. There were
no more guards at the barns which held only helpless women and chil-
dren. They only guarded the drinking water, which was very scarce.

We found three pits. Around their edges we saw scattered phy-
lacteries and prayer shawls and bits of brain as well as scattered
passports and documents. The largest pit looked as if it was spitting
blood. It seethed. I fainted.

When I returned to the camp, I felt half dead. I told the others
what I had seen. The place was filled with heartbreaking cries as the
reality of what had been done to us sank into our minds and hearts.

We women and our children were by now starving. They trans-
ferred us to another camp in Geruliai. There the conditions were sim-
ilar to Auschwitz. Watery soup, one hundred grams of black bread,
coffee. No sanitary conditions. Infested with lice. Spotted typhus and
scarlet fever took the lives of the children daily. My six-month-old,
Reyzele, died in her sleep. My four-year-old son, Ruvele, caught

diphtheria and typhus. He was transferred to an infirmary, but the Lithuanian doctor refused to help Jewish children, who lay scattered dead under their beds. Ruvele died on Wednesday, August 27. His grandmother buried him with her own hands in the Jewish cemetery.

All the time in Geruliai, the "partisans" told the women about preparations to murder them all. Sometimes they said only the older women would die, so these women began trying to make themselves appear younger, putting on makeup and dressing up.

In the middle of Friday night, August 30, 1941, the "partisan" murderers Platakys, the camp commandant, and Jodeikis arrived. They brought bottles of whiskey with them and got drunk.

They then demanded gold, silver, and rubles. Rebbetzin Rashi Bloch and a few others went around collecting the valuables and handing them over. At 5:30 a.m., on the Jewish Sabbath, all the women and children were driven out into the yard. Believing we were about to die, we threw whatever we had left of value into the swamp rather than leave it behind for the benefit of the murderers. The two of them then separated out a group of five hundred of the youngest, prettiest women and sent them to Telzh on foot under heavy guard.

The "partisans" took off the remaining women and children's coats and shoes and clothing. Then the women were told to remove their underclothes and leave them neatly folded in a certain spot. They were arranged in rows, seventy-five in each row. The women and children were led off to a pit that had been dug beforehand. They were told to stand at the edge of the pit and were shot from behind with automatic weapons. Men were discovered masquerading as women. They, too, were shot.

He stood up. "I . . . I . . . don't . . . know. It's . . ." He walked around in a circle, holding his head in his hands.

She took him by the hand and led him back to the bench. "Shall I stop?"

He looked at her hopefully, wondering if that was a possibility, then realizing it wasn't because he didn't want it to be. He wanted, had to, listen to everything.

He sat down again. "Go on!" His voice was hoarse.

The women still standing in rows in the courtyard surrounded by armed murderers could see everything that was happening at the pits. They began begging the guards to shoot them more quickly. Those who had valuables left gave them to the guards in exchange for being shot sooner, rather than being left to suffer hearing the screams of the victims and witnessing their children and friends being slaughtered.

One woman, Mery Sholomovitz, managed to escape by jumping over the pit and running into the forest. They shot after her but missed. She sat watching and later told what had been done to the smallest children. They had not been shot. Because as the "partisans" explained, they didn't want to waste bullets on them. Instead, they picked them up by the feet and smashed their heads against rocks and threw them into the pit or put an end to them by crushing them in the pits with heavy boots or the butts of their rifles. Some women went into labor, they and their half-born children were dragged into the pit. The "partisans" thought this was extremely amusing. All the while, the "partisans" had a smile on their faces.

Eight thousand women and children were murdered on that day. In this way were the women and children of the Geruliai camp murdered by the Nazis and their helpers, the Lithuanian "partisans." Only a handful survived. Some went to the Telzh ghetto to join the other five hundred girls. But a few hid in the villages.

He seemed dazed. "Listen. Maybe it's enough for one day, Milia. We'll find someplace for the night. Come back tomorrow . . ."

"As if I would spend a single night in this place . . . ," she said venomously.

It shocked him. Never before had he heard her speak with such hatred. It was jarring, but understandable. In fact, he gave her a great deal of credit for being willing to share a bench with him, for allowing him to touch her. For being friends with him at all. If the situation had been reversed, he wasn't certain he would be able to do the same.

"I haven't told you what became of the five hundred women who were sent to the Telzh ghetto. I haven't told you what happened to little Milia, my beautiful fourteen-year-old namesake."

He nodded helplessly.

She opened the beer he had brought her and drank it down.

"They were brought to a bathhouse in the worst part of town, right near this beautiful lake," she said, nodding toward the water. "The place was surrounded on three sides with a high wooden fence topped with barbed wire. They were old, ruined wooden houses, with low ceilings full of holes and no windows. The street was always knee-deep in mud.

"Four of the women were taken back to Geruliai camp the day after the slaughter to pick up supplies. Do you want their names?" she suddenly asked him.

He shook his head, horrified. "Of course not!"

"You know, your Red-Brown Commission will refuse to believe this eyewitness testimony. So perhaps if we give them the names . . ."

"Fuck them," he said, his voice harsh.

She inhaled. "Anyway, this is what they saw: Female bodies scattered around the pit, which wasn't deep enough to hold them. The bodies of the sick, the old, invalids, and women in labor who had been unable to walk as far as the pit, dead in the barns.

"Women from town, Lithuanian women, had come running to Geruliai to tear the underwear off the dead bodies, and scavenge for belongings that had not yet been taken away and distributed or kept by the 'partisans' for themselves and their friends. There was nothing left for the four women prisoners to bring back to the ghetto. But even the rags they collected were cherished by the women in the ghetto, mementos of their murdered mothers and sisters and friends and children. Malke said in her testimony that these things 'drove the women in the ghetto mad with pain and sorrow.'

"There was nothing to eat. The rags were sewn and sold to the peasants in exchange for food. There was no bedding, no candles, no firewood. No food. No food. No food. They slept on the cold earth. They starved. The weather was changing. It was freezing and damp. They had no shoes. No clothes. And not a shred of hope. They started to tear down the huts and use the wood to warm themselves. A week later, they started to get one hundred grams of bread. But not every day. Sometimes, only a few times a week. They were between fourteen and eighteen years old. My little Milia."

None of this was new to him. The things he had read in Zuroff and Vanagaitė's book, the stories she herself had told the students in Raseiniai . . . And yet, this was unbearable because it was so personal. Through Milia, he suddenly felt connected to each and every young girl who had starved here, on the edge of this beautiful lake. It made him feel as if his whole life had been a monstrous lie, and only now did he see the truth of where he was living and among whom.

Perhaps, too, because now he was sitting next to someone he admired, even loved, a person of such fine qualities and intelligence, and goodness, and these things had been done to *her* family, to people like *her*, whereas before it had happened to strangers, long ago.

He was seized by a sudden, strange, seething fury. He wanted to stand up and shout at the people around him enjoying their day on the lake, to tell them: *You are standing on sacred ground where thousands of martyrs have died!* Instead, he reached out to her tentatively. He wasn't surprised when she shrugged him off.

"I'm almost done."

We women were given permission to go out to work by the new head of the ghetto. The peasants paid him for each one of us. Young girls were made to go out barefoot, half-naked to do the hardest work, as the water froze. The peasants hardly fed them, and wouldn't let them into their homes, making them sleep in the cold barns. A wealthy landowner took ten girls, but he only returned five. When the women heard the landowner's story, they went to check. The girls had been horribly raped and murdered. All the girls sent to work in the country were forced to sleep with the peasants or their sons. It was even worse in the ghetto where men came in all night and did whatever they wanted. Many of the girls became pregnant.

My little Milia . . .
He saw the tears running down her cheeks and wanted to die.

The High Holidays came and we women gathered in the synagogue to pray. There were no men. A young woman led the prayers. We were certain we would be killed. We prayed for ourselves, for our dead families that we would never see again, for our dead friends. But even as we said the prayers for a good year, a long life, we went back to the ghetto with no hope for life. On Yom Kippur, the young woman acting as cantor, Miss Golde Hamerlan, prayed with a voice that threatened, demanded, and tore its way into the dead heavens. Many of us lay on the floor in a faint. The strongest prayed until nightfall, swaying like our men used to. Our prayers were heartrending. Most of us expected this to be our last Yom Kippur on earth. The world had never seen such a Day of Atonement. Who knew if the world would ever understand or remember it? Who knew?

Rumors were spread among the Lithuanians in town that the

ghetto was a source of disease. Women began chasing away the hungry girls and refused to hire them. In the middle of the night a German . . . a German! woke up the girls and told them they must escape. That there were plans to kill them. Not a single "partisan" took such pity on the Jewish girls. The German even let one spend the night in his hotel room and didn't touch her. Some tried to escape. But the "partisans" caught them and either shot them or brought them back to the ghetto.

"I hate them," he whispered. "With all my heart. And I'm glad my children have left this cursed country. I hope they never come back."

She stared at him speechlessly. "I don't want that."

"It has nothing to do with you! It's the fucking lies, the fat morons trying to hide and obfuscate and thinking they can bully us into forgetting what happened. Not a single one of the people in your testimonies has been tried in our courts for these crimes. Not one!"

"I know," she whispered despondently.

Some small part of him wished he could go back in time to a place where these revelations would have made him angry—at her, at her unbelievable, preposterous story. What he wouldn't give to believe again with full confidence that it was all lies! Putin propaganda. That Jewish Communists had made it all up. That it never happened! But that was impossible, now and forever. Because here was a woman sitting next to him who had been named after a young girl who lived in this town. A woman who had lost her family here. If it was a lie, then where was little Milia? What had happened to the Litvaks, the great vital communities that were no more?

He felt the seeds of insanity sprouting as he thought about all she had told him, as if there was no longer solid ground beneath him. The idea that most people were kind, except for criminals, and that the universe was benevolent, lay like a tangled corpse at his feet. "How did Malke Gilis make it out alive?"

"Right after her little boy got sick, she also fell ill and was admitted to the local hospital. A Russian nurse took pity on her when the Lithuanian doctor and nurses refused to do anything to help her. In fact, she even describes how the doctor came to her and laughed about the killing of the women in Geruliai: 'All the women were driven out of the Geruliai camp and shot. Your mother is never going to visit you now.' The doctor said it with as much joy as if he had won a big lottery, Malke remembered. The nurse also smiled. There were also twenty-one Red Army soldiers recovering in the hospital. When they did, they were all taken out and shot."

"So we Lithuanians were certainly no better than the Russians when it came to war crimes," he said bitterly. He felt betrayed by his education, by the entire patriotic narrative he had been brought up with.

I was a milliner, and a local hat maker took me on. The hat maker took the orders and I did the work. The woman was a widow who lived with the German commandant of Telzh. All the murderers used to visit them. The hat maker's home was filled with things stolen from murdered Jewish women. People like Jodeikis and Platakys and the Inzhiulvichiai brothers brought these things to her as gifts. She had gold, silver, sewing machines, all looted from the murdered. She lived in the local hotel. Only the German military were allowed to live there, and I had to go down to the restaurant every day and eat together with them. They didn't know I was a Jew, and they used to invite me out on dates, to the theatre and cinema. With the money I received for my work, I was able to buy potatoes and bread and other food and share it with the girls in the ghetto. One day a tailor who often worked together with me told the Germans I was a Jew and might poison their food. From then on, I was forbidden to eat in the restaurant, but ate alone upstairs with the hat maker.

The hat maker once offered me poison. She said it was better than being shot. She also offered to buy my boots because "I would not be needing them in any case." And then one day I heard the hat maker telling her maid to be careful not to say anything to me about the plans to kill all the women in the ghetto. That was it for me. I left and went to work for a German woman who was a teacher in the gymnasium. The German woman had a son who worked in the German labor office. He was a young and worthy boy who brought me all the news. But at the end of the week, I was let go.

People competed with each other to hire me, not out of sympathy, but because they hoped to grow rich on my unpaid labor. In December, rumors started again that the ghetto was going to be liquidated and all the girls murdered except those who converted. Some of the girls, starving and freezing and scared to death, agreed. They went to church, and the priest gave them baptismal certificates, promising that no harm would come to them now.

I asked the German teacher if the rumor was true. She said: "We will all meet in heaven." That's how I knew. The day they chose was December 25.

"Christmas!" Darius said, feeling sick.

Milia nodded.

Sure enough, the ghetto was surrounded by a reinforced guard of Lithuanian "partisans." A few days before Christmas, hundreds of girls tried to escape from the ghetto. Some waded in the freezing lake or crept through the fence. But almost all of them were caught and returned. It was impossible to escape. Hopeless, some girls strangled the children that had been born to them to spare them worse cruelty. Others went insane. The "partisans" laughed and joked as they watched the girls beg for their lives.

Starting on December 23, the "partisans" started packing the women and children into wagons and bringing them to the pits near the Rainiai compound, near where the men had been murdered. Peasants zealously brought the young girls who had worked for them back in wagons, their hands and feet tied so they couldn't escape the slaughter. Some brought them directly to the pits.

He jumped up. "I can't. If you say one more word, I'll jump into the lake. Please, Milia. Please . . ." He wept.

She understood him. She had read this same story and also found it unbearable. But instead of jumping into a lake or out of the window, she had jumped out of her life and begun a passionate quest to honor the memory of the victims by sharing the truth of what had happened to them and who was responsible.

"Now you know why I am public enemy number two. It's because of what I know," she said. "And that I'm not afraid to share it."

"It's lethal."

She nodded. "And thus the unbelievable lengths to which certain Lithuanians will go to hide it, even from themselves." She looked at him. "Those little girls from the ghetto? Those hundreds of girls hired out into the countryside? Lithuanians murdered them all. Including the ones clutching baptismal certificates, because the priest who issued them did not raise a finger to help them when the time came."

He winced. "If only . . . ," he began wistfully, trying to conjure some miracle that would transform the past. "How did Malke escape?"

"She had a work permit that convinced the Lithuanian guards to let her out of the ghetto. Her employer took her in for a little while, and then she ran into the forest. She and another girl were taken in by her employer's old father."

"Christmas miracle," Darius said cynically.

"He saved their lives, but Malke had mixed feelings about him. Often the old man treated the girls very badly. He tormented

Malke with demands that she convert. He beat her and never gave her enough food and she received nothing at all for the expensive hats she created, which made his daughter, her employer, rich. *'Not even a crust of bread,'* she writes. Also, the old man's son was a local policeman who was murdering Jews."

"He didn't give her away?"

"I suppose he didn't want to get his father into trouble. And maybe by that time it was clear the Germans were going to lose, so keeping Malke and some other Jews under his roof was like an insurance policy. Still, he was risking his life. And the last thing Malke says in her testimony is this: *'We women were saved by the peasant Juosas Baltmishkis and will be eternally grateful to him. The good peasant saved five Jewish women, risking his life. He will be eternally remembered for the good.'"*

For a few moments, they sat together in stunned silence.

Finally, Darius asked almost in a whisper: "How many of these young Jewish women survived?"

"About sixty. Some hid with peasants they knew, paying them in gold and other valuables. Others kept the women to save themselves from hiring maids, exploiting them mercilessly. Many saved them on condition they'd sleep with them. They were made 'wives' of entire groups of men. Some of the converted were saved by Christians. Others worked as prostitutes in the villages." She put the pages back into their manila envelope.

"And reading this convinced you to take over from your father."

She nodded. "It didn't even feel like a choice anymore, but an obligation and also a privilege. I was passionately committed to keeping faith with the victims by finding the guilty and exposing their crimes."

He hung his head. "I'm exhausted," he said. "Let's get out of here and find someplace to spend the night."

"I can't do anything until I go to the forest in Rainiai, to where she is, my little Milia. You understand, Darius, don't you?"

"Yes. Of course." He was almost afraid to look at her. "But perhaps . . . that is . . . would you care to stop somewhere for food maybe? Or just to stretch our legs . . ." He desperately needed some time to recover. But the look she gave him made his skin go cold. Silently, he walked back to the car, opening the door for her.

"I've looked it up. They say the memorial is near the villages of Geruliai and Viešvėnai," she told him.

He found it on Google Maps. There it was: Memorial Rainiai Massacre.

It was only a drive of around four kilometers outside the city, but it felt longer, she thought. There it was, unmissable at the side of the road. But wait . . . it was a chapel! And the place was filled with wooden crosses.

"This can't be right," she murmured.

"I'll go ask someone. Wait here."

"No. I'll go with you."

It was definitely a Christian chapel, with crosses everywhere, she saw. "Chapel of Rainiai Suffering," a sign said in several languages, consecrated in 1991: "To commemorate the 50th anniversary of the massacre, to immortalize the memory of all the victims of Soviet terror."

Soviet terror. This was a memorial for those same Lithuanian prisoners murdered by the Soviets that the Jews had been tortured over, she realized.

Inside it was white, the walls covered with frescoes depicting the local martyrs whose portraits draped the walls.

"Rainiai martyrs, Siberian exiles, and partisans, all intertwined with the suffering of Christ and his Mother," she heard someone explain in English. It was a tour guide, she realized, leading a group of South Africans. "The artist, Antanas Kmieliauskas, said that when he was painting his frescoes he thought for a very long time how to convey not only the suffering of Rainiai, but also the suffering of our whole nation: *How can we solve the riddle of this evil? Could God otherwise not have saved mankind just by allowing his only begotten son to be crucified? Couldn't Lithuania avoid a terrible war and postwar experience? Therefore, I decided to make a comparison: in the center I depicted the suffering of Christ, and on the sides the experiences of the Lithuanian people and dozens of Samogitian martyrs, whose fate led to such a terrible death a couple of hundred meters from this chapel. And to ensure that all this wouldn't be too shocking, I used light tones so it would dissolve in the clouds.*"

The chapel's stained-glass windows had hints of red drops of blood against a white background and included instruments of torture like nails and pliers. There was also barbed wire, "all of it symbolizing the depth of our nation's suffering," the guide said solemnly.

The word "Jew" was never mentioned. Milia hurried to leave. She felt dizzy.

Darius was waiting by the car. "You shouldn't have gone inside."

"You're right. I feel nauseous."

"It's not here. But it's nearby."

"They actually have one? A memorial for the Jews they murdered?"

"That's what I was told. The person I asked even gave me directions. Come."

They got back into the car and traveled toward Geruliai.

"It should be around . . . here," he said looking out at the forest, perplexed.

Then she spotted something at the edge of the forest, a crumbling wooden fence. "There!" She pointed.

They parked and walked toward a forest thick with pines on an unpaved path filled with brambles and stones toward a ne-

glected square of cracked concrete paving stones overgrown with
weeds and surrounded by an old wooden fence. Inside was a stone
rectangle, about four feet high. She and Darius opened the old
wooden gate and walked inside. The words were written in Lithuanian with no translation. It was dated 1941. "What does it say?"

"*In memory of the victims of Fascism, 1941.*"

"That's all?"

"I'm so sorry."

This was where they took the girls. This was where they dug
the pits and had them take off their clothes. She thought of little
Milia, her namesake. These trees, this ground, were the last things
she had ever seen on this earth. She thought of her family, her
great-grandparents, her uncles and aunts and cousins, and what
had been done to them on this cursed soil by these cursed people
they had lived among for hundreds of years.

She took out a small prayer book and began to say kaddish,
the sacred prayer for the dead:

> *Yit'ga'dal v'yit'kadash sh'may ra'bbah, b'olmo dee'vro chir'usay
> v'yamlich malchu'say* . . . May His great Name be blessed
> forever and to all eternity. Blessed and praised, glorified,
> exalted and extolled, honored, adored and lauded be the
> Name of the Holy One, blessed be He. Beyond all the bless-
> ings, hymns, praises, and consolations that are uttered in
> the world; and say, Amen.

She sank to the ground, her legs suddenly giving out. Her
heart literally ached, drowning in sorrow. For so many years, she
had been able to keep it all at arm's length, to be the dignified
professional, the speech giver, the confident figurehead of an organization. She cared, but this was also her job. She didn't make
it personal. All that suddenly vanished as the reality of what had
happened here invaded her soul. She wept, bent in two, hugging

herself, her head almost touching her knees, the rough weeds and small stones tearing up her stockings, bruising her flesh. She wept and wept and wept, her heart raw, helpless to stop.

He stepped back into the shadows, watching her. A great tenderness welled up inside him. In her, he saw all those young Jewish girls who had stood here at the edge of the pit. She, too, was still a girl, he realized. Beneath the dignified facade of the tough, world-famous dignitary, the "public enemy" was a vulnerable, tenderhearted woman, crushed by a tragedy so profound, it was impossible to fully comprehend.

He was not a religious man. That is, he had dispensed with religious ritual along with most of his generation. But at that moment, hearing her keening, surrounded by the sight and smell of the deep, dark earth where these atrocities had taken place, he felt himself suddenly fall to his knees, as if overcome by a sudden sickness. Almost instinctively, he clasped his hands in imitation of piety, gripping his fingers together so tightly they ached. He wanted, needed, to pray. He so wanted there to be a higher power looking down, into the ground and into his shaken heart, from whom he could ask forgiveness. He wanted to believe that even this befouled and desecrated earth, where the cries of the innocent still echoed through the silent forests with every wind-tossed branch, could be made right somehow. Such a thing, he knew, was beyond the power of human beings. Only God—if He existed—had such power. "Forgive me," he finally said, closing his eyes. "Forgive my parents and grandparents, and everyone in this village. And if that forgiveness necessitated punishment, then punish us, and let our pain expiate what has been done here."

The irony of asking for punishment did not escape him. But it was preferable, he thought, to the catastrophic idea that no one would ever pay for these terrible crimes. For if that were the case, how could one go on living and believing in the future? How could you bear to be part of a planet inhabited by human creatures prone to such actions? It would almost be better for the earth to cease to exist altogether.

He rose, looking to where Milia still sat doubled over with grief. An inconsolable sorrow mingled with compassion and unconditional love flamed through him for this small woman named after a fourteen-year-old girl who had been tortured and murdered in this place, by his people. *His* people, he finally admitted to himself. He could not escape from that fact. *They* had done it, to the Jews. Not the Germans, not a few "degenerates." The whole nation had taken part, even if many, even most, had not committed the acts themselves. They had been bystanders: rejoicing and approving or weeping and disapproving. Whether in joy or sorrow—they had been equally useless to the victims, refusing to interfere. And in their lack of protest, they had joined hands, agreed, decided, and helped to carry out this death sentence without mercy. Perhaps the motivation had been at its core a mindless hatred, but the form it had taken was calculated and venal: they had killed, and they had filled their pockets and their homes. And even those who had done nothing at all had been happy to line up to share in the murderers' loot; to get new shoes, a fine tablecloth, and a gold necklace with pearls and sapphires . . . The idea might have come from the Nazis, but they had eagerly volunteered to be willing executioners. They did it with enthusiasm, with a smile and patriotic songs. And now, all these years later, they still hid the truth from themselves and their children, as if no one would notice. As if it, too, could be buried and forgotten like these killing pits where the bones of babies, young girls, and grandparents mingled in the earth beneath an indifferent sky.

He looked at this forsaken place, thinking of the chapel, its manicured lawns and newly painted walls, its stained glass and frescoes and tour guides.

Lithuanians were fanatical about respecting graveyards and gravestones. They visited, polished, cleaned, and brought flowers.

But no one came here. It was forgotten because they wanted to forget and thought they could get away with it. The way they had murdered and gotten away with it. And so far, they had been right.

He heard Milia take great gulps of air as she tried to compose herself. He bent down, putting an arm around her to help her up. But she pushed him away, stumbling to her feet.

For certain crimes, he thought, stepping back to give her room, forgiveness was not possible, nor was retribution or even true justice. All were beyond our paltry human powers. What was left for us as humans was compassion, and a willingness to believe in and trust one another's sincere sorrow and regret. But that could only happen when coupled with the task of exposing the crimes and demanding whatever shred of justice and compensation were still attainable. He wanted to do that for her. He was determined.

He stepped back, uncertain where to go from here. He would wait, he thought. Calmly, patiently. Wait for her to tell him.

TWENTY-SEVEN

THEY SAT AROUND the outdoor picnic table in Karin's backyard in Be'er Sheva, Amir and Renee; Karin's husband, Solomon; and Gilad. The two little girls were jumping on the trampoline with their cousin, Tal, screaming with laughter.

Karin brought some pita bread, humus, pickles, and frankfurters to the table, setting down plastic dishes and cups and cutlery.

"It feels like a Yom Ha'atzmaut picnic." Gilad grinned, carrying in bottles of soft drinks and soda that he'd brought with him. All the women immediately groaned.

"One little glass of orangeade isn't going to ruin their health, Karin." He shrugged, dismissing his sister's protests. "It's one of the best things I remember about my childhood."

"Orangeade?" his brother, Amir, asked with raised eyebrows, exchanging a secret glance with his wife, Renee.

Gilad's face reddened. No matter how old he was, and how many degrees he had earned, he always felt like the pathetic idiot brother among his siblings, who didn't approve of his still being single, living way out in the middle of nowhere, not owning his own apartment, and, especially, not bringing home a fat paycheck.

"Listen, I can't stay long," Gilad said warningly, "so let's get to the point."

"Okay," Karin agreed, sitting down. "Hey, kids, keep it down, will you?" she shouted at them, which had zero effect. She turned back to the adults. "I thought we should all get together to talk about Aba and Ima."

"Listen, Karin, is there something happening we don't know about? Something new?" Gilad asked.

She hesitated. This was going to be a stretch, but so what? She could only say what she *thought* she knew. "I think Ima is seeing someone. And he's not Jewish. He's a Lithuanian."

There was a collective gasp and some titters, as well as a few disgruntled words of dismissal.

"Why do you say that?" Renee asked politely.

"Well, have you seen the video?"

Now they looked at her.

"Yes." Gilad nodded. "So what?"

The others, who didn't know what they were talking about, began to clamor.

"What video?"

"Do you have it on your phone?"

"Let's see it!"

Gilad took out his phone. They crowded around him, watching silently until the end.

"Wow," Amir breathed.

"I'm so proud of her!" Renee said.

Karin looked at them. "Didn't you see it?"

They looked puzzled, staring at her and at one another.

"The way he put his hand over hers!"

"And who is 'he,' exactly?" Amir challenged her.

"Dr. Darius Vidas, the person who is running the conference she's attending."

"The Lithuanian professor who invited her?" Gilad asked

neutrally. "But that was just a gesture of encouragement! It wasn't sexual."

"You can't believe such crap is real," Amir protested, looking around the room, shocked that none of the faces he saw seemed to share his skepticism. "Ima and a . . . Lithuanian?!" he scoffed. "She hates them."

"I don't think it's fair to call it hate," Renee insisted. "It's true she's been challenging them, but that started with your great-grandfather, and then your grandfather. It was never her idea."

"She hates the fucking bunch of them, those antisemitic shits!" Amir fumed.

"Well, apparently not all of them . . . ," Karin's husband, Solomon, said gently, a bit amused.

Amir stared at him hostilely. "Hey, almost-doctor, this is not your business, so butt out!" Amir said heatedly.

"Hey, bro, that's my husband you're shouting at," Karin said mildly, but her face tightened as she looked at her brother.

Just then, there was a loud thump and one of the kids started wailing. Both the mothers jumped up to see who it was. Renee brought back her weeping four-year-old, taking ice out of the bucket and wrapping it in a napkin to put on her bruise only for the child to grab it out of her hand and start licking it.

Karin laughed, then disappeared into the kitchen, bringing back a box of dark red cherry ice pops.

Everyone took one. Sitting there, their tongues turning bright red, the assembled family members cooled down.

"Listen, what if it *is* true?" Renee shrugged. "So what?"

"I can't get my head around it," Karin answered, and Amir nodded. "Besides, Aba wants her back."

"Oh, I heard." Gilad shook his head. "Bad timing."

"They love each other, I'm sure of it. We can't let her get involved with this goy!"

"Oh, my goodness, the very woke Karin said the 'g' word," Amir mocked.

"It's true. She'll be vilified and you all know it!"

"I hadn't thought about that aspect," Renee admitted. "But at any rate, it's nobody's business. Certainly not ours. You all know how much she's suffered over this past year. I, personally, would be glad if she found some happiness. You have no idea how much your father's betrayal has cost her emotionally."

"And I suppose you do?" Karin accused, feeling the usual jealousy over her mother's closeness to her sister-in-law.

"We've talked about it, yes. Listen, Karin, your mom obviously has problems talking openly to you and your brothers about this because, after all, the man who betrayed her is your father. Besides, you are all so busy, and I'm home most of the day. Your mom has so much respect for what you are doing with your lives, she never wants to burden you with her problems, that's all," she placated.

"She's lucky she has you, Renee," Gilad said generously, meaning it.

"So, wait, do *all* of you think we should just butt out, then? Is that it?" Amir fumed.

"I'd like to point out to you, that whatever we decide or don't decide, there is nothing much we can actually *do* about this," Gilad informed him, leaning back and eating a frankfurter he'd rolled up in a pita bread. "That is, if there is something more than collegial support in the gesture we just witnessed."

"It's not just that," Karin said.

They turned to stare at her.

"I called her, and she was someplace not on her itinerary. 'Rest and relaxation,' she told me. With him."

Amir shook his head, incensed. "You'll be sorry you're spreading these rumors, Karin."

"No, *you'll* be sorry you are refusing—as usual—to listen,

Amir. I just want Aba and Ima to get back together," Karin whispered. "And I think that whatever they've been through, there is still so much love left between them. Aba is devastated. He really is. He's kicking himself over what happened."

"He's a good man," Renee agreed.

Amir nodded bleakly. "Look, I'll admit what he did was unbelievable."

"He was an ass." Karin nodded. "How he behaved . . . it . . . was . . . I don't know, infantile."

"Idiotic," Amir agreed.

"Unforgivable?" Gilad said.

They stared at him.

"You know, of all of us, I was the most furious at him," Karin reminded them. "I wouldn't even let him come over to see Tal."

They nodded, agreeing.

"But he came to speak to me. Just walked in, without warning. I was pretty pissed, let me tell you. But after we sat down and spoke, even *I* couldn't help feeling sorry for him! He's so— broken." She shook her head sadly. "He totally knows how badly he screwed up, how much he hurt her—and himself! Actually, I'm really afraid for him if she doesn't take him back."

"What do you mean, Karin?" Renee asked, alarmed. "He wouldn't . . . *do* anything to himself . . . would he?"

She shook her head. "I don't think so. He's not the type. Not deliberately. But he's a surgeon and if his mind isn't one hundred percent focused . . ."

"It could be disastrous for more than just him," Solomon concluded.

Gilad and Amir exchanged glances. This was serious stuff.

"Have you spoken to him, Gilad?" Renee asked.

"Yes. In fact, *he* called *me*. But it was a short conversation. Meaningless. He didn't share anything special with me, and I didn't press him. I think he's only opened up to Karin."

"His pride and joy. My-daughter-the-doctor," Amir said cheerfully, with an edge of sarcasm that did nothing to hide his pique.

"Get over yourself, Amir." His sister shook her head. This had been going on for years. "Look, I think he needs help, and he certainly needs to take some time off from work until this whole thing settles down," Karin said.

"Did you suggest that to him?" Gilad asked.

"Duh!"

"So what was his answer?" Renee pressed.

"Hostile, dismissive. Pure Aba," Karin answered.

"Which is why you asked us all here," Gilad said softly. "For him, not for her."

She nodded.

"When is your mother coming home?" Renee asked.

"In three days, if something doesn't change," Karin said.

"What could change?" Solomon asked, at pains to respect boundaries as the outsider.

"She could stay there. With *him*. In Lithuania."

"No way in hell!" Amir shook his head.

"Or . . ." Renee hesitated. "She could bring him back here with her."

Everyone turned to stare at her in horror.

"It would ruin her reputation. The board of her foundation would be furious," Amir said, his voice tight with fury.

"Not to mention that the press will have a field day," Karin muttered. "And all her friends, and all the people she works with."

"And what about all the survivors' organizations?" Solomon added.

"That's true. They'll be outraged," Karin whispered, shaking her head.

"Survivors' organizations? What about *us*, her family? What about what people will say—our friends, our neighbors, after everything she's said over the years about that miserable country, those Holocaust distorters, scum of the earth. Which is why I can't believe she'd actually bring *him* back with her," Amir insisted.

"People sometimes surprise you, brother," Gilad interjected. "They do unexpected things when they've been hurt. And if you study the video, you'll see this person comes in to help her and support her at a very difficult moment. I think we should prepare ourselves to be by her side if she needs us, no matter what."

"You think we should be supportive of her and the Lithuanian? Are you mad?" Amir shouted.

"No. I think we should be helpful to our mother, whatever choice she decides to make."

"But, Gilad, this could seriously ruin her. It could destroy her credibility, the good work she's accomplished over the years. People can be so unforgiving," Renee said sadly.

"People!" Amir scoffed. "I will tell you all straight out: if she gets off that plane with him at Ben Gurion airport, I will never speak to her again!"

* * *

"Karolina, is that you?" Jurgis asked his sister.

She angled her phone a little differently to give him the full picture. "Like it?"

"Why would you dye your gorgeous blond hair black?" her brother asked, shocked. She was his pet, his beautiful little sister. He felt very protective of her.

"I got bored. Want to see my latest tattoo?" she offered.

"That depends where it is . . ."

"On my belly. It's totally awesome," she declared, starting to pull up her shirt.

"Wait, are you in a public place? I hear a lot of noise."

"I'm at work, but they've already seen it, so . . ."

"Let's just save it for another time," he said as some big shlub high-fived his sister. "Who was that?"

"Oh, a regular. He's into weight training."

"Looks scary."

"I can take care of myself." She made her fierce face.

His heart lurched. She looked around twelve. "Anyhow, are you thinking about coming home for a while?"

"Actually, no."

"Why not? It's been a while. I miss you. Daria misses you. Matas misses you."

"How is your little superhero? Still addicted to Spider-Man?"

"No. Now he wants to be a pilot."

"Well, that's safer, no? You won't have to worry he'll try to climb out the window . . . Look, I'd love to see you all. I miss you, too. But I'm not Paris Hilton. I'm saving my money for a trip to South America. I've got it all figured out. You see . . ."

"Listen, little sister, I'd love to hear all about it, but that's not why I'm calling. It's Dad. And it's serious."

"Wait a minute, keep your pants on . . . ," she muttered to someone off camera. "Go on. Is it Covid?"

"No, nothing like that. It's . . . he's gotten himself involved with a Jewish woman who is a Nazi hunter and hates Lithuania."

There was a beat. "Say that again?"

He did, slowly. Still, there was silence. "Karolina, are you still there?"

"I'm still here. Just speechless. What do you mean by 'gotten involved'?"

"They were doing this conference together, and this woman, Milia Gottstein-Lasker . . ."

"Oh, I remember her! She was all over the news when I was in elementary school. She hit someone . . ."

"Yes, exactly! Anyhow, Dad invited her to speak at his conference . . ."

"Why would he do that?"

"I don't know, and that's not the point."

"Which is?"

"That during this conference, she said some horrible things about partisans being murderers, and it went viral, and Dad was doing her translating. And . . ."

"What?"

"He put his hand over hers."

"And . . . ?"

"Someone posted another video of them in Nida."

"Having sex on the beach?"

"Don't be ridiculous."

"No, you're the one being ridiculous. So he is hosting her, showing her the country. And if he's getting something on the side, way to go, Dad!" She chuckled.

"Be serious! When my boss saw the first video, he almost fired me, and I'm just the son! And it's possible the university might fire Dad, at least Mom thinks so . . ."

"Right, like she's suddenly worried about him."

"She thinks his publisher could shut him down, too."

"I'm sure they were only telling the truth."

He was flabbergasted. "What do you *mean*?!"

"That Jewish woman and Dad, at that conference. I did a paper in high school about the partisans. Got some pretty horrible information off the internet . . . Actually, it's one of the reasons I moved to Paris."

"Oh, and I'm sure the Eiffel Tower and the clothes had nothing to do with it," he mocked.

"Well, maybe a little," she said, grinning. Then she got serious. "Look, don't you ever wonder about what happened during the war? All those Jewish families that disappeared?"

"It was the Nazis. It happened all over Europe. In your precious Paris also."

"I know that. But their neighbors didn't shoot them. And the French underground didn't target Jews; they targeted Nazis, not like our 'partisans.'"

"Don't tell me you're becoming a Communist!"

"What does what I'm saying have to do with Communists?"

"Only our enemies try to bring us down by spreading these lies. Who told you these things?"

She hesitated. "I have many friends, some of them are Communists, and some are Jews, so what? It doesn't make what they are saying lies."

"Okay, listen, I don't care," he lied. He cared intensely, but he couldn't let that sidetrack this conversation. "I just think our dad is getting a little too friendly with this Jewish woman."

"Romantically, you mean? Now this is *really* getting interesting. You don't have a problem with that, Jurgis, do you? I mean, because she's a Jew?"

"Actually, I do. And I'm not alone. Our mom, the university, his publishing house . . ."

"Screw them all! It's none of their business," she fumed, waving her hand angrily at a man who was shouting at her. "It's my boss. I'm going outside."

The screen went blurry. She took out a cigarette and lit it, taking the smoke deeply into her lungs, then exhaling slowly, savoring the forbidden pleasure. "So, what do you think *I* can do about it, anyhow?" she asked him.

"Come back home for a few days. Try talking some sense into Dad. Tell him to distance himself, to do a podcast and renounce what was said about the partisans. I can make sure it goes viral. He'll listen to you."

"Why should he?"

"Why should he what?"

"Renounce what she said. Or listen to me if I tell him to do it?"

"Because, as I just explained, he is going to get himself in terrible trouble with everyone who employs and supports him. He's going to ruin his reputation and get fired. And yes, I think he'll listen if it's coming from you. Especially if you fly over and do it in person. Don't pretend you don't know how much he misses you, his little princess. And stop shaking your head acting surprised. Just admit it."

"Okay, I admit it. So what? He's not going to do something that important just for my sake."

"You just don't get it! It's for his *own* sake! They will blackball him everywhere if he keeps this up. And blackball me!"

"Ah, so now the truth comes out! It's your own skin you are worried about! Admit it!"

"So what if I am? Is that a crime? I have a family to think about. And I've worked really hard to get where I am. But that doesn't mean I'm not right. Besides, he has much more to lose than I do. I'm still young, I could leave the country, start over. But what's *he* going to do? Without the backing of his department and the university, no one will hire him. And his publisher can easily do to him what Rūta Vanagaitė's did to her, and she was a much more popular writer than he is."

"I heard about that. The bastards. Listen, I hear you, but honestly, I don't think I can help. He won't listen to me. He loves me, but he doesn't respect my choices. Have you called Domantas?"

"Yes, but he isn't interested in getting involved."

"You mean he's having too much fun with his Swedish girlfriend."

"No, listen, he's on scholarship. He's teaching. He really can't just pick up and leave."

"Oh, but I can because I'm just some bimbo working in a bar at some low-paying job, right?" she huffed. "Not like the rest of you . . ."

"What will it hurt to come back? See what's going on? You owe him that. After all the money he's sent you . . ."

There was a beat. "He told you about that?"

"No, it was just a guess. Thanks for confirming."

"I'm going to pay him back. It's just until I get on my feet . . . Anyway, it would be a waste of time. He won't listen to me."

"Why do you say that?"

"Because I've asked him a million times to visit me in Paris, and he just won't."

This was the first he'd heard about it. "Maybe he thinks that if he stays away, you'll get lonely and come home."

"Maybe."

"So?"

"So . . . what? Listen, I want to help, but even if I had the cash for the flight, which I don't . . ."

"I'll send you a ticket."

"Round trip?"

"Round trip. And you can always find another job."

She threw down her cigarette and squashed it brutally. Truth was, she was getting pretty sick and tired of her current boss and his wandering hands.

"When?"

"Your flight leaves tomorrow morning."

She took off her apron and threw it into the alleyway. "See you soon, brother."

TWENTY-EIGHT

THEY SAT AROUND a large conference table in a room decorated with Lithuanian flags and portraits of former Algirdas University presidents. It was a big table and there were only five of them, but still, the room seemed crowded. A secretary discreetly knocked on the door.

"Come in," called out the head of the university's political and social history department, a rotund, balding native of Kaunas who was hosting this meeting.

A woman of indeterminate age, dressed in a sharp blue suit with a skirt just a bit too short, entered, bringing in a tray of doughnuts, coffee, tea, and water.

"Thank you, thank you," said the broad-shouldered éminence grise who represented the International Commission for the Evaluation of the Crimes of the Nazi and Soviet Occupation Regimes in Lithuania (recently and blessedly shortened to Commission for Historical Truth), and called the Red-Brown Commission by its (mostly Jewish) detractors. He plucked nervously at his graying mustache and goatee, his tone unmistakably impatient. Finally, he waved his hand, shooing the secretary out of the room.

"There is no need to be rude!" admonished the petite brunette in her late fifties representing the Genocide and Resistance Research Center.

She was wearing too much red lipstick and fidgeting like a game show contestant, he thought, watching her adjust her polyester suit jacket over her ample breasts. Too bad her boss wasn't able to come. A prolific and respected scholar who had just published the definitive history text about the Jewish Holocaust in Lithuania (well, not quite accepted by everyone as definitive; he'd left out some material about the murder of the Jews in some areas, and some fanatics were unhappy about that and the fact that he'd addressed a patriotic rally celebrating the seventy-ninth anniversary of Hitler's invasion flanked by large posters of Jonas Noreika and Kazys Škirpa). While the Commission had sponsored the work, it had been, alas, unhappily unable to give it a full and complete endorsement.

He looked down at her superciliously. "I don't think you should be giving any advice," he told her curtly. "Considering."

The brunette gave him a withering look.

The two organizations had not been on the best of terms lately for another reason, the Department Head knew. Silvia Foti was to blame. Ever since she'd published her book, *The Nazi's Granddaughter*, exposing Lithuanian partisan hero Jonas Noreika for being a Nazi collaborator and mass murderer of Jews, the two had been bickering publicly, to the humiliation of the government that was funding them both. The International Commission was aghast at the Research Center for promoting the ridiculous idea that not only didn't Noreika know about the killing of Jews in the area of which he had total control—his home had, after all, been across the street from the synagogue where Jews were held captive for weeks without food or water and died en masse!—but that he had actually *aided* Jews to escape death!

"Listen, we need to put aside our differences and work together on this. It is in all our interests," the woman from the Genocide Museum interjected. She had short, blond hair and a long-suffering face. Her museum had recently been forced to change its name to the very unmellifluous Museum of Occupations and Freedom Fights. She held the Research Center responsible, since it was they who had very publicly pointed out that the museum really didn't house any exhibits of genocide victims, i.e., the Jews, but rather those of Lithuanian victims of Soviet oppression, which, as much as many disgruntled Lithuanians wanted to believe, was not the same at all. No one, after all, had mass murdered Lithuanians because they were Lithuanians.

"Look, as rare and delightful as it is to spend time with all of you, might I suggest we proceed? We are, after all, in a bit of a rush," interjected the man from the Ministry of Foreign Affairs, who, while noticeably small, was athletically trim with a full head of hair, a relative youngster compared to the others. He wore a suave, expensive suit, obviously not locally made because it fit him perfectly.

The others turned to him resentfully, not only disapproving of his outfit, which made them feel shabby and outclassed, but his youth and superior tone, which underlined the barely acknowledged and highly unpleasant truth that he, as representative of the government, held all the cards at the moment.

"Certainly," the Department Head agreed, forcing an affable smile to crease the layers of fat on his round face. "Who would like to begin?"

"Why don't we play the video first?" the blonde from the Museum suggested.

They all nodded in agreement. The Department Head shut off the lights and adjusted the projector.

They sat silently, shifting uncomfortably in their chairs as they listened to Milia Gottstein-Lasker describe the events that took place in Raseiniai in 1941. When the disruptions began, the shouting from the audience, the students and teachers getting up and leaving, the principal's ineffectual attempts to bring order, they sat up straight in their seats until the finale, which was, as far as they were concerned, the shocking movement of Dr. Darius Vidas to the podium where he took the place of the absconding translator—a woman they all admired—and put his hand over Milia Gottstein-Lasker's.

"Okay, I think we've all seen enough," the suave little man from the Ministry declared. "Put the lights back on."

They all blinked.

The broad-shouldered éminence grise of the newly coined Commission for Historical Truth rose from his chair. He seemed filled with nervous energy. "Who," he pointed at the screen, "is responsible for this travesty?" His eyes scanned the room accusingly, finally focusing on the Department Head, who squirmed uncomfortably in the too-small armchair.

"I think that you misunderstand, my friend," the Department Head said politely. "We are not in the habit of censoring our professors. But I must say, I am as shocked as the rest of you at this terrible situation. As far as I understood it, Professor Vidas was arranging an EU conference on forgiveness and reconciliation concerning the Holocaust."

"Does that sound very forgiving and reconciling to you?" the brunette from the Research Center accused.

The blonde of the newly, unfortunately named Museum of Occupations and Freedom Fights nodded in agreement.

"I expect your Professor Vidas probably had good intentions," the éminence grise conceded grudgingly, "but he has failed, and caused a national scandal. This video—as the young people are fond of saying—has 'gone viral.' It has been seen over fifty thousand times!"

They all looked appalled.

"But only in Lithuania," the brunette pointed out. "Still, it is responsible for corrupting the minds of people who watch such things, our most important and vulnerable citizens: our youth, our future generations," she said fiercely, like an outraged middle school teacher whose students have left obscene words on her blackboard.

"Yes, yes, of course," the Ministry's man said impatiently. "But that's water under the bridge. What we all must focus on now is the upcoming conference in Vilnius where these two are to speak. I understand the entire foreign and local press have been invited?"

"That is standard for EU conferences," the Department Head told him apologetically. "The university had nothing to do with the invitations."

The Ministry man turned on him. "Is it also standard for *no one* to have vetted their speeches?"

"What?!" the blonde said, outraged.

"That was an unfortunate oversight," the Department Head admitted sheepishly. "I was told that it was a precondition to Gottstein-Lasker's agreement to participate."

"Well, her participation is obviously out of the question now," the éminence grise thundered, slapping the table so emphatically that their coffee, tea, and soft drinks surged dangerously close to the edge of their cups. "We'll just announce it's been canceled."

"Not so easy," the Ministry man sniffed, rubbing some dust off his gleaming Swiss watch. "Since all of you have allowed it to get to this point, we can't just cancel at the last minute. The press will want to know why. And then of course, there is the EU to be considered, who funded this whole program." He looked around the room. "I hope all of you have come to finally understand the extreme delicacy of this matter. Might I also add that our vice minister has just met with the representative of the American Jewish Committee to discuss preserving Holocaust memory in Lithuania?" His brows arched meaningfully.

They looked sullenly into their drinks.

"I don't care!" the brunette suddenly burst out, while the blonde watched her cautiously. "This is now a matter of Lithuania's reputation worldwide! We can't just allow this Gottstein-Lasker woman, a well-known enemy of Lithuania . . ."

". . . public enemy number two," the éminence grise of the Commission added helpfully, happy to agree.

". . . who should *never* have been invited here in the first place, to spout any more lies about our partisans to the entire world! It's bad enough she's confused our children!"

"I'm in complete agreement. This time," the blonde said meaningfully, and they could all see it cost her.

"As am I," muttered the Department Head.

"Oh, my, how very convenient," scoffed the Ministry man, "that *now* we are all in complete agreement just when—as I think I've already explained—it's *impossible*." He pointed an accusing finger at them. "We are having this meeting because our government believes that it is *your* responsibility to come up with some viable alternatives. Otherwise, I have been authorized to tell you that our government is looking into cutting the budgets of all your institutions, whose sole reason for existence is to guard the precious reputation of our fatherland and the heroes who sacrificed their lives to win our independence from those who invaded and enslaved our people. Our leader holds you *all* responsible for this fiasco. Do I make myself clear?"

Everyone except the Department Head, who really *had* been in a position to do more, felt badly used, as well as a bit frightened. Budget cuts were the kiss of death for all the fun things their dreary jobs afforded, and goodness knows there were few enough perks as it was.

"We need to get in touch with this Vidas. To make it clear to him that he must renounce everything that was said in Raseiniai and put it right. He must openly oppose Gottstein-Lasker. He must say that as a historian, he has checked out what she said, and that it is all lies," the brunette of the Research Center demanded.

"That seems to be the standard way the Research Center handles all Jewish accusations these days," the éminence grise said pointedly, enjoying her furious blush. "But yes, by all means. I can't see another way out."

"Wait, are you saying that *you* think what Gottstein-Lasker said is true?" the brunette challenged him.

"I haven't had sufficient time to look into it," he demurred. "So I can't be sure."

"Exactly." The blonde nodded, finally agreeing with the Commission on something. "In the meantime, it is our national pride that is at stake. The honor of our patriots and heroes. But how can we ensure he cooperates?"

At this juncture, everyone turned to the Department Head.

He shifted uneasily, his florid face turning a shade of purple. "I have investigated. Vidas doesn't have tenure. If he doesn't cooperate, he will have to find a new job."

"I'm sure he's already thought about that," the little man from the Ministry said slowly, unimpressed. "We need something more."

The éminence grise smiled. "Just yesterday I had dinner with my good friend, who is a senior editor at Vidas's publishing house. We even watched the video together. He found it quite disturbing."

"Disturbing? How disturbing? Disturbing enough to do to him what Alma Littera did to Rūta Vanagaitė? Recall all his books and cut all ties?" the Ministry man wanted to know.

"If not, I think I can help," the Department Head interjected. "We here at the university have an important relationship with his publishing house's textbook division. It is very lucrative," he said eagerly, viewing a blessed light at the end of this tunnel. "But

I'm sure it won't come to that. I'm sure Vidas can be made to see reason."

"That's him. But what about *her?* How can we stop *her* from speaking?" the brunette asked.

"We can't. However, *he* can," the little man who held their paychecks said smoothly. "He invited her. Surely, it is up to him to withdraw the invitation. And when she doesn't show up, everyone will blame her, not us."

"Yes! Of course. There are, after all, many legitimate reasons." The Department Head nodded ingratiatingly.

"Well, then, we must leave it to you, Professor," the éminence grise said, rising from his chair. The others followed suit. "I, from my end, will contact my friend at the publishing house."

"I think I can also help," the brunette suddenly offered, not to be outdone. "My husband is the editor of the newspaper where Vidas's son Jurgis works and he has already spoken to the boy. I'm sure Jurgis will speak to his father. The boy has a young family, and this job is very important to him."

"Ah, the beginning of his career." The little man smiled, looking at her admiringly. "Excellent! So here we are, all pulling together for our beloved homeland. Truly inspiring!" he said with a smile that no one believed. "You have two days. Don't disappoint our government."

"We wouldn't dream of it," the Department Head murmured, watching as the room emptied at last.

*   *   *

They'd found accommodations just a few kilometers outside the city in Viešvėnai, a hotel called Lavender Inn, *"a cozy seven-room, family-run guest house focused on quality relaxation and service,"* where guests were urged not to miss touching the grasshopper in the center of the lawn for luck.

Neither were in the mood for touching grasshoppers.

It had been a hellish night, both of them locked in their rooms, barely speaking.

They met for breakfast, sitting outside. It was very pretty there. Like everywhere else in the Lithuanian countryside. The sky was blue. The grass was green. The ferns and birches swayed in a gentle breeze and a nearby brook gurgled and splashed. Unfortunately, none of it was enough to distract them.

"We don't have to go," Darius told her. "Not if you don't want to. I'll understand."

She looked at him wearily, her eyes puffy and red as she poked listlessly at her breakfast plate of herring and fruit—the only things she could safely eat in a place redolent with the smell of bacon. "Sure, why not? It can't get any worse, can it?"

He wasn't sure about that.

"I've never even met this person myself. So it's a bit of a risk."

"Look, I've given it some thought and I think it's important we talk to your cousin—"

"—once or twice removed!" he emphasized, distancing himself.

"Whatever. He lives right here. Even though he was born after all this happened, his family lived here. They must have spoken to him about their lives, about what happened here. And he lives here now. He must have neighbors, friends, who might be able to tell us things we don't know that have been passed down to them, or that they witnessed."

"What things, exactly?"

"Stories about the participation of the locals, whether they resisted or tried to help their Jewish neighbors. You can't imagine how important that is to me. To all Jews. Look, the most important, vital thing we Jews want from Lithuanians today is simply for them to change the narrative. To stop disseminating the lie that it was the Nazis and 'some criminal elements' who killed almost every Jew in your country. To change your textbooks and history books and what you teach your children. To let this generation learn the truth. And so yes, I would like to talk to your cousin, one of those descended from such 'ordinary people' who had a house in Telzh when all this was going on. I'd like to hear what narrative has been passed down to him from his family."

He nodded, afraid of what the answer would be. But also curious. "Okay, but only if you're sure."

She held out her hand to him. "Let's risk it, Darius. He could prove things are much better than we think they are, at least among some people. He could be the link between your family and mine."

He twined his fingers through hers. Now he was even more nervous. A link? Or the detonation of an old enemy bomb lying in wait for them?

On the phone, his cousin had sounded friendly, affable, certainly more coherent than Emilija. And he wasn't really a native of the area. He, like Emilija and Daiva, had grown up in the big city, Kaunas. He wasn't clear about who had owned the farm Marijus had inherited and when they had left.

It was a very short drive from the hotel. "I think we're here," he said, spying an old wooden barn. A few hundred meters farther down the road was an equally old wooden house plastered with aluminum siding and plastic windows, a hybrid monster. The only nice thing about it was the apple orchard in front of it, now in late bloom. The fragrance was enchanting.

Darius parked, then came around to open the door for her, a gentlemanly gesture revealing just how nervous he was. He felt like he was walking on glass and any moment the fragile peace between them could shatter.

"I won't understand what he says. Please remember to translate."

"Of course."

He let her walk ahead, hurrying to catch up as she rang the doorbell. A man in his early seventies or late sixties opened the door. He wore jeans and a kind of sleeveless undershirt Americans were fond of labeling a "wifebeater." He was not at all what she had been expecting, which was a wizened farmer in spattered overalls and galoshes.

The man faced her, examining her with wordless curiosity.

Darius got in front of her, extending his hand in greeting. "Cousin Marijus? It's Darius Vidas. We spoke on the phone?"

His indifferent stare suddenly focused. "Ah, Cousin Darius!" He bowed. "An honor to meet you, the famous professor," he said enthusiastically. Darius allowed himself to be pulled in for a manly hug.

"And this is my friend and colleague, Milia," Darius introduced her, deliberately leaving out her last name.

What did that mean? she wondered, feeling the old man's look linger over her for more time than was necessary or polite.

"Come in, come in," he said suddenly, all smiles, his arms open wide.

The house was clean, but almost bare, with a cheap, serviceable IKEA table covered in an ugly brown and purple oilcloth and a few simple metal chairs. The floor, she saw, was covered in old-fashioned linoleum, frayed at the corners, and along the wall was a sink and stove. The only object of note was an elaborate china cabinet filled with porcelain and silver objects. It stood out with grating incongruity, an alien from another planet. Milia couldn't help staring.

Darius also couldn't help noticing it, but glanced away nervously.

"Do you live here alone?" Darius asked him, trying to be friendly.

He nodded, making a dismissive gesture with both hands. "Not everyone is smart enough to see the benefits of country life.

The rent my wife pays in Kaunas! Thrown-out money! But it's her choice. She's still working, so I let her pay for it. Maybe when she retires . . ." He shrugged, indicating it was all the same to him.

"Ask him if it isn't lonely," Milia said.

Darius asked. Marijus shook his head. "I'm fine. It's fine. I'm retired, you know. I have simple needs. I work in my garden. Pick fruits. Live off my pension. I don't like the big city: the noise, the traffic . . . and the prices. Oh ho! They rob you blind! So I came here. This is my inheritance from my mother's sister, who was your grandfather's niece," he told Darius. "Her children all went to live in America, so she left it to me, out of spite." He cackled. "Her children in America aren't angry. This is of no use to them, and they wouldn't get much by selling the place," he rushed to explain, as if accusations had been lodged against him. "Besides, they are all rich Americans now. They even sometimes send me American dollars. To fix it up, they say. Did you see the aluminum siding? The new windows? And the floors, the best, most modern materials," he bragged. "When they come to visit, they won't be ashamed of the old place." He chattered on, seemingly unhappy with any silences.

Milia looked around. There was something about the place and this Marijus that made goose bumps rise on her arms. She couldn't exactly put her finger on it. Perhaps it was the insolent way he'd looked her up and down, focusing on her breasts. Or the time it had taken him to invite them inside. Or the fact that he still hadn't offered them any refreshments. Or maybe, just maybe, it was that china closet.

Either Darius said something to him, or his manners suddenly sprang to life, because he was now bustling about, setting the table with blue cups and saucers and a plate of store-bought cookies, and a bowl full of apples.

"Tell him not to go to any trouble," she said politely.

"Don't worry, he doesn't appear to be the type who bends over backward for guests," Darius said dryly.

The coffee was hot, the cream was sweet. She held the cup in both hands, feeling its warmth. For some reason, even though it was quite warm outside, her hands were freezing.

Marijus talked nonstop.

"He's telling us about his father's family . . ."

"It's through his mother he's related to you, right?"

"Yes. His mother was my grandfather's niece, as was the woman who left him this place. Apparently, his father and grandparents and uncles and aunts and cousins were the ones who used to live in this house. His grandfather owned many hectares of land. In 1941, before the Nazi invasion, the Communists confiscated everything. They shot the animals, smashed the beehives, stole the land. And one day, Soviet soldiers showed up and took his grandparents, his aunts and uncles and deported them to Siberia."

"But not his father, your aunt's husband?"

"He was a student in Warsaw who'd just gotten married. None of his family ever returned."

"What a heartbreaking story! Why did the Soviets deport them?" she asked, filled with sympathy.

"He says that he thinks it was because they stole his land and didn't want any trouble about it, but mostly it was because his grandfather had dealings with the Jews, who put his name on the deportation list."

"Which Jews?" she asked.

Darius asked him. He was evasive. "He doesn't know. He says all the Jews were Bolsheviks who supported the Russians and were happy to help them take over Lithuania."

Her spine stiffened. "Ask him if he knows that the Jews were also deported by the Soviets. Thousands of them also never returned. But for them, it turned out to be a blessing, because those who remained, got murdered by 'partisans'."

"I can't tell him that. He'll just deny it," Darius sighed.

"Then ask him what the family told him about what happened to the Jews in Telzh."

He asked. "He says his aunt told him everyone knew that the Jews were going to be punished for helping the Soviets, and for drawing up the deportation lists." He hesitated. "And also for the matzah."

"The matzah?"

"You don't want to hear this, Milia! It's disgusting!"

"No, I do. Tell me," she insisted.

"He says the Jews put blood in the matzah, the way the ancient Hebrews put lamb's blood on their doorposts to scare away the Angel of Death. So they put the blood of Lithuanian 'lambs,' children, into their matzah. They'd kidnap children and roll them down the hill in a barrel to mix the blood well, then they slit the child's throat and drain its blood to use."

She bit her lip, then tasted something bitter and metallic in her mouth. The old blood libel from the Middle Ages. Nothing had changed here in Europe. The ignorance was appalling. She thought of just leaving, but something stopped her. Maybe because it was Darius's family. Or maybe, just maybe, because she never gave up hope that you could educate people out of their determined ignorance.

"Ask him if he knows that Jewish law, the Torah, forbids Jews to eat blood of any kind. Even the blood of animals. Animal flesh has to be soaked and salted for hours before Jews can cook it and eat it."

Darius listened to her. He, too, had been told the story of the blood and the Passover matzah when he was a child. It was commonplace among Lithuanians. But this was the first he had heard about Jews being forbidden by their religion to eat blood. It made the lie all the more egregious. He tried to imagine the ignorant imbecile who had cooked up the story in the first place.

"What did he say?" Milia asked.

"He says he heard I was a professor, so what I say must be true. But everyone he knows believes this story."

"Ask him again what the family told him about what happened to the Jews."

"It was before he was born, he says, but what they did say was that among the Jews of Telzh there were many Bolsheviks who wanted to help the Russians return, and who fought against the partisans. To prevent the Russians coming back, the townspeople gathered all the Bolshevik Jews together in town and gave them a choice: they could follow the Russian army and leave, or they could stay here in Telzh under guard. The ones that chose to stay were brought pots of beef stew and warm blankets by the townspeople, who wanted to help them. But in the end, most of them ran away, too. He doesn't know where they went. He thinks maybe to America."

"In 1941? In the middle of World War Two?!" she scoffed.

She saw Marijus shrug.

"Ask him what else he's heard."

Now there was a long pause as Marijus looked hostilely at both Darius and Milia.

"His aunt told him that some of the neighbors tried to save the women and children, especially the young girls. They took them in and hid them, but the Germans had spies and found out. People became afraid they would be killed for hiding the Jews, so they turned them over."

"Ask him what happened to those girls."

She saw Marijus shrug, then get up from the table and start cleaning off the dishes, putting them into the sink.

"Ask him again what he heard happened to the Jews of Telzh." Her tone had grown more insistent.

"He says he told you already."

"Ask him again," she insisted stonily.

This time, she noticed, Marijus was talking longer, gesticulating. He dried his hands and went into the bedroom, bringing back a photo album.

"He says these are the photos his aunt left behind. Some of them are from the war."

Marijus placed the old album on the table. With an uncomfortable feeling in his gut, Darius sat down, listening to the old man as he turned the pages and explained the photos. Mostly, it was relatives long dead, people he had never met or heard of, sitting on grass surrounded by smiling children. But one seemed different. It was a group photo of about fifty people who sat in five rows for a group portrait, all dressed in holiday finery. He asked his cousin for an explanation.

But when he heard it, Darius's face changed colors.

"What?"

"Wait." He lifted the photo carefully out of the album and turned it over.

It was dated June 1941.

"I think we should go," he said, putting back the photo and getting up.

"Why . . . ? What . . . ?"

"It's a photo of the celebrations that were held here, he says. And the photo is dated June 1941."

They looked at each other in horror. Right after the killings.

"He says I should be very proud."

"Of what?"

Reluctantly, he took the album and pointed to the photo. "That is Jonas Noreika, and there is . . . my grandfather." They were shaking hands, smiling at the camera, surrounded by people enjoying a moment of rare joy in the middle of the war. She felt sick.

"Noreika was responsible for the murder of the Jews in this

entire province," she said softly. "He gave the orders. He even prepared the armbands and gave them out. And he is shaking hands with your grandfather . . ."

It was undeniable. Yes. They were shaking hands. And all around them, people were celebrating, smiling, happy.

"They weren't celebrating the murder of the Jews," Marijus suddenly interjected out of nowhere. "They were just happy the Communists had fled. The Germans were good to the people, not like the Russians, my parents told me."

Darius turned to him slowly. "I thought you said you were told the Jews ran away? And the rest lived in comfort, under protection?"

For a moment, Marijus actually seemed speechless. "I have a neighbor here who lives with her mother, a very old woman who is nearly blind. Her mother told me that one day when she was a child playing in the forest she saw them dig the pits, then throw in the Jewish children. She says she cried and still has nightmares. She said her mother wanted to steal away some of the children and hide them, but her father was afraid of the partisan armbanders. They carried machine guns and killed whomever they didn't like, just like that. But who can believe such a crazy story! She has obviously lost her marbles. Anyway, why should we talk about the Jews? Let's talk about my cousin, the professor and famous author! We in the family are so proud of you, Darius! And your grandfather, he was also a hero! A partisan, the mayor of a town, my mother told me. And here you come to see your old cousin. Such an honor! Come, let's celebrate!"

Marijus returned with a bottle of vodka and some glasses.

With a big smile, he poured three glasses: "*Į sveikata!*" he said, downing his in one gulp.

"L'chaim," Milia murmured, raising her glass to him but not touching a drop.

Darius froze.

Marijus stared at her for a few moments, then refilled his glass immediately, polishing it off, pouring himself a third.

"What country is she from? What language is that?" Marijus asked Darius.

"It's Hebrew. She's from Israel. What she said means 'to life.'"

"He asks me if you are a Jew," Darius told her.

She nodded, taking out the little gold Jewish star she wore around her neck and showing it to Marijus, studying his reaction.

Now there was a long pause as Marijus looked from Darius to Milia. He was no longer the smiling host, the proud "cousin."

"Ask him again what happened to the young Jewish girls."

Darius asked him. Instead of answering, he poured himself another shot of vodka, downing it defiantly. He pushed himself up unsteadily from the table, putting his hand over his heart and began to sing:

"Lithuania, our Fatherland,
You are the land of heroes
From the past may your sons
Draw the strength . . ."

When he finished, she saw him shrug, turning his back and walking to the sink where he began washing the dishes. It was clear this meeting was coming to an end.

Darius looked at Milia, rolling his eyes. "Well, we'll be going now, Cousin, thank you," Darius called.

"Ask him where he got the china closet and all the porcelain and silver," Milia insisted.

Darius lowered his head, then asked the question.

Marijus dried his hands and walked over, grasping Darius by the shoulder and whispering something in his ear with a smile.

Darius listened, then suddenly—rudely—shook him off. "Come, we're leaving," Darius told her.

She got up hurriedly, following, avoiding Marijus. They went swiftly back to the car. But just as they were about to get in and drive away, they saw Marijus coming toward them, calling Darius's name.

"You wait in the car," Darius told her, heading to meet his cousin. She watched them as they spoke, rather heatedly it seemed to her, although in the end Darius simply nodded silently, his head bent, looking at the ground. Then they each turned their own way, parting without a handshake or a backward glance.

Darius climbed in beside her, slamming the door and staring at the steering wheel. When he finally started the engine, he backed out into the road with unseemly haste bordering on recklessness.

"Hey, slow down! What happened just now?"

"You don't need to know." She saw his jaw flex in fury.

"I'm a big girl, Darius. Don't keep me guessing."

"He was disgusting. He wouldn't answer the question about the china closet, but I guess we both know where it's from, don't we? Instead, he asked me . . . what he wanted to know . . . was exactly what we do in bed together—'like the people here did with the young Jewish girls.'"

She felt sucker punched and showed it.

"I shouldn't have told you."

"No, I asked."

"But he did say something else that might be useful, and that's what he came out to tell me right before we left. It's about another relative of mine, Ramunos Jonaitis, the black sheep of our family, or so my mother called him. Marijus called him a 'Jew-lover, son of Jew-lovers.' He suggested we should go visit him if we were so curious about what happened to the Jews during the war and the people who helped them."

"Where does this Ramunos live?"

"He said he thought it was in Karalgiris, which is about an hour and a half away."

"Don't we need to get back to Vilnius for the final program?"

"It won't really take us out of our way. And I'm curious to see this relative of mine and to find out why he is on the outs with our family."

"Why did your charming cousin Marijus call him a Jew-lover?"

He shrugged. "That's something else I'd like to find out."

She took a deep breath. "I wasn't going to say anything, but I guess there will never be a good time to tell you this."

He glanced at her anxiously.

"Last night, I heard back from Yad Vashem. They say they searched their database and they are quite certain that the family you are looking for, the Kenskys . . ."

Emil, Beyle, Itele, Henokh, Ruchele, he thought, feeling almost as if he knew them; as if he had held little Ruchele in his arms, had seen Itele and Henokh dressed in jeans and sweatshirts, like American kids, and their two smiling, prosperous parents, Emil and Beyle. Of course, they would all be so much older now, parents of children themselves, Emil and Beyle would be portly and gray, grandparents, even great-grandparents, as they stood onstage to thank his family and talk about their good lives in Denver, lives made possible because his grandfather had been a Righteous gentile who had had the courage to persist in being a man when the world had turned into beasts.

". . . they never survived the war. They were all killed in J—, in July 1941."

He did not turn his head, unable to look her in the eye. He felt breathless, gripping the steering wheel as if it were a cane to lean on and he was suddenly crippled. So it had all been a lie, from beginning to end. And the necklace? Not a gift given in gratitude from the mother and father of small children whose lives had been saved, but simply stolen loot or worse, bribes for which false promises had been made, trust betrayed. He felt needles prick his eyes as he held back tears as something he cherished died inside him. Optimism? A connection to righteousness, goodness, generosity? His family, like all the others, had taken part in these horrendous crimes. He was their offspring, no different, no better than the rest of his countrymen. It broke his heart.

"I . . . am . . . so . . ." He searched for the word, the one word that would express more than any other how he felt at this moment. "Ashamed," he said.

"Darius, it isn't fair to blame yourself, or even your parents. None of you took part in these things. You honestly didn't know."

That was true. Perhaps that was the real reason his country was so dead set on maintaining its ignorance; so determined to ferociously guard the reputations of those "partisan" Nazi collaborators they had put up on pedestals for young people to worship and imitate. For the minute they let the truth seep out, shame would overwhelm the nation. The truth would sweep over them like a tsunami of filth, washing away the dams they had so carefully constructed over the years with their self-serving genocide research, and genocide commissions, and genocide museums, all of them publicly funded attempts to deny, obfuscate, and bury the ugly truth that lay like a poisonous toxin beneath their very soil, sending up its fumes, which were little by little destroying any hope for a good and prosperous future for their children and their country. One by one, their children were drifting off, finding other places in the world in which to live their lives, as Karolina and Domantas had done; places with more opportunities; places where they could plant their hopes without having to dig through tangled corpses. Places where the dead were buried one by one, with prayers and flowers and granite markers.

"But Yad Vashem has found one of the Kensky relatives.

The daughter of Emil Kensky's brother Hirschl, Esther. She was the one who filled out the Page of Testimony. Apparently, her father escaped through the Soviet Union and then made his way to America. I have a phone number and an address for her."

"Really?! Thank you. Thank you so much."

Milia reached for his hand. It was damp with tears.

* * *

Julius sat beneath an umbrella at his favorite beach, Nachsholim. It was one of those perfect June days—before the summer sun roasted everything beneath it, and the humidity made life a constant sauna.

He had taken a leave of absence from the hospital, put off non-threatening scheduled surgeries, and found top-notch replacements for the rest. His patients were not happy—and that was putting it mildly. But as he explained to the hospital administrators, in his present state of unrest and melancholy, it was dangerous for everyone involved, including the hospital, for him to keep working. He needed to get his focus back. Reluctantly, they agreed. Did they have a choice? Insurance premiums were high enough as it was, and if something went wrong after they'd been warned . . . Besides, there was no way he was going to risk his patients' well-being for someone's financial bottom line, or his own ego.

He lay back, his straw hat over his eyes, listening to the waves breaking against the shore, filled with a sense of relief. Perhaps that's all it had ever been, he considered, overwork and tension. Perhaps all he had really wanted or needed was a vacation, not a new life and certainly not a new partner.

He and Haviva had ended it in the worst possible way. She was even threatening to sue him for breach of promise. He chuckled to himself. Like she was some pregnant eighteen-year-old left at the altar! What a stupid woman she was! He had struggled to find some excuse for his infatuation, some mitigating circumstance that would have softened the brutal self-assessment with which he was now saddled. Alas, he simply couldn't. It was as if he had been taken over by a body snatcher from Mars, all his good sense drained, his lower body parts running the show.

He was more than a little embarrassed. If it had just been about sex, then why not one of those nubile nursing students in their twenties? Why a woman his own age, for goodness' sake? What a waste. What a fool.

A mosquito, buzzing in his ear, landed on his naked chest. He tried to slap it away with an open hand and the blows felt like self-flagellation.

How could he expect Milia to forgive him when he couldn't forgive himself? At least he had patched up his relationship with his kids. Amir had been annoyed, but as usual his self-preoccupation had luckily prevented him from getting too involved in the first place. He had been easy to placate. Gilad had been the kindest. That, too, was no surprise. He was a professional and his empathy was sincere as well as informed. Karin, as expected, had been all fire and ice. The wisest thing he had done in all of this was confiding in her first and getting not only her grudging forgiveness, but also her womanly sympathy. She was his mainstay now, the one who was going to be the most help in turning Milia around.

The first thing he had done after he left—letting Haviva and her carefully painted toenails come back to an empty house after her bridge game—was to go home. Even though Milia hadn't been there physically, she was still everywhere: her clothes, the smell of her shampoo in the bathroom, the way she lined up the colorful ceramic mugs on the kitchen shelf—two green, two turquoise, two yellow, two white. He even imagined he could feel her imprint on the old velvet sofa when he lay down, smelling her scent when he covered himself with the fuzzy, warm mohair throw they'd bought on that trip to Ireland so many years before.

He was glad now that he'd been scrupulous in continuing to pay all the bills for the house, despite Haviva's nagging that Milia could well afford it. Thankfully, Milia still hadn't changed the locks. He wondered if that meant something.

Even though they'd moved there fairly recently, still everything he loved was in this place: all the family photos of the children when they were small and rambunctious and sweet, tumbling over one another at the beach and in the park, or on hiking trails in the Negev and Galilee. All those photos of both of them being handed awards and citations and various other honors and promotions. All the photos of them as a couple: getting married, standing in front of mountains and waterfalls on the adventures they'd had since the children had grown up and moved out. Milia always looked so young, he thought, with her lustrous dark hair and flashing blue-green eyes. They had not had much time for vacations, so the evidence was precious to him.

If only . . . he thought, and then couldn't stop. If only he had taken her away on that cruise to Antarctica they had both longed to take, to see the penguins, instead of starting some ridiculous affair with that stupid woman! If only he had not brought Haviva with him to that last meeting he'd arranged with Milia. If only he'd waited before rushing into the whole, idiotic . . . He stopped himself, standing up and walking around the living room. She hadn't changed anything since he'd left. Did that mean she was happy with everything exactly as it had been before? Did it mean she wanted him back? He knew he was grasping at straws, but when straws are the only thing between you and drowning, even they were worthwhile having in hand.

As he lay there in the shade, listening to the sounds of the restless ocean, he suddenly remembered something Karin had told him. He sat up, taking out his cell phone and going to You-Tube, where he found the video he had been obsessing over ever since Karin told him about it. He pressed Play, watching in fascination, his admiration for his wife growing with every second that passed. Her principled defiance. Her refusal to stop or back away, facing down that disgusting, hostile audience was so, so . . . Milia. He felt a huge surge of that admiration he had always felt for her but had somehow let slip his mind in the last year. What courage she had!

And then came the part where the translator walked off in a huff and Darius Vidas stepped up to the podium placing his hand over hers. He focused on it the way he had the first ten times he'd seen this video, pressing Pause to study it. But it was not crystal clear. It could have been a courteous gesture of support from one professional to a beleaguered colleague. Or it could have been something more. He let the video run, pausing it on Darius and studying the man.

He was fit and undeniably good-looking, that is if you liked that Aryan look. Did she? Could she? Was it even possible? Wouldn't it bring up too many unwanted references? And most of all, a goy and . . . a Lithuanian! But who could predict such things? After all, could any rational person—the kind he used to be—have predicted his running off with Haviva? He didn't know. He wasn't experienced in romantic adventures, this only being his second one. The first had lasted over thirty years. As for understanding the minds and hearts of women, he had never scored too highly in that subject, and had gotten Ds and Fs this past year. But the more he looked at that video, at the interaction between his wife and the tall, blond professor, the more agitated he felt.

When did Karin say Milia would be coming home? A few days. He'd planned to just sit tight and wait for her, filling the house with flowers, groveling if need be. But what if that wasn't enough? What if that casual touch on the podium was not the innocent, collegial gesture it appeared, if there was more to it? Then three days could mean the difference between a spark of new life or the snuffing out of all hope.

As a surgeon, he was acutely aware of such instances. Sometimes, you didn't have three days, or even three minutes! When a patient can't breathe, or his heart stops, or his bowel is obstructed, there needed to be immediate intervention!

He packed up his beach gear and headed toward his car. He was just about to speed-dial his travel agent when he had an incoming call. Haviva. He let the phone ring until it annoyed him, then clicked on the option to ignore the call.

If he wanted his wife back, he thought, as he headed toward the house in Zichron—and he did, rather desperately as a matter of fact—then he should be on a plane to Lithuania before anything else happened. He threw his bags down in the living room, then called his travel agent who booked him on a 9:00 p.m. flight via Warsaw. From the internet, he was able to get the itinerary of the conference. They probably booked her into a hotel near the conference site in central Vilnius. He remembered the first time she'd gone with her father. When she'd returned, the only thing positive she'd said about the trip was the hotel. What's its name again? Ah yes: the Radisson Blu Royal Astorija. He went into an online hotel booking site and made a reservation.

TWENTY-NINE

DARIUS'S PHONE DID not stop ringing. The entire time they were on the road, Milia saw him involved in tense conversations that at times turned belligerent. She had tried to probe him for details, but he seemed unwilling to give her any information.

"It doesn't matter. It's not important," he said, waving off her concerns. What was the point of worrying her? he thought. There was nothing she could do to help. But he wondered how long he could keep the wolves at bay. The Commission, the Museum, the Research Center, and perhaps most serious of all, the head of his department. All of them suddenly had urgent business with him. And last but not least was the smooth talker from the Ministry of Foreign Affairs who made it clear that he was not to be put off. Of them all, he seemed the most dangerous.

Eventually, he would have no choice but to face them all, Darius realized. But right now he didn't want to confuse the issues by bringing Milia into the discussion. She had nothing at all to do with it, he told himself. This is me against them. His jaw flexed in fury and fear and determination.

It wasn't easy to find Ramunos Jonaitis's cottage in the forest.

It was buried deep in the woods and even cell phone reception was erratic.

"Maybe we should just give up," Milia finally suggested.

"No! That's the last thing I want to do!" Darius insisted.

She looked at him curiously. "Why is this so important to you?"

He was embarrassed to explain it to her, this foolish, almost desperate hope that somehow, somewhere, he could find a relative who had done the right thing during the war; that his heritage was not a total black hole of perpetrators, looters, and bystanders. What he wouldn't give to find a Jew-lover!

"I'm going to try to call again farther down the road in the clearing on top of that little hill," he told her, wandering off.

She sat in the car, watching him disappear. The only call she had gotten since yesterday had been from Gilad, who was solicitous, but also persistent in probing for answers, which she had no intention of giving any of her children. First of all, it was none of their business. And second, even if they had a right to know what was going on with her personal life, how could she be honest about it when she herself didn't know?

Sometimes she thought it would have been better never to have made this trip at all. And sometimes she thought it was the most important thing that had ever happened to her. But as much as she had come to like and admire Darius, and believe in his sincerity, that last meeting with his Neanderthal cousin had created a barrier between them. This was his family. There was no getting around that, and that cousin of his was every bit as despicable as she had always imagined Lithuanians to be regarding Jews. Of course, it was unfair to hold Darius responsible for this distant relative's boorish antisemitism, but a certain part of her was unable to rise above it, however she tried. At this point, she wanted nothing more than to give her speech and get out of this cursed country, back on a plane to Tel Aviv and then home, where she could curl up on her blue velvet sofa, look out into her blooming garden, and push Lithuania and its people out of her mind and her heart back into the sphere of research.

And what of Darius? she asked herself. Would he also be that easy to turn into a dispassionate work-related encounter? Could she, did she even want to, forget? On the other hand, did she even have the right to have these personal feelings that interfered with her work? Only when she articulated these questions to herself did she realize how few choices she had allowed herself. Yes, she had a job, an important one. Yes, she belonged to a certain tribe, a certain religion, with a particularly ghastly as well as unimaginably heroic history. But beyond that? When you peeled away the layers of imposed instructions and expectations and demands, was she not also a human being, a woman, who needed love and affection, admiration, and care? At her most fundamental, was she really *that* different from every other woman, no matter their background, ethnicity, and heritage? How she had loved that trip to Nida! That unexpected sojourn with the enemy, which had gone beyond all her expectations and fears, demolishing the clichés that had been ringing in her head for decades. A few days off from herself had been such a liberation! But she had stopped herself from going all the way. She wondered if she should regret that. I deserved that experience, she thought. I've earned it after everything Julius has put me through.

And wasn't the same true for Darius? Beyond the certainties of his society and family and country, all things he had been born into through no choice of his own, was there not a human being, a man, capable of great affection and kindness and loyalty? A handsome, kindhearted man who cared for her and admired her? Why did everything have to be so complicated, so difficult?

She watched him approaching, weaving back through the trees and bushes, his long limbs strong and graceful as he made his way back to her. His handsome face was all smiles. She smiled back at him, her heart suddenly missing a beat.

"I spoke to Ramunos! He says that we should wait, he will drive out to meet us."

"How does he know where we are?"

"I found some markers on the road up ahead."

"Don't tell me this is near another mass grave!"

He looked abashed. "No. The signs were just road directions, kilometer markers. He says he knows exactly where we are."

Ten minutes later, an ancient Volkswagen clattered to a stop. The driver looked like a central casting choice for the kindly old uncle. His graying hair was still abundant, and there was a sparkle in his sad blue eyes. He was even taller than Darius, close to two meters.

"You didn't do badly," he said to Darius, offering a handshake. "My house is just down the road. But good you called. It's pretty well hidden. If you didn't know, you wouldn't be able to find it." He smiled at Milia, offering her a courteous handshake, then got back behind the wheel, gesturing them to follow in their car.

His house really was nearby, but at the end of a number of forked turns that made it impossible to find if you didn't know exactly where you were going.

"Wow!" Milia said when she got out of the car. It was one of those old wooden houses that Lithuania was famous for, and which were rapidly decaying into hovels and then into dust; a lost architectural heritage that was really sad to contemplate.

Made of pine and spruce with a shingled roof, it had wood-framed windows divided into six, and wooden shutters painted red. It looked like a Christmas gingerbread house. The foundation was fieldstones, Milia noticed, which probably kept the damp from seeping into the floorboards. But most unusual were the carved wooden lintels and the wide porch. It was nothing like Marijus Norbut's plain dwelling, plastered over with cheap, modern materials.

"My great-grandfather built this house with his own hands," Ramunos told them.

"I'm sorry, I don't understand Lithuanian," Milia apologized.

"My English is only a little," he apologized, "but Professor Vidas—"

"Please, Cousin Ramunos, Darius."

He smiled, nodding. "Darius will translate. My great-grandfather and his sons followed all the traditions. They cut the timber from the forest in mid-February, when the trees are sleeping, so that the windows would not cry and the wormwood would not attack the logs. They kept the wood dry for a few years before they started. Then they chose a plot where lightning and fires had not caused havoc, a place on which there were no old tree stumps—because a tree connects man to God, and souls reach heaven through it. They built it in the south end of the plot, so the family would prosper and be warm and comfortable. And when the first beams were raised, they placed a cross in the corner with a piece of mourning candle, blessed herbs, Easter thorns, and a silver coin against the evil eye so that the devil might not sit in the corner." He sighed. "He came in anyway and didn't limit himself to a corner. He took over the whole house. But we have taken it back and chased him to hell. Please," he said in English to Milia, beckoning them both inside.

They followed him through the wooden fence that surrounded the property. Nearby, they could see other structures that seemed to be barns or storehouses. But there wasn't another dwelling as far as the eye could see.

"Are you the only person living here?"

"There used to be a number of these old houses. But when the Soviets came, they convinced people that the wooden houses were primitive and old-fashioned and cheaply made. They told them to replace the wooden windows with plastic, and the doors with iron. Pretty soon, mold and dry rot crept in, and the houses became unlivable, so the people moved away to the cities. But my father had helped my grandfather and great-grandfather build this house and knew it was solid. So they didn't listen, and left it as it was."

They entered through a solid, polished wooden door with an elaborate carved lintel that welcomed them inside. The smell of freshly washed floorboards, and newly cut logs perfumed the air. A large, carved wooden table sat at the center of the room near a huge fireplace that doubled as a stove.

"Please, sit. I have for you eat and drink," he said in English.

They sat on a long, hand-carved wooden bench by the side of the table. He brought them crackers and cheese, and bowls of fresh berries and cream, and a large loaf of brown bread. He placed mugs in front of them with coffee he had brewed himself, adding herbs and cream. It was delicious, Milia thought, taking a sip. She filled her bowl with berries.

"I am so happy that finally someone from the family has come to see me," Ramunos told Darius, joining them at the table.

"Yes, I was going to ask you about that, Ramunos. Can you tell me what this rift is all about?"

His cousin looked down at the floor. "It was the war. My grandparents were devout Christians. And so when they were asked by the local priest to hide Jews, they could not say no."

Darius looked at him, blinking.

"Did he say his family hid Jews?"

Darius nodded speechlessly.

"Tell us more, Ramunos," Milia urged him.

"This is what my father told me," he began in English, then switched to his native tongue, which Darius simultaneously translated: "At first, they were gathering the Jews together into a ghetto from all the little towns and villages. My father said the family thought they would put the Jews in prison and when the war was over, they would let them go, because all the time they were saying the Jews are Bolsheviks, helping the Russians, who were our enemy. They said the Nazis were our friends and would help us win our country back. But that was not what happened. My father told me that by July 1941 everyone knew that the Jews were intended for slaughter. It began in June. People saw it, heard it. He said, 'Whoever tells you they did not know is a liar.'

"First came the daughter of a local Jew who used to buy lumber from our family. She asked my grandfather to hide her and her daughters. So my grandfather, who knew the family well, built a hiding place for them beneath the kitchen. And then, as things got desperate, the priest came to us and asked us to take in more Jews who wanted to escape from the Kaunas ghetto. My grandparents could not say no. But it was very hard to find food to feed so many people. But my father said his parents were saints. They told him that they needed to share their food with these poor women because as Christians that was their duty. At a certain point, there was no more room. My grandparents had to decide which neighbors could be trusted with the secret. One of the Jews was sent to our neighbors, the Vaidotas. Everyone was frightened. But my grandfather told the Jews, who were terrified and sincerely regretted all the trouble they were causing him, 'We'll manage somehow. Almost all of you are young. You still have a life to live. I'm not doing this for the money. I'm pretty old myself. I won't take the money with me into my grave. I just don't want to see any more innocent blood spilled. If I could, I would save more Jews. But since I can't, I'll protect those that I can. I want to show you that not all Lithuanians are like those partisans of ours.'

"The Jewish women made flowers from wood shavings, sold by my father, who was able to travel because he was a merchant. In this way, the Jews survived the war. When the Soviets came back, the Jews were so grateful they wrote and signed a letter of testimony, praising my grandfather and my father and the other neighbors for keeping them alive."

He stopped, wiping away tears.

Milia and Darius were astounded. A happy end! And yet, he seemed devastated. "There were many people around here who didn't like the fact that we helped to save Jews. They were part of partisan groups like the Forest Brothers, and their leader, Jonas Neicelis-Šarūnas . . ."

"You can read his 'heroic' biography online," Darius told her disgustedly. "He, too, is now one of Lithuania's great heroes."

"And so what happened?" Milia asked Ramunos.

"They killed my father and my grandfather. They were ambushed in the forest as they were cutting down trees. They were executed. No one ever took responsibility. But in 2007, my father and my grandfather were awarded the Life-Saving Cross." He went into the bedroom and returned with a thick, black velvet case. He opened it to show them the medal: a cross in red with gold trimming and a striped red ribbon. "They gave it to me, because both of them were long gone."

Darius got up and walked to his cousin, shaking his hand and hugging him. "Thank you for telling me this story, Ramunos. You cannot imagine how much this means to me." He embraced the older man, kissing him on both cheeks. Then he moved back as something occurred to him. "Ramunos, are you telling me that our family stopped speaking to your family because you were awarded this medal?"

He shook his head. "No. It began long before that, when my father and grandfather were killed. They were afraid they could also be targeted. So they cut off contact."

"They do both, you see. Honor the saviors as well as honoring those who murdered them," Darius said grimly. "I'm going to have a long, long talk with my family when I get back," he told his cousin. "But I want you to know, I am so proud to be part of *your* family, Ramunos, if you'll have me, after what my grandfather did."

Ramunos looked down. "We all did what our consciences told us. And some were weaker than others," he said generously. Then he brought out a delicious liqueur made of honey, and a picture album of his late wife and children and many grandchildren, who lived in Kaunas and England and America.

"Here, let me take a photo. Stand together, smile," Milia urged them, snapping some pictures of Darius and Ramunos with her iPhone. They were so tall she couldn't get a full-length photo! Then they took selfies with Ramunos in the middle holding the medal, all of them smiling and on the verge of tears.

And when they parted, Milia, too, hugged Ramunos. "It was worth it to come here all the way from Israel, if just to meet you," she told him, then asked Darius to translate. Then she reached behind her neck and undid the clasp of the gold chain holding her Jewish star. "Tell him to bend down, Darius." The older man looked at her shyly but did as he was told. Reaching up, she fastened the chain around his neck, kissing him on the cheek. "From a Jewish woman who lives in Israel, whose family were once Litvaks. But they didn't have your father and grandfather to save them. May God bless you and your family."

THIRTY

HE SAT BACK in the chair, looking at the man who was in charge of his academic career. It was the department conference room, and the walls were filled with framed diplomas and certificates testifying to this or the other academic marvel achieved through the years. Of course, the Lithuanian flag was prominent, as well as a framed photo of their current prime minister, who looked down benevolently.

"My dear Dr. Vidas," the Department Head began.

Darius sat up.

"I welcome you to my office and thank you for coming so promptly. I understand you have been much occupied of late with a national tour in conjunction with our partners in the European Union?"

Darius nodded cautiously, waiting.

The Department Head cleared his throat. "While I am sure you began your program with the best of intentions, as you know there has been considerable controversy concerning your program. I speak of Dr. Gottstein-Lasker's speech in Raseiniai, which I understand shut down your original itinerary, and produced some very unpleasant videos that have been circulating to the shame of our university and our country."

Darius said nothing.

"Well, what do you have to say for yourself?"

"I think Dr. Gottstein-Lasker did an excellent job of enlightening our high school students as to the true history of their country."

The Department Head rose from his chair and paced the room. He looked, Darius thought not for the first time, like the perfect actor for the role of head pig in a theatrical production of *Animal Farm*. His bald forehead, glistening with sweat, puckered as he began to shout, making his vociferous and threatening points.

So this was how it was going to go, Darius thought, trying not to feel despondent. He sat up. "Well, then, let me get this straight," Darius said mildly. "You want me to lie about the veracity of the statements made by Dr. Gottstein-Lasker, and to pretend that the eyewitness testimony she read in Raseiniai is not to be trusted, even though it is completely reliable. Otherwise, you will ruin my academic career. Have I got that right?"

The Department Head seemed momentarily taken aback by such a direct and unadorned summary. He took his seat and picked up a pen, which he tapped nervously on the edge of the table. He coughed, clearing the bile clogging the back of his throat. "There is no question of, as you crudely and falsely put it, 'lying.' I am simply asking you as a scholar, who is in the employ of a public institution on which the honor and integrity of our great country relies, to suggest that Dr. Gottstein-Lasker—*who is not a historian*—has simply gotten the story wrong. That she has simplified it and failed to give it the in-depth analysis which would take into consideration *both sides* of the narrative, not simply the *Jewish side*, told solely by the Jews."

"Oh, so there is another side to what happened in Raseiniai, Telšiai, Ponevezh, and here in Vilnius to the Jewish people in 1941? I'd be happy to hear it." He was incensed.

The Department Head raised his hand, annoyed. "This is not an academic discussion, Dr. Vidas." He suddenly lowered his voice to a growl: "Nor is it a negotiation. I hope you understand that."

"Oh, yes. Completely understood. There is nothing even vaguely academic about it. I am being threatened and bullied in a most unacademic way."

The Department Head squirmed. He had not expected such resistance. He wiped his forehead with a cloth hankie he kept in his jacket pocket out of habit since his mother put it there when he started first grade. "Just so you know, I am not alone in this. Your publisher, the heads of the Commission for the Evaluation of the Crimes of the Nazi and Soviet Occupation Regimes . . ."

"I thought they were going to shorten that to Commission for Historical Truth, no?"

"Ah, yes. That is true."

"So, the Commission on Historical Truth also wants me to *deny established historical facts* and lie because the truth makes them uncomfortable?"

"How dare you! Besides, it is not only the Commission . . ."

"Let me guess: the Research Center, the Genocide Museum, and last but not least, the Ministry of Foreign Affairs are also involved, and all of them are in favor of denying Dr. Gottstein-Lasker the right to tell the truth as she sees it?"

"This has nothing to do with her! She is not Lithuanian. She is an Israeli . . ."

"Yes, and *a Jew* and *a woman* . . ."

"What are you hinting at?"

"What, you thought that was a hint? I am saying quite clearly that you want me to publicly discount and deny the accuracy of her statements in Raseiniai, which were based on the notarized, first-person testimony of survivors, because they were Jews and she's a Jew."

"No, because they are all *liars!*" the Department Head shouted, slamming his fist against the table. "We Lithuanians also suffered! Our partisans sacrificed their lives to rid Lithuania of its oppressors and enemies. Yes, many suffered, many died. *Not all of them were Jews.*"

Darius didn't move a muscle. "I'm afraid I don't see it that way. I don't see that Lithuanians were systematically murdered because they were Lithuanians, which is what happened to the Jews."

"That was the Germans. The Nazis."

"There were only a thousand Germans in Lithuania when over two hundred thousand Jews were slaughtered and tortured and raped. Even some of the Nazis were appalled by how we behaved toward the Jews. *That's* historical fact."

They stared at each other, taking the other's measure.

"You have everything to lose, Dr. Vidas. Are you prepared for that?"

"If you try to fire me, or hurt my academic standing in any way, I will sue you personally, and sue the university, and make sure the foreign press is aware. These heroes you put up on pedestals, didn't they make the ultimate sacrifice so that Lithuania would not be under the thumb of a totalitarian power any longer? We are a free and independent country. I can think and say what I like as long as I can prove it."

"I think you are confusing your patriotism with that of our judiciary," the Department Head said mildly, folding his hands placidly over his stomach.

Of course, he was right, Darius realized. In any court in the land, he would lose such a case. Look at what had happened with Grant Gochin, that persistent South African–born descendant of Lithuanian Jews who had had the courage to sue Lithuania in its courts on their false hero narrative for Noreika, and for recognition of his Lithuanian citizenship. His book, *Murder, Malice, and Manipulation,* documented his Sisyphean battle with the Lithuanian court system, showing how at every turn, his just requests had been denied and repudiated by the flimsiest of legal arguments. Darius had found it embarrassing to read. No, the Lithuanian legal system would not help him, either.

The Department Head immediately caught the change in his demeanor. "Look," he said in a tone that was suddenly conciliatory, "I understand you have formed a relationship with this Jewish woman . . ."

"This is not personal! And that's none of your business."

"You know, the Jews will never forgive us no matter what we do. They are a lost cause."

"Silvia Foti went to Israel. She was embraced there."

He snickered. "Of course. Because she is a traitor, besmirching the name of her own grandfather."

"No, telling the painful truth. She was embraced, even though her grandfather was a Nazi who killed thousands of Jews, the descendants of these Jews still embraced her. Do you know why? Because the Jews are remarkably easy to placate. They *want* to forgive and forget, to get on with their lives. So they take whatever crumb of apology and repentance thrown their way and treasure it. Otherwise, they could not keep living in the world. All they want is for us, the descendants, to say, 'Yes, our grandparents murdered, tortured, and raped your people. It was horrible. We are so sorry. We will take down the plaques to those who participated, those who gave the orders, rounded them up and guarded them, took their belongings, and murdered them. We will rename the schools and streets that honor perpetrators. We will build decent memorials at every mass grave and bring schoolchildren to sing songs and place flowers once a year. We will return whatever we stole when we can find the real owners.' Do that, then you will have tourism. You will have economic and educational ties. You will have blessing and friendship with people who turned a little strip of desert into a vital, flourishing miracle of progress."

The Department Head stared at him. "What are you trying to say?"

Darius stood up, exasperated. "What is unclear? I'm trying to tell you that letting her speak will begin the long overdue reconciliation with the Jews that will bring this country blessing and advancement. Just look at the countries that hate Jews, they are backwaters, primitive, unsuccessful. And then look at those who reach out to Jews."

"Oh my, oh my, you really are on a campaign to change the world. Relax," the Department Head said soothingly. "I want you to know that I appreciate the difficulties involved in changing course at the last moment. Yes, it might very well damage your relationship with this woman, but nothing like the damage that will be caused by her to our beloved homeland if she isn't reined in and prevented from giving an uncensored closing speech in front of the world press."

"After everything I've said"—Darius shook his head in despair—"and you are still *asking me to deny her the right to speak at the closing conference?*"

"Obviously. It will be better for everyone, especially for her."

"Meaning?"

"The government informs me that the Pro Patria and National Unity groups . . ."

"You mean the neo-Nazis and the supporters of Arvydas Juozaitis, with their black skull-and-crossbones flag with the Lithuanian swastika and their Lithuania for Lithuanians posters?"

"Now, now. They had police permission to march last time, you know. They are entitled to their opinions, even though I don't agree with them completely. We are, as you just pointed out, a free country."

"Freer for some than for others," Darius muttered. "What about them?"

"I'm informed that they are going to be massing in the thousands if she's allowed to speak and insult our partisans. It could get very ugly."

"That's why we have a police force and an army."

"Yes, of course. And I am sure they will both do their utmost to prevent any violence. But as you know, things could very quickly get out of hand. Do you really think it's a wise idea to risk her safety?"

For the first time, Darius felt the strength of his ardor wane. He was prepared to fight, to defend himself and his career. But risking Milia's safety was something else.

"I will give it some thought," Darius said, rising to leave.

The Department Head leaned back in his seat, relaxing. "Excellent idea."

* * *

Milia had just gotten out of the shower and was sitting on the bed in her bathrobe. She had just called room service with her order for a late breakfast. In the meantime, she'd delved into responding to a long string of unread emails.

One of them caught her eye. It was from one of the students in Raseiniai, she realized, excited. Her secretary had forwarded it to her. It was in Lithuanian. She googled a translation, then read it, her mind adjusting the obvious Google translation mistakes. It went something like this:

Dear Dr. Gottstein-Lasker,

When I listened to your talk at my high school it made me feel sick and angry. I went home and asked my parents if what you said was true. I was very surprised when they told me it was, and that their parents had told them the same stories but they never told me because they thought I was too young and it was too frightening. I think it's good that we now know the true history of what happened in our town so that it can never happen again. Many thanks, Goca Balkus

Amazing, Milia thought with satisfaction. That's all it took. One child going home with the facts in her hands, like precious seeds that could be planted, and which would grow and spread until the soil of her city—now filled with the tangled roots of lies—would have to give way to deeply rooted truths. Hopefully, Goca Balkus was not the only student she had reached that day, nor were her parents—undoubtedly good people who felt they were doing the best for their child—the only parents who were afraid to tell their children about the war and the death of their Jewish neighbors. But once the truth became inevitable, they would all find a way to discuss these things openly and the healing could finally begin.

If this was the result of a little speech in the middle of nowhere with no press coverage, she thought with satisfaction, imagine how much good her closing speech would do, center stage in the capital surrounded by local and foreign press! She smiled to herself, reaching for the printed text of her speech and going over it carefully with a red pen. She wanted it to be perfect.

She was so engrossed that she almost didn't hear the knock on the door.

"Come in," she called out unthinkingly, then looked down and realized she was practically naked. "One minute, I'll be right there."

She hurried to unpack a bra and panties, then slipped into an easy summer dress with blue polka dots on a cream background. She struggled to zip it up as she walked barefoot to the door.

"Sorry," she said as she opened it.

But it wasn't room service. It was Julius.

She looked at him wordlessly, then moved back, opening the door wider.

He walked in, closing the door behind him gently, then locking it.

She sat down on the sofa, pulling a pillow into her lap and running a hand through her hair. It was still soaking wet. *I must look like a drowned cat,* she thought with vague regret. *I should ask him what he's doing here.* But somehow, she knew. The question was not what *he* wanted, but what *she* wanted, she realized.

"Can I sit down?"

She waved him toward the desk chair.

"Can I get a drink of water?" he asked.

She looked at him more closely. His eyes were bloodshot, and a two-day stubble covered his usually fastidiously shaven cheeks and chin. His thick salt-and-pepper hair, of which he was inordinately vain considering all the baldies his age, was disheveled. He looked as if he'd just come off a two-day bender.

She gestured toward the minibar. "Help yourself."

He bent down, taking out a bottle of Coke and pouring it into a glass into which he dumped an entire mini bottle of vodka. Sitting across from her and not taking his eyes off her face, he gulped it down.

"Have you brought Haviva with you?" she asked him.

He winced, shaking his head. "Okay. I deserved that. Just know that it wasn't my idea."

Milia nodded. "Poor Julius. Such a browbeaten man who can't resist a pretty woman. Except if it's his wife," she said meanly. "Your Haviva would not be happy to hear you're blaming her."

He rested his elbows on his knees, his head bent low. Only when the glass was absolutely drained did he finally raise his head to look at her. "I'm an idiot. And she is not 'my Haviva.' She wasn't . . . isn't. It's over. I need you. Desperately. I need our life together. I've taken a leave of absence from the hospital. I can't work. I can't sleep. I can't eat. Please, Milia, forgive me."

She crossed one leg over her knee, dangling her foot nervously. His unexpected, larger-than-life presence was sucking the oxygen out of the room, she thought, feeling suddenly breathless. She went to the window, opening it, then stood there taking deep breaths as she followed the movements of strangers in the foreign streets below.

How she had daydreamed of this moment! Julius like a beaten dog begging to get back together, having left Haviva in the dust! But after all she had experienced, suddenly, it wasn't enough. Not nearly enough. "Why are you here, Julius? Couldn't this wait until I got home?"

He didn't know what he'd expected, but not this. She seemed completely unmoved, he thought, astonished. As if she hadn't heard a word he'd said, as if she was *used to* him begging forgiveness, which he never in his life did! Of course, he had hoped, dreamed, that just seeing him she would fall into his arms in gratitude and agree it had all been a terrible mistake. After so many years of marriage, children, grandchildren, such a history together! He'd hoped she would even reciprocate, tell him how much she missed him, needed him. At the very least, he'd hoped his sudden, unexpected presence would make her malleable, or at the very least appeal to her deeply held love of order, the idea that everything could go back to exactly where it had been before his temporary insanity had upended their lives.

But the woman before him didn't seem the least bit touched. In fact, her interest in him seemed no more than mild at the most, he realized painfully. It was as if there were an iceberg between them. He was at a total loss on how to breach that icy barrier.

"Maybe I should have let you know I was coming," he said, getting to his feet and retrieving whatever shred of dignity he had left.

"So, going already?" she said.

"If that's what you want," he responded dully, overcome by despair. He was not a man used to failure, which was why people put their lives into his hands every day and had been doing so for decades.

"Sit down."

He sat.

She paced the small room as if it were on fire and at any moment she would be called upon to jump out of the window to save herself. Suddenly, she turned to face him. "Do. You. Have. Any. Idea. What. You've. Put. Me. Through?"

Her voice was not a shout, but there was an edge of hysteria to it. "Do you have any inkling how you've hurt me?" she continued. "How many nights I wished I wouldn't wake up? How many hours of self-loathing I suffered? How I questioned my work, my choices, my entire adult life? Do you know how many hours I looked into the mirror and suddenly saw an aging hag, without beauty or appeal or dignity?"

He got up and reached out for her.

Her arms shot out forcefully as she shook her head. "You turned everything I had into dust, Julius. I had to rebuild from dust. What you're looking at is a woman who is entirely new, created like Eve, from dust. That woman doesn't have a past with you. The one you are appealing to, the one you once knew, is dead because you and your 'girlfriend,' that silly cow, killed her. I'm sorry if this is all a surprise to you, and you find it painful. Truly, I think you have many good qualities . . ."

"Oh my God!" He sat down again. "Really? That is what you are giving me? A brush-off? Like some teenage boyfriend you are tired of?"

"Ah, hurts to be rejected, does it?" Her eyes sparkled.

That seemed to take the wind out of his sails. He fell back heavily into his chair.

She also sat back down. She studied him. Julius. Her first boyfriend. Her first love. A man she had always admired so much, and whose admiration had always been the bedrock of her adult life, the most important measure of her beauty, her intelligence, her success in the world.

She wasn't, she realized, as indifferent to him as she wanted to be.

They sat there silently until someone knocked on the door. "Room service."

"Have you had anything to eat?"

He shook his head.

She opened the door to let the waiter roll in the cart. And there, right behind him, stood Darius.

THIRTY-ONE

"DARIUS, I WASN'T ..."

He strode into the room forcefully, his mind filled with contradictory thoughts, wanting to lay the situation bare before her, when he noticed Julius.

"I'm sorry, I didn't know you weren't alone," Darius apologized.

"So that's what you were hoping, was it?" Julius said nastily.

"Julius, stop it! Darius, this is my ex—"

"No, not quite," Julius rebuked her. "Her husband. Present tense."

Her husband, Darius thought, his mind racing. The person who had been lucky enough to have been married to this remarkable, beautiful woman and who had treated her like dirt, leaving her for some floozy. And now, he was back. He was here in Lithuania, sitting in a chair in her room at ten thirty in the morning.

"Julius, this is Professor Darius Vidas, who is running the conference here in Lithuania."

"The one with his hands all over you in that video," Julius said abruptly, nodding.

"If you didn't look so pathetic, I'd punch you in the face for that," Darius told him, wondering what else could go wrong this morning.

"Stop it, both of you! Before I throw you both out!" Milia told them.

"I'm sorry, Milia. It's urgent that I speak to you about the conference. Something has come up that you should know about. Can we find someplace to talk privately?"

"If this concerns my wife, it concerns me," Julius said firmly. But even at his full height, he realized, he was at least half a head shorter than Darius Vidas, and certainly not used to using his fists to get his way, as was, apparently, this Lithuanian. Julius looked him over. Blond, tall, good-looking, smart. So what if he was a goy? A man like that could probably have any woman he wanted if he was nice to her, especially coming on the heels of a previous partner who had treated her badly. He could see in how Milia looked at him that he had been very nice to her.

"Julius, this has nothing to do with you. Just leave."

The confusion in Darius's mind suddenly slowed, a strange clarity forming out of the chaos, the way crystals will magically form in refrigerated tap water and magnesium sulphate.

All the time they had been on this journey, he had asked himself one question, the most important question of all: Had he been in his grandfather's place, would he have behaved like him, or like Ramunos's father and grandfather, risking everything to save the lives of the Jews? Now he was being forced to face that question.

His face suddenly changed, going blank, avoiding Milia's eyes. "No, let him stay." Darius nodded toward Julius. "What I have to tell you is very simple. You can't speak at the conference tomorrow."

Milia turned to him, astonished. "What did you say?"

"I said your invitation has been rescinded. I think it would be best if you left now, especially since your husband is here to accompany you and you obviously have unfinished business together."

"Darius, you can't be serious. Talk to me!"

He shook his head stubbornly, refusing to meet her eyes. "There is nothing to discuss. I have been threatened by my department head, the Ministry, the Museum, the Commission, my editor, not to mention my son's employers. I will be fired, my books will be taken off the shelves, even my son faces losing his job! They are insisting I correct all the 'unpatriotic' things that were said in Raseiniai. I'm sorry. I had a choice to make, and I have made it," he said, looking down at the carpet, hoping she would not see the tears welling up in his eyes.

She went to him, touching his face. But he backed away abruptly. "We had a nice trip together, Milia, but this is my life. We just got caught up in something very unreal, something romantic and foolish. But now it's time to get serious. A Jew and a Lithuanian? We both knew it wasn't real and would never have worked. I'm sorry if I disappointed you. As I said, it's best that you leave now with your husband. I'll arrange the flight back for you."

Milia sat down on the bed, her heart like a stone. How could this be happening? She had thought . . . after all they'd experienced together . . . Was she such a bad judge of character? She looked from Darius to Julius. Two men she had trusted, and yes, loved. And they had both betrayed her. She felt nauseated.

"I have a contract," she told him bitterly.

Darius swallowed. "Yes, and you violated it by the things you said in Raseiniai. And now you are planning to say even worse things."

"How do you know what I'm planning to say?"

He swallowed hard. "We discussed it, no?"

She had never discussed her speech with him but had relied on

his trust because they both believed in the same things—or so he
had made her believe—and both wanted a better future for Lithuania and her people. She picked up the pages labored over with
such care, rolled them into a baton, then smacked him across the
face with it. They scattered to the floor. He bent down, gathering
them up carefully and holding them tightly in his hand. "I think
I'll hold on to these. After all, I paid for them."

She winced. "Go right ahead. Burn them if you want to!
You . . . you gave me the only hope I've had for your shitty little country in decades. But I guess that was just a fantasy. You
people are all the same."

He looked pained but nodded. "Except for Ramunos and his
family."

"Yes." She nodded, giving him that. "Except for them, and a
handful of others."

He turned to go. "Goodbye, Milia. Will you write me?"

In response, she slammed the door in his face.

All the way to the airport, Julius held her hand and she let
him. She felt numb, as if she were wading through the thick,
viscous heaviness of an endless nightmare, unable to pull herself
free.

How could she have been so stupid? So gullible? This was what
he'd planned from the moment he'd been threatened, to throw her
to the wolves to save himself. She couldn't really find it in her heart
to blame him completely. Facing the kind of total ruin that awaited
him for defiance, she could see why he'd weakened. But somehow,
she'd imagined . . . what? That he'd be her knight in shining armor? That he'd meant all those things he'd said in Nida? At least
she hadn't slept with him, she thought, trying to find comfort in
that. And now, I never will, she thought, with a strange devastation.

Luckily, the flight was crowded, and as their tickets had been
purchased at the last minute, she and Julius weren't seated next
to each other. At least that, she thought, as she opened her purse

and took out her bottle of sleeping pills. She took two, swallowing them without water, then closed her eyes and tried to sleep.

"Milia, we're home," she heard someone say in what seemed to her only moments later. But it had actually been hours. She opened her eyes, and there was Julius looking at her kindly, his face blurry and distant, as if she were staring at him through the wrong end of binoculars. She blinked, stretching and looking around. People were gathering their bags from the overhead compartments. She could see that Julius already had hers. Mechanically, she waited for her seatmates to get up, then followed them down the narrow aisle and out of the plane.

She walked slowly, silently toward customs and baggage claim.

"Are you feeling all right?" Julius asked anxiously. "Here, have something to drink." He handed her a plastic bottle of water from the plane. She gulped the lukewarm liquid down, the residue of the sleeping pill still coating her tongue with a metallic taste.

"How are we going to get back home?" he asked her. "Did you put our car in long-term parking, because I came by taxi."

"I have *my* car here," she said, correcting him. "But I don't know if I should be driving."

"I'll drive," he offered.

"But then how will *you* get home?"

He paused, letting people hurrying to get on the line for customs overtake them. "Actually, I've moved back into our house in Zichron."

She stared at him. "Really? Without discussing it with me?"

"It was impulsive, but I thought, since you hadn't changed the locks, and we were actually still married, and I've been paying the mortgage . . ."

"How convenient for you," she murmured, giving him the first inkling of how wrong he had been about what was going to happen now.

She let him drive her home, allowing him to collect his things while she found him a hotel room and called him a taxi. She was not as detached as she would have wished, she realized, finding that the door to their relationship had not been slammed shut. But getting back together—if it ever happened—would be a long, slow process that could go either way, she thought.

After he was gone, she walked into her garden. The gardener had been here recently, she saw. New flowers had been planted in the terra-cotta pots that lined the staircase, tiny petunias replacing the faded blue lobelia. The freesia, tulip, and daffodil bulbs were gone, probably safely stored until next spring when they would bloom again, bringing color to her life and joy to her damaged heart. Summer would see the bougainvillea and climbing roses reach new heights, and the geraniums spill over in magenta, pink, and white out of the new flowerpots she'd planted on the porch facing the sea, she thought, trying to look forward. It wasn't easy.

She took a long shower, put a pita in the microwave, then stuffed it with a drained can of tuna and some newly picked lettuce and baby tomatoes still warm from the garden. She found *Legally Blonde* on Netflix and sat up watching it, mining half a pint of strawberry cheesecake Häagen-Dazs as she smiled at the clever antics of Reese Witherspoon, who managed to easily overcome all the chauvinists in the world.

Only when she went to the bathroom to brush her teeth did she have a chance to actually look into her own face and read the desolation and havoc written all over it.

I'll survive this. I'm a survivor, like my ancestors, she told herself. *This is nothing. I will be fine,* she ordered herself before taking two more sleeping pills and crawling into bed even though it was only five in the afternoon.

A phone was ringing, she realized, blinking at the fierce morning light pouring through her bedroom windows. She leaned on one elbow, turning over and looking at the radio clock. Ten past eleven! she read with shock, sitting up and automatically reaching for her iPhone, only to realize that she'd forgotten to plug it in before going to sleep. Its battery was out of power. But somewhere in the house, a phone kept ringing. It was the landline in what was once Julius's office, for which very few had the number, her fogged brain finally realized. Fearing some kind of emergency, she jumped out of bed and hurried down the hall to answer it.

"Where have you been?! I've been calling all morning!"

"Karin? I forgot to plug in my iPhone."

"Have you read today's paper or looked at the internet?"

"Hello, Karin. What?" She was still half asleep.

"The news. It's all over the place."

"What are you talking about?"

"Listen, just open your computer and look!"

"Well, okay."

"And by the way, welcome home, Ima! Have you and Aba spoken, because—"

"I'm sorry, Karin, we'll talk later," she cut her off, then put the phone down and ran to her computer.

There it was, the pictures of the riots in the streets of Vilnius, and the full text of the speech that had reportedly caused it, with a photo of Darius's bloodied face captioned just above it.

"Oh my God!" She wept. "Oh my God!"

She glanced at an article beneath the photos, which was apparently front-page news all over the world.

Dr. Darius Vidas, a senior lecturer at Algirdas University, after being attacked by far-right demonstrators as he left Vilnius town hall following a controversial keynote speech that concluded a weeklong conference on Holocaust reconciliation in partnership with the EU. The speech, prepared by Dr. Milia Gottstein-Lasker, director of the Survivors' Campaign, was delivered by Dr. Vidas instead, who said she had left the country following threats to her safety. Below are excerpts from the speech that aroused the ire of locals.

What followed were extensive passages from her speech, the one she had slapped him across the face with. And he, in turn, had risked his life, his reputation, and his livelihood to deliver it in her place. She covered her mouth with her hand. He had known just what to say to make her angry enough to just leave, she thought, smiling through her tears. He had done it to keep her safe.

Darius.

She looked over the familiar text, now, thanks to Darius, being broadcast all over the world:

Just outside of Telšiai are the graves of seventy-five Lithuanian prisoners killed by Soviet forces before their 1941 retreat. In their honor, Lithuanians have built a magnificent chapel with artistic stained-glass windows, which stands on manicured grounds where tour guides lead groups of international tourists. I am sure some of you have visited there just as I am certain most of you have never been to the graves nearby, the mass graves of Lithuanian Jews murdered by their neighbors, that hold not seventy-five martyrs, but thousands. But I have been there because that is the resting place of my namesake, once a pretty, fourteen-year-old girl named Milia, who lies beneath the earth together with my great-grandparents, uncles, aunts, and cousins. There are no manicured lawns, no flowers, not even an engraved granite memorial stone with their names. No paving stones mark the muddy path through the forest and only an ugly, dilapidated fence, and some words in Russian about "victims of Fascism" let you know you've arrived.

The story of my family, and this gravesite, has been repeated hundreds of times all over Lithuania. And even though Lithuanians conscientiously respect their dead and care for their graves, these gravesites are not marked nor visited, even though their occupants lived side by side with you and were your neighbors and friends. They were Lithuanians, no less than you. But they were also Jews. For that reason only, they were tortured and murdered in 1941 not by Nazis, who were in the minority, but by Lithuanian collaborators wearing white armbands whom today Lithuania insists on honoring as "partisans."

My grandfather and father spent their lives searching for justice for their murdered family, but Lithuania has failed to indict and punish a single perpetrator. Not one, despite having been given accurate lists with hundreds of explicit names and details of these despicable crimes by the Wiesenthal Center and the Survivors' Campaign.

By ignoring these graves, Lithuania may think it has hidden its crimes from its children and from outsiders. I want you to know, that will never be true. The voices of the victims still call out from the unhallowed, disrespected earth into which they were thrown. You who are alive today are not the perpetrators. But by continuing to bury the truth, you are complicit in perpetrating the crime of obfuscating and denying the Holocaust in Lithuania. The voices of the living, all those good people in the world who wish for justice and freedom to prevail, have joined the voices of these dead. These voices will never be silenced until Lithuania publicly recognizes and repents what happened here. Until it educates its children, instead of feeding them false narratives about how a handful of Lithuanian degenerates were responsible for these deaths, and how many Lithuanians saved Jews.

A tiny fraction of one percent of the Lithuanian population were found by Yad Vashem to have rescued Jews. This leaves 99.96 percent of Lithuanians either perpetrators or bystanders.

According to the International Holocaust Remembrance Alliance: "Holocaust denial seeks to erase the history of the Holocaust. In doing so, it seeks to legitimize Nazism and antisemitism . . . Holocaust distortion acknowledges aspects of the Holocaust as factual. It never-

theless excuses, minimizes, or misrepresents the Holocaust in a variety of ways and through various media."

In the last 20 years, almost every Lithuanian I have met has claimed that their family tried to save their Jewish neighbors. This revisionism is widespread within Lithuanian society, abetted by the dishonest official teachings of numerous government-financed authorities tasked with Holocaust research and remembrance, which amounts to a concerted official attempt by the Lithuanian government to distort and deny the horror of what actually took place here, resulting in the highest percentage of Jewish deaths of any country in Europe. Out of 220,000 Lithuanian Jews, only ten thousand survived, plus another two thousand who had fled to the Soviet Union.

Lithuanians now wish to be pitied as equal victims to the Jews because of their suffering under the Communist regime. They wish to blame the death of the Jews entirely on the Nazis. I acknowledge they suffered, were deported, lost their lands and jobs. But they were not targeted for annihilation. There were only a thousand Nazis in Lithuania. The work of rounding up, looting, raping, and murdering the Jews was left entirely in the hands of locals. In fact, there are multiple documented cases where Nazis protested the savagery and cruelty of Lithuanians. Some Lithuanians were also so disturbed by the bloodlust displayed by their countrymen that the Lithuanian officials in charge of the murders demanded that Jews not be killed so publicly so as to reduce the angst suffered by the spectators. These demands were ignored. The slaughter of Jews was often perpetrated in public festivals with parties held afterward to celebrate and share the plunder, parties organized by the people who were their neighbors.

Not content to murder their own Jews, Lithuanian murder squads traveled to neighboring countries like Belarus to murder Jews there.

These facts are inconvenient for Lithuania. Who, after all, wants to be known as a country of such savagery? Since there is no possibility of Lithuania denying the Holocaust—the most documented genocide in history—the government of Lithuania has decided to implement

instead a state-sponsored program of Holocaust distortion. Your Genocide Research Center needs more than a name change. It needs to be
shut down and all its so-called research discredited and destroyed. Your
Genocide Museum talks only about non-Jewish Lithuanian victims
of the Soviets, not Holocaust victims and has no value or credibility
concerning the Holocaust. Your conferences and rallies and commem-
orations of Holocaust victims are equally without value, as are your
public relations attempts to paint Lithuania as a welcoming tourist site
for Jews interested in their heritage. As long as Lithuania continues to
distort history, Jews should not visit these unmarked graves, these false
museums, these fake conferences that deny the simple facts.

When will the world know that Lithuania wants reconciliation and is truly sorry for what happened here? When the country
ceases to honor and idolize Nazi collaborators and perpetrators as
Lithuanian heroes. I am speaking of Kazys Škirpa, head of the Lithuanian Activist Front, an ally of Hitler. I am speaking of Juozas
Ambrazevičius Brazaitis, who actually became Lithuania's prime
minister, who called for Jews not to be murdered so publicly and who
established the first concentration camp for Jews in Lithuania. The
government of Lithuania has falsely stated that the US Congress
"completely exonerated and rehabilitated Brazaitis." This is a lie,
as the US congressman Brad Sherman officially told the Lithuanian
government in 2019. Lithuania has so far ignored him.

I am speaking of Antanas Baltūsis-Žvejas, who led camp guards
in the Majdanek concentration camp. The government of Lithuania
declared Baltūsis innocent of any crimes on the grounds that he served
on the outside of the camp and did not know what was happening
inside. This is a ridiculous lie that brings shame to your country.

I speak of Jonas Noreika, who as regional leader in Lithuania,
was the man responsible for signing the official death warrants for
the murder of my family, including my little cousin Milia, a fourteen-
year-old girl who was starved, beaten, and probably raped before
being shot along with thousands of others. Noreika wrote his own

Lithuanian version of Mein Kampf, Pakelk Galva, Lietuvi, in which he called for the mass murder of Jews!!

And yet Lithuania has made Noreika one of its heroes, awarding him Lithuania's highest medal of honor, the Cross of the Vytis. He has had a school named after him, the Jonas Noreika Grammar School. Plaques with his name grace places he worked and his birthplace. This is who your country honors. Moreover, they have had the temerity to now declare Noreika a secret rescuer of Jews! Yes, so secret no Jews survived his "rescue" attempts.

Both the International Holocaust Remembrance Alliance and the US State Department have identified and declared Lithuania as Holocaust revisionists.

These declarations by the Lithuanian government that murderers were actually rescuers and that guilt cannot be determined is finding its way into Lithuanian academia. These frauds have now become primary source facts published by a European Union member government that is also an ally of America. It is only a matter of time before these falsifications find their way into American textbooks and destroy decades of combined and cumulative work toward factual Holocaust education. The biggest threat against Holocaust education in the world today is the Lithuanian government's Holocaust frauds.

Allowing the rewriting of the Holocaust facilitates the next genocide. For if a European government can commit Holocaust fraud so openly, this encourages genocidal regimes all over the world to think they can easily cover their tracks in a similar fashion. For history to veer toward peace and justice, truth must prevail.

Dr. Vidas concluded his talk with words of his own:

For a country such as Lithuania to find a path out of this morass, it will take fresh leadership. For future generations to not be tarred with the taint of Holocaust deception, falsified history must be repudiated, and truth told. For Lithuania to show sincerity, the national leadership responsible for Holocaust denial must be charged under their own national Holocaust denial laws. This problem did not begin recently, and it will take time to correct. It is the task of international academia to ensure that history is reported accurately. We do have real allies inside Lithuania. People who would like to see their country break with their past. I am one of them and I know of many more. We need to encourage them, not ban them. The children of Raseiniai were given a gift when Dr. Gottstein-Lasker read to them a first-person testimony of what really happened in their town. We should have thanked her, not made it necessary for her to leave the country to ensure her safety. As President Brazauskas said in 1995 to the Jews of Israel:

> *I address you as the president of a reborn Lithuania—a Lithuania which is aware that truth should unite and not divide us, a truth to be constantly and gradually restored by historians in order to prevent the past from repeating itself. Education, especially that of youth, is of particular importance in Central and Eastern Europe, where democracy has not yet passed the initial stages of development . . . Only after having absorbed and evaluated that which occurred can we become truly free.*

> *My fellow Lithuanians, let us join hands to help each other create a country that is truly free.*

Milia sat back in her chair and closed her eyes. She saw Darius's large, handsome face, his fair hair, the blue eyes sparkling with life and humor and intelligence. He had deceived her in order to enter the Colosseum alone to battle their lions. *How foolish!* she wept. *Darius, Darius.*

How badly hurt was he? She searched through the numerous news reports, but while they all said he had been hospitalized, no one detailed his condition.

She went to get her cell phone. The battery was still low, but at least it opened. Before she dialed his number, she saw she had a WhatsApp message. It was from him.

Please forgive me for lying. If I had told you the truth, you would never have left. I'm sure by now you have seen pictures of my face. The rest of me is just as bad. But you should see the other guy! I will live, it's just black-and-blue marks. The important thing is: we did it!! We broadcast your speech all over the world. It was magnificent.

I'm so grateful you are home and safe, my darling Milia. I will never forget the time we spent together. Thank you for showing me who I am. I gave your husband a package to deliver. Please take care of it. The doctors are after me, we'll speak soon.
All my love, Darius.

My darling Milia.

She fought the irrational urge to get on the next plane back to Vilnius. But by then Darius could just as well have left the country. She decided there was nothing to do but wait. But this package he had given Julius? Where was it?

"Julius?"

"Up already?"

"Have you seen the news?"

"You mean about your Lithuanian? Quite impressive, I must say. Great speech, Milia."

"Thank you. But I haven't called to chitchat. Did Darius give you a package?"

"Ah, yes. The mysterious gift. I almost refused to take it. You know what El Al security says about accepting packages from people you don't know."

"Did you think it was a bomb?" she scoffed.

"I don't know the man."

"Yes, but I do. Why didn't you give it to me?"

He hesitated. Why hadn't he delivered a gift from his love rival to his estranged wife? Duh. "It was late. We were both tired," he improvised lamely.

She pressed her lips together. "So where is it?"

"I left it on top of the bookcase in the living room."

Just high enough for me not to see it, she thought, furious.

"Listen, Milia. We need to talk."

"Yes, we do. But not now. Goodbye, Julius." She hung up, hurrying down the stairs.

She dreaded the coming conversation with her children, where she would have to explain why she was not immediately going to get back together with their father. It wouldn't be easy for them to understand. Strangely, it was a decision that had nothing to do with whether her relationship with Darius had any future. Spending time—however short-lived—with a man who admired her and honored her work, who looked at what she was trying to do with enthusiasm, appreciation, and respect, had somehow changed her. Throughout her marriage to Julius, it had been understood that his work was celebrated, and her work and her dedication to it tolerated, a concession he had made for which he expected gratitude. Suddenly, that wasn't good enough. She deserved more.

She hurried to the bookcase. There it was, dangling over the edge just high enough for her to need a stepladder. She dragged the ladder over the living room floor from the storage closet, reaching out for the square package wrapped carefully in brown paper and secured with string.

She carried it carefully to the living room couch, placing it in her lap and undoing it.

Reaching inside, she pulled out a square jeweler's box of blue velvet tied with strings of faded gold ribbons. She undid them carefully, raising the lid. She caught her breath. It was a necklace of white gold leaves set with tiny pearls, which rose out of a golden vase at whose center a stunning blue emerald gleamed, encircled by sparkling pavé diamonds and a lustrous circlet of larger matched pearls. There was a letter.

Dearest Milia,

This necklace has been in our family since 1941. My grandparents and parents led me to believe that the original owners, the Kenskys—Emil, Beyle, Itele, Henokh, and Ruchele—had given it to my grandfather Tadas out of appreciation for his saving their lives. Now you and I both know the truth.

It wasn't easy prying this away from my mother, but in the end I think she finally understood that it doesn't belong to us. It needs to go back to its rightful owners, the family of Emil Kensky's niece Esther, who filled out the Page of Testimony. You mentioned you had an address and phone number for her? Would you please arrange to have it delivered to her? I would be very grateful. We cannot bring the dead back to life. But we can try as much as possible to do whatever is in our power to seek justice. Please ask her to forgive us for taking so long. I hope very much to meet her and her family one day.

Please don't worry about me. I did what I had to do. Besides, look what happened with Rūta. Yes, they destroyed her career in Lithuania. So now, instead of being a famous Lithuanian author, she is a famous international celebrity lauded all over the world! I'm not worried, and neither should you be. Whatever happens, I will be living a good life, a real life. The life I want. I may do it here in Lithuania, or I may go back to Paris with my lovely daughter, who surprisingly just came to visit me. Perhaps I'll explore what my daughter has become so addicted to there. This publicity can only do me good.

I hated the way we parted. There was so much that I wanted to say but couldn't. Please believe I did it to keep you safe. I don't

*know what will happen with us in the future, Milia. The more I
think about it, the harder it is to imagine that I could make a life
with you. For one thing, your people would never accept me, even if
I changed my religion, which honestly I can't say I would be able
to do. It is not that I am such a good Christian. Looking at all the
laws you obey, I think I would make a very bad Jew.*

*Having said that, I implore you to hold on to what is most
precious between us: a true and loving friendship that has brought
me so much closer to becoming the man I want to be. My love and
admiration for you will never run dry. I will hold it in my heart
forever.*

Until we meet again (soon! Come to Paris!),
Darius

She took the letter and held it close to her heart. Then she
closed the box, tying it with the faded gold ribbons. Though
she tried her best, not all the strings could be tied up so neatly,
some dangling. She let the loose ends lie. Sometimes that's all
you could do, she thought, kissing the letter and putting it back
into its envelope, then locking the velvet box carefully in her safe.

She would call Esther today. But first she had to take a
shower, get dressed, say her morning prayers, and eat a good
Israeli breakfast.

But before she did anything, she somehow found herself
opening up her front door. She stood there, breathing in the
sea air that flowed up from the Mediterranean over the Carmel
mountains, setting the leaves of her tall olive tree dancing with
joy. The journey she had started was not over, she knew, the final
destination not yet in sight. But her heart, once desiccated, had
been filled with youthful hopes and dreams once more. She was
eager to get to her office, to read her emails from all over the
world. She was eager to get back to work.

ACKNOWLEDGMENTS

As the descendant of Lithuanian Jews, and the daughter-in-law of two Holocaust survivors, I have long meditated on the responsibilities of our generation toward the victims as well as the correct, moral attitude toward descendants of the perpetrators.

The Enemy Beside Me is a work of the imagination, and all the characters, except for those specifically mentioned by their real names, are fictional. The events described as taking place in Jurbarkas, Raseiniai, and Telzh in 1941 are entirely factual, paraphrased from first-person survivor testimonies contained in the book *The Lithuanian Slaughter of Its Jews*, collected by Leyb Koniuchowsky based on his personal, notarized interviews of Lithuanian survivors conducted in displaced persons' camps from 1946 to 1948. It was translated from the Yiddish into English by Dr. Jonathan Boyarin, and compiled and published by David Solly Sandler (sedsand@ iinet.net.au). I thank him for allowing me to use this material. I have used the real names of those providing these testimonies, and the real names of their family members, descriptions of events, and dates. None of this has been embellished or invented, simply edited for clarity and space considerations.

All the representatives of Lithuanian institutions in chapter 28, as well as Darius's department head, are all fictitious inventions not based on any person living or dead.

The description of Lithuania's behavior and its institutions are my own opinion, based on extensive research, as well as the expert advice of Dr. Efraim Zuroff, head of the Wiesenthal Center in Israel. I thank Dr. Zuroff for his generous help, advice, and inspiration and for the amazing work he has done and continues to do. More than any other person, Dr. Zuroff has spearheaded efforts to convince Lithuania to take long overdue responsibility for its attitude toward the historical facts of the Holocaust in their country and for the need to bring perpetrators to justice, educate their young people, honor the victims, and make reparations. All these things are vital in a country that wants to be accepted as a respected member of the new Europe, not to mention to invite tourism. Until these things are done, I suggest those looking for information about their Jewish Lithuanian heritage read Leyb Koniuchowsky's book instead of wasting money on a heritage tour.

Other books that I consulted and which proved very valuable were *Our People*, by Zuroff and Vanagaitė; *The Nazi's Granddaughter*, by Silvia Foti; *The Murderers Among Us*, by Simon Wiesenthal; *The Jews of Lithuania*, by Masha Greenbaum; *Malice, Murder, and Manipulation*, by Grant Arthur Gochin; *The Destruction of European Jews*, by Raul Hilberg; *The War Against the Jews*, by Lucy S. Dawidowicz; *When I Grow Up*, by Ken Krimstein; *Righteous Among the Nations*, by Mordecai Paldiel; and *Awakening Lives: Autobiographies of Jewish Youth in Poland Before the Holocaust*, edited by Jeffrey Shandler.

I thank all the other brave people on the forefront of trying to make the horrors of the past a thing of the past through truth and reconciliation. I thank Dr. Dovid Katz, whose blog *Defending History* is a resource to all those seeking updated, truthful information about Holocaust revisionism in Lithuania. I thank Rūta Vanagaitė, coauthor with Dr. Efraim Zuroff of *Our People*, and with Christoph Dieckmann of *How Did It Happen?* She has paid an enormous price for her honesty and courage.

I thank Silvia Foti, author of *The Nazi's Granddaughter*, who has now made it impossible for the Lithuanian government to ignore the mass murders and atrocities committed by her grandfather, Jonas Noreika, bravely removing the pedestal on which he has been falsely placed by Lithuanian revisionists. Her dedication to revealing painful truths deserves widespread recognition and thanks.

The description of Ramunos Jonaitis's wooden house in chapter 29 is based on the article "Lithuanian House: Customs of Construction and Mythologies," by Libertas Klimka, from the book *Wooden Heritage in Lithuania*, edited and compiled by Alfredas Jomantas, translated into English by Vertimo Namai and published by R. Paknio Leidykla in 2011 with support from the Lithuanian Ministry of Culture, Department of Cultural Heritage.

Lyrics to the song "All I Ask of You," from *The Phantom of the Opera*, written by Andrew Lloyd Webber, are reprinted here with copyright permission from Hal Leonard Permissions.

Deepest thanks must go to my excellent editor, Anna deVries, whose suggestions were invaluable, and my diligent copy editor, Janine Barlow. Thanks to my agent, Mel Berger of WME, for his support and kindness.

As always, thank you, Alex Ragen, for being my first reader and for your careful attention to detail and most valuable insights.

While Milia Gottstein-Lasker and Darius Vidas are both fictional characters, their spirits are real and live on in all people whose histories have made them enemies, burdened by crimes committed before they were born. While historical truths cannot be ignored or overlooked, and should never be distorted or denied, it is up to the living to make peace with one another. We must never be deaf to the voices of our dead, and yet we must also be open to the living hands reaching out in friendship and a sincere desire to make amends.

Naomi Ragen
Zichron Yaakov, July 2022

According to the United States Holocaust Memorial Museum (https://www.ushmm.org/m/pdfs/USHMM-Holocaust-Memory-at-Risk-2021.pdf)

State-sponsored or otherwise politically influential Holocaust distortion is wide-ranging and widespread across Europe. It can appear as:

- *Public statements denying or minimizing national and societal responsibility for crimes against Jews or collaboration with Nazi Germany*
- *Attempts to limit academic and public discourse on Holocaust history by means of legislation and penalties*
- *Political interference with the accurate representation of history in museums and exhibitions, and at historical sites*
- *The rejection of the importance of Holocaust remembrance and memorials by influential political and societal leaders*
- *Efforts to glorify, honor, exonerate, or otherwise "rehabilitate" Holocaust-era historical figures or entities despite their association with crimes against humanity, collaboration with Nazi Germany, or direct involvement in the persecution and murder of Jews*

The proponents and enablers of Holocaust distortion include governments, political leaders, and non-state actors. They have increasing political power and societal influence, and are bringing ideas once considered to be unacceptably extreme into the mainstream of politics and public discourse.

1. What are Darius's motives for inviting Milia to be keynote speaker?

2. Despite her initial reluctance, what are Milia's reasons for accepting this invitation? How many are personal, how many ideological? Was going the right decision?

3. Darius is warned that inviting Milia is a mistake. Do you think he made a mistake? Describe the consequences, both positive and negative, of that invitation.

4. What is the motivation behind Julius's betrayal? Is what he did forgivable, and do you see their marriage healing? What needs to happen for the marriage to go forward? Or is it a lost cause?

5. How much of what happens between Darius and Milia is personal, and how much is connected to what they are hoping to accomplish in their work?

6. Both Milia and Darius were born long after the Holocaust. And yet, both face consequences and feel responsibilities for the terrible crimes of that era. Describe those consequences and responsibilities. Is that fair or unfair?

7. What do you think is the motivation of the Lithuanian government's present actions as Holocaust distorters? Does the suffering of Lithuanians under the Soviets and Nazis justify their present agenda? Has this agenda brought the country benefit or harm? Justify your answer.

ST.
MARTIN'S
GRIFFIN

8. If you could speak to Lithuanians, what would you tell them about facing their past?

9. How would you react if your children were threatened because of your political or ideological agenda? Would you back down? Or keep going?

10. What do you think of the statement: "So this was what impending divorce brought: not only dissolving the personal bonds between two people, but contaminating all the familial bonds . . . all of them going up in smoke on the altar of the selfish urge for more, better, different."

11. Do you see Milia and Darius getting back together as a couple? List the reasons for and against.

12. Do you agree or disagree that today every Jew is living with Anne Frank in the attic?

13. Do you agree or disagree with the statement: "The very slogan 'never again' was like a child daring the monsters in the dark to pounce, a false bravado, a way of admitting the fear by pretending to conquer it."

14. What is the responsibility of people today to the memory of victims of genocide and oppression? How can people forgive and go forward? Can you envision any situation in which the correct moral stance would be a refusal to ever forgive or forget historical wrongs?

15. How is the final decision facing Darius similar to decisions made by his family during the Holocaust? What does his answer prove?

ABOUT THE AUTHOR

Alex Ragen

Naomi Ragen is an award-winning novelist, journalist, and playwright. Her first book, *Jephte's Daughter,* was listed among the one hundred most important Jewish books of all time. Her bestselling novels include *Sotah, The Covenant, The Sisters Weiss,* and *Devil in Jerusalem.* An outspoken advocate for women's rights, and an active combatant against anti-Israel and antisemitic propaganda through her website, www.naomiragen.com, she has lived in Jerusalem since 1971. *Sojourn with the Enemy* is her fourteenth novel.